Flight of Youth

Flight of Youth

by

Ron Graham

Whittles Publishing

Typeset by
Whittles Publishing Services

Published by
Whittles Publishing,
Roseleigh House,
Latheronwheel,
Caithness, KW5 6DW,
Scotland, UK

ISBN 1-870325-42-7

Cover photographs courtesy of the
Imperial War Museum, London

Printed by Interprint Ltd., Malta

Dedicated to the memory of

AM1 Christopher Graham, Engine Fitter, RFC

and

Lieutenant Philip Brereton Townsend, RE8 pilot, RFC

Blow out, you bugles, over the rich dead!
there's none of these so lonely and poor of old,
But, dying, has made us rarer gifts than gold.
These laid the world away; poured out the red
Sweet wine of youth; gave up the years to be
Of work and joy, and unhoped serene,
That men call age; and those who, would have been
Their sons, they gave their immortality.

The Dead, Rupert Brooke (1887–1915)

Prologue

The cold November morning promised little comfort for the thin crowds of people now lining London's streets. Helped by a watery sun, the grey overcast brightened now and then as, behind fleeting shreds of low cloud, it reflected from the medals of marching civilians. Although rain was not expected, the forecast promised little hope for fine weather on this cold morning of the eleventh day of the eleventh month.

The 20th century had but a few years remaining, so it was perhaps not too difficult to understand the falling interest for a parade commemorating past wars and old heroes. With each successive year the marching columns became smaller until, inevitably, participants of World War One were represented less and less through natural attrition.

The original Armistice Parade was one of remembrance for the fallen of WW1, later extended to include an even greater conflict, WW2, and a number of smaller, but no less lethal, wars to the present day. But to a nation long at peace with the world, the parade now meant little, just another TV event for many, while the thinning crowds that lined the streets were mainly sympathisers, friends, families and loved ones – in sorrow.

On this day the parade was special. At its head, two uniformed airmen carried a fluttering banner proclaiming WW1, while behind, a solitary wheelchair was pushed by a veteran of the Army Air Corps.

The occupant of the chair, well covered in hat and overcoat, sat upright, white haired and old. He was the last of them, the sole representative of a generation now lost. An aviator who served in the Royal Flying Corps: one of the Early Birds.

Chapter One

Bill Proctor didn't think much to the city of Leeds at all. It was his second visit to the grimy centre of Yorkshire's woollen trade and, at eighteen years of age, no longer the exciting experience of automobiles, trams and stores, that had enthralled him during his first visit two years ago. But it had been different then, he had come on a day trip with his parents – a family wake in fact, and it was his first taste of a large city. All the same, he thought, a lot has happened in the past year, what with the war and all, but Leeds and its folk didn't seem the least bit bothered! It was quite different to what he had expected and Bill was vaguely disappointed that the city didn't reflect the martial urgency of the times.

It was March 1915 and the 'short war' predicted by politicians on all sides to be over by Christmas, *last Christmas* that was, had long since been dismissed as a cruel myth, with over a million dead to prove it. Yet the war and all its terrible excitement seemed to be as far away from the commercial hubbub of Leeds as it was from his native village in the dales some thirty or so miles to the north.

Born in 1897, Bill's entered the 20th century during a period of unprecedented social and industrial change. Destined to experience changes and events far beyond the expectations of his parents, he was determined to make use of every possible opportunity. His father was right of course; the future, his future, was in engineering and this war was going to develop it like mad. It made sense therefore to keep up-to-date, at the government's expense if possible, and if the war was a means of furthering his technical education then he had to enlist now.

Bill's journey from the tiny Nidderdale village of Dacre-Banks had started at 7.20 a.m. with the first train to Harrogate, a journey of some 25 minutes over a single track to the wealthy spa town fronting the Yorkshire dales. Although mostly inhabited by the rich and retired who lived in its numerous hotels, Harrogate also acted as a commercial centre for many of the Nidderdale villages. As a consequence Bill had often visited this pleasant and spacious town with his father, Chris Proctor, to purchase spares for the garage where his Dad worked. It was from Harrogate he had taken the 8.15 to Leeds, enjoying the journey until rain made the dirty carriage windows opaque to the view outside.

Idly gazing through the rain-lashed window he contemplated the reflected face as though it belonged to a complete stranger. As indeed it would be to others he thought, many others, who would be meeting him for the first time and making up their minds about Bill Proctor before they even knew him! The fleeting panic subsided and the face changed to a more serious expression as it turned for a more serious approval. Being neither self-conscious nor introspective the young Dales lad was not given to any form of self-analysis, and so, perhaps for the first time in his life, he took stock of himself.

He wasn't anything special he mused. A round-cheeked open face stared back at him, his father's face, or so the family always said, with an insignificant nose set above a wide mouth which had a slightly pro-truding lower lip. A shock of unruly blond hair denied any attempt of a decent parting and fell upon a broad forehead to give an overall boy-ish appearance, now tending to a scowl as Bill's thoughts took on a serious vein.

'You're an ugly bugger Proctor and thar's nowt to worry o'wer.' he exclaimed, lapsing into the broad Yorkshire vowels which he rarely used – even at home. And as the homely face relaxed into a wide three-cornered grin Bill turned, grinning at the empty carriage.

Once at the station he purchased a copy of the *Daily Mail*, a small pork pie and a cup of tea, then sat down under the protective roof of the station concourse to eat the frugal breakfast. The bench on which he sat was unoccupied and allowed for a comfortable meal as he read the paper without distraction. The news was still concerned with the most recent allied attack at Neuve Chapelle, but it seemed to have lost the initial shock and success first reported when the advance was sprung nearly a week ago.

Bill recalled the words of their first village casualty, Jack Renshaw, who had been wounded at the Marne last autumn;

'It's going to be nothing but trench warfare from here on, and I'm well out of it thank God!'

And so it seemed with this most recent initiative, the attack had been prepared as no other within the history of warfare; highly detailed planning had been made with the aid of air photographs, the first time such reconnaissance had been used for strategic planning, he read, but it appeared that the offensive was now petering out against the German wire which the artillery had failed to flatten. Elsewhere in the

4

columns Bill read of rumours to the effect that British shells had failed to explode on many occasions and that there were faults in fuses and detonators due to imperfect manufacture. In the face of this damning accusation against the British war workers it was disgusting, Bill thought, that they should be now going on strike for more money in so many industries. The headlines only made him more angry as he read of 10,000 Clyde engineers on strike for another two pence per hour, of the striking south Wales miners, the Merseyside dockers – he threw the paper down, confused and disgusted with it all.

'Can I have a read of it?'

Bill was startled to find that in his anger he had completely overlooked the fact that the bench was now full and that a workman was as intent on reading his paper as he was of discarding it.

'Go ahead' he muttered 'I don't want it!'

The station platforms were now crowding with khaki-clad figures in full kit, no doubt embarking for the southern ports and France. Too early to go yet he thought, the recruiting centre was quite a walk from the station and it might stop raining before long. The troops were grouped in sections of about ten men, each with a Sergeant or Corporal it seemed. They were festooned with webbing, packs, rifle and ammunition pouches and Bill knew there was little likelihood that they would shed any of it this side of the Channel. It appeared to him that the Army never recruited non-smokers, since each of the assembled groups seemed to be either handing out cigarettes, lighting them, smoking or throwing them away. As a non-smoker, like his father, it all seemed rather futile he thought – and the expense!

'Thems going t' front I bet' said a voice somewhere down the bench.

'West Yorks,' said another, 'God help old Jerry now, eh.'

Bill was intrigued by the soldiers; they appeared to be most unwarlike in their attitude, more like a party of working miners assembled before the pit-head. Indeed, from what he had read in the papers they were just that, miners for the most part with a fair smattering of factory workers, all part of the new Territorial Army now reinforcing the old regulars of the BEF in France. Jack Henshaw had said that the old BEF was now gone. A regular in the lst Battalion West Yorks, Jack was one of the first to see action in France and had advanced through the Marne only to be shot by a sniper as both sides settled into trench warfare. As a boy Bill had enjoyed listening to Jack's exploits as a trooper in the Boer war. Jack had been a boy soldier ever since old Sam Stockten had died and had left him jobless when only halfway through his apprenticeship as a farrier.

5

Bill was only a baby then of course, but he had grown up with first hand experience of the transition from horse to motor, and knew every detail of George Graham's purchase of the old blacksmith shop to create the first garage in Dacre, in fact the first garage in the entire dale.

George Graham had learnt his skills as a mechanic in Ripon where his father owned a bicycle shop. More of an enthusiast than a man of business, his father was wealthy enough to indulge in his passion for engines and he took a keen interest in the emerging motorcycles now being manufactured in England. His first machine was not unlike the conventional bicycles he sold in the shop, an 1899 Werner of French design. Only three-quarter horse-power, the Werner 'Motorcyclette' was, nevertheless, a first class introduction to powered transport and young George needed little persuasion to spend a year with Scott's at Shipley, where he worked on a number of engines, including the early two-strokes then being investigated by Alfred Scott. He was to have spent a few months more at the Quadrant works in Birmingham, where his father had good business contacts through their manufacture of ordinary pedal cycles, but when Sam died and the Dacre 'smithy' became available he was called home to establish the new 'Dacre Motor Engineering Works'.

During Jack Henshaw's last year at the smithy there had been a decreasing amount of work, mainly due to the closure of the Darley Carriers some two years before. The introduction of the railway line between Harrogate and Dacre was a blow to the old horse-drawn carrier trade and with it, Sam's smithy as well. There had been work enough from the Dacre Sawmill at one time, but this too was in decline as the timber hauling was mainly done by steam tractors now, except for some work on the slopes. Jack was not of the worrying kind however and decided to follow his trade with the colours, joining as a boy soldier in a mounted infantry regiment and completing his apprenticeship as a farrier with the Army. Most of his early soldiering was done in Natal, during the Boer war, to be followed by further overseas service with the West Yorks in India. Finally came the war in France as one of the 'Old Contemptibles' of the British Expeditionary Force in 1914, where he was wounded and lost his right leg through gangrene; then honourable discharge home. As the first war hero to return to Dacre, Jack was quite a celebrity and being well-liked was treated kindly by the village. George Graham's business was good and he could afford to be generous, so he provided a job for Jack in what passed for the stores section of the garage. It wasn't much, mainly sorting out nuts and bolts and cannibalising parts from old engines, things Bill used to do during his

6

early apprenticeship, but Jack was content.

Bill thought on the parting advice Jack had given him yesterday.

'Well then young Bill, if you intend going for a soldier, join the cavalry and stay in it! Don't ever join the bloody infantry like I did, but there you are, the West Yorks needed a farrier and a Corporal's tapes don't come that easy in peacetime, so I went to the PBI–the poor bloody infantry. Never even saw a bloody 'smithy' in France either! But for God's sake lad – don't ever join the infantry!'

The rain had stopped and Bill prepared to walk to the town hall, where the regional recruiting office had been established. His gaze fell on the large poster glaring balefully from the hoarding opposite. A picture of Field Marshal Kitchener with forefinger outstretched was pointing directly at him. 'Your Country needs YOU' was the message Indeed it was time to go he thought as he stared back with determination.

'I'm told that the old boy got quite a shock when half a million joined the colours in the first month.' said a voice beside him. Bill turned. His neighbour was, perhaps, slightly older than himself with dark strong features and a cheerful open face.

'Evidently he doesn't think much of the 'week-end soldiers' like them.' he confided, nodding in the general direction of the territorials now bustling to the commands of their junior officers. 'Old Kitchener wants a new regular Army recruited, so I'm told, but I imagine the 'terriers' are going to have to hold the fort for a while yet.'

Bill smiled. 'It's all the same to me be they regulars or 'terriers', cannon fodder the lot of them, silly sods!' The look on the young man's face prompted him to continue. 'I'm for the Royal Flying Corps, today as a matter of fact.' He rushed his words, embarrassed and proud at his declaration of patriotism.

'So you are for the town hall too are you? Well, this is well met, my name is Gerry Harcastle and I'm for the RFC as well.'

Bill introduced himself with a shake of hands, 'I've just got in from Harrogate and have been idling about until the rain stopped, do you know the way from here?'

'Not the slightest old lad, I'm from Skipton but spent the night in mucky old Leeds with my Aunty Jo, anyway we'll get a taxi and you will be my most welcome guest.'

Bill had never been in a taxi before and the journey from the station to the town hall gave him great pleasure. The cab was a 4-litre Unic, recognised from one of George Graham's motor catalogues, and he made a mental note of its comfort as they threaded their way over the

7

cobbled streets. It was obvious that Gerry Hardcastle's background was more elevated than his own. It wasn't just a question of being able to afford a taxi either, there was his accent for example; definitely Yorkshire but with the almost lilting rhythm that differentiated the educated from the flat tones of the local working class. How many times had he been lectured to on the subject of speech Bill wondered? His mother, Muriel Proctor, had never really cared for dales-talk and, being something of a snob in these matters, had made sure that her son's accent didn't follow the almost biblical speech of his father. That she herself had a slight 'Geordie' accent did not deter her from taking a somewhat superior attitude to the dales folk, whom she loved, but this went largely unnoticed in the tightly knit community that accepted her as the wife of one of their sons. Bill considered the matter with idle interest and guessed that his companion would probably be a grammar school lad, perhaps even public school? Either way he had been educated beyond Bill's level that was certain. But as his father had often said,

'Not much use being educated if tha's goin't spend thee life engineering!'

Typically, Chris Proctor, like most of his fellow countrymen, confused engineering with that of being a mechanic, but there were few professionally educated engineers about who could match his natural flair for the subject. Conscious of his own educational shortcomings, Chris made sure that young Bill's apprenticeship was accompanied by as much book learning as he could provide – despite his own proud boast of being a practical man.

It would be difficult to live in Leeds these days and not be in uniform, thought Bill. As a regional recruiting centre the town hall was covered in posters extolling the need for young men to join the colours. Many of the posters, indicating the patriotic role that British womenfolk expected of their men, gained special significance in the traditionally matriachal society of the northern working class. Yet for all the propaganda, much of it moral blackmail, Bill was somewhat concerned about the lack of inducement to join the RFC, or even the Royal Navy for that matter.

'I shall only enlist in the RFC mark you, and if they don't accept me for the Corps then I won't join!'

Regardless of the emphasis of this declaration, Bill knew how desperate the Flying Corps had become for skilled mechanics in any number of trades, a consequence of rapid expansion for one thing and its increasing role in the war for another. Indeed, the motor-trade journals were increasingly being used to advertise for air mechanics and it was in one of these that Chris Proctor had read of the opportunities for his son.

'Don't you worry Billy lad, the RFC are not going to reject two future hotshot pilots like us in a hurry, just you see!'

Bill turned to face his enthusiastic new friend.

'Pilot! who said anything about being a bloody pilot!'

The idea of flying aeroplanes was quite unexpected. Like cars and motorbikes, aeroplanes were simply machines that needed skilled mechanics to make them work. The work ethic was everything in Bill's family; getting a skill, keeping a job, steady work with a future that's what it was all about – but flying, being a pilot, it was almost laughable. Even though Bill had more than a passing interest in cars and had often driven one to the end of the village and back, as a test, that was as far as his motoring went. His relationship with the car was more to the machine than to its use, not unlike that of the groom to his master's horse.

Gerry Hardcastle studied his new friend with fresh interest. There was something about his companion that put him ahead of the usual working class lads he had met from the council schools in Skipton. Coming from a comfortably well off home, Gerry's parents had paid for his entry to the local grammar school, where he had managed to pass his school certificate with modest results. He was well aware of his advantage but had no illusions as to his ability, particularly in practical matters and he could see that Bill was no fool. The dales boy had a quiet confidence behind an easy manner and an open face. Fair-haired, with a square-cut face and broad brow, Bill's head was stuck on a solid, almost squat, frame joined by a short neck. About five feet eight inches in height, with broad shoulders, he typified the solid north country stock that could never look comfortable, let alone smart, in a three-piece suit. Not that such apparel was common to the likes of Bill, who had never owned a suit in his life.

'Surely young Sir, you couldn't possibly want to join the RFC and not be a pilot,' countered Gerry, 'why it's the best thing there is to this bloody mess and it's free of charge!'

'I'm a mechanic Gerry, it's all I know really, and after this lot is over the whole world will be full of mechanics, so I shall need to know all there is. That's what my Dad says, and his boss too, so I consider the RFC as being my education for the future.'

'Yes, I can see all that, but pilots are the future as well you know, and much better than being a mechanic. Besides look at all the fun we could have training together.'

As the taxi drew abreast of the town hall there was an immediate lull in the conversation as the two companions saw the large crowd of eager patriots waiting to join up.

'Bloody hell!' exclaimed Gerry, 'We'll be here all day looking at this lot.'

'Maybe the King has run out of shillings.' joked Bill, 'After all, buying an Army must make a big dent in his pocket money.'

Gerry laughed. 'It's a cheap system all the same, the recruit makes his mark and takes up the King's Shilling – no fussy legal contracts for this apprenticeship, eh!'

As Gerry paid off the cab-driver Bill appraised the ever growing crowd of men. Mostly youngsters, like themselves, there was also a fair percentage of older men too, many of them showing the discomfort of long journeys and bad weather by their soaked clothes and unkempt appearance. A tall recruiting Sergeant, flanked by two MP Corporals, was trying to marshal the crowd overspilling the town hall steps as Bill and Gerry attempted to find a place in the queues now being formed.

'Any of you lads know 'owt about motors!' shouted the Sergeant.

'Hey! that's me.' said Bill.

'Shut up you bloody idiot.' warned Gerry. 'They will put you into some transport unit or other, soon as look at you. Say nothing and just go for the Flying Corps.'

Other doors were opened and the queues shifted forward into the spacious entrance of the town hall. Once inside, groups of NCOs filtered the advancing humanity into files, each being further controlled by uniformed hatless clerks at various desks within the main hall. After some minutes of patient waiting a young subaltern climbed onto a chair in the corner of the hall and hung a large sign over a door.

'RFC! That's us,' exclaimed Bill, 'Do we just go over?'

'Better wait, they will sort us out sooner or later, besides I don't think we should be too hasty or we might find ourselves as batmen or such.'

'Batman, what's that?'

'Officer's servant old lad.'

'I'll not be any bugger's servant,' replied Bill. 'Anything but that!'

A fresh, single file of men were now being directed under the RFC notice where, after a few minutes, Bill and Gerry found themselves. They could see three desks in the room beyond, at which men were delayed before moving on to either a further row of desks at the back, each manned by an officer and attending clerk, or to an ever growing queue leading out of the room.

'Rejected! that's what I heard one of them Sergeants say. Them that goes to the queue at the left are not wanted.' exclaimed a red-faced volunteer in front of Gerry.

'Not leaving many going for selection then.' mused Gerry.

'If they don't want me I'm coming out the same way I came in, its the RFC or nothing.' said Bill.

Chapter Two

'Well our Bill, how did you get on?' Eileen Proctor's greeting to her elder brother initiated a similar chorus from the rest of the family the moment he entered the front door of their small terraced cottage. Hot and tired though he was from the return journey, his flushed face and bright eyes were warmed more from excitement than fatigue as he fell into the time-worn leather armchair generally recognised as 'father's chair'.

'Just let me get this collar and tie off lass and I'll tell you all about it.' he replied, tearing off the offending items.

As Muriel Proctor set the table for her son's late tea, nine year old Maggie ran to sit on Bill's lap as Eileen helped her mother with the brisket of beef left warming in the black kitchen range.

'Now then,' his father protested, 'You lasses let the lad alone, let him have his tea first, then we can hear what's to do.'

As Bill wrestled with his collar, Maggie rummaged through the coarse home-spun jacket for the present she was sure her big brother would have brought her. Idolised only as big brothers can be, Maggie's world tended to revolve more about Bill than her sister who, at sixteen, considered Maggie to be something of a pest. Finding the two ounce packet of acid drops Maggie gave Bill a kiss and leapt off his lap.

'Look what…'

'Not before you have had your milk young lady! And then only one mind you. It's close on to eight o'clock and about your bedtime!'

As Maggie pulled a face, her mother, anticipating the request, added… 'And you can hear all about Bill's adventures tomorrow – so off with you. 'Come and get your tea first Bill, although at this time of night I suppose its more like supper!'

As with most Yorkshire working-class families, meal times were a ritual governed by the working day. For Muriel Proctor, her day started with getting 'the lads' off to work by 7.30 each morning, and since Chris and Bill worked through until six in the evening, breakfast was generous and dependable. This meal usually consisted of a thick porridge, followed by bacon and eggs and a fresh loaf of homemade bread, which also served for their midday 'snap' of bread and dripping, or bread and cheese, eaten at work. Always wrapped up in a clean linen cloth, Muriel's menfolk could always expect extras in their 'snap' tins, the contents being eaten during the three-quarter hour dinner break.

The evening meal was usually divided into tea and supper, with teatime accepted as a family affair where the day's events, domestic, workshop and school could be discussed in a relaxed fashion. Considered as dinner by the more wealthy, or the more sophisticated, it was always 'tea' in the dales, despite the fact that this would usually be a cooked, two-course, meal involving the cheaper cuts of beef and liberal helpings of thick Yorkshire pudding. Supper took on different forms and different times depending on the time of year, but generally consisted of cocoa and biscuits for the children, and soup or even a hot meal for those working late.

Excited by the day's events and impatient to tell his story, Bill made short work of his supper, only waiting for his mother and sister to return from the kitchen, and the washing up, before he began.

'Well, to start with I've been accepted for the RFC and I go to a place called Farnborough, that's in Surrey I think, as soon as my train tickets come in the post.'

'When do you think that will be son,' said Chris, 'And did you tell them you hadn't finished your apprenticeship yet?'

'From what the officer said, it could be in about ten days time, and they said that since I have less than a year to go with my articles they considered my apprenticeship complete. In fact it's likely I will be a 1st class AM as soon as I complete my training.'

'And what is an AM love?' Muriel asked.

'Air Mechanic, and if you have a skilled trade you start as AM/2 then go up to AM/1 when you are good enough, although it seems you are called an AM regardless of what you do; blacksmith, carpenter, photographer or electrician, everyone starts off as an air mechanic.'

'Did you meet any pilots?' Eileen asked eagerly.

'No, I don't think so, but I did join up with a lad from Skipton, Gerry Hardcastle. He took me in a taxi from the station to the recruitment centre...'

'Was he good looking?' Eileen interrupted.

'Oh, do shut up girl, you think too much about boys.' her mother snapped.

'He was a good bloke really, and he wanted to become a pilot, in fact the daft bugger even suggested that I should be a pilot with him!'

Although Muriel Proctor would never allow swearing within her earshot, this relapse seemed to go unnoticed in the welter of excited discussion now taking place. 'And I hope you did no such fool thing.' she retorted.

'Strange to tell they weren't even interested,' Bill continued, 'Gerry was interviewed just before I was, and I think the officer thought we both wanted to be pilots. He asked Gerry if he did horse riding, or motor-bike riding, and when he said he didn't the officer said he was not likely to be considered for expensive pilot training since he had no proven aptitude, whatever that is!'

At this point Chris Proctor, who had been quietly listening to it all, laughed. 'Now that's typical, trust the British army to think like that – can you ride a horse! What in God's name have horses to do with flying an aeroplane?'

'As a matter of fact that's just what Gerry said, and he got quite excited about it, said we had come to fly aeroplanes not horses. He's a good lad, but daft about flying, in fact he got quite shirty about it, so this officer bloke took us both into an office where a more senior chap, a Captain I think, took over. Anyway, Gerry was still going on in that posh voice of his…'

'Is he posh then this pal of yours?' Eileen asked in a somewhat hushed voice.

'Well our Eileen, I'll say this about him, he could afford a taxi, and he went to grammar school 'til he were sixteen, he'd be just about right for you would Gerry.' Eileen blushed at his teasing, it being a family joke that she was looking for a rich husband.

'Get on with it lad, tha's said nowt about owt so far,' Chris said impatiently.

'When the Captain learned that Gerry had just finished his school certificate, he suggested that it might be possible for him to be a pilot, but it usually meant getting his pilot's licence first, then he would be accepted. In fact if he had his own aeroplane he stood an even better chance since he would do his RFC training on that!'

At this Chris Proctor's face adopted an expression of disbelief.

'It's true Dad, and from what this RFC chap said, nearly all the pilots come into the Corps by this route. Poor old Gerry though, he got quite a shock when he found that a pilot's ticket cost about seventy five pounds in training fees!'

Like most of his contemporaries, Chris Proctor accepted his 'working class' position without question, just as he accepted the ways of those who occupied more elevated stations in society. But in times of

14

war! Chris found it intolerable that these fine young men should be invited to offer their own aircraft as well as their lives.

'Then he turned to me and asked me about my schooling.'

Whereas Bill Proctor's education at the small village school was not out of the ordinary, his own performance was well above average. Benefiting from a lively intelligence and an exceptionally gifted teacher, he was constantly top of his class in arithmetic and reading and was encouraged, both in class and at home, to further his knowledge with books and private study. Although far from being a bookworm, the little amount of leisure time he did have was generally spent on interested study rather than games. His ability at cricket was far below that required for even the second eleven of the village team, and in a county renowned for its cricket, this put Bill firmly down-stream in terms of local acclaim. Not that this worried him at all, for truth to tell Bill was not over keen on a game where you could be expected to stand in direct line of a speeding cannon ball! As a consequence he became less of a 'team man' and, along with a few of his pals, was content with a little amateur boxing at the village hall, swimming in the Nidd, and reading his beloved books.

'So I told him about my grades, and that my headmaster had given me a note, but the Captain didn't seem all that interested until I told him that I was a trained engine fitter. He still thought I wanted to be a pilot for some reason, probably because I was with Gerry.'

At this stage of the war the RFC had possibly less than two hundred aircraft capable of operations, and since their true value on the western front was only just being recognised, each aircraft was very valuable and, with over-use, required constant servicing. As a consequence of this, and until such time as new machines could be manufactured and sent to France, recruitment centres were instructed to enrol as many skilled tradesmen as possible. Pilots, although small in number at this time, were at least sufficient for the aircraft available and were gaining valuable experience for the future, as were their artillery observers, but the immediate need was for fitters, riggers, and allied tradesmen. As a consequence the good Captain could see more use for Bill than he could for Gerry – who had looked increasingly fed up as the interview continued.

'Anyhow,' continued Bill, 'What the Captain then suggested was that we both join the colours for four years.'

'Join the what?' Muriel exclaimed.

'The colours. What that means is regular service just as you would do in peace time. Four years full-time service with an extra four on the

15

reserve. The alternative was to sign on just for the duration of the war, but if we became 'regulars' then we would have a better choice for doing what we wanted to do now and even a career in the Corps after the war. He then said that if Gerry wanted to fly he could do trade training as a photographer, there's a need for them at this time, and in France some of the photographer AMs were flying as observers. In this way he would get squadron experience that could lead to pilot training later. Well, at this Gerry bucked up a bit, and then when the Captain said that we would both be going to Farnborough for our courses that settled it.'

'I like the sound of your Gerry,' Eileen remarked.

'And it will be nice for you to have a friend when you do your training,' added his mother.

'How much does tha get paid lad?' asked his Dad.

'We get two shillings a day and all found to start with, but this goes up to four bob a day when you become an AM/l. After that it's six bob a day for a sergeant and…'

'Steady on lad' said Chris. "Tha's not even got through't trade test yet, and how long is this course?'

' We can expect to be at Farnborough for about eight weeks doing trade training, followed by a further three weeks of square bashing.' At this point, seeing the look of dismay on his mother's face, Bill explained that 'square bashing' was drill. 'We still have to do military training of course.' he added.

Chris Proctor rose from the table. 'Well Billy, that's it then, thee and I will see George Graham in't morning. He knows tha's going o'course, and he'll keep thee job for thee 'till after't war. Job's thine for as long as tha' wants it, he told me. Come to think on't tha's going to be better off than tha's ever been, four bob a day is good money lad!' With that he left the small living room to visit the outside lavatory before going upstairs to bed. 'Now don't be long going to bed all o'thee, and there's a lamp still burning in't kitchen Mue.'

Muriel Proctor left for the kitchen to lock up. Her day was done the moment she extinguished the large paraffin lamp suspended from the oak-beamed roof – and she was tired. Framed in the open doorway of the living room, a small squat candle burning in one hand and a large water jug in the other, Muriel made an appealing figure as she returned to say goodnight to Bill and Eileen.

'God bless you both,' she said quietly. Both of her children came to her and kissed her goodnight.

'And God bless you too Mum.' Bill said, as he gave her a larger than usual hug. At that moment Muriel Proctor felt she was the luckiest of God's creatures, and went up to pray before joining Chris in bed.

'Are you scared Bill?' Eileen's question brought him out of his reverie and he thought a little.

'No, not really, but it's going to be different, and that's always a bit frightening at first.'

'But war Billy! What if you have to kill somebody? Or worse, they might kill you!'

'Nay lass, don't fret, it's not as though I'm going to the front for a bob a day. I'll probably never even see a gun.'

Eileen was of medium height and, like her mother, pretty, with a good figure and large grey eyes that tended to mirror every passing thought. But whereas her mother's hair was constrained in a bun, Eileen's thick blond tresses fell almost to her waist.

'We will all miss you Billy, and as for poor old Maggie – you will have to write often, promise?'

'Yes, I promise.' He kissed her affectionately. 'But now it's bed for me, it's been a long day!'

Half awake, Bill stretched himself beneath the heavy quilted eiderdown. A light breeze wafted through the open window, lifting the lace curtains and drenching his room with the freshness of early morning. There was no better time, Bill reflected, and were it not for the exigency of work he could have been excused for languishing under the soft warm covers letting the crisp dales air wash the sleep away from his face.

The smell of freshly cooked bacon was not common to everyday breakfast in the Proctor household, and sensing that his mother was making this a special treat, he leapt out of bed to pour cold water into the china washbowl, rinse his face, ruffle hands through unruly hair and, half-dressed, run downstairs to the kitchen where his mother, laughing, already had the meal on the table.

Kissing his mother lightly an the cheek, Bill sniffed the air in mock surprise. 'I fancy someone's in for a treat this morning Mum!'

Muriel looked at her son and sighed. 'Well goodness only knows if they will feed you proper in the army son! So we shall have to fatten you up a bit before you go, when did you say that will be love?''

'Oh, not for about ten days I expect Mum, maybe even longer.'

As Chris joined his son at the table, Muriel poured the hot water into Bill's shaving mug in preparation for the shave he didn't really need, but took in deference to the soft stubble that grew within a few days.

Soon, he was followed by his father, shaving with an open razor in a lather of fragrant soap and watched by a captivated Maggie who seldom missed the morning's entertainment.

As the two men took leave of the house, Muriel watched them go with a heavy heart. Dressed in thick blue overalls and well-worn caps they made a fine pair she thought as they walked, with their snap-tins, to George Graham's garage. 'And although he'll never say it, I know Kit, your Dad that is, he's going to miss our Billy something terrible.' she said, as Eileen joined her mother at the doorway.

Although the term 'foreman' was never admitted, since the firm was only small, it was generally accepted that Chris was in charge of the day-to-day running of the workshop, leaving George Graham to conduct the business side of the garage, the small 'spares shop' and the forecourt. Most of the work still dealt with farm machinery, but an increasing amount of motor repairs had encouraged George to expand his business more in this direction.

With the two new lads taken on as apprentices, and his fifteen year old daughter, Jane, helping Jack Henshaw in the spares shop, he was confident that the garage was set fine for healthy growth. His only worry was the immediate problem concerning Bill Proctor's leaving. True, he was the first to encourage the lad, but it would still leave a gap that could only be filled by himself until Bill returned. But, he reasoned, maybe that will be all for the best since 'Kit' Proctor and himself had always enjoyed working together and there were too many things still to be learnt yet. The fact that Bill might not return never passed his mind, but he couldn't help noticing the interest Jane took in the boy... maybe? He had even voiced the possibility to his wife, and together they agreed he would make an ideal son-in-law and, as one of the family, he would have the garage's best interests at heart. Yet secretly, they both knew it was the son they never had that they really wanted.

'Well Bill, we shall be right sorry to see you leave, but I want you to know there will always be a place for you here with us. And talking of leaving, when do you have to go?' George Graham had joined them with a pot of tea, which his wife made each day for them, and as was his custom, he discussed the day's work as they ate their midday meal.

'They said to expect my movement orders within the next ten days or so Mr Graham. I'm not really sure, but if possible I would like to work right up till my last day.'

George smiled. 'Aye you're right welcome lad, but you'd better make sure you say goodbye to our Jane before you leave, and Mrs. Graham as well, or the two of 'em will make my life hell. Oh, and another thing, these are for you!' He passed Bill a large buff envelope. 'It's your articles lad, your apprentice days are now over, and I can tell you that me and your Dad are right proud of what you are doing.'

Bill's surprise must have been gratitude enough, but as he thanked his boss he managed to hide his embarrassment by finding refuge in the precious documents that qualified him as a fully skilled fitter.

In the few days that followed Bill found it difficult to put much attention to his work, there was an unrealness about everything, coupled with not a little apprehension. Even at home he felt uncomfortable, where there was an unspoken reluctance to discuss his going and the waiting began to weigh heavily upon him.

On the 28th May his orders arrived. He was instructed to entrain for London, King's Cross station, where he must report to the RFC Movement Control within the next forty-eight hours. Accompanying his orders were a travel warrant and a postal order to cover incidental costs.

It had been only seven days since his return from Leeds and his mother, upset by the swiftness of it all, cried quietly throughout the day as she busied about the house. Bill made his farewells to the Graham family and was surprised when Jane, crying openly, asked him to write to her so that she, in turn, could send him comforts. Bill had never paid any attention to the girl, and was totally unaware of her affections. But as she kissed him he promised that he would write – to them all.

George Graham pressed an envelope into his hands before he left. 'It's your pay packet lad, it's up to date and a little extra for the journey – good luck now!'

Bill had not looked forward to saying farewell to the family, and particularly to Maggie. But she had done her crying and with Eileen's help managed to come to the small railway station at Dacre to see him off. With his parents' blessings and a few tears from his sisters it was over.

As the train puffed its way along the single track to Harrogate, and his first change of stations, he pulled out his orders once again. The magic words were still there, unexpected and exciting.

2nd class Air Mechanic 4003 Proctor W.C. RFC.

Chapter Three

It was late evening by the time the two buses dropped off their passengers within the camp gates at Farnborough. Filled with about forty men in all, their journey had been slow and uncomfortable as the transports progressed south of London, stopping now and then to allow the men to relieve themselves at convenient points along the Surrey wayside. Most of the new intake had been travelling all day, and some for much longer than that. As a consequence, the sergeants in charge of each vehicle had no trouble in assembling the sorry looking recruits now fussing with their suitcases and parcels.

'Pay attention you lot! Leave all your belongings here – and form a line for your tea and wads … and stop that chatter when I'm talking!' This last aside was certainly not called for thought Bill, since most of their conversations had died long ago and the majority were too tired to even think of food. At this command an awkward queue was formed shuffling forward to receive a bowl, and then a helping of thick brown soup followed by two slices of bread.

'Tea's in the dixie.' announced the corporal cook, pointing to the two large copper urns set on chairs.

Seating himself at a mess table, Bill took the opportunity to continue his search for Gerry Hardcastle. But it was obvious that Gerry was not a part of the tired contingent now grumbling about their lack of cutlery – spoons being their most immediate need!

'A've no doot this is some form o' initiative test.' commented one of the Scottish lads, as he dipped bread into his soup.

Worse, since they had not yet been kitted out, only a few had either cup or mug, and being too tired to care the majority paraded for their allotted billets where the promise of a good night's rest had more appeal.

Bill was awakened by a terrible din. A coarse voice, shouting and cursing along the length of the hut was accompanied by the clashing of two dustbin lids. The effect, as intended, was startling!

'I think he wants us to get up.' offered Bill, who was earnestly trying to understand what was being said. And as some of the rudely-awakened humanity buried themselves below rough hairy blankets, others sat bolt upright – neither understanding where they were, or what was happening.

'Get up – get up youse 'orrible t'ings!' The strong Irish brogue made the request perfectly clear, as a tall skinny corporal brought the hut to life. 'I am Corporal McElroy and in this hut *I* am god – do youse get that!'

It seemed wise to offer some kind of affirmation of this good news, and as nodding heads and mumbled voices suggested their understanding, the corporal bellowed once again ... 'Do youse get that? Yer sorry looking little men, youse miserable misbegotten t'ings! And yer says *yes* corporal! What do yer say?'

In unison, they said it, loud and clear.

Somewhat mollified, their newly-acquired deity told them that he was their Disciplinary NCO and any 'requests' on their part were to be addressed directly through him. After numerous doubts regarding their parenthood, intelligence, and prospects of future life, Cpl Mac, as he was to be affectionately remembered, gave his men various helpful directions regarding the wash-house, then told them to parade in twenty minutes for breakfast.

'Youse is unlucky this fair mornin' cos we usually go for a nice little run before breakfast see? But youse all got a busy day ahead of ya – so you'll just have to be patient till tomorrow!'

Cpl Mac ran his semi-civilians to the cookhouse where breakfast, in the form of bread and dripping sandwiches was handed to each man with a mug of tea.

'Youse have fifteen minutes to get it down, and when I blow me whistle every mothers' one o' ya will swill out ya mugs in the big dixie by the door, rinse it under the tap, and fall-in outside. Did ya all get that!?'

The residents of hut 32 confirmed, 'Yes Corporal!'

The rest of the morning was spent in being kitted out. Various storemen threw articles of clothing at each man as he recited his service number and surname. The uniform came first, two outfits per man. An army style outfit for work and a 'walking-out' uniform based on the French Chasseurs design. The latter, with its clean cut 'maternity' jacket was the distinctive dress of the Corps and, being jealous of its reputation for smartness, the RFC ensured that each man's 'best dress' was tailored to the individual. There seemed to be two of everything. Two pairs of breeches, jackets, boots, putties, RFC forage caps, shirts, long-john underwear, towels – the pile increased in their arms until, mercifully, a kit-bag was provided in which to carry all.

After the clothing came the military kit. Webbing equipment, packs, belt and revolver holster, water-bottle, mess tin, and button-stick. Finally, they were fitted with gasmasks and the 'swagger cane' common to RFC 'other ranks'. But for most it was the issue of 'eating irons' and a brown tin mug that created the greatest interest.

'Thank Christ for that,' said one. 'We could have starved to death!'

The afternoon was taken up with medical inspections, inoculations, vaccinations, and for one a medical discharge due to a weak heart.

Following their evening meal, Bill and his companions were marched back 'home' where Cpl Mac instructed hut 32 on the niceties of RFC domestic life.

'Well now, youse all got a working uniform and kit, and I wants to see ya dressed proper – with kit formed up like this …' Cpl Mac pointed to one of the instruction posters on the hut wall. 'With lockers made tidy and beds dressed for inspection – like this one 'ere.' Another demonstration followed. 'I'll be inspecting at nine pip-emma! And for those t'ings that fail we have arranged some nice duties in the tin room.'

Like most of his entry Bill was confused. 'What's all this 'ack-emma' and 'pip-emma' stuff?' he asked.

'Time mate, that's what it is, time! Since morning is a.m, they calls it ack-emma, same as p.m. is pip-emma. Come to think on it, they even call us AMs ack-emmas.'

A red-headed lad, Dusty Miller, spoke up, 'Will someone please tell me what the bloody 'tin-room' is? Uncle Mac just mentioned it a minute ago but I don't think its anything to do with metal working - even if we are mechanics.'

Sam Walker, an older man recently transferred from the Royal Engineers, laughed.

'Some hopes Dusty! I've done a bit of tin-room time myself and it's no joke. It's cookhouse fatigues – the worst! Scrubbing out greasy cooking tins with a wire brush and hot water – bloody murder that's what tin rooms are, and it's my guess that some of us are destined to spend some time there after tonight. Let's face it lads, that's what kit inspections are all about!'

Sam was right. Six failed to satisfy Cpl Mac's inspection, and spent various shifts in the dreaded tin room for the rest of the week.

'Before this course is over I bet we all do a spell in this hell hole,' Bill remarked, as in company with the other five defaulters, he toiled in the steamy atmosphere, arms deep in a large grease-filled basin. Yet strange to tell he almost enjoyed the filthy work, or rather the friendships and humour they shared in their new found status as criminals!

By the end of their second day in North Camp Farnborough the new entrants got to know more about themselves. They learned that eighteen of their number were to form Engine Fitter Course No. 12, the remainder being airframe fitters, or riggers as they were more generally known. Between them, these two trades were the backbone of RFC groundstaff.

On the morning of their third day in North Camp all eighteen members of No. 12 (AM) Course assembled inside the main lecture hall of Blenheim Barracks. They were called to attention as their Commanding Officer, Captain Frederick Stokes R.E., entered the room.

'Right men, be seated. Today you will begin your technical training as Ack-Emmas Engine. This course will, for most of you, be of eight weeks duration. During the first few weeks you will be instructed in workshop practice, benchwork, lathe operation, basic blacksmithing, drilling and grinding.'

At this a few sighs and subdued moans were quickly silenced by Cpl Mac.

'Oh I'm well aware that all of you are here because you have done some training as mechanics, indeed, I believe that some of you are already fully skilled. But the RFC needs men not only with sound workshop ability, but also the ability to improvise under field conditions where workshops don't even exist! This is why we must be sure of your basic skills. In addition, you will also have to learn something about the working's of aircraft and the principles of flight before you can be let loose on one of the King's aeroplanes!'

The C/O then outlined their theoretical work and explained that apart from the theory of the four-stroke Otto cycle, magneto, ignition, carburation and so on, they would be expected to know something of the riggers trade as well if they were to be of all-round use on operational squadrons.

'Those of you who are familiar with automobile engines will find that the in-line water-cooled types used in our aircraft are not really much different. But most of our machines are powered by types of engines that you will not have experienced before. I imagine none of you will have worked with rotary engines for example, a type where the cylinders rotate about a stationary crankshaft! However, I will leave all this to your NCO instructors. Meanwhile, I must tell you that you will be trade-tested frequently. Those of you who do not meet our high standards will either be given a second test, or retraining. For hopeless

23

cases I'm afraid the RFC will have to find something else for you to do. Remember this – the lives of the airmen who fly these machines are in your hands. I want you to remember this at all times!'

Captain Stokes then explained their immediate future. 'You will remain in the hut you have been allocated, and if any of you wish to see me then Cpl McElroy will arrange it. At all times you must remain properly dressed, sick parade, messing, clothing parades ... all of these things will be dealt with by Cpl McElroy. All technical matters will be dealt with by your tradesmen NCOs. Any questions?'

Sam Walker stood to attention. 'Air Mechanic 2nd class Walker sir! I transferred from the REs and know my way round a workshop. Do I have to go through all the basics again sir?'

The C/O studied Sam carefully. 'I think we know each other don't we Walker?'

Sam stiffened. 'Yes sir, I was with you at the depot two years back, before I was posted to the School of Artillery at Larkhill.'

Sam had been a regular in the REs for six years, and at his wife's behest had sacrificed the substantive rank of corporal in order to avoid been posted to the front with his unit. He remembered the Captain well, he had been a Lieutenant then, and a very popular officer in charge of workshops.

'That's it! What brought you here Corporal – sorry, Air Mechanic 2nd class Walker?' The C/O laughed as he covered his error, and No. 12 Course laughed with him.

'The RFC wanted trained fitters sir, and the artillery wasn't really in my line.'' Sam lied.

'Well Walker, within the next week or two we shall have an opportunity to find out if *you* suit the RFC! As I said, we shall be looking at each of you, your experience, qualifications and abilities. Those of you that can be exempted basic workshops will proceed directly to engines and some, only some mind you, could possibly be promoted to 1st class Ack Emma, we shall see.'

Bill stood up. 'Sir, do we go to France directly we finish this course?'

Corporal McElroy jumped! 'Stand to attention that man! and didn't I tell youse – give your rank and name when addressing a superior officer!'

Fred Stokes gave a silent curse. Transferring from the REs just after the outbreak of war he fully expected to join an arm that would ignore traditional parade-ground nonsense. Discipline was essential of course, but it didn't need to be of the kind that sapped every natural sense of initiative in a man. But as he had come to learn, the RFC was

24

very much under the eye of the General Staff, many of whom were opposed to the new Corps from day one. As a consequence, and as a sop to the hide-bound attitudes of traditional military thought, discipline was more firmly established in Home Command units of the RFC than it was in the majority of various Army Corps. A form of self-protection no doubt – but completely at odds with their role in war.

'Thank you Corporal. This is as good a time as ever to remind you all that Cpl McElroy here is your good shepherd. He will instruct you on RFC discipline and, pray God, save you from the attentions of stray Sergeants looking for cookhouse defaulters, and service policemen trying to earn their keep. Pay attention to him at all times and remember – you will have to learn how to be soldiers as well as tradesmen during your time here.'

Bill was still on his feet and, like all soldiers the world over, beginning to see the wisdom of keeping his big mouth shut!

'But to answer your question lad – er, what is your name?'

'Air Mechanic 2nd class Proctor sir!'

'Yes. Well Proctor, the answer is no! After you complete your training as Ack Emmas, you will continue here, at North Camp, doing your basic military training. This could be anything from three to four weeks depending on service requirements at that time. So learn what you can from the good Corporal here, before you start with basic training. As for France – some will go for sure. Just as some will stay in Home Command units. Postings will be to squadrons, training units and servicing parks, but these matters are completely out of our hands.'

The Course was then handed over to the Warrant Officer i/c Instruction and his attending group of NCOs.

W/O Simon Baker wore pilots wings over the red and purple ribbon of the Distinguished Conduct Medal. Immaculate in his smart 'maternity' jacket, he made an impressive figure with his broad chest and 'Kaiser Bill' moustache. One of the first senior NCO pilots in the RFC, Flight Sergeant 'Doughy' Baker flew BE2cs in France until shot down earlier in the year. Grounded for medical reasons, he was given his 'Warrant' and posted to Farnborough where he looked after the administration of AM (Engine) Courses.

A popular figure in the Sergeants' Mess, at 40 years of age he had almost 22 years of army service behind him and was tipped as a certainty for the post of Station W/O now being established. A happy man, Simon Baker had the gift of putting everyone at their ease, be they recruits, senior NCOs, or junior officers new to service life. His knowledge of engines was minimal, 'Just so long as they keep the bloody fan going, that's all I need to know.' was a typical remark. But W/O Baker's special contribution to each course was his front-line squadron experience, and for the short time he was to be available Captain Stokes intended to learn as much as he could from the man.

'My name is W/O Baker and apart from instructing you lot on aircraft handling it's my job to see that your talents are put to the best possible use as future RFC fitters. We have no time to waste and I intend to hand you over to the Sergeant and Corporal instructors who will now find out what you know – and what you don't know.'

The Course was then split into small groups where each man was interrogated by one of the NCOs. After a short discussion and an inspection of his hands, Bill declared his apprenticeship as an auto-mechanic.

'That's as maybe Proctor, what counts round here is how you shape up with the trade tests – we'll soon see what you're made of! Anyhow, bring your articles to W/O Baker tomorrow, he'll need to know about your qualifications. But this afternoon we'll start on some workshop tests.'

By now it was 12.30 and their allocated slot for lunch. Clutching their issue of tin plate, mug and irons, No. 12 Course formed threes and marched to the cookhouse.

'Get 'em up youse bloody t'ings, get 'em up! I wants to see them arms waist-high… left … left … left, right, left… halt!!'

It *was* a shambles. Some unfortunate in the front had dropped his plate, its now dented form still spinning by the side of the column. The approved drill was to march with the left arm rigidly kept to the side, with left hand clutching mug, plate and irons. It seemed that one AM/2 Butcher was the culprit. Fat and uncoordinated it was always Butcher.

'Pick it up stupid! Ya no good to man nor beast. Youse is a bloody fat idjit Butcher – what are ya!?'

Butcher confirmed Mac's appraisal with 'I'm an idiot Corp.' while the rest sniggered at his discomfort.

'Bloody Air Mechanics – I've shit 'em! I'd no sooner trust you lot with me old bike, let alone a bloody aeroplane!' Mac placed his long nose inches from the shaking miscreant. 'Mr. Butcher, ya keeps one arm still – the left one! It's the right arm that moves up and down. Ya reports to himself at seven pip emma – we've got some marching to do *this* evening, and every other bloody evening 'till ya gets it right!'

The column continued to the cookhouse where interminably long queues awaited them.

'Watcha betting its bloody stew agin!'

Every intake had one – a moaner! And No.12 Course was no exception. Already assigned the nickname 'Grieving Gardener' or, GG, for short, AM/2 James Gardener was a small skinny cockney who seemed to only have one interest in life – food.

'Nah, its 'growlers' today GG! You can always tell by how fast the fucking queue moves.' True enough, sausages and mash were on the menu. Each man held out his tin plate to receive a large black sausage onto which a muddy looking pile of mashed potatoes was shaken, a service taken at top speed.

'Hey! My dog's a bit short ain't it?' complained GG to the serving cook, as he poked at the small incinerated cylinder dumped on his plate.

'How would I know mate? Anyhow, you know what they say… 'short and thick they do the trick and satisfy the ladies, long and thin'…'

'Go too far in and mass produce the babies..' came the chorus from the queue, always ready for an amusing diversion.

'Damned if I know where you put it all GG.' said Bill, as he watched the little cockney wolf down the mash uneaten on his comrades plates.

'They never gives yer enough 'ere,' moaned GG. 'And we won't eat agin 'till six pip-emma, then all it'll be is bread and jam, unless we 'ave that cauliflower cheese agin.' he brightened.

God almighty, that must be the worst bloody meal they do here' said Geordie. 'It tastes like shite and looks like baby puke!'

Their return to 'school' came fifteen minutes earlier than the usual 1330 hours, resulting in only ten minutes for their meal. An issue of working overalls was to be made from workshop stores and Mac had been told to get the men there early so as to get the best pick.

'Double-time now, let's see youse move!' They hurried along, their meal undigested, clashing along the road with irons and tins jangling like a tinker's cart.

'It really doesn't matter sir, I can always roll the sleeves up a bit,' said Bill. 'I never did get a pair of overalls that fitted me right anyway.' The heavy blue cotton overalls were of good quality but, as usual, always too long in the sleeve for Bill's short arms.

'That's all right son,' said Doughy Baker. 'When you are pulling an engine over by its prop, you need lots of room round the shoulders, stretch your arms up and lets see how they look. A bit big, but once you've spent some time on a cold, exposed, airfield you'll be filling them out with all the clothes you can get inside them. The legs will need shortening though, or you might easily suffer an accident when prop-swinging.'

W/O Baker addressed them all. 'Now pay attention! Don't let me see any of you wearing loose work clothing. Catching loose sleeves on machines, tripping over boot laces, or come-down overalls, can kill! I've seen it happen, and you will too before this lot's over. And you married men – if you're wearing a wedding ring, take it off. I've seen a man lose his foothold coming out of a tall cockpit, grab at a metal edge and strip his finger to the bone as the ring, not his fingers, held the fall!' The advice was received with dramatic effect as two of the older men tore at their wedding bands.

The rest of the afternoon was spent undergoing a series of trade tests. With Sam Walker and four others, Bill was detailed to a filing and fitting exercise. Following a blue-print, each man had to file two pieces of mild steel so that an accurately dimensioned square peg fitted into a square hole. Sam finished five minutes before him, but Sgt Ray waited until Bill had completed his task before inspecting their work.

'Good enough, now we shall have a look at some soldering and brazing and, if there's time, some welding practice.'

By the end of the afternoon Bill was exhausted. Taken at his own time the welding would have been left for the morning. But Sam was setting a cracking pace for him to follow, completing three different types of welding to Bill's one.

'Well done Walker. I can see you've had a lot of experience at this game, REs wasn't it?'

By now the others, who had yet to start on the welding exercises, crowded around Sam's bench to inspect his work.

'Well, yes, at the depot I was one of Captain Stokes's instructors.'

Bill laughed, 'You don't need to tell me what you taught there either Sam.'

Sergeant Ray picked up Bill's work. 'This is good stuff young 'un, let's see what you can do with 'scarf' and 'lap' welding in the morning.'

During the remainder of the week, Bill's feet never seemed to touch the ground.

Each morning, reveille at 0530 was followed by 30 minutes of PT directed under Mac's supervision. Breakfast, now a highlight of their day, was even looked forward to despite occasional gastronomic horrors. There was a watery porridge, kippers, and sometimes fried or boiled bacon. Bread and jam and always the ever present figs which no one, not even GG, ever touched.

Bill had sent home a postcard on his second day at North Camp, and his first letter followed two days later. But now, his news was being created much faster than he could write it. His period in the dreaded

28

tin room was over, and true to his predictions, another six were currently on 'jankers' each evening. At this rate he calculated he would be on 'defaulters parade' in about two weeks time, and he made a mental note to be particularly careful with each daily bed-space layout. But God knows if he would pass muster at the next full kit inspection!

The skill tests were going well, and although he could never keep up with Sam, Bill's work was generally well received. One of their group, 'Timber' Wood, failed all his lathe work, and since tool making was important for promotion to AM/1, he was transferred to a rigger's course. Thanks to the training he received from his father, Bill was always good at 'turning' and for his test produced some fine examples of male and female Whitworth threads, even gaining better marks than Sam for this work.

As instructed, Bill had reported to W/O Baker with his articles of apprenticeship, and in recalling the interview he warmed to the man and his easy going manner.

'Ah yes, I see you've had good schooling Proctor, we need young lads like you in the Corps.' Dropping his eyes to the wings on his tunic he was almost apologetic as he admitted 'I'm not a mechanic as you can see, but by God there have been times I wished I knew more about the machines I flew, particularly the 'donkey' bit.'

'It's a mucky job Sir, but not dangerous like flying. Though I can't see why you would want to know about the donkey – surely there can't be much you *could* do if your engine conked out in the air?'

'Ah, but you see if a pilot knew enough to recognise a fault when flying he could always land and put it right – that's something that does happen you know! It even happened to me once when my fitter was flying with me to the maintenance park at St. Omer. I force landed and he put it right in next to no time! I tell you this, if it were not for the fact that my flying days are over, I would make sure I did the fitter's course before I ever flew again!'

But the most important part of Bill's interview was the news that he and five others were to be tested for 'advanced standing' on the course. And providing they passed their workshop tests with sufficient marks they would go directly on to aero-engines, cutting out at least three weeks of training.

As Bill was dismissed, Doughy Baker smiled to himself, he admired the young fitters for the pride they had in the work they did so well. But young Proctor had something else – he would keep an eye on him!

A confirmed bachelor, Doughy nevertheless cut a fine dash with the girls and had aptly been described as 'a man's man, on permanent loan to the ladies.' He took great personal pride in his appearance, the result of starting as a 'boy' soldier in the West Sussex Regiment. He served in India and, like Jack Henshaw, in the Transvaal, where he won his DCM. But he could read the signs, and as an infantry sergeant didn't fancy his chances in the next one.

In 1913, Sgt Doughy Baker joined the RFC with the intention of learning a useful trade. Something that would not only keep him safely away from the sharp end of any future conflict, but also serve him well as a future civilian, perhaps a married one at that! But, as a hero, and experienced soldier, our brave sergeant fell victim to the mores of military reasoning.

Firstly, his military bearing. Coming to the RFC as an experienced sergeant he was seen as an ideal drill instructor, and was offered a level transfer in this capacity. Doughy had avoided the despised role of drill instructor all his service life and was not keen to start now. But to be accepted for trade training would mean loss of all rank, starting as an AM/3, since he had no skills whatever – other than killing people!

But in the end it was the medal. Proud of it though he was, it was always the bloody medal!

The distinctive ribbon had to be lived up to. Military people respected it, and expected him to behave accordingly. At this time the Corps required a few NCO pilots, and since he was fit and obviously fearless, pilot training was suggested. He had never admitted to a fear of flying, not even to himself, the question never arose! Only officers flew anyway, or so he had thought. He was trapped – to refuse was unthinkable. Besides, to the ladies he was a hero, and recognising his own weakness for them he accepted.

At this time the majority of RFC fliers were 'gentlemen' many of whom had gained their civilian pilots ticket at Brooklands. As a consequence the young, and not so young, gentlemen who wished to fly in the RFC were expected to gain their own licence prior to joining the Corps.

The small core of NCO pilots were trained by the Central Flying School at Netheravon, Wiltshire. Trained on the BE3 biplane, Doughy was found to be a careful pilot of average ability, all he needed was more hours in his log book and he would get these on his squadron. But by the time he left CFS to join 2nd Sqdn, the war had started and he found himself in France, at the sharp-end once more.

Flying reconnaissance missions in the stable, but vulnerable, BE2c was a dangerous game. On his sixth mission they were brought down by ground fire. Doughy managed to bring his machine down inside their own lines, but in the crash he lost the aircraft, the observer and, worst of all – his nerve.

At 39 years of age, Doughy was already too old for operational flying, and sensing that his sergeant might welcome a way out, the C/O gave him a choice: keep on with the squadron, or return to Blighty as an instructor.

And so it was; transferred to Farnborough for instructor duties. Doughy Baker had ended up as an instructor after all, but at least it wasn't drill! Best of all, in recognition of his fine service record, his loss of flying pay, some four shillings a day for every day flown, was compensated by promotion to Warrant Officer.

Yes, W/O Simon Baker DCM had reason to be a happy man, and as he watched Bill Proctor march out of his office he was glad the way things had turned out.

Chapter Four

With Sam and now only three others, Bill looked forward to the advanced part of their course. They still lived and worked with the rest of the group, joining then for all the non-technical lectures they shared, along with their meals, PT, and parades. But it was noticeable that the 'elite', as their comrades called them, were no longer tormented with the hut chores still exacted by Cpl Mac from the rest of the entry.

'Bloody wrong that's wot it is, it's all bloody wrong!' Naturally GG found it so, but whereas most of the others, although envious, could laugh, joke and generally tease, poor old GG found it hard to take.

At their first lecture, on the theory of engines, they were surprised to find three others in the advanced group. They were 'retakes' taking the second part of No. 11 Course again. They also found that Captain Stokes was their lecturer, assisted by two Sergeant demonstrators.

'That's handy,' said Sam. 'These retakes can give us quite a bit of help – they've done it all once before!"

'And failed it once before too.' said Bill, with a wide grin.

Captain Stokes was an excellent teacher, and his lectures filled Bill with enthusiasm. As the days passed he learnt much more of the basics than he had ever known, for although George Graham and his father were both excellent in showing him *how,* it was the *why,* that gave him problems when reading the few books he had at his disposal. Now it all seemed to come together, his pencilled notes growing steadily by the hour, and within days they were studying aero engines.

They listened intently as Stokes introduced the subject by bringing to their attention the all important concept of power/weight ratios. Starting with Bleriot's well known channel crossing in 1909, he discussed the famous Bleriot XI machine in some detail since it had been used extensively by the embryonic Flying Corps.

Bleriot's aircraft was powered by a light, three cylinder, Anzani engine developing about 25 hp. And although distributed like a fan, these three cylinders were still very prone to overheating. Indeed, it's said that if it were not for a provident shower of cooling rain he would never have made it across!

The students were then given a demonstration of a working Anzani which, like a number of other demo engines, was mounted on a robust wooden stand.

'However, searching for a lightweight yet powerful engine, designers turned to the rotary engine, the overheating problem being solved, in part, by the rotation of the cylinders...' As before, what could have been a dreary dialogue was made interesting with anecdotes and humour. Vital detail was carefully explained through demonstrations, questions and hands-on application of theory to practice.

'Right! Now who thinks he can sort out the exhaust valve system on this 50 hp Gnome Rotary?'

Time flew! Theory, demonstrations, stripping, assembling, questions, notes, more questions – Bill was in his element. Even to the point that he begrudged the time he had to spend on his very first pay-parade, an event of no small moment in service life.

Pay parade was never a matter to be considered lightly in the RFC.

'It was just like this in the army as well,' Sam explained. 'So you can thank your lucky stars we only get paid every two weeks!'

They were drawn up into 'Flights' each made up from the various Courses, then marched from corner to corner within the vast space of North Camp's gymnasium until they were drawn into queues according to their surnames.

'Oh my God! Why couldn't I have been born Abbot, or even Abuthnot?' Sam whispered, as Bill fell out to join the Ps now being called.

'Wouldn't make any difference,' replied Bill, 'We'll still hang around till everyone gets paid.'

Bill was now in sight of the pay-table immediately in front, and concerned himself with the ritual now being enacted. Cpl Mac had carefully explained everything, embellishing his instructions with dire threats as to the consequences of missing one's name at roll call.

'When ya name is called youse will spring to attention and answer: Sir! followed by the last three figures of your service number.'

Cpl Mac had drilled this litany into them well. But some got it wrong just the same – muddled replies, incoherence, it was all the same and as the order 'Next man!' followed, the culprit was sent to the back of the queue – to await further abuse and the attentions of scavenging NCOs looking for fatigue fodder – before being paid.

'Proctor!'

Bill stiffened and responded with a high pitched 'Sir, 003!' Marching smartly to the pay table he saluted the Pay Officer, who then counted out the sum called by his clerk.

'One pound four shillings.' the clerk announced, and the sum was duly handed over by the Officer.

One pace back, salute and a smart turn to the right. Bill marched off to his Flight, now forming up at the edge of the gymnasium.

The evening hut discussions were mainly fiscal.

'I work'd it out and I've been underpaid. In fact I'm about one and threepence short!' moaned GG.

Sam tried to explain, hopeful that he could cheer GG with the news that the army, and the RFC, only paid to the nearest shilling.

'Then, every now and again, we get our 'credits' paid to us. This makes up for all the bits we get paid short see? They always like to think that they have some of our money in credit so that they can deduct certain amounts for fines, loss of kit, breakages and such like.'

Jim Pearce, one of the married men, broke into the discussion. 'An army oppo of mine, he's in France, said that they never pays you everything, then if you get killed in action they don't have to try and get it back.'

Sam disavowed this as nonsense. 'It's simply common sense Jim, you and all the other married blokes will find that your pay will always be kept back a bit, just in case it's needed at home, and don't forget, credits also include your clothing allowances as well.'

At this point Cpl Mac informed them that providing the Saturday morning parade went well, and they stayed out of trouble, they would be allowed out on Saturday, after 1600 hours.

'Mind youse this – every mother's one of ya will have to pass my personal inspection first!'

Mac then formed them all up and recommended haircuts for all, before proceeding with warnings on their conduct when in town.

'Youse *will* be smart at all times, and salute every officer ya sees. When ya walk in town that means with ya shoulders back, non o'ya slouching now, cos himself will be about and I'll be watching for dem t'ings as lets me down! And remember, ya gets back within the gates by 2300 hours or 'tis a charge you'll be on! Now! Tomorrow, at two pip-emma, youse will all parade at the barber's shop for haircuts!' With that he left them.

It will be nice to see Farnborough, thought Bill. And with money to spend he hoped there would still be a few shops open.

34

'God knows what the beer is like, but at opening time that's where I shall be.' said Alan Collins. 'Who's joining me for a booze-up in town?' he invited.

'I'd take care if I were you son,' warned Sam. 'The pubs will be fair game for the MPs on a Saturday night, so watch it.'

'Where the girls are is where I'll be,' spoke a good looking youth from his bed.

'Yeah, don't we know it though.' his constant companion, another Welsh lad, spoke with feeling. 'Be warned all of you! Evans here is a bloody menace, he cost us all a week's CB at our last unit. Though I'm the only one who knew it was him that got us confined to barracks, or he'd have been lynched! Before we came here we spent three weeks in Cheltenham, at an RFC reception centre. We had our medicals there, then did nothing but paint every bloody thing in sight look you. Dead boring it was, just waiting for our course here see. Well, on our first evening in town we meets up with these two young girls in a tea shop…'

By now 'Taff' had the attention of the entire hut. 'And when I say *young* I mean about fifteen or sixteen – definitely jail-bait I can tell you! A nice pair of wenches though, talked very posh. Boarders they were, at this convent school near to the camp. Well, we took them to the picture house, to see the Pathé news, and when we came out it was dark see, so we took them back to their school. I said goodnight to my girl, and that was the last I saw of Evans here – until reveille next morning.'

John Evans became the focus of all attention as his friend, aware of the now eager faces around him, was pressed to continue.

'Dirty bugger,' joked one, winking lewdly at the smiling Evans, and making suggestive motions with his forearm.

'I can't help it if the wenches like me,' he said innocently. 'She invited me to her room to look at some pressed flowers.'

At this, even Bill saw the humour of it and laughed with the rest, yet felt awkward and embarrassed by the crude ribaldry that followed.

'I'm bloody certain she was no virgin either.' added Evans.

Taff Jones continued with his story. 'Well she certainly wasn't after you'd been banging her every night for the following week. Next thing we knew, we were all called on parade. The C/O warned us off very clearly. It had been reported to him that some man or other was known to have been regularly entering the local convent school and spending the night there. Suspicion had fallen on us - and if he found it was one of his men that was guilty of seducing innocent little schoolgirls …'

'Innocent my arse! She bloody well made a physical wreck of me within the week that kid.'

'Shut up Evans, you're a bloody sex maniac! To continue, the C/O said he would have the culprit up for court martial. So we got one week of CB – the lot of us, all because of this cock-happy bugger. Mark you, he'd never have been found out if it wasn't for the fact that every morning, after he left Dora's room…'

At this a chorus of 'Dora, oh Dora!' rent the air, now smoky with the fervent puffing of cigarettes.

'The daft sod had a piss in the lavvy down the hall. Problem was, he left the seat up – a dead give away! The matron reported it to the Mother Superior and she to our C/O, who must have had a good laugh about it because the news soon got around the camp.'

Conversation was now dominated by the subject of sex, and though at first nauseated by the crude barrackroom stories, Bill soon realised that they were mainly a form of bravado, particularly the tales from fellows his own age. And although dubious of some of the stories, he was concerned about his inexperience and resolved never to reveal his virginity to the others at any cost.

The following day's lectures and demonstrations were concerned with the subject of engine lubrication. By way of introduction, Sgt Ray reminded the class of the two-stroke system, where a petrol/oil mix provided adequate lubrication for small engines.

'But this is not sufficient for the highly loaded bearings and cams of a rotary. Here a suitable lubricant must be pumped into the crankcase where rotation and splash distribute it around the critical parts.' Using a cut-away model, the sergeant then demonstrated the rotary lubrication system and continued: 'For this job castor oil was found to be suitable since it has the best film strength and is hardly soluble in petrol, so it's not washed away by petrol vapour in the crankcase.'

The class was then directed to an early 'Gnome' rotary set on a large wooden stand.

'This little fella consumes four gallons of petrol an hour at cruise revs, but in the same period it also consumes two gallons of castor oil. It costs more on oil than it does on fuel! And most of that gets flung out via the exhaust valves. Now we all know what castor oil does to you! I'll bet you remember taking spoonfuls of the stuff as kids? Well, I can tell you this, those of you who work on rotaries will never suffer from constipation!'

Good-hearted laughter and groans met this aside, only to be followed by a sympathetic sucking-in of breath, as Sgt Ray added… 'But pity the poor bloody pilot and his observer, if he has one. They have to swallow the foul stuff for hours – trapped in their cockpits!'

John Evans couldn't resist it... 'Did you say cockpit or cesspit Sergeant?'

'Oh you can laugh, but just remember this, when a crew come back from a mission over enemy lines and they smell like they've shit themselves – they probably have! But don't get to thinking it was due to the Hun, it was more likely the bloody lubricant!'

The advanced class were then introduced to a number of fully working rotaries, all secured to sturdy demonstration benches. Most were fitted with two-bladed propellers, but a few had four-bladed props. There were Gnomes, Sequins, Monosoupapes, Bentleys, Le Rhones, and Clergets, the latter extending to 140 hp. But, as Sgt Ray explained, with something like 350 lbs of engine rotating at 1200 rpm, these type of engines created high gyroscopic forces which increase in proportion to their power.

'As a consequence the high torque reaction tends to turn the aircraft round its prop-shaft. And unless the pilot is ready for this he could turn his aeroplane into the torque and spin – if he is not careful. This is why the rotary cannot be made too powerful, higher power is left to the in-line engines, which we shall deal with later.'

At the end of the demonstration Sam and Bill compared notes as they inspected the engines on display.

'The one thing I'm not looking forward to is swinging the props, particularly those four-bladed brutes.' Sam said.

'Looks easy enough, but I know what you mean,' Bill agreed. 'Though I'm sure they will teach us how to do it without getting injured – I hope!'

Prior to getting their 'walking out' passes on Saturday afternoon, Cpl Mac gave his men a full dress inspection. Buttons, cap badges, boots – all were given careful scrutiny, and some were 'advised' to try again if they were to pass muster. The cheap rough cloth of their uniforms was difficult to keep smart, and since there were no facilities for pressing tunics and trousers, they had to employ the time-honoured method of sleeping on them. By taking great care to fold the garments correctly, and placing them between the hard mattress and a blanket, it was possible to get some semblance of a crease. However, this depended upon the kind of sleeper you were and the state of the mattress – made up from three square 'biscuits'.

'I don't know Sam. I've been sleeping on my best for three nights now, and they still look like I've been sleeping *in* them rather than *on* them. Still, Mac seems to think I look smart enough, and that's what counts.'

'Aye, its bloody typical Bill! Just the same as in the army. I can never make out why they spend so much time telling us to look smart when they give us junk like this to wear. The officers have serge material, now that does look smart! But this stuff – just look at my tunic, it flares out like a ballet dress!'

The entire hut qualified for their passes and walked into town. Most of them found there was little to see and even less to do, and after a fish and chip meal many returned to camp early. A few, at the behest of Collins, Jones and Evans, went into the pubs as soon as they opened, while Sam and Bill looked for bookshops.

'I should say we have about forty minutes before all the shops close,' observed Sam. 'So if we are to find something on aircraft we had better get a move on young Bill.'

By five o'clock they had enquired at two likely shops but there was nothing to be had. Finally, they found a small shop specializing in technical books.

'Well, we have about ten minutes to go,' said Sam, looking at his pocket watch. 'I think you had better ask the girl if she has anything on aeroplanes.'

As Bill approached the counter a dark-haired girl, about his own age, gave him a welcoming smile.

'And what can I do for the Royal Flying Corps gentlemen?'

Bill grinned, blushed and dropped his cap.

'Er, we hoped you might have some books on aeroplanes, miss?'

She remained smiling. Petite and pretty, with large brown eyes above a generous and well sculptured mouth.

'Now that's a surprise!' she teased, the long dark eyelashes fluttered again. 'I know we don't have much – but I will look for you.'

Sam was enjoying himself. In the short time he had known the young Yorkshireman he had taken to the lad's quiet good humour. Clean-minded and good-natured, the boy had never mentioned girls, and he guessed that they had but little influence on his life so far. Bill was still gazing at the pretty thing behind the counter while she, if he wasn't mistaken, seemed keen to flirt with the lad.

'Gosh Sam!' Bill fumbled with his cap as she returned, then taking the offered book, looked her square in the face. The smile was different now, more gentle as she spoke.

'I'm afraid it's not very useful – it only deals with aero-engines.'

Sam snatched at the book. 'Just what we wanted young 'un.'

Bill couldn't take his eyes from her. Again, the lashes drooped then opened, as if shutters to her passing thoughts. Not one of them, in the dim stillness of the shop, was more surprised than Bill as he stuttered

'Will you be...be here next Saturday?'

'Yes!'

The book was four shillings and sixpence, not that Bill knew, he was still staring at the girl as Sam paid her the money.

'Where are you from?' she said.

'Er, North Camp ...'

'No, silly. I mean where do you come from, up north somewhere isn't it?'

Flustered and hot under the tight fitting tunic Bill tried to calm down.

'Dacre Banks,' but seeing the question in her eyes he added, 'in Yorkshire that is!'

As usual when excited, Bill's accent had become stronger as he fumbled the words.

'Where the puddings come from.' she teased, her eyes mischievous as she smiled. 'But now I must close up – it's gone five-thirty.'

'Perhaps we could look at some similar books next Saturday, if you have them that is.' Sam knew that if it were left to Bill, the unspoken romance would end here and now.

'I'm afraid that's all we have on aeroplanes, but you are welcome to look around if you come next week.'

Bill nodded, speechless almost. 'Yes we will, and thank you very much.' He dashed out of the door as Sam, laughing, gave the girl a wink.

'Young Bill is not like this really – I think you've smitten him to the ground lass.'

She smiled, her eyes crinkling with humour as she rocked her head from side-to-side. 'He's very sweet, but are they all so shy in Yorkshire?'

Sam laughed with her. 'Can I tell him your name?'

'Alice.'

As they returned to the centre of the town, Bill talked of nothing but their good fortune in discovering the shop. Finding a seat he sat down to look at their purchase and, quite forgetting that it was Sam who paid for it, remarked.

'I shall go next Saturday and buy another book, that girl was quite helpful don't you think? Not bad looking was she?" He went on and on. Finally, Sam thought he should bring the lad down to earth.

'We may not even get a pass next week you know!'

Bill now became quite agitated until finally, 'I've just got to see her again Sam!' His companion smiled, nodding his head sagely.

'I wondered when you would come to admit it – her name is Alice by the way!'

Bill had spent the first night rehearsing, then rejecting the various approaches he would make to Alice next Saturday. Sam's assurance that she liked him, that she had even flirted with him, added to his confidence. 'I'll ask her to go out for a walk, for tea perhaps?'

Sunday Church Parade was over and as they returned to their hut Bill thought about the letters he had to write home – should he tell mum about Alice? No, best not, nothing may come of it after all.

Corporal Mac was not a happy man as he strode into the hut.

'So! Youse went and let me down! Two of ya decided to get drunk and fight wit the locals did ya! Well, those two are now under close arrest in the detention cells, and it's my opinion that the C/O will give 'em at least two weeks pack drill. But the rest of ye will also suffer cos none of ya will be getting a pass next Saturday – that's to teach youse all a lesson!'

Bill's thoughts were murderous. 'Pack drill will be the least of their worries, wait till I get my hands on those Welshmen!'

'Didn't I just tell you now – nobody gets a pass next Saturday! I'll hear no more about it and dat's dat!"

Bill's attempts to reason with Mac fell on stony ground.

'Don't worry, she'll still be there the following Saturday,' Sam sympathised. 'And it's not as though you arranged anything definite with her is it?'

Bill was not sure of anything anymore and turned to the letters he was writing. There were a number to answer, one to his parents, where he needed to respond to some technical questions asked by his father, and another, now very much overdue, to Maggie.

'When you've finished writing Bill, come and look at the book we got yesterday – it's going to be very useful.'

Bill had quite forgotten the book. 'Right, and I owe you half the money. Sorry Sam.'

The following morning's tuition continued with rotaries and their heating problems. Bill was fed up and paid little attention, but he knew that Sam would be taking accurate notes and he could catch up later. The afternoon session was more interesting however. It dealt with the power regulation of rotaries, and since Bill knew he must have a thorough understanding of the subject to pass the course he forced himself to listen intently.

Captain Stokes introduced the subject with the Gnome Rotary.

'Like most of its kind, the Gnome's carburettor has a butterfly throttle valve, and a sleeve air valve, that require careful juggling of throttle, air and fuel if it is to run smoothly. But in flight these combinations are even more complex since they need to be altered as forward speed or altitude are changed. I suppose you could say that all rotaries are constant speed engines since, when landing the aircraft, power is regulated by cutting the engine with a 'blip' switch located on the control stick. However, Mr Baker will tell you all about that in an hour or so.'

Doughy Baker continued after the C/O had finished. Taking the group to the Gnome 'mock-up' cockpit he showed the class all the important controls and instructed them on basic 'starting up' procedures. Then, moving to the 80 HP Le Rhone engine, with Sgt Ray in the mock-up cockpit, he positioned the trainees for live start-up practice.

'Now the 80 HP Le Rhone should give about 1,100 rpm when run on the ground, and about 1,200 rpm flying all out near ground level. We shall run it at about 1,050 for this lesson, and only for a short time.'

'There are only three engine controls. The fuel main tap, the fuel fine adjustment lever and the throttle lever.'

Each man was then shown these items by Sgt Ray.

'The fuel supply is gravity fed. Now, theoretically, once the fine adjustment lever has been set correctly, that's that! The engine will then run smoothly for all further settings of the throttle – that's what it says in the book anyway. Oh, it will run well enough that's true, but in practice it's usual to vary the position of the fine-adjustment with every change of throttle position.'

With that, Doughy discussed engine running at some length before demonstrating engine start-up.

'I appreciate that all of you are a little shy about starting-up! But if you follow the procedure it's as safe as houses – so pay attention all of you, I want no accidents.'

With Sgt Ray in the cockpit, Doughy went to the front of the mock aircraft and faced the class – now standing safely behind a chalked semi-circle drawn in front of the engine cradle.

'Pay close attention. The following procedures must be employed at all times, taking care to observe the rules for each engine type. First, we make sure the wheels are chocked! I've seen ack-emmas being chased all over the field by a runaway – don't let it happen to you!'

Doughy let their imaginations run riot for a while then, as the laughter subsided, he continued. 'A runaway may not catch you, but it might get someone else – remember that!"

'You now 'suck-in' the fuel by turning the prop over a few turns. The ack-emma, or pilot, will then half open the fine-adjustment lever and slightly open the throttle. Any questions?'

One of the 'retakes' asked. 'Sir, do all engines rotate clockwise? I know this one does, both for sucking-in and for starting, but is that the same for all engines?' Doughy passed the question to Sgt Ray.

'A good question. The short answer is no, they don't! In this park they do, all the engines you work on anyway. But when you go to the squadrons, or maintenance parks, take care. Some go anticlockwise, and some go one way for sucking-in and the other way for contact – so beware.'

Doughy continued with his instruction, fully aware that his class hung on to every word.

'The mechanic now stands by the prop, like this ... and shouts, 'Petrol on, switches off, suck-in!' The mechanic will now give the prop a few turns in the direction of engine rotation, in this case clockwise ... like this.' He turned the two-bladed wooden prop a couple of turns. 'He then calls ... 'Contact Sir!' And when he receives the reply 'contact' from the cockpit he grasps the right hand side of the prop, near the tip, and standing as clear as possible gives it a big swing downwards.'

'Very well then. Let's see what you have remembered. Why do I grasp the right hand side... Proctor?'

'Because it's a clockwise rotation sir!'

Doughy nodded to Sgt Ray, who was waiting for the signal.

'As soon as the engine has been turned over and the mechanic has shouted for contact, the cockpit drill is to push the fine-adjustment lever half open and advance the throttle to about a quarter open. Then, as the engine starts, close the throttle and cut the fine-adjustment until the engine begins to miss. The throttle is then pushed well open and the fine-adjustment advanced until maximum rpm are obtained. The engine is now adjusted for ground running. So stand well back and we shall go through the routine proper.'

Doughy faced the propeller. 'Petrol on, switches off, suck-in, Sir!' Sgt Ray, with his head out of the cockpit replied

'Petrol on, switches off, suck-in!'

Doughy executed the sucking-in and, as he placed his hands on the tip of the prop shouted, 'Contact Sir!'

After a couple of seconds Sgt Ray returned with...'Contact!'

With shoulders back and head high, Doughy heaved the heavy propeller down, moving backwards as he did so. The engine, being warm and finely tuned, fired immediately.

'Easy isn't it?' he said, turning to the class.

Doughy and Sgt Ray repeated the procedure three more times, explaining their respective roles as they did so. Then each of the AMs took Sgt Ray's place in the cockpit, until they all had practised engine running. Finally the dreaded moment arrived when they had to practise prop-swinging!

The retakes went first, each making the task look simple. Sam went next, after further instruction regarding his stance.

'Make sure you don't drop your head forward as you swing,' warned Doughy. 'That's a sure way of getting a permanent headache!'

Bill's hands were sticky with sweat and he desperately wanted to be somewhere else as his name was called out. He felt unsure in his heavy ammunition boots, and was afraid of slipping on the concrete floor which was now filmed with a dressing of castor oil. Grasping the prop he addressed the cockpit.

'Petrol on…'.

'Stop!'

Sgt Ray lifted both hands above the cockpit, as Doughy roughly pulled Bill from the propeller.

'Just look at this man! Loose overall sleeves half turned-up at the elbow, wearing a wrist watch, and the floor swimming in oil! Disaster in the making!'

Bill wasn't sure if the reprieve was worth the admonition, but by the time he had rolled down his sleeves, removed his watch and wiped the floor his fear was gone.

'Contact!' It was over.

The class then continued the practice taking it in turns to act both in the cockpit and at the propeller. As they made the control adjustments Sgt Ray diagnosed their errors from the exhaust smoke.

'Remember! Black smoke … too much petrol; white smoke … too much oil.'

As the class cleaned up, prior to being marched to the mess-hall, Doughy Baker called for their attention.

'Any of you ack-emmas know anything about the 1913 FN motorbike?'

Bill stepped forward. 'My boss had one sir, I used to service it for him.' Doughy signalled him forward.

'I'd appreciate you looking at one right now Proctor. But don't worry I'll make sure you get to the mess-hall in time for tea.'

Doughy had purchased the bike from a sergeant recently posted overseas. A good bargain at five pounds but flawed with poor performance.

'I was hoping I might run into someone who could take a look at it for me, I have no skill with engines as you know – apart from starting and stopping them. And if you would care to earn a few bob, in your spare time … well I leave it up to you lad.'

Bill didn't hesitate, apart from his interest in bikes he admired the easy-going Warrant Officer and was happy to do him a favour.

'I'd be glad to sir, I know the FNs backwards, but I shall need my tools on an evening.'

Doughy thought for a moment. 'Best thing is to use our motor-pool, they have all the tools. I'll arrange it with Sgt Dodds, he has maintenance crews working there until 2200 each day. So you could work from, say, six till nine pip-emma. How about two bob a night?'

Bill flushed. 'No sir, I don't want payment, it's no trouble.'

'Are you certain Proctor? I'd have thought you'd have had enough of engines during the day! Anyway, I'm grateful to you lad, but you get paid just the same, and that's an order! And I'll fix things up with Cpl McElroy. Now, get on the back son, you can form an opinion of the damned thing as I drive you down for tea.'

After two more days on rotary engines Captain Stokes introduced then to radial types. Their days were filled with engines and for Bill, his evenings too. Eager to learn what he could, Doughy spent almost as much time at the motor pool as Bill.

'I think I might make an ack-emma yet lad,' he joked. 'In a hundred years or so!'

By Friday night the bike was perfect and Doughy competent enough to do minor servicing jobs himself.

'Great stuff young Proctor, how much is it I owe you?'

Bill still refused payment.

'Now that's all well and good son, but I cannot be owing you any favours, so here it is – twelve bob. And if you would like to give the bike a run tomorrow afternoon it's yours.'

'Our passes were stopped this weekend sir, but I would have liked that … there was a girl …'

Doughy laughed. 'Already! You bloody young rogue.'

Warrant Officer Baker took an official-looking pad from his pocket and wrote a short note.

'Give this to Cpl McElroy, Proctor! You are detailed for technical duties and will report to me at the Sgts' Mess, 3.30 pip-emma. *You* are going to test my bike tomorrow!'

Bill parked the FN close to Webb's Bookshop, noting, for the first time, the name above the door. 'Alice Webb' he said to himself.

Doughy had provided him with the bike, a pass until 2300 hours, and a 'Good luck Proctor, leave the bike in the cycle sheds when you return!'

Flushed with excitement, he paused at the shop door. It was only 4 o'clock, Alice would not finish work for a while yet. What if she spurned his offer for a ride on the bike, or even go out with him? Maybe she had a fella already? He walked away …perhaps he should leave things until after 5 o'clock, but what if she wasn't in? Bill returned to the door and was about to enter, when a customer came out of the shop. He turned and walked off.

A warm evening sun brightened the busy streets as Bill passed a flower shop. An impulse prompted him inside, he'd never bought flowers before.

'Ah well, in for a penny …' he mused.

Sensing the young airman's shyness, the sales lady helped him choose a small bunch of mixed blooms and wrapped them in plain paper. Bill paid for the flowers and left the shop at a run, an almost guilty look an his face. It was an act of commitment, now or never!

Alice Webb looked up from the counter as the door bell tinkled. She smiled her surprise, then laughed, as Bill held out the floral gift.

'For you Alice!'

The boy-like shyness almost brought tears to her eyes as she took the flowers.

'Thank you very much. I'll be honest, I saw you when you first came to the door, about an hour ago. How sweet of you to go and look for the flowers. Just a minute, I'll find a vase for them.'

Bill sighed. The first part hadn't gone so badly at least. He looked at his watch, five past five, too early – what now?

As she returned Bill looked out of the window. 'Nice day isn't it?'

Ignoring the remark Alice couldn't resist teasing. 'Have you come to purchase another book?'

'Er no, that is I … well, in a way I wanted to er … Alice, would you like to come out with me?'

'Where to?' Her large eyes seemed to question the propriety of his question.

Saved by the entrance of a customer Bill had time to ponder on the unanswered question. A ride on my motorbike? Or tea?? Damn the man why doesn't he buy the bloody book and push off!

Alice came round the counter and whispered 'Come back at six

45

o'clock. I have to check the till for Dad, then get changed.'

Dressed in a simple 'sailor suit' Alice was as fresh as the summer evening she stepped into. Her loose white blouse was square-cut, and trimmed with navy to match the neat straight skirt that fell to a length of just acceptable modesty.

'Phew! just look at you!'

She smiled his reward and took his arm. 'Well Billy-boy where are you going to take me?'

It seemed he could never take the initiative, and as the shops were now closed he suggested. 'A walk perhaps – but I'm afraid I don't know Farnborough very well. I intended to take you out for tea, if you wanted to of course, but is there anywhere open now?'

Alice stopped. 'I'm not sure that my mother would like me going anywhere with a young man whose name I don't even know!'

'I'm sorry, but I really thought – just now, my name, you just …'

Alice squeezed his arm and laughed. 'Your friend told me you were called Bill, last Saturday, just after you fled in such a hurry.'

They introduced themselves with mock formality. Now more comfortable and at ease, Bill suggested going for a ride on his motorbike. Alice raised her shoulders, spread her arms and looked down at her feet, laughing at herself.

'Like this?' She thought a moment. 'My mother would say it just isn't done; young ladies do not ride on motorbikes! But it *would* be exciting Billy – if you are sure I won't fall off? Or get my skirt dirty? If you can promise me that then I would love to, but not around here for heaven's sake.'

With Alice side-saddle behind him, her arms tightly about his waist, Bill could hardly believe it was all happening. It was pure joy; the thrill of riding about the Surrey countryside without a thought for the machine itself – just the sheer pleasure of it all, with his beautiful passenger shouting, unheard, into his ear.

Approaching a tiny village he slowed down and, hearing Alice's words for the first time, pulled to the side.

'Could we stop for a drink Bill? Just ahead there is a nice little pub where you can sit outside in the summer.'

It was all very new to him, and everything was happening so fast. It seemed like Dacre was a million miles away and a thousand years ago.

As he parked the bike he noticed that Alice had found them a bench under a large oak. She smiled as he approached, throwing her hands into the air.

'That was wonderful Bill, my very first ride on a motorbike!'

46

As he sat beside her Bill took stock of his surroundings. It was his first real look at the southern countryside and its people. Everything was so much softer. The air, the buildings, the tree under which they sat, even the voices of the people enjoying their evening out.

Coming from an unsophisticated background, with no great experience of life outside of Dacre Banks, Bill was slightly unsure of himself, and although proud and happy beyond measure, he felt a little out of his depth.

'What can I get you Alice?'

She paused. 'A shandy, I'm so thirsty Billy, could I have a large one please?'

On entering the pub he noticed fresh sandwiches for sale, and ordered two rounds of cheese with their drinks; a pint of shandy for Alice and a cider for himself.

As he waited for his order, he contemplated the differences between his own county and those of the south. Everything was softer here. The air was more languid and the countryside, with its profusion of hedges rather than dry-stone walls; less harsh. People's accents were very much softer too. He found the comparisons agreeable nevertheless, and the locals were certainly ready to engage him in friendly conversation. But not so much for the patriotic reasons Bill had in mind, as much as just listening to his dialect.

Like all parts of Britain where army camps had been set up, local populations were fascinated by the invasion of accents and dialects foreign to their own. A new accent was akin to discovering a rare animal and Bill's flat vowels targeted him as one of a special species. Disengaging from the small talk about the bar Bill courteously refused the offer of a drink and, with his tray of food and drinks, returned to Alice.

As they enjoyed their drinks, Bill explained how he had come by Doughy's motorbike and his good fortune in being able to get into town.

'I'm so glad you liked the ride, but I doubt if I will be able to borrow the bike again.'

Bill realised that he would soon have to start planning his next date with her. What did she like to do in her free time? Where could they go? They could hardly come here again, it was too far from the town. Maybe she would not want to see him again?

Alice spoke of her father's business and her job in the bookshop.

'Father wanted an assistant, but with the war we couldn't get anyone suitable which is why I am behind the counter. Mother dislikes the idea, but there, she's a little old-fashioned poor dear. But enough about the Webb family, tell me about Dacre Banks and Yorkshire puddings.'

Bill showed her a photograph of his family. It had been taken only a week after he had left home, and showed his mother, seated in front of their house, with father standing beside her – one hand on her shoulder. Eileen and Maggie were dressed in their best smock-like dresses, standing by their parents. It had been his mother's idea. She knew that George Graham had a camera and he, in his turn, had been pleased to arrange the formal looking group into a delightful photograph.

Bill was quietly proud of his family and had shown the photograph to Sam when it had arrived. He also showed him the photograph of Jane Graham which, at Jane's insistence, her father had taken, to be included with that of the Proctor family. As Sam had observed, 'You're a lucky lad Bill. A lovely family *and* a nice girl to go back to – but I don't think you ever mentioned her to me before?"

Bill explained that Jane was not his girl, just his boss's daughter, but he never showed Jane's photograph to Alice for all that.

'They are a lovely family Billy. I hope you appreciate them? I think your mother is very beautiful.'

Indeed, Muriel Graham made a fine picture. In her best black dress, the high neck line fronted with lace, she looked as elegant as her husband looked uncomfortable. Despite the best suit, watch-chain, and speckless white shirt, Kit Proctor could never be mistaken for anything but a workman in his Sunday best. An intelligent girl, Alice learned more from the photograph than she could ever have gleaned from conversations with Bill.

'You resemble your father so much Billy! And your sisters, how old are they?'

They chatted on. He found it so easy to talk to Alice and discussed his life in the dales with enthusiasm. She listened intently. It was another world she thought, totally different from the sophisticated town life of Surrey. As a distant clock chimed the hour she caught at Bill's wrist.

'Billy, we must go soon! It's been lovely, but you have to get back to camp – and mother worries …' Seeing the disappointment mirrored in his eyes she leant forward and kissed him lightly on the cheek.

'Listen Billy. I've been thinking. There's a military concert to be held in the town next Saturday evening. It should be exciting, there will be marching bands, parades and such, shall we go? It starts at seven o'clock, so if you could meet me out of the shop at six, I could bring a small picnic – what do you think?'

He didn't even trouble to think. Was it always going to be so easy? Alice always pre-empted his shyness it seemed. The irony of escaping from tedious parades to watch one for pleasure didn't even get a second thought.

'What a good idea, yes I would like that. Six it is then, but I'm afraid I won't have the bike next week.'

As Bill parked the bike at the Sgts' Mess, his thoughts were filled with Alice and their evening together. Although not exactly frightened of the opposite sex, he had never been entirely comfortable in their company. Oh yes, there was Jane of course, but that was different. He had known Jane mostly through Eileen, almost another sister. Alice was wonderful. It was she who had arranged their next date, so she must have wanted to see him again. And with her everything happened so naturally, even to kissing her goodnight – fully on the lips. He savoured the moment as he walked back to the hut, whistling softly to himself.

With the Sunday morning Church Parade now over, Sam and Bill discussed the past week as they caught up with their chores and tuition notes.

'We start on the 'in-lines' tomorrow Bill. I'd like us to do a bit of swotting later – if you can take your mind off Alice for a moment that is. I suppose you'll be seeing her this coming Saturday, eh?'

Bill felt a little guilty about his trip to town, and although he came in for a bit of good-natured joshing, he knew that some resented his good fortune. However, most of the ill-feeling was reserved for the two Welshmen who, fortunately for them, were kept busy by the service police during their free time.

'Look Sam, I hope you don't mind me going off with Alice next Saturday? I should have included you in our arrangements. Though I'm not sure if you would have been interested in watching the Combined Guards Brigade band.'

Sam made a show of parting his thinning hair and, wetting the tip of his finger, ran it over his eyebrows. 'Do yourself a favour lad, you wouldn't stand a chance with me around, and I would hate to steal your girl! Besides, I'm about as keen on watching the Guards as you are – only I don't have the added attractions! By the way, you may not have much more time with her don't forget. Only three more weeks to go, then it's square-bashing for a month. Oh my God! I remember it well from my army days ... 'If it moves salute it, if it stays still paint it!' I don't think we are allowed out during our square-bashing either. And after that, God knows where we will be, France more than likely.'

Chapter Five

'Well Bill, two weeks of in-line donkeys followed by trade tests and we'll be finished – all but the dreaded square-bashing that is!'

Bill pulled a face of disgust as he took his place next to Sam in the 'Advanced Engines' lecture room. 'It just doesn't make sense to me Sam, I mean what the hell's the use of us being trained to shoot people? We're bloody engine fitters not squaddies!' Sam smiled, his young friend had soon adopted the casual use of service adjectives despite his strict upbringing, it was harmless enough, even natural in the circumstances, but he hoped the lad would not become too coarse.

'I suppose we could be called upon to fight you know. If we go to France we shall be close to the front line, and although the aeroplanes can fly off we might have to fight our way back, then you'll be glad you know how to use a rifle lad! Anyway, you're in luck Bill my boy, I know you don't want to leave Farnborough too soon – having just met Alice and all – but according to Doughy Baker our recruit training is definitely here at North Camp, by the Malplaquet Lines, so at least you will be able to see Alice for another three weeks after we finish here.' Bill's face brightened up at this, only to darken as Sam continued... 'But I remember when I first joined the colours, we were all confined to barracks while square bashing!'

The ack-emmas all rose as Captain Stokes entered the room accompanied by Sgt Ray and a civilian dressed in overalls.

'Be seated. As you know we start instruction on in-line aero-engines today. They are very different from rotaries and I can assure you that you will see increasing numbers of them on the squadrons. Indeed, progress at the Royal Aircraft Factory suggests that many of the new machines now being planned will employ in-line engines, all of them much more powerful than the types we have here for your instruction.'

'Mr Thomson here is a highly experienced workshop fitter and is on the staff at the Royal Aircraft Factory. You possibly are not aware of this, but the RAF is based here at Farnborough; as a consequence you will be taken on a conducted tour of the factory before you pass out from this course. Mr Thomson will be assisted by Sgt Ray in showing you the intricate details of the different types of in-line we have at the school, most of them still powering operational machines.'

At this point Captain Stokes approached two demonstration stands each containing a genuine aero engine that had been cut-away to reveal vital parts. Fully working pistons nestled in highly polished cylinders, valves and plugs were revealed for all to see, and the entire assembly surrounded by components stripped for detailed instruction.

'The working units you see here will be fully demonstrated by Mr Thomson later in the day, but for the moment it is sufficient to say that they represent the general principles of in-line engines. Oh, I know that most of you know the principles well enough but I must remind you that these are *aero engines* and need to be considered in a different way to their automobile cousins. Take this four cylinder one for instance, you are looking at the earliest British aero in-line, the 1909 35hp Green water-cooled engine. It has a bore of 105mm and a stroke of 120mm but its power to weight ratio is as high as 6lb/hp! Far too heavy to be a great success of course – but it was soon improved to this 60hp version which has twice the capacity for a lower power to weight ratio. The 60hp Green did quite well with the Avro 500, but is generally inadequate for military purposes where the machine must carry an effective war load as well as its crew.'

Captain Stokes moved on to the other side of the room where a number of working aero engines were installed on demonstration benches. 'Here we have an early 1908 60hp Renault air-cooled V8, later developed to the 70hp air-cooled version seen here. This engine is one that you will need to give special attention to since it powers the BE2c, a machine that is now in mass production and for those of you who go to reconnaissance squadrons in France, it will be your prime concern. For those posted to home units, particularly flying training, you will find it on the Maurice Farmans. Another Renault, built under licence by Wolseley Motors, Birmingham, is the 80hp you see here. This unit can be employed either in tractor or pusher installations.'

Bill found the lecture fascinating; this was what he was here for after all, and although he was confident about automobile motors he could see that the design of aero engines began with the ever-present problem of weight before such things as power and cooling could be considered. By the end of the day their notebooks were full and the evening was devoted to swapping notes in readiness for the following morning.

Mr Thomson was an experienced instructor and spent most of the second morning using the blackboard and the cut-away models.

'One advantage of the in-line engine is that their design demands the use of carburation, and so the delivery of power to the propeller can be controlled via a throttle. Power can therefore be increased by design – whereas with the rotary engine it is limited by torque – as we have seen.'

Thomson warmed to his theme as he saw the interest returned by his students. 'Naturally there are problems inherent in the design of in-lines, not least being the cooling of the cylinders, particularly those to the rear of the engine block…'

By the end of the third day they were stripping and reassembling various motors to order, and their workshop time increased unto the late evening with a special supper arranged for ten pip-emma.

Sergeant Ray opened the first lecture of the fourth day with a talk on daily servicing of the Renaults, followed by what was to be the first of a series of practical exercises with engines installed on working aircraft. Mostly the machines were old BE2s and an assortment of MF 'Longhorns' and 'Shorthorns' which, Bill mused, looked more like chicken cages than aeroplanes, with their pusher propellers hidden in a maze of bracing wires.

'Oh God,' moaned Jim Pearce 'How the hell do you get to the prop when starting one o' them things?' Bill said nothing; he secretly hated prop swinging and hoped he would never have to admit to his fear of this basic chore. So far he had been able to avoid most of it by electing to chock the aircraft wheels, this usually worked since an ack-emma with a handful of essential chocks was never detailed for another task – so far! Failing this stratagem there was always the cockpit of course, but this duty was usually directed on a roster basis. Always careful not to advertise his fear, Bill would sometimes volunteer to swing the prop, with not a little show, but only when the engine was running warm and required but a touch to fire up the start.

As the week progressed so did the keen interest of the ack-emmas to the point that even their spare time was spent in technical discussions and argument, the latter mainly concerned with the relative merits of rotary versus in-line power plants.

After four days of intensive instruction the 'elite' not only felt qualified to discuss in-line engines with the rest of No.12 Course, now just starting on rotaries, but felt impelled to parade their new-found knowledge during the endless barrack-room discussions. For Bill, with four years of recent automobile experience behind him, in-line engines made sense. He felt comfortable with them and, for a Yorkshireman, un-characteristically profound on the subject. 'Oh I know rotaries are lighter, but from what I hear quite a number of pilots find them difficult to control – give me a throttle any time! And how can they develop? Mr Thomson says they have no real future, and that the RAF spend most of their time with in-lines since that's where the future of aviation power is going to be.'

'In-lines are all very well, but just look at the problems; weight, cooling, servicing...' Sam's discourse was rudely interrupted as Bill took up the argument,

'Well the Huns don't consider in-lines to be a problem do they! Just look at their Mercedes for instance or their Daimlers. I know how good they are, in fact I was working on a brand new 30hp Daimler in our garage only a few months back – lovely workmanship with forged steel cylinders, single overhead camshaft, two valves and two plugs per cylinder My Dad said...'

Sam remained unconvinced, 'You still have to consider the weight, what's the point of having a bigger engine just to provide more power to shift it into the air? And all that plumbing just to keep them cool! In fact Sgt Ray was telling me that it only takes one bullet to puncture the plumbing and then its a dead donkey!'

Feeling the need to enter into the spirit of the argument, and to show he wasn't completely ignorant of the subject, Dusty Miller remarked, 'No doubt about it, Sgt Ray is right, one bullet in the radiator and you loses all yer water, just look what happened to Doughy Baker!'

Bill gave him a contemptuous glance as Sam explained, 'Well, not quite Dusty. Doughy was flying a BE2c when he was shot down, and they are powered by Renault V8s.' '

'Air-cooled 70hp in-lines you ignorant bugger.' yelled Bill.

'He still got shot down though.' mumbled Dusty as he retreated into silence.

As they washed and shaved before breakfast Bill continued with his arguments in favour of water-cooled in-line motors until, in desperation, Sam brought him down to earth.

'Saturday tomorrow Bill. I hope you don't bore Alice to death with aero-engine talk! You remember Alice don't you? The girl in town!'

Bill grinned widely. 'I suppose I deserve that, and the answer is yes, I remember her and yes, I won't even mention engines to her. Phew, what a week. I only hope I can get my finger nails clean before I see her.'

Captain Stokes was looking forward to his Friday morning lecture and associated demonstrations. He had two engines to discuss, both entirely British in design, the 100hp RAF1, already in squadron service and more important still, the 120hp Beardmore that promised much for the future of British military aviation. Securing the Beardmore was a personal triumph not easily won, particularly since the large water-cooled in-line was destined for a new machine as yet not released for squadron service. Indeed, were it not for his contacts with the RAF here at Farnborough, and for his outspoken conviction that even the best aero-engine is mere junk without first rate servicing, Fred Stokes knew he would never have gained such a prize so early in the life of a new motor.

More to the truth however, many RFC commanders were extremely concerned about air supremacy over the Western Front and increasing reports of a new German air weapon in the form of the Fokker E1. This machine was reported to be far superior to anything the Allies had to offer and employed a forward firing gun synchronised to fire directly through its propeller blades. The matter was urgent and the new FE2 fighter was to be brought into front line service as soon as possible. The FE2 was to be powered by the Beardmore and an even more powerful 160hp version was just leaving the drawing board, but Fred Stokes was not to know that!

'Ah there you are young Proctor. Just the man I'm looking for!' It was Doughy, just the man Bill wanted to see as well but he didn't know how to approach the subject of borrowing his bike for the following afternoon. They had been busy all day, stripping components, listening to lectures and making notes on magnetos, carburetters and water pumps, all in readiness for the following week's schedule of first-line servicing, field workshop practice, tuning and testing. Doughy was entering the workshop just as the AMs returned from their evening meal. 'Hoped I would run into you since I could do with a bit of advice on fitting a sidecar to the bike. One of the civvy office wallahs has one up for sale and I would like to know if it's suitable?'

'Well if I could see it sir…' Doughy took his arm,

'I know you have a lot on right now lad, but I also thought we could do each other a service. If you like I could take you into town to see the sidecar tomorrow afternoon, then we could bring it back here if its suitable, then you take the bike for the evening if you like – hows that!'

The warm summer evening gave promise of a fine night for the Guard's concert as Bill carefully parked Doughy's bike outside Webb's Bookshop. Now complete with a leather upholstered sidecar he was still a little wary of its handling properties and resolved to take extra care while 'testing' the new combination.

Alice was delighted, she had already planned to take a picnic for the evening, but was uncertain how she could carry the basket while riding side-saddle. 'But this is wonderful Billy. This solves everything! Not only can I can put the hamper on my lap but I can wear my new frock as well.'

Bill could easily understand how a sidecar helped when it came to carrying a bulky picnic hamper, but was completely lost to her feminine logic concerning a new frock. Seeing the unspoken question in his eyes Alice laughed 'Oh Bill, you *are* an innocent – never mind, come and see Mummy and Daddy, they are so looking forward to meeting you.'

It was perhaps just as well that Alice had sprung the introduction without warning for, as with all young men, meeting a girl's parents was not a matter to be taken lightly. Confused and ill at ease he was rushed into the living room where Jean and Alfred Webb greeted him.

They were rather older than he expected, quiet, considerate and perfectly content to be manipulated by their adored and only child. After brief introductions Bill was invited to take tea. It was all prepared; careful and polite questions were asked in a disarming fashion and answered in his typically forthright manner. Alfred Webb was keen to discus politics and the war, losing no time to seek Bill's opinion on the coalition government recently forced upon Asquith's Liberal party.

'It had to come of course. That man Churchill was too clever by half, never did trust him really, and our frightful losses at Gallipoli was the last straw.

Bill was entirely out of his depth, 'Don't get much news really Mr Webb, not while we are in training...'

'Well, all I can say is that since Lloyd George took over the munitions job everything has gone downhill!' Jean Webb's startling outburst came as a welcome relief to Bill, whose knowledge of politics was matched only by his lack of interest in the subject. 'There are just no standards left at all since he encouraged women to work in the factories. No moral values left these days, short skirts, short hair, and just look at what they are being paid – some young girls are getting thirty five shillings a week working those silly typewriters. And I certainly don't approve of them driving vans or riding on motorbikes!'

'Well my dear, he had to dilute the work force to allow young men like Bill here a chance to join up. It was getting impossible, why the unions wouldn't even release apprentices to the army!'

Seeing Bill's difficulty Alice stepped into the conversation opened by her mother's pointed remarks.

'Now Mummy, you mustn't worry about me riding on Bill's motorbike it's all perfectly safe, and quite respectable.' Alice cocked her head provocatively at Bill and with a broad wink continued, 'It's not your riding skills in question here Billy – but Mummy is a little worried about the length of ankle revealed while riding on the back. So much so she forbids me to wear my new frock on account of its short length.'

As Bill blushed and looked away, Jean Webb gasped an outraged, 'Alice!' as her husband sought refuge in relighting an already incandescent pipe.

'But don't worry mummy dear, Billy now has a sidecar so I shall be very respectable. Go and show it to Daddy Billy as I go and change!' With a mischievous smile she then left them to wallow in a chaos of minor embarrassments.

'Perhaps you would like to see the bike Mr Webb,' offered Bill, 'It's not mine really but my Warrant Officer lets me use it since I service it for him.' Alfred Webb smiled as he rose from his chair,

'I know nothing about things mechanical young man, but I should like to learn something about motorbikes.'

As Bill explained bike mechanics, Alfred Webb feigned a keen interest while he summed up the young man his daughter thought so much about. As far as he could see the lad was nothing out of the ordinary, a clean cut young chap, possibly quite bright – with mechanical things that is – but there could be no future in it and anyway the boy would be posted away before long so what was the harm…? His wife, Jean, was not impressed by the young Yorkshireman that was obvious, and he guessed that Alice had sensed as much too. Everything was changing so fast that he could barely accept his child was already a woman, let alone going out with a young man! But she was a good girl for all that, even if she was a bit too 'modern' for her mother's taste. Not her fault really, not these days he thought. Her short hair for instance! Originally fashioned as a measure of safety for wartime factory girls the style had soon become fashionable in its own right. Nevertheless, when Alice had her own hair cropped she found it necessary to counter her mother's criticisms with veiled threats that she too might become a patriotic munitions worker.

And now she had to give her mother further aggravation with this silly frock of hers. He smiled to himself, 'fashionable' it may be but for heaven's sake, it barely covered the girl's knees!

Alfred Webb tried to follow Bill's explanation of the two-stroke cycle knowing it was something beyond his understanding, but since his daughter found the damned things so exciting he could at least look interested in the noisy beast. Always tolerant of his daughter's whims, even to the point of being amused by them, he could refuse her nothing. A pity Jean wasn't a little more understanding he thought. It wasn't as if Alice deliberately set out to annoy her mother, so much as she needed to identify with the world around her – or so she had once confided to him. Certainly it was not the world Jean had planned for her he knew that! But this young mechanic – where did he fit in? Was she serious? Surely not! And what she saw in him he could not even guess at.

Within minutes Alice appeared at the door wearing a pencil-slim green frock, followed by her mother carrying a wicker picnic hamper. Bill stared – it *was* short! And as Alfred Webb quickly made his excuses and fled indoors, Alice inexpertly lowered herself into the sidecar, oblivious to her mother's fears for her modesty and Bill's widening eyes as slim ankles gave way to 'frillies' exposing legs and, for one heart stopping moment, a flash of bare thigh. Trying hard to conceal her displeasure, Jean Webb placed the hamper over Alice's lap and stepped back, her only comment being a chilly 'don't stay out late' in response to their noisy and exited farewells.

'Why Billy boy! I do believe you are something of a prude.' Alice teased, as Bill parked the combination under a large oak overlooking the bandstand. She had caught him looking away as he helped her dismount from the car, his fair complexion a ruddy hue as her foot caught on the handle-bars.

'Well… I mean… no not really Alice it's just that given a chance I could look at your legs all day I suppose, but you would think me rude, surely?' Alice spread the rug she had brought and opened the hamper.

'Come down here and do something useful you idiot, and for your information you will not be given a chance to look at my legs all day or all night for that matter, but I am pleased you find then attractive just the same.'

Although most people crowded about the bandstand, the tree-lined slopes of the park offered more attractive spots where, like Bill and Alice, a number of families and courting couples had brought picnics to enjoy with the popular tunes and marches now being played. As they ate, Alice talked about her family and the shop, her relatives and something of the family history.

'You see Billy, they are all rather old-fashioned in their way. I love then very much, of course, but times have changed and I know I am

57

going to be a great disappointment to them – particularly to Mummy. She sees me marrying my cousin Frank so that he will take over the shop leaving me to bring up a family of bookworms.'

Bill took her hand 'You never mentioned Frank before, is he important to you Alice?'

She kissed him on the nose 'You have no need to concern yourself about Frank my lad. We grew up together that's all, he's one year older than I am, and his sister Cissy and I are best friends.'

The band was playing a selection from Gilbert & Sullivan as lengthening shadows extended towards them from the bandstand, now illuminated with coloured lights. 'I don't even think of Frank in that way, but since the idea keeps Mummy happy it does at least give me some freedom to see other friends – like you.' She stretched out on the grassy slope and looked at him. 'Do *you* want to get married Billy?' The question came too fast, she was teasing again, and he had already learnt that he would need to answer in kind. Keeping his serious face he returned her look, and taking her hands in his proposed:

'I know this will be a shock Alice but yes – will *thee* marry me lass?'

'Why sir! I hardly know you and…' Alice stopped mid-sentence as she considered him afresh. There it was again, a seriousness in his voice and a lapse into dialect, she looked at him more deeply the banter falling from her eyes – could this really be a proposal?

'Well you did ask tha knows! And you should know better than to ask a simple Yorkshire lad daft questions – you'll only get dafter answers.' he laughed. Alice was not certain if the joke was as entirely welcome as she made out as, with a twist of her slim body she pushed him down the slope.

'That will teach you to make free with my affections you rotter! I shall never trust one word you ever say to me again!' With that she joined him down the slope, each wrestling to gain a foothold as they rolled away, laughing and fighting on the soft turf.

Most of the family groups were now leaving the park, no doubt anxious to return home before darkness, and as the flurry of arms and legs attended by Alice's screams drew close, the smiles of some barely outweighed the scowls of others less disposed to see their antics as anything but indecent. As they collected themselves and walked back up the hill Alice hooked her arm in his.

'I don't even like Frank that much you know, but the idea helps to keep Mummy occupied with plans for my future – poor dear if only she knew!' Bill said nothing as she continued, 'You see it's easy for you boys, you can do as you please, and this war – well I want to be a part

58

of it too. Oh, I know I could join the VAD or the FANY…'

Bill choked. 'Join the what?'

Alice laughed, 'I think you know perfectly well, the Women's Voluntary Aid Detachment. They offer help to the sick and wounded.'

Bill was still choking with suppressed laughter, 'No, not that one, the other, the…'

'First Aid Nursing Yeomanry to you – you ignorant airman. And don't laugh they really do splendid work and I may join them!'

On their return to the picnic spot they sat and discussed the war. Bill was soon to learn that his lively companion was not only well informed with facts but could discuss war and politics as well as any man.

At home, in Dacre, none of the womenfolk would even try to offer an opinion concerning the war, particularly in mixed company, and even if they did he couldn't imagine them being taken seriously.

'You see Billy, I know that very soon you will be posted away from Farnborough; all the boys get posted don't they?'

Bill drew her to him. 'Some stay as instructors, in fact it's on the cards that Sam will be promoted and stay here as one.'

'Yes, but I don't think that's what you want from this war is it Billy?" She looked keenly at him, knowing the answer already.

'I joined to see active service Alice and we are more than likely to go the front, unless I get posted to a home unit. The RFC are creating new squadrons all the time, many of them for home defence units. It's no secret that since Zeppelin attacks an the east coast have increased there's a possibility of attacks on London, and in time we shall have aircraft that can shoot them down, I hope.'

'That's what I tell Mummy and Daddy. We are all in this war, but the dears don't see that and it's why I need to do something other than just stay in the shop – you understand don't you, Billy?'

It was now nine o'clock, and as the concert finished Alice cleared up the picnic debris and closed the hamper. Thinking that this was a signal for departure Bill got up, brushing the dry grass from his tunic. 'Not yet Billy, not yet. Let's cuddle up in this rug for a while it's so lovely and quiet here.' Needing no further prompting Bill rearranged the large rug about them as they came close, closer than they had ever been – to kiss and to feel the warmth of each other against the rising chill of the night air.

They said nothing, there was no need. For Bill was getting used to new experiences and events that only yesterday he would have thought impossible. Yet now he could believe it was all happening – to him, Bill

Proctor, and Dacre Banks was a thousand miles and as many years away. Alice clung to him, happy and excited as she felt his rising manhood.

Bill was afraid to move. Totally aware that he was sexually aroused he was reluctant to display the fact to this wild and wonderful girl. He let his thoughts wander to stories overheard in the barrack room; of girls that did, and those that did not, of virgins, prick teasers, prostitutes and 'tarts on the game'. Numerous half-understood phrases failed to come to his rescue and in their crudity he was repelled by the thought of 'groping' or 'feeling' … not with Alice! Confused and distraught he did nothing.

With regard to women and sex, the only instructions Bill had ever received were frightening lectures on VD given by the medical officer and the need to use a 'French letter' at all times.

She moved against him and he was frozen with embarrassment. Despite her virginity she knew, her senses telling her everything she wanted to know about herself and the latent sexual power at her command.

Alice relented. Not now – perhaps never with Bill. Not yet! At first, when she felt his erection against her thin frock, she thought it the stiff edge of his tunic, only to realise her mistake as her hand took measures to remove the source of discomfort. At the shock of her discovery she was surprised to understand what it was, and why it was, and as her hand moved away she held her breath with mixed emotions. She wanted something to happen and was half-ashamed, so she waited not knowing why or for what. After a while she relaxed, she was Alice once more and in command of her feelings.

'Billy. Kiss me, and then we must go!' They both knew, and each was aware the other knew. They shared their secret as if the act they both wished for had been fulfilled and were not ashamed as they rode back to the shop.

'Did you tell your girl you couldn't see her next Saturday.' Sam asked.

'Yes, I told her. I even suggested sneaking out through the perimeter hedge, but she soon told me off about that! Bloody swotting, I tell you Sam I'm fed up with engines.

'Cock happy that's what you are mate!' Bill turned in a fury. He knew 'Birdy' Parrot's voice and his habit of joining into private conversations.

'Thar's going to get thee sen a busted gob Birdy – piss off!' As Bill

60

turned on him Sam rose from his chores, shocked at the anger displayed by his mild-mannered friend.

'Steady on lad. And you push off Birdy, he means it!' His young friend was a never-ending source of interest, just as capable of displaying an ugly temper as he was a thoughtful and sensitive gesture. But when he lapsed into his native dialect he knew he could be violent. Birdy Parrot had come within inches of a bloody nose he thought.

'Sorry Sam, but that bloke really makes me mad sometimes.' Sam smiled.

'I'm getting worried about you. If there was one person here I thought would never get their fill of engines it's you! She means a lot to you I can see that, but she's right you know. You'll not be any use to her if you fail your trade tests cos they confine you to camp until you have retaken them – did you know that? Anyway, you've only known her a week or two and in a few more you'll be posted.'

'I don't want to lose her Sam; I've met her folks and I think we are going steady now. She's really wonderful!'

Sam smiled, 'You really have got it bad, but right now you have two weeks of hard graft before you see your lady love again and then you may only have a couple more times with her before posting! God knows if you'll see her during square bashing but I wouldn't count on it lad.'

Bill continued with his writing, he was already overdue with his letters home and although his news embraced the entire family Maggie insisted on her own special letter. Indeed, it was to Maggie that Bill confided most of his secrets. It was a family joke really, ever since she had been seriously ill with pneumonia Bill had promoted their 'secret world' which, over the past few years had developed into a rare closeness shared by no others in the family group. It was to Maggie that Bill disclosed his real feelings for Alice, fully knowing she would never disclose them to her mother or older sister.

It had been arranged that in a fortnight's time he would meet Alice at the shop, have tea at home, then see the musical show 'Quaker Girl' which was now touring the provinces. But the most important thing was that they should write to each other. Before he left for camp, Alice had presented him with a gift, a dictionary, endorsed with her neat copperplate handwriting: 'To Bill, may you never be lost for words. Alice'. But now, as he turned through the pages, he realised that he had never written a love letter before and it wasn't the same as writing to Maggie!

The final week of their course was intensive, mainly with copying out hand-written notes, attending numerous lectures and towards the end of the week, practising first-line servicing on various aircraft. Doughy Baker was in charge of the latter exercises and, with Sgt Ray, had devised an excellent training scheme based on fault finding. A representative group of aircraft made up of rotary as well as machines with in-line engines was assembled for inspection by the class. Each machine had at least one servicing fault and students were required to find the errors as part of a scheduled preflight inspection.

A scoreboard of errors made the exercises both interesting and amusing, particularly since a number of faults included errors of rigging which, as the group were quick to protest, was not really their trade! But as Doughy pointed out.

'Perhaps, as engine fitters, you could say the work of your pal – the airframe rigger, is none of your business! But let's say he's had a bad day – his girl has jilted him, he's put on a charge for losing a valuable popsy, and he turns to drink. Ah, I hear you cry. Poor lad, but what about the even sorrier pilot eh!' They all laughed. Doughy's lectures were always amusing, but he had made his point and had their attention entirely.

'You see, we ignorant pilots would never know if a dozy rigger – or fitter was not up to scratch, so if you see anything wrong, anything at all, make sure the appropriate tradesman knows about it. If a bomb release is fouled, a Lewis gun has an empty magazine, or a camera has damaged bellows, report it! You know what they say; it's the ground crew that own the bloody aeroplane, the aircrew only have it on loan!'

Sam had to ask. 'Sir! Do the riggers do the same for the fitters, I mean do they look at the engine as well?'

'God! I bloody well hope not, it's bad enough with you fitters trying to kill us.' replied Doughy.

By early Friday afternoon they had completed tests on an Avro 504, a BE2c, a Bristol Bullet, a Farman 'Shorthorn' and an old Bleriot. They had done well, finding common and uncommon faults alike; dead plugs, oil leaks, wrongly wired magnetos and even a slack landing wire.

As a final test, Sgt Ray had prepared a competition using the Vickers FB5 'Gun-Bus'. It was a useful machine for his purpose, a two-seater that had already seen operational service in France, but was now being replaced by better machines of similar type. And since its open framework-pusher prop configuration was a popular design, powered by an equally popular engine, it was an excellent example of the kind of aircraft they would service in France. The competition was based on a running engine and the class had to complete a form which listed possible engine faults, fuel supply problems or control errors.

Sgt Ray explained the procedure. 'Now you all know this engine well, it's the rotary Gnome 100 hp Monosoupape. And it's in perfect shape having been through its fifty hour inspection only yesterday. It's even got a new propeller so they tell me. I shall start up with Mr Baker doing the honours on the prop and what I want you lot to do is to look, listen and concentrate on its performance – then complete your form – without any discussion between you. Right then, Mr Baker!'

Doughy removed his cap and gloves, checked that the front wheels were correctly chocked and walked to the rear of the cockpits where the FB5's 'chicken cage' extended towards its tail unit. Carefully climbing through the bracing wires he stood next to the engine and continued with a few points prior to heaving on the massive two-bladed pusher propeller.

'Right lads, now stand each side of the framework and watch out for tell-tale smoke, false starts, farts and the like as we go through the usual starting drill.'

Doughy grasped the end of the broad-bladed propeller adjusting his stance as he called out…'Petrol on, switches off, suck in!' He then pulled the engine through a couple of turns and called… 'Contact Sir!'

'Contact!' replied the cockpit, as Doughy pulled down on the prop.

Bill was standing a few yards from the engine as it fired, its harsh explosion almost as shocking as the warm wet object that struck him in the face throwing him backwards.

Almost blinded by gore he found himself staring at what remained of W/O Baker's head now resting at his feet.

Sam rushed to the cockpit as the whirling blades steadily chopped Doughy's body against the bracing wires. Staring white faces speckled red as the horror continued and stomachs heaved. At Sam's signal to 'cut engine' Sgt Ray responded immediately, his weather-beaten face creased with concern as he made to exit from the still shaking cockpit.

Bill turned from the aircraft, wiping his face on the sleeve of his bloodied overalls. He couldn't recall being sick but it was there, mixed with the bits of hair, flesh and brains that made him gag again and again as he tore at his clothing.

Corporal Mac took immediate charge, ordering the shock-stricken Sgt Ray into his flight office, then detailing Sam to contact the medical section before marshalling the ack-emmas into open order parade.

'Get them overalls off, let 'em lie where they fall – and you, stop that whimpering there, youse'll be seeing more of this in France. Squad will advance, right turn, at the run – double time quick march!'

Chapter Six

'Roight lads, stand by your beds!'

Corporal Kevin McElroy's command was almost friendly as he stood in the doorway of No.12 Course hut. 'We have a wing funeral parade for Mr Baker tomorra'. Tis a sorry affair, and the camp C/O is to make a big thing o' it – indeed himself will be there and so will youse, at 11 ack-emma. We 'ave some slow marching to practise, in one hour! Then it's best dress at 2 pip-emma, collect yer rifles and some reverse-arms drill. All roight lads, I want yer best tomorra' give old Doughy a good send off eh!' McElroy was almost out of the door when he turned, 'The five of yer in 12A course are excused, youse studying this week-end for yer trade test next week.'

'If possible Corp' I'd like to pay my respects tomorrow.' Kevin McElroy looked at Bill, and with an uncharacteristic smile answered softly,

'Sorry lad you just study hard – it's what Mr Baker would want, and besides 'tis Captain Stokes' order.'

Sam looked at Bill and sighed. The lad had taken Doughy's death very hard, and considering the horror of it, was possibly suffering more from shock than grief – doubtless that would come in good time he thought. But now there was work to do and Sam Walker was going to take charge.

'Come on then let's get cracking, we've lots to do and three days of tests starting Monday!'

By Thursday it was over. Sam came out top of course, and despite everything Bill did well enough to qualify as Air Mechanic 1st Class. After a talk from Captain Stokes they were marched into the Wing Administration offices for 'documentation' where, for the first time, Bill really began to feel he was now fully accepted into the RFC, par-ticularly since his paybook (to be carried at all times) was now endorsed with his new standing. AM/1 (Engines), 4003 W.C. Proctor: 18th July 1915.

After 12A had been paraded they were marched, in full kit, to the Malplaquet lines where, after being allotted their new hut, they were to start three weeks of 'soldiering'.

'Youse is not airmen yet yer sloppy lot but if yer tink I was hard on yer, just wait, tree weeks in these lines will soon make men o' yer! Unlike yer kind and motherly Corporal McElroy, yer now in the hands of real soldiers – guardsmen everyone! Yer now have the weekend all to yerselves but God 'elp yer come Monday and the best of luck lads. To the right, dismiss!'

In her last letter, Alice mentioned that she had already purchased the tickets (her treat) for *Quaker Girl* and as Bill ran to catch the camp transport into town he began to look forward to the event and to seeing Alice. As he sat in the back of the Crossley Tender, Bill had time to reflect on the past two weeks and examine his thoughts. The course work, Doughy's death, trade tests, moving to Malplaquet, it all seemed unreal and it seemed that the worst could always happen – tomorrow! Everything was different somehow, home was a lifetime away and everything was changing. He had decided not to mention Doughy's death to Alice, but found himself consciously needing to confide in someone, to understand how he felt. He would write to Maggie.

The Crossley stopped at the YMCA, close to the town centre. It was nearly 4 o'clock and Bill had some shopping to do. Alice began to fill his thoughts, and as he looked for a suitable box of chocolates he considered if he should purchase another box for her mother? Bill was unsure of Mrs Webb. She was pleasant enough for a southerner, but he was never comfortable in her presence. He would buy her flowers.

Promptly, at 5 pip-emma, Bill entered the shop. It was empty, save for Alice. On seeing him she swept round the counter, kissed him squarely on the mouth and locked the door.

'Oh Billy, I was hoping you would be on time – did you miss me? Are those for me? Mother is expecting us for high tea at about half-past five so we must be off as soon as I have put the till money in the safe.' She looked lovely, the world had suddenly changed again…

'Alice!' Dropping his gifts, he took her in his arms and hugged her close. 'Yes I *did*, I really missed you lass.' She looked at him, saw the dampness in his eyes – and something else?

'Is everything well for you Billy?' Filling his lungs with air he shrugged.

'Couldn't be better and its 'Air Mechanic *1st class* Billy' if you don't mind!' She was genuinely pleased for him, kissed him again and closed the shop.

'Thank you Billy, I'll put them in water right away.' It seemed that Jean Webb was in a much more open frame of mind as she asked about Bill's course and where he was going to after he left Farnborough.

'I wish I knew Mrs Webb, it seems that I could go almost anywhere in England, but it's also likely I may go to France. After this 'square bashing' I will know soon enough I suppose.'

Alfred Webb showed interest. 'It sounds as though you would like to go to France Bill? But would this mean fighting? I mean to say, there must be some point in you having to learn how to shoot as well as drill?'

'We have to learn how to fight, even using the bayonet, but we are not PBY it's just a question of defence really. That is to say, defending the airfields if the aircraft have to withdraw to another base.'

Bill had to smile when, in answer to Jean Webb's question, Alice volunteered with, 'PBY is what they call the poor bloody infantry mother.'

'So why do you have revolvers?' asked Alfred Webb, no doubt anxious to avoid further discussion concerning the PBY.

'We have to wear them on active service, like Boy Scouts – always being prepared. And we can hardly carry rifles as well as a tool kit I suppose. And we are expected to fly at a moment's notice…

'But I thought you said Air Mechanics were ground staff?' quoted Alice. 'Billy Proctor you're telling fibs again.' she admonished.

'So we are, but sometimes we have to fly in case the engine conks out and on active service we may have to use the observer's machine gun, but we learn that on the squadrons.'

'Typical!' Alice snorted, 'Boys have all the fun!'

High tea was soon over and although he was encouraged to eat more, Bill was careful not to appear greedy, even though the temptation was great. Alfred Webb took advantage of Bill's mechanical knowledge to ask questions about the Ford Model T now two years in production in the USA, until Alice rescued him for their visit to the theatre which started at 7 o'clock.

It was Bill's first visit to a theatre and his first musical show, Alice didn't think to ask, but it was a completely new experience and one that left Bill in a state of utter confusion. He was aware that it was something people down here actually paid good money to attend, so they *must* like them! But for the life of him he couldn't see why. After the show they walked through the park and sat on a bench, absorbed with each other, Bill trying to get a word in edgeways – how this girl could chatter!

66

'Oh Bill, it was so lovely, we must go again, I could see it all ten times over!'

'But I doubt if that will be possible Alice, even the three weeks I have left here are only going to give us a few opportunities to see each other – it seems I have no control over my life these days.'

Alice put her fingers to his lips, then kissed him. 'I refuse to consider such things. What shall we do next week? I know, can you row a boat? There are boats we can hire and the evenings are nice and long but you must promise that I can have a row!' She stopped, as if to catch her breath, 'They have punts too, but I believe they are very difficult to manage…'

Catching her mood, Bill stopped her with a kiss…'I'm not only a very capable rower but the best puntman in Nidderdale! Tha's seen nowt yet lass.' She hugged him close, and by 11 o'clock they just made the YMCA in time to catch one of the Crossley transports before they all departed for the camp.

'Saturday, I'll hope to get to the shop as early as I can love. I'll write and let you know as soon as I can. Please write, I look forward to your letters.' She walked him to the Crossley, eyed by a score of the waiting troops who, with envious looks made Bill both embarrassed and proud.

'Take care Billy boy, until Saturday!' With that she kissed him – and left head high, aloof to the hoots and yells of the waiting airmen, one of them red-faced and desperate to get aboard the 12 seater Crossley .

'We have to move into tents!' were the first words Sam uttered as Bill entered the hut.

'Oh well, that'll be fun – providing the weather holds.' answered Bill, unconcerned about anything but Alice and the following weekend.

'Well you won't be so damned happy when you're crowded into a bloody great bell tent, up to forty men sleeping with their feet pointing at the pole – I *know* laddie I've had some!

'When?'

'Tomorrow! One of them great hulking guardsmen said we are to go to the Recruit School cookhouse at eight, another bloody tent, then parade at outside here at 9 ack-emma. Oh God, I hate tents!'

The cookhouse was indeed a tent. More of a marquee really, and the queue was already large by the time Sam and Bill arrived.

'I have a feeling this is the first and last time we arrive here on our own. After the parade we'll be marched everywhere, even to the shithouse.'

'I wanted to ask you about that Sam, I had a leak last night outside the hut. But I must go for a number two before parade, where is it?'

Sam laughed. 'Follow your nose Bill, just follow your nose. Fortunately the winds in the wrong direction at present but it's three huts down from us, between E21 and E22'.

Regardless of the environment, Recruit School food was the best they had ever tasted since coming to Farnborough. Fried bread, bacon, beans and even boiled eggs, all washed down with strong tea available from the numerous tea-dixies scattered about the rim of the marquee. As the line moved past the wooden benches, each man extended his mess-tin for offerings that were expertly slapped into each part of the tin. The mess orderlies, with their dirty aprons and bored demeanour, were a mixed bunch of Army privates, mostly sullen and somewhat contemptuous of the 'pansy' RFC men, with their 'trades' and their 'maternity jacket' tunics. Many of them were ex-BEF, old soldiers due to return to their units at the front, and some (showing wounds) could look forward to this cushy number for the rest of the war.

To Bill's dismay half of the latrines were locked and the remainder full, with men lining up to use them. Now desperate, he enquired where else? He was directed to the tent-lines where there was bound to be space available, or so he was told! As he approached the tents he realised that Sam's suggestion was no joke, indeed the tent-line 'bog' required no directions other than his nose. Surrounded by a four foot high canvas, the latrine was moderately private from the outside, but within its confines the atmosphere was decidedly more social than that of a typical country 'thunderbox'. Whereas the primitive army latrine was sometimes a shock for those who came from town or city, growing up in the country had at least conditioned Bill to the rigours of an outside lavatory. Even so he was not prepared for this!

The engineering of this particular facility couldn't have been more basic! Two steeply banked, six foot deep pits, were topped with three parallel poles running the length of each trench. The first pole ran about two feet from the rear pair - which supported a series of wooden squares (each with a suitable hole) sufficient to seat a whole rank of airmen squatting side-by-side. His amazement apparent, Bill was easy meat for the jokers among the five or six 'squatters' who, with feet firmly planted on the foremost pole, greeted their unexpected guest with a chorus of cheers, grunts and farts.

It was something akin to a warped *Alice in Wonderland*. Some were reading newspapers (old or new their terminal role was eventually the same), some were reading novels, one was even darning his socks, all had bottles of booze tucked in their tunics, or at their lips! Their banter and rough good humour suggested that this was a common meeting place for a group of regular soldiers enjoying a quiet crap. And the stench was awful.

'You're not a Tommy Dodd are you son?' This from a hard-faced man wearing a cook's hat on an almost bald head and drinking from a large broken mug. Taken by surprise Bill's reply was cut short with,

'I bet you don't even know how to crap correctly either – it's quite an art form you know.' It went on until Bill recovered sufficiently to ask (politely)

'I can't get into the E-lines latrines can I?'

'Course you can son, but who the 'ell told you to come down 'ere then?' It was obvious he'd been the butt of some joker in E-lines - *this* was definitely a private bog and the residents, regular soldiers if ever he saw one, were obviously stark raving mad, drunk and most likely both!

After some welcome instructions Bill managed to negotiate a respectful position over the pit and not without some embarrassment relieved himself to the accompaniment of cheers amid the buzzing of countless flies. Taking his cue from the humour of his present company Bill turned to his nearest neighbour, the one with the cook's hat, to enquire...

'What's a Tommy Dodd when he's at home?' At this there was another round of laughter and applause.

'God 'elp us if 'e ain't a young saint.' said a large sergeant to his left. 'What Charlie 'ere is talking about is queers, yer know, sodomites.' Bill had heard something about them in the past two months, barrack gossip. 'But you ain't one son so don't worry 'bout it.' Bill left it alone and after accepting a few pages from a month-old edition of the *Herald*, hitched his pants and prepared to leave. As he got up, carefully negotiating his way to the edge of the pit, he was astounded to note that all his new-found friends were Senior Non-Commissioned Officers (SNCOs). Indeed, Charlie even wore the leather wristband of a Sergeant Major who, on seeing Bill's surprise laughed,

'Yes son, this is a *real* Sgts' Mess, better knock next time!'

The rest of the morning was spent in moving into the tents allocated to them. Evidently the huts had been condemned by the station medical officer, not so much for their condition but the fact that the area was to be devastated in favour of new latrines. In the meantime E-line's bogs were to be used under a restricted timetable so that reconstruction could take place. And on no account were recruits to favour the nearby tent latrines, which had been condemned, awaiting destruction and positively out of bounds.

Introduction to Recruit School took place on the parade ground at 2 pm. Something like eighty recruits were assembled for a brief lecture by the C/O who, not disguising his distaste for RFC tradesmen, dismissed the course as a waste of real soldiers' time. They were then left to various Guards Brigade SNCOs who shouted well, but conveyed little, no doubt relying on their Junior NCOs to make their meaning understood.

In short, the next three weeks were to be devoted to drill, rifle shooting, pistol shooting, grenade and bayonet practice. There would also be more drill, kit inspections, gas drill, foot inspections and FFIs.

After instructions on how to arrange their cots, maintain the single hurricane lamp attached to the tent pole, lay out their kit and roll up the tent skirts for morning inspections, a 'senior man' had to be appointed for each tent. Although there was no real authority to such a post, there was a good deal of responsibility, and with his obvious maturity Sam's appointment was generally welcomed by the group. Unlike their AM course, the tents were filled with an extensive range of trades with only a small number knowing anyone else in the 'Flight' let alone the tent in which they lived. It was all part of being in the RFC and preparing new airmen for squadron life.

By Wednesday most of Bill's tent had got to know each other well. And after a 14 hour day were quite content to lounge in their tents or visit the Recruit Club for an hour or two, before lights out at 11 pip-emma. Their first three days had been drill and lectures on RFC law, how to salute, who to salute, arms drill and recognition of ranks and badges. But tomorrow was much more exiting, they were to collect rifles for a full day on the range. It was Sam's job to keep the tent informed about daily orders and having just received them he joined Bill in the Recruit Club to let him know the worst.

'For god's sake Sam they can't do that! Bloody 'ell I've got to see Alice this Saturday.'

'To be honest Bill I was expecting something like this, but I didn't want to say anything in case it never happened. You must remember this is Recruit School and discipline is very tight now, so promise me you'll not try to break camp, cos if you did, and got caught, it wouldn't be just your neck but mine too! Is that Alice you're writing to now? Well just tell her why you can't make it this weekend or any weekend till this course is over. She'll understand.' Sam left him and went back to the tent, he wasn't going to be popular there either.

By Saturday Bill had received two letters from Alice, the latest was a short note to say she was disappointed he could not see her for the next two weekends but he must write and let her know what would happen next. She was worried he could be posted before seeing her again.

By Sunday they had completed their first revolver shoot and were told that one more practice on the 25 yard range should qualify them with the heavy Webley 0.455. Furthermore, those posted to France would receive a personal issue of this weapon rather than the usual rifle. Bill enjoyed firing the Webley and was delighted to come third in the entire flight. Possessed of strong wrists and a calm nature he was well-suited to handle this difficult weapon and managed to gain some good four inch groups on the 15 yard range.

Sunday afternoon was a rest period and while most of the tent played cricket, Bill and Sam wrote letters home.

'If we go to France we won't be able to say much in our letters Bill. They will be censored just to make sure we don't complain too much or tell anybody what we are doing. So if you want to say anything to your folks, now is the time.'

'I did mention Doughy to our Maggie, and I told her he died in an accident but I didn't want to say how, it would worry Mum'. Sam put down his pencil.

'Well, I meant to tell you, there was a Court of Enquiry a few days ago. I got some details from the Orderly Room clerk – it's not to be spread around though. Evidently some idiot in the maintenance unit put the prop' on back-to-front. The rigger who fitted it and the Sgt in charge are both up for Court Martial. They didn't even check it on a running engine silly buggers. Mark you, the result would have been the same, only the rigger would have had his head off instead of Doughy!'

'I don't understand Sam. What made the prop' turn the wrong way?' Sam stood up to make his point.

'The prop' went round as it always does of course – but come on Bill, use your loaf! The FB5, the 'Gun Bus' is a pusher, right? So the prop' does just that, it pushes, providing its on the right way that is, but…'

Bill had it now, 'So if the prop' was back-to-front it would pull the bus backwards into poor old Doughy!' They were both silent for a while. 'I hate prop pulling, I tell you Sam, I'm going to dodge it all the way from now on.'

'It's a lesson well learnt lad; think of that and Doughy's death won't have been for nothing.'

More to get Bill's mind off the subject, Sam introduced another item related to Courts Martial. 'I also heard that there's a group of

SNCOs under open arrest, here in this School. Its rumoured that some of the support staff are under suspicion of buggering recruits. But since there's no evidence – no one likes to admit they've been sodomised – they'll most likely be split up and posted to the front. But I hear they have been thrown out of the Sgts' Mess awaiting postings to God knows where; possibly much worse than ten years jail eh!' Bill recalled his forbidden visit to the tent latrines and smiled to himself,

'Tommy Dodds the lot of them.' he murmured. 'In the shit proper, Sam, a *real* Sgts' Mess you might say!'

Bill finished his letter home and realised that most of his news couldn't be told anyway, censors or not! He could hardly understand it all himself, he had learnt so much in the past few weeks and knew there was even more to come. There was something else too,

'Sam – what the devil is an FFI? I'm sure we're supposed to have an FFI or something tomorrow evening – is that right'?'

The long line of recruits extended out of the medical tent for about fifty yards. They were entering through a wide open flap and within a minute were exiting from another in the back. Bill couldn't stop laughing, 'Free from infection, that's a hoot. What's this infection look like anyway? God, I don't envy the MO this job, looking at knobs all evening.' As they entered to within a couple of feet of the inspecting officer each recruit was told to drop his pants to his feet whereupon the MO used a 12-inch ruler to lift each penis and inspect it closely. Those under suspicion of having the clap (gonorrhoea), syphilis, crabs or lice were sent directly to the STC (special treatment centre) where further inspection and treatments were carried out.

'It's all a bit of a game really,' said Sam, 'I mean to say not much chance any of you youngsters getting a dose here, you're all much too young to have experience with prostitutes. But over in France it's becoming a problem, or so I hear.' Albert Cross the tent pessimist was adamant.

'You can easily get it from these terrible lavatories you know.' Albert was married, close to thirty, and a bank clerk in civvy street, but for the duration of the war he was now a trained telegraphist. Well-spoken and dapper he kept to himself most of the time, rarely offering an opinion on anything.

'Stupid bugger,' said Alan Butcher, 'That's a right old wives tale. Crabs maybe, but you can only get the clap one way – the right way thank God.' The ensuing laughter rippled down the line but was short-lived when, within minutes, Butcher was dispatched to the STC with the dreaded clap! Perhaps it was poetic justice that he should live up to

72

his boast. But despite immediate and painful treatment Butcher took such delight in his new found notoriety that by Wednesday evening he was giving impromptu lectures on the subject. Bill suggested that Sam should sell tickets, particularly since the story became more gory and dramatic with each telling. In the end, after a particularly nauseating session (which included public views of the afflicted member) Albert Cross spoke to Sam, whose threats eventually put a stop to the constant stream of visitors to his tent. Albert was to plead with the Padre to be moved to another tent, but no more came of it.

Nobody fancied bayonet drill, and although they had marched with fixed bayonets there was great respect for the 18-inch long knives stuck to the end of their Lea Enfields. Albert Cross summed up their fears precisely,

'It's one thing to march around with these things, but I hear we have to fight each other with them. They scare the life out of me!'

Perhaps *fighting* was an exaggeration, but Thursday morning saw them practising the art of it and it was certainly not a drill. Lined up against a series of sandbags which swung from an overhead pole the instructors shouted their advice.

'Don't plunge a bayonet straight through the body, three inches is enough. Don't forget, you have to get the bloody thing out again! If you can't remove the blade, pull the trigger and recoil will do the rest. And another thing; in hand-to-hand you don't get much time to think, there's always another bugger around, so be quick. You jab him in the guts, stir around a bit then use the butt of the rifle on the next German – like this!'

Lunging at sandbags with the naked blade was one thing, but as they were drawn up into two facing lines they realised that this was going to be a serious business. Three pairs of instructors demonstrated their technique on the defenceless sandbags; 'on guard', 'thrust', 'parry'. It was very impressive. They practised against each other with scabbards over the blades, then their fears were realised.

'Remove scabbards; take up the on guard position.' But Air Mechanics were an expensive commodity and their value was not to be squandered on the end of a large knife. So as soon as they showed a healthy respect (verging on sheer funk) for this noble art, their tormentors relented and returned them to the parade ground. It was the end of their weapons training and the rest was all downhill.

It was evening, and for the first time it seemed they could discuss the war without reservation. The morning's exercise had made a deep impression on them all – the name of this game was killing people!

There were the important things in life of course; beer was three pence a pint, fags were four pence for twenty, and women could get well-paid jobs in the munitions factories. Some of the girls in town were even getting as much as 35 shillings a week as typists. Girls' hair was getting shorter and more important yet so were the skirts.

But the war was stepping up, with repeated concentration at a place called Ypres, a west Belgian town in Flanders. A vital centre of communication, Ypres held the key to Calais and Boulogne and only a month or so back, at the so-called second battle of Ypres (or wipers, as the British tommy called it) 'Jerry' used poison gas, for the first time. Reports were few, but returning casualties said it was totally unexpected. They spoke of being unprepared, of pissing on handkerchiefs which were held to their nose as they fell back. The choking horror of gas was now a constant threat, and anti-gas drill concentrated on early detection, warning (rattles) and speed in putting on the mask. The entire Recruit School was scheduled for an intensive gas drill the following afternoon.

Asquith, the liberal Prime Minister, had formed a coalition government with the conservatives and Lloyd George was appointed Minister for Munitions.

'Trust 'im to look after the ladies!' said one. Then, to top it all, Italy declares war on Austria and Hungary, and Alan Butcher goes and gets the clap!

Since morning a breath of war had touched their face, and its reality could now be discussed with less reserve; they were RFC tradesmen but felt as soldiers for the first time.

'When do we get to know of our future postings Sam? I know we get a week's leave before we go to France, but if it's to a home unit when do they tell us? Alice keeps asking which weekend I will be free and I don't know!' Sam lit his pipe and after a while said he would see if he could get something out of his pal in the Orderly Room. 'Anyway Sam, I hope we stick together we've... bloody hell look what the wind blew in!'

A very smart Gerry Hardcastle stood grinning at him from the tent door.

'For your interest you uncouth Yorkshireman, you are in the presence of one 4004 G.P Hardcastle AM/1 (Photo), late of the Regent Street Polytechnic, London.'

Open-mouthed, Bill leapt to his feet and welcomed Gerry with a strong handshake.

'Where the hell have you been you silly bugger? Did you say Lon-

74

don? Look, this is my best pal Sam Walker.' After introductions Bill suggested they all go to the club for tea and wads, but Sam declined,

'I've some letters I must write Bill, and I'm sure you and Gerry have lots to catch up with anyway. I'll come over later if I can. Are you just passing through Gerry, or come to join us?' Gerry grimaced

'Doubt I'll be able to avoid Recruit Camp Sam, but as a matter of fact I'm down at South Camp where they are fitting out some buildings for the new school of photography. I came with W/O Laws, he's our chief instructor and in charge of the advance party that will set up the first photo course later this year. He really is a nice chap, spent some time in France and is doing pilot training as well.'

'You're looking very fit Bill, must be all this exercise you chaps do down here.' Bill had brought over two cups of Bovril and a plate of bacon sandwiches.

'Sorry old lad, they say the tea urn won't be ready for another ten minutes, which usually means about twenty, hope you don't mind.' Gerry laughed.

'Bovril! There's always a first time for everything, never had it at home. You won't believe this but Mr Laws and I came down from London in a requisitioned van and it had Bovril in large letters on the side! Anyway, what's your news Bill?'

Bill enlarged on his engine fitter's course and gave Gerry a good account of what he would face when he was posted to Recruit School. But his main news concerned Alice.

'You lucky old devil, you will have to see if she has a friend, for me. We could then make a foursome together...' Bill was quick to point out that he only had another week and problems enough seeing his own girl before he left for goodness knows where. Gerry could see they were not going to have much time together.

'Well I know I'm supposed to join Recruit School on Monday, and this weekend is going to be tied up with helping Sergeant Major Laws. But not to worry Bill, I'll pop over to your place on Monday evening, and we'll have at least a week together before you go.'

'What I don't quite understand Gerry, is how you got to AM/1 when the photo-school isn't even started yet?' Seems like a dead easy course to me!' Gerry's pleasant face beamed.

'It *was* easy Bill. But as you know, photography is a hobby of mine so it wasn't too difficult to impress the powers that be! In fact all the chaps on the course were professional photographers of one sort or another. But you know, we still have to establish a good air camera yet. There's the Watson air camera, Mr Laws has flown with that a few times, and the model 'A' which takes 4 × 5 inch plates, but the difficulty is that most of the trained photographers won't be the lads who fly with them. And they are too fragile for crude AMs like you to play with!' Bill grinned,

'Like I said before, I won't be going in any bloody airyplane so here is one crude bugger you don't need to worry about.'

Gerry smiled at his friend. 'I don't, but as you know I *do* have plans to be a pilot, and the only way is to go through observer training and as photographic observer I will soon be on a squadron.'

'I thought observers sat in the back and fired a machine gun.' said Bill.

'Well that too of course, and I've been approved for the gunnery school at Hythe, as soon as I finish recruit training here. There's even talk of a three month wireless course after that, before I go to France. It seems the reconnaissance squadrons need wireless-trained observers for artillery spotting.'

Bill was genuine in his alarm. 'God almighty Gerry, that means BE2cs – bloody deathtraps! Those things are hopeless anyway, the observer sits in the front cockpit surrounded by struts and wires and his field of fire is so restricted he has to move the Lewis gun from one post to another. He can't *see,* anything either. Above and below him are the mainplanes, so he can't see what he's supposed to be observing anyhow!'

Gerry was looking quite irritated and snapped out, 'Well how would a grubby fitter like you know? I'm sure the aviators understand more about the job than you do, and yes, Mr Lawson did tell us the BE2 had some problems, but evidently it's very stable and easy to fly and serves its purpose – that's the main thing.'

Bill wasn't to be fobbed off and continued his argument. 'One of our best instructors used to fly BE2s, in fact he got killed recently (Bill was careful not to say how Doughy met his death since the facts didn't suit the point he was trying to make) and he told us the same thing, except he said they were too damned stable and not manoeuvrable enough to avoid being shot down. Just imagine what it must be like Gerry, a Hun up your arse and your observer is shooting over *your* head trying to get his sights on him! And another thing, did you know that when it's flown over 6000 feet, the rarefied air increases the stalling speed to almost its top speed? Not that its top speed is much of course, only about 70 mph.'

Gerry was impressed. The young country boy had changed a great deal in the short time he had known him. There was self-assurance and even a degree of coarseness that had not been there before. And he could only envy Bill's understanding of aircraft.

'So, you've only got a week to go young Bill – then what?'

Bill outstretched his arms. 'I wish I knew but nobody tells you a bloody thing here. If I get a home posting I just might get a 72-hour pass, and if I do, it's going to be a question of do I stay here and see Alice or do I go home? And the answer to that depends on where my posting is going to be!'

Gerry put an arm around Bill's broad shoulders, 'We both know you have to go home Bill, it's the decent thing to do. But I shall still be here, and at great personal sacrifice I shall be pleased to look after Alice for you, just give me her address and…'

'Bugger off Hardcastle, I wouldn't trust you with my granny; get your own girl, if you can find one daft enough to go out with anyone who wants to fly in a BE2!'

The two friends laughed and made their way back to Sam's tent.

'It looks as though I shall be pretty busy tomorrow Bill. We have to supervise the construction of darkrooms and unload a lot of equipment due to arrive in the morning. But with luck I should be able to see you tomorrow evening, about seven.'

Bill mentioned the anti-gas drill programmed for that afternoon; there was even talk about it being a 'live' exercise, he said. 'But it couldn't be much worse than some of the bogs round here – I've even thought about taking my gas mask next time I go!'

Gerry laughed, then became serious. 'In London it's being rumoured that we had over 5000 dead and 10,000 wounded from that last attack, but let's hope that's all it is – a rumour.' With that they parted, Bill for the tent-lines and Gerry for a mile or so walk down to the airfield where the new school was to be sited.

So far, Friday had gone very well. The gas-drill was no more than a simulated exercise and to everyone's surprise it was cut short at 3 pip-emma. There seemed to be some confused orders, then the entire wing was paraded in order of Flights.

' Something fishy about this.' said Al Cross, 'that's the Wing Adjutant coming to talk to us – wonder what *he* has to say?' From the RSM there was no doubt about his message. '

Atten-shun! Open order march – stand still!'

It was a short address, and the orders were very clear. About thirty of the Wing were to complete their course tonight! Those whose names were called out would take one step forward and turn right to form up against the 'right markers' now assembled. The Adj' then moved over to where the 'markers' were standing and handed the parade back to the RSM.

'Stand still and look to your front, listen for your names.' Two of Bill's tent had been called out when… 'Proctor! 4003 Proctor' was called. As he marched onto the new group Bill was directed to the second rank and fell-in at the 'stand easy.'

The list was completed, and as the original parade marched off, the Adjutant came forward to talk to the waiting airmen.

'You men are going to France, where your particular skills are needed urgently in the rear areas and on the squadrons. You are no longer recruits, but fully trained Air Mechanics of the RFC. As soon as we are finished here, you will be marched to administration where you will receive your documentation. This will mean clearance from this school, notice of postings, pay, kit check, leave pass for seven days and rail tickets to your home and to your port of embarkation. Tomorrow at 8 ack-emma you will have a medical, then clear your tents and be ready for final inspection – in full marching order by 11 ack-emma. Transport will then take you to the railway station. One final thing – you are still confined to camp until tomorrow. March them off Sergeant Major.'

It was six o'clock by the time Bill and his two comrades got back to the tent where Sam was first to greet them. 'Sorry Bill, I had hopes we might be posted together, but it's you for France and guess what – I'm to stay here, at the fitters' school. Captain Stokes asked for me right after the parade. I'm to be made acting corporal as soon as I finish here and then be an instructor!' Sam was obviously pleased, and although Bill was disappointed he knew that Sam would be happier at the school – him being married and all. 'So what now young Bill? Do you go home or are you to stay here and spend your leave with Alice?' It was strange really, he'd never been given any choice!

As he explained to Sam, 'My pay, travelling money and my leave ticket were all ready for me when I got to admin' so I go home! We have our jabs at the medical tomorrow, then parade, go to the armoury for our revolvers and then off. But I shall pop round to the shop as soon as I get into town, and see Alice before I go. It's all too quick Sam, too bloody quick!'

Gerry visited around 9 o'clock, thoroughly taken aback at Bill's news. 'You go to France on August 11th!' After some discussions, and appreciating the unknown future of their postings, each promised to keep in touch through their home addresses. Then, seeing that Bill had much to do with his kit, Gerry made his farewells and returned to South Camp.

It was 11.30 ack-emma, and for Bill and the other draftees, their past six hours had been a period of organised chaos.

'What day is it?' asked one.

'Saturday the bloody 4th of bloody August mate! A day to remember this is and as soon as I gets 'ome I'm going to bed, it's a day my missus won't forget either!' They were packed into a three-ton Leyland lorry, sweating under their full kit with webbing, gasmask, revolver, back pack, side pack and heavy kit bag. The solid rubber tyres of the lorry made their journey even more uncomfortable as it bounced along the cobbled entrance to Farnborough's railway station.

Excepting Bill, the airmen made brief goodbyes and entered the station. Bill had already found the left luggage office and deposited his kit bag and packs for the afternoon. He would work out the train time-tables after he had seen Alice.

It being Saturday, both Alice and Alfred Webb were attending shop as Bill entered. Dressed in full kit his appearance said everything, and Alice's face showed concern as she excused herself from the counter.

'Oh Bill – what's all this?' She took him aside, clasping both his hands in hers, tears now falling down her cheeks. 'I was not to expect you until *next* Saturday – what's this?' Her concern was so genuine and heartfelt that Bill was overwhelmed with his love for her at that moment. And as he looked at her, he began to realise what this fresh young girl meant to him,

'I love you Alice, I just love you!' She turned to her father who, though busy with a customer, simply smiled at her and waved his finger at the door.

'See me later both of you.' She never even thought to grab her hat, and with her eyes never leaving his face grabbed him by the webbing and pulled him out of the shop door. '

And I love you,' she kissed him there and then, and with Bill holding his forage cap to his head, ran him to the tea shop only four doors away. It was spontaneous, they were gloriously happy, and his explanations, his posting, going home – all were lost in the moment. Blissfully unaware of the wistful smiles from all around they just held hands and looked at each other.

It was a waitress who broke the spell and after ordering – a barrage of questions and plans for a future that could only be counted in days. They went for a walk, sat in the park and made what plans they could.

'I shall write tonight, I have your home address in Dacre, and I know I'm being terribly selfish Billy but if you could get down to Farnborough on Thursday evening, I shall arrange with mother to put you up in our spare room. We would then have Friday and some of Saturday together and you could go to Dover from here!' Bill wondered what Mrs Webb would say about that but he knew Alice; she was an only child and spoilt to death bless her!

'I shall have to make sure I can get to Dover by 6 pip-emma' said Bill. 'Oh, you and your pips, it's only down the road you silly, you'll make it on time – if I don't keep you here that is! Oh, Billy I wish you didn't have to go – I shall worry so, I just know it.' They sat in the shade, and protected by overhanging branches were unconcerned as they cuddled on the park seat, Alice adjusting her position to avoid the heavy revolver at Bill's side.

'You'll be my best girl when I'm away? Alice, will you marry me?' She showed no surprise, but dropped her head as she deliberated her answer.

'Bill, we have so much to consider … I…' He grasped her hand.

'That was silly of me Alice, I'm going to war dammit. I shouldn't have asked such a thing – not yet, its just that...' She understood, yet had no answer other than to say,

'I *do* love you dearest Billy, and I think I shall marry you, but can we keep this our secret for now? I'm sure Mother would throw a fit if we mentioned it right at this moment.' She laughed at the thought, 'I can just imagine what she would say! 'And how do you propose to keep my daughter young man?' '

Caught up with her laughter, Bill joined in the fun, glad to have mentioned the possibility – to have her love confirmed – yet secretly pleased that his passionate outburst didn't require further commitment, he knew she was quite right.

Bill looked at his pocket watch. 'I shall have to go; best take you back before your Dad thinks I've kidnapped you.' They returned to the shop, where Bill explained his posting to Alfred Webb. The shop was busy now and he was pleased to leave on this excuse. Alice saw him out, kissed him and with tears welling in her eyes softly murmured

'I shall write tonight…' Bill waved and marched away – he too had tears.

Trains to London were frequent and he was at King's Cross station shortly after six. With an hour or more to wait for the Leeds train and since there was a shop still open, he thought to buy some gifts for the family. Tobacco for Dad, a jar of humbugs for Maggie and after some difficulty a small brooch for Eileen and a floral apron for Mum. The train left on time, but being full of servicemen it meant standing all the way to Doncaster before he found a seat. His train entered Leeds just after midnight and missed the Harrogate connection by forty minutes. Content that he might as well be stranded in Leeds as in Harrogate he prepared to spend the night on the platform. Laying his greatcoat over a seat, with the kitbag under his feet and packs under his head, Bill loosened his webbing and secured the revolver under his tunic before making himself comfortable. Not much different to tents he thought as he rested – soon to fall asleep.

Bill awoke to the hurt of a boot kicking at his foot. 'Get up lad!' Two burly Military Policemen stared down at him. 'Let's see your pass airman.' Bill struggled with his tunic to get at his documents, which the MPs carefully inspected. Bill asked the corporals if there was a canteen on the station. 'Not open until 8 o'clock – but get yourself cleaned up first lad – there's a washbasin in the lavvy. You look a mess!' His train to Harrogate was at 7.25, and Bill arrived at the northern spa town with only ten minutes wait for the Dacre train.

Bill was alone when he stepped from the train at Dacre Banks. And as he breathed in the clear dales air, the young airman experienced an unusual pride in his return. This was home, more special now than ever before. Wherever he went, Dacre would always be with him. He felt elated, proud to be wearing the King's uniform and above all – hungry.

The tiny platform, immaculate with its neat little lawns and tubs of bright flowers was just the same it always was this time of year – yet it seemed he was seeing it for the first time. Jack Peables, the station master, was a keen gardener and with Dacre the last of five villages on the line he felt it his duty to make it the best. Always immaculate, Jack was proud of his little station and critical of anything and anyone that failed to meet his exacting standards. He stopped dead in his tracks as he recognised the soldier walking to the gates.

'Well I'll be blowed. It's young Bill Proctor – tha's got thee sen in't Flying Corps ah see!' Never an overtly sociable man he took Bill by surprise as he grasped him by the arm, 'By gum lad tha's a good'un, we're all proud o' thee in't village.' Embarrassed and tired, Bill dropped his kitbag to shake the proffered hand and exchange words with a man he had known almost all his life, but had never uttered more than a few words to before this. After answering a multitude of questions he managed to take his leave,

'Best be off Mr Peables, the folks will be wondering where I am!'

Bill hoisted his kitbag and walked the few yards to his home; it was Sunday, there were few people about, no doubt most were preparing

81

for the late morning service. It was only when he was at the small garden gate that he remembered – there hadn't been time to let his folks know he was coming home!

Chapter Seven

The lone BE2c was making only 40 mph as it struggled against the prevailing west wind. At 6000 feet the air was chilling, despite the clear blue sky and hot sun, forcing the pilot deeper into the largely exposed open cockpit. He sank as deep as he could behind the windscreen, concentrating on the simple instrument panel of his flimsy aircraft as it wallowed in the thin air. Altimeter, tachometer, air speed indicator, compass and watch, they were his only friends in this hostile environment. He looked over the side, keeping track. The hands on the watch moving oh so slowly. From his position and estimated ground speed it would be all of half an hour before they were safe behind their own lines. Safe? He knew the German fighters rarely penetrated far into allied air space – they just waited, patrolling on either side of the trenches. He knew they would be waiting.

Major Cecil Hunt MC, CdeG, looked up. The shadow of his observer was now cast over the cockpit; it couldn't be worse! It was close to 4 pip-emma and his compass bearing was taking him directly into the afternoon sun. Putting his fears aside he considered the plight of the observer, standing in his cockpit facing the tail with a Lewis gun mounted on one of the rear struts. The BE2 observer's cockpit was in front and beneath the upper wings, an almost useless position to either 'observe' or exploit a field of fire. Standing in that position, exposed to cold air, slipstream and engine fumes it was an unenviable position made worse by a total lack of speech communication between the crew.

As C/O of 4 Sqdn, Cecil Hunt could exercise privilege of rank and select the best observer in the unit. As a consequence, Sgt Andy Mills had been 'borrowed' from his usual pilot to accompany him on this mission. Andy Mills was the most experienced observer on the squadron and had already shot down two enemy machines, gaining a DCM while flying with 3 Sqdn. As C/O, Hunt rarely flew these days, but this particular reconnaissance was too dangerous, difficult and important to be delegated. In addition the mission area had to be photographed, and since it was common knowledge that the 4 Sqdn C/O was an expert in this field, he knew that Wing HQ would expect him to do the job himself.

Cecil Hunt's promotion to lead 4 Sqdn was entirely due to his work earlier that year when, as a Flight Commander on 3 Sqdn he was mainly responsible for photographing the area immediately to the front of the British 1st Army at Neuve Chapelle. Using a BE2c fitted with the very first RFC air camera, he'd conducted a series of reconnaissance missions up to 1000 yards in depth, photographing the entire German trench system. Despite the fact that the BE2c was slow and a sitting duck to enemy attack it did have the advantage of being extremely stable, sufficient to enable pilots to fly 'hands off' and operate the camera.

In February he had used the 'A' type camera for vertical photography, but from the BE2c it was *his* job to operate the camera since the observer's cockpit denied vision of the ground below. Usually pilots cursed the excessive stability of BEs since they resisted those swift manoeuvres essential for evading enemy machines or anti-aircraft fire (Archie). But for photographic missions, its ability to fly by itself was a blessing, particularly as the pilot now had three difficult tasks to perform: control the aircraft (the least of the problems), navigate the photorun and hardest of all – operate the camera. The stability also ensured a straight 'flight line', an essential condition for producing a series of overlapping photos from which mosaics could be laid and detailed trench maps produced – a major feature in winning the battle of Neuve Chapelle.

The wooden 'A' type camera employed 5 by 4 inch plates and could be fixed to the side of the pilot's cockpit for control, but it still took eleven separate operations to make a single exposure. And at high altitude and cold weather lengthy operations required a heavily gloved hand in order to avoid frostbite. Such were the conditions in February, but Captain Cecil Hunt was lucky. There was sufficient midday sun to enable good exposures which, with insensitive orthochromatic plates, an f/9.7 lens and yellow filter made photography only just possible. Nevertheless, without 3 Sqdn's photography it was doubtful if the attack at Neuve Chapelle would have been successful, and a delighted allied army showed its gratitude in decorations and promotion for Hunt and other members of the squadron.

Now 1st Army was aware of large enemy troop concentrations along their front, and an attack could take place at any time. It was Hunt's task to secure high quality photography at a scale of 1:10,000. Originally the army photo-interpretation unit at GHQ asked for 1:5000, but Hunt's argument won the day.

'With an eight inch lens the camera is only going to capture half the ground you need covered at 1:5000 scale, admittedly each exposure will yield better detail, but at a cost of only half the cover! Furthermore gentlemen, since we would have to fly straight and level for about eight minutes at 3300 feet, we shall well and truly be quartered by archie, increasing the possibility of being shot down! But if we fly at 6600 feet, we cover the same area in half the time – leading to better chances of getting back with the information you need. If we can get good quality stuff all you have to do is use a magnifying glass – the detail will still be there!' His arguments made sense, and although there was little concern for his safety, getting back with the photographs was of the utmost importance.

Making good his promise Cecil Hunt had chosen his flight time with great care. At 3 pip-emma there was enough light to secure good exposures but, more importantly, the sun's angle was sufficiently low to cast the shadows that disclosed the size and nature of his military targets.

Taking off from his field just north of Amiens it took them an hour to reach 6000 feet over Bapaume where, as arranged by 1st Wing HQ, they were met by a flight of four Vickers FB5 twin seat fighters, their 11 Sqdn escort. The FB5, or Gun-Bus, was a pusher type with a free-mounted Lewis gun in the observer's front cockpit. As an escort it was at best supportive, but as a fighter it was too slow and could not even keep up with a lightly-loaded BE2c. Nevertheless, they were a comfort and would at least be able to counter any fighter attack.

Crossing the allied trenches at Bapaume, he climbed to 6600 feet and flew to a position a few miles north west of Cambrai. The FB5s climbed above him to 8000 feet and split into pairs, providing Hunt and the two decoy BE2cs below him with top cover. The plan was to deploy the decoys at 5000 feet, one flying to the north east, the other due east, while the photo aircraft flew due south for five miles from Bapaume then, turning onto 200 degrees it would fly the four mile photo-run.

The Jerry archie was sporadic; being unsure of their targets they were hedging their bets on the correct range. Hunt made his final checks on the 'C' type camera hung outside the cockpit. Identical to the earlier 'A' type, the latest camera had a semi-automatic plate-changing top and two magazines. One magazine held twelve plates stacked face down directly over the focal plane then, after exposure the plate was slid in a frame over a second magazine into which it fell. The operation was much easier than with the 'A' type, reducing controls to aperture setting, shutter winding knob, shutter release (with automatic capping) and a shutter blind tension control.

Hunt had done his calculations with care. Just as correct planning was essential for gaining accurate photography, so it was for escaping with their precious plates. The photo-run was planned for a line which took advantage of the sun's azimuth angle and the suspected disposition of the enemy supplies and ammunition dumps. Even well-camouflaged artillery cast shadows, and the interpreters were becoming more skilled with every mission. The over-target time of 3 pip-emma was vital in this respect, as was the direction of his return to the Allied lines.

It had gone well. Using a dog-legged approach to the first exposure his intentions were suitably disguised and the archie gunners confused. He was into three minutes of his run before the filthy black smelling stuff even found his range, and by then it was too late as Hunt exposed the last of the twelve plates. Turning onto a heading of 285 degrees he fled to the nearest point of the British lines, turning his head to check on the decoys and his top cover. Andy Mills fired a short burst from the Lewis, attracting his attention to the escort now engaging a pair of the new Fokker Eindekkers slowly climbing to engage him. With their synchronised forward firing gun, the Fokker posed a considerable threat to the BEs which were already suffering from the 'Fokker menace' as the British press called them, but Hunt knew they would never catch him.

Andy Mills searched the sky as best he could, shielding his eyes against the westering sun. He knew the escort would mind their 6 o'clock position but what about ahead of them? He unhitched the heavy Lewis from the rear post and placed it on the starboard front strut. He knew they would attack out of the sun, some ten to fifteen degrees above them, his blind-spot, and out of his field of fire! Hunt knew it too.

'Clever buggers these Huns, they know where I've been, they suspect what I've been doing and, what is worse, they know our weaknesses.'

The FB5s were far behind now, and had adopted their usual defensive strategy of flying in a circle. It wasn't particularly aggressive but it kept the Fokkers busy! Hunt had put his nose down as soon as he made his dash for the lines, levelling off at 5000 feet. He also signalled Andy Mills to crouch down in his cockpit, although of average size his observer still created drag and he needed every bit of speed he could muster. Archie was getting closer again, lifting the BE some fifty feet or so with each burst. Weaving was painfully slow but the only option. Climbing was out of the question and to descend was to court certain death from the concentrated small arms fire now coming from the German forward trenches.

They could both see their own lines now, first indicated by the white archie bursting ahead of them – British stuff obviously aimed at enemy machines.

'God! Let's hope they are firing at German recce two-seaters.' Hunt concentrated on his weave, fully aware that Andy Mills would have the greatest difficulty in spotting any Huns coming from the west. Mills tuned his head as though listening, throwing a meaningful look at his pilot. The archie had stopped. Both knew this meant the enemy machines were now closing on them.

Unlike the allied two-seaters, the German Army Air Service machines were usually commanded by the observer, it was he who made the decisions, the pilot's role being simply that of 'driver'. This relationship worked well for reconnaissance work, but often had grave faults when the two-seater was employed as a fighter. Oberleutnant Otto Schonger came from a long line of Prussian cavalry officers and as observer of the C1 Aviatik now approaching the British BE, he was very much in command of his machine. To his long-suffering pilot, Unteroffizier Richard Becker, Schonger was an idiot who would soon have him killed with his stupid pretensions of being an 'airborne cavalry officer'. True enough he *was* from a quality Uhlan regiment, but his efforts with the twin Spandau were about as useful as a lance in this game!

Schonger had instructed his pilot with a number of definitive hand signals which 'if he would follow to the letter, would result in a series of glorious victories'. On two previous occasions Becker had almost stalled the Aviatik following dangerous manoeuvres orchestrated by his glory-hunting superior, and had already applied for transfer to single-engined fighters in order to escape his suicidal commander. In company with another Aviatik from their own Feldflieger Abteilung 24, they had just completed a reconnaissance of the British lines at Gomiecourt and were returning to their base at Doual when Schonger saw the lone BE crossing the German lines.

Schonger signalled the other Aviatik his intention to attack. The agreed strategy being that, as patrol commander Schonger would make the attack while the accompanying machine provided cover.

Becker put the heavy Aviatik into a wide right-hand turn, allowing the aircraft to drop into the path of the approaching BE. From Schonger's point of view the attack looked simple, out of the sun and high, his pilot would drop across the BE then, banking sharply to port provide him with a clear field of fire as they turned to the rear of the enemy machine. With luck the crew of the BE would never see them until too late, and would have little opportunity to return fire. Richard Becker had over 90 hours in the Cl and knew its characteristics well. Capable of 100 mph and a ceiling of nearly 15,000 feet, the Aviatik was a formidable adversary for even the best of the allied aircraft at that time. But in capable hands, and flown against the BE2c it was highly dangerous.

As Becker banked to his left the Spandaus were still out of range, but his sharp bank produced a yaw that would soon put that right he thought. Schonger, aware that the BE's observer had not seen them was impatient, and signalled furiously for Becker to tighten the turn and reduce the range now! This was not the approach his pilot had planned; at the current rate of his descent he knew he could put Schonger's guns onto the port side of the BE, and at very close range, but this was not the time! Cursing, he obeyed the order with full left rudder, and the Aviatik immediately departed from controlled flight.

'Jesus bloody Christ!' As the falling shadow of the Aviatik fell across the sun's glare, Andy Mills stared at the enemy machine now dropping to port in the first turn of a deadly spin. Four pairs of eyes followed the big Aviatik as its spin rate increased. Those in its companion aircraft watched with concern, knowing only too well that few Cl pilots ever managed to recover from a spin at a height now approaching 4000 feet. Cecil Hunt's emotions were mixed. Surprise quickly followed by professional interest as he counted the turns of the spin, to be followed by a strange compassion, a sadness for fellow aviators despite their enmity. Fascinated, Hunt banked his machine to port the more to watch the fall of his enemy 'another victim for the Squadron and not a shot fired!'

Leutnant Bruno Lorenz signalled his friend in the front office, mouthing unheard directions for attack. But the pilot of the second Aviatik had already anticipated their strategy as he gently turned his aircraft into a beam attack on the starboard side of the 'tommy' machine. They had advantages of speed *and* surprise, but their manoeuvre was still risky if the enemy observer should spot them before they closed the range. Rainer Arnu hastened to his task, steepening the dive to bring Bruno's guns onto the unsuspecting enemy below.

Hunt levelled his machine. They had spent too much time watching the stricken Aviatik and although they had just crossed their own lines, the situation was still dangerous. Putting his house in order he signalled Mills to keep a watch as he brought the BE back on course. From habit he glanced behind and as his head turned back he caught it! A glint of sun on the rapidly approaching speck. Staring, he waited long enough to recognise the danger for what it was.

'It's a bloody two-seater!' He prodded Mills with his swagger stick, his usual instrument of communication reserved for immediate concern! As Mills struggled to re-position the Lewis on the starboard rear strut, Hunt kept the aircraft as steady as possible, but a quick look to his five o'clock gave him a shock. The enemy two-seater was fast, and identifying it as another Aviatik he realised his mistake. In fearing the frontal attack of a Fokker Eindekker he had forgotten the classic manoeuvre of a fast two-seater!

Above, and almost level with the BE, Leutnant Rainer Amu made a small rudder turn to the right giving Lorenz a clear shot into the exposed cockpit. The Spandaus rattled off a four-second burst, it was enough. Hunt's body slumped forward, he was dead in an instant! Fearing return fire from the obscured front cockpit, Arnu pulled the Aviatik into a right bank turning for home.

Andy dropped the Lewis onto its spigot at much the same time as Lorenz's bullets found Major Hunt and his own right leg. Collapsing against the cockpit edge he no longer worried about returning fire. He didn't even know where the enemy machine was – he never saw it! The blood streaming from his pilot's head confirmed his worst fears. There were no dual controls in a BE, and parachutes were unknown to the RFC. Whereas German airmen were experimenting with early forms of parachutes, the British Corps denied them to its own crews on principle. It was suggested they would be bad for moral!

As he looked over the cockpit he recognised friendly terrain. Ground he had flown over many times before and incredibly, the BE was actually flying itself home! Even if he *could* reach Mr Hunt's cockpit he could hardly fly the aircraft, but with its exceptional stability it would probably keep on like this ... until the fuel gave out. Ten minutes later he could see their own field some three miles to port, they were at about two thousand feet now, but still on the same track, dead into wind and gently losing altitude.

'It could be possible of course. It could even land itself in this area; it's flat without many trees. It just might.' Andy Mills settled down in the cockpit, resigned to whatever fate had in store for him, the pain and loss of blood dulling his mind. Twelve minutes later, Mills now mercifully unconscious, the BE2c ploughed into an open field, catapulting him into the ground and breaking his neck.

Within minutes a detachment of infantry arrived at the wreckage, and as the dead crew were lifted into a tender, two privates were detailed to guard the remains until they were collected by the squadron.

After an hour, hungry and bored, one of the soldiers prized open a 'box' found next to the cockpit.

'Hey Smithy! there's no bloody sandwiches in this, I thought you said these fliers always carried rations with 'em? All we 'ave 'ere is a load of glass plates!'

Chapter Eight

It was a hot day, and in common with most of the small terraced houses the front door was open. As Bill entered the living room he surprised his mother who, dressed for church, was putting the finishing touches to Maggie's pigtails. She turned as Bill's kitbag dropped to the floor.

'Bill!' It was Eileen's voice, coming from the foot of the narrow staircase that led directly upstairs from the small front room.

Muriel Proctor just looked at him and cried. He *should* have sent a telegram Bill thought, but further thought was impossible as Maggie leapt from her chair, laughing and crying, pulling him into the room.

'Look Mummy, isn't our Bill wonderful. He's got a gun as well – does it work Billy – show me… !' She stood back as Eileen gently pushed his mother towards him.

It was a full five minutes before he even took his webbing off.

'Gosh Bill have you killed any Germans yet?' Maggie wouldn't let him be, and fussed about him as Eileen departed for the kitchen and to the garden where Kit Proctor was to be found. She returned in a moment, followed by her father wearing his suit and one shoe, the other half-cleaned in his hand as he too prepared for church.

'By gum Bill, thar's a right credit to us all, you look a real soldier in yon suit. But we didn't know thar were coming home, I thought thee had another week or more at that school?'

Eileen made tea as an unremitting dialogue continued among the excited family. Maggie, after stern warnings from her father had settled next to her big brother on the old settee – listening to every word.

'Breakfast! You must be starved Billy; how would bacon, fried egg, sausages and black pudding do?' Muriel had at last gathered her wits and started issuing orders to her dutiful daughters who went to the kitchen with a will. Kit Proctor studied the changes he could see in his son.

'Thar's a gradely sight in your RFC suit and no mistake. Welcome home son. How long have you got, eh?' Turning to his wife he announced…'There'll be no church today – our lad's home!"

The entire family watched as Bill made short work of a large breakfast, most of it consumed with an adoring Maggie standing behind – arms around his neck. Then, after distributing his gifts and an hour or so of talk, a perceptive mother took control and packed him off to his room.

'The poor boy's tired out, and I'm sure you'll want to wash up and shave son. So *you* be quiet our Maggie and give your brother some rest.' By late afternoon Bill reappeared, washed, shaved, refreshed and in his civvies.

It was sunny and warm with a light breeze flowing down the floor of the valley. Eileen suggested the family should go for a walk as they always did on Sundays. But Bill would have to put his uniform back on! There was no getting out of this, indeed if Maggie had her way it would have been complete with webbing, revolver and full packs! And so the proud family set out into the village.

Like all dales folk the Proctors enjoyed walking, but Sundays were more of an opportunity to socialise rather than exercise so Bill was fully aware what this walk was all about! The ten minute journey to the river took all of an hour, and being the first village son to return on embarkation leave he was something of a celebrity, not least due to the novelty of his RFC uniform which, with 'maternity tunic' and swagger cane caused quite a stir. Most questions centred on his assumed experience of flying an aeroplane, surely a terrifying experience? After a while he felt somewhat irritated by these questions and took pains to explain that his job was more important than being just a *driver!* Keeping these heavier than air machines flying was far more important! Yet at heart Bill could see that his own interest in the machines was not really shared by his friends.

George Graham, his wife and daughter Jane met them by the river. As expected George, his father and himself soon fell into deep conversation about engines, much to the dismay of Jane, who looked for an excuse to talk to Bill and more – get him to herself,

'If you're not too busy tomorrow Bill, why not come over to the garage for lunch? I'm really interested to hear more about these Royal Aircraft Factory 'in lines' you mentioned.' At this Bill realised that he had perhaps said too much already… 'careless talk costs lives'. This was the message drummed into them at training camp, but with their mutual interest he had forgotten!

'I will Mr Graham, and thanks.'

In answer to Kit Proctor's question, 'When did he have to go to France?' Bill felt uneasy as he lied.

'I have to return to Farnborough first Dad. My orders may be changed and I may have to fly over with a BE2 aircraft. Pilots usually like to take an ack-emma, Air Mechanic, with them just in case of an engine or airframe problem. So I shall have to return to camp on Thursday I'm afraid, get my orders then go to Dover from there on the Saturday morning.' He was surprised how easy it was to lie. And even more surprised to find he could live with it, despite his mother's tears and cries of 'unfair' from young Maggie, who was packed off to bed at eight. Muriel Proctor dried her eyes,

'I'm that sorry Bill, I seem to be crying all the time, but no more I promise. You have little enough time at home and you don't want me blubbing every time I speak.' She turned to Eileen, 'Did you tell Bill about your job pet?' Eileen sighed,

'I'm to be an apprentice dressmaker in Harrogate! It doesn't make much money though and what I do make goes on rail fare.'

It was obvious Eileen was not too happy about the job and Bill recalled the wages that could be earned down south.

'Girls in the munitions factories are earning tons, and even young typists are earning good money these days.' Kit Proctor was quick to respond,

'Aye so they may be, but what happens after t' war, eh? Thar knows right well Bill, Harrogate has no industry, it's a posh town for posh folks; alus was and alus will be. Our Eileen's got to have a trade that she can rely on – a skill, just like thee and me – and there's nowt around here for her.'

Bill turned to his pretty sister, 'Well it's a good place to meet your rich husband lass! There's lots of nice officers in Harrogate...'

Eileen made a face and changed the subject, 'Have you seen your pal Gerry yet?' Bill told them about his friend and their arrangement for forwarding letters.

'You haven't found a girl friend yet Billy?' Eileen was intent on helping her best friend and although she knew Bill and Jane had corresponded, there was little evidence of any romantic progress so far. She also knew Jane would have mentioned the slightest sign of affection on Bill's part. Eileen didn't start her new job for two weeks, so she determined to do some serious matchmaking in the next few days.

'Don't be daft, we don't have any time for girls at camp.' Bill lied. He knew Maggie had kept his secret and although he had considered telling his folks about Alice, he was concerned lest they realise why he

93

was returning to Farnborough early. All the same, he wondered if Maggie had guessed?

'If it's nice tomorrow Jane and I thought we might play tennis, you'll join us Billy won't you?' He never even considered the possibility of a plot, and although his tennis was nothing special the game appealed to him,

'That would be nice, but remember I'm having lunch with Dad and Mr Graham tomorrow.'

It had been an exciting day and as the family retired to bed, Muriel kissed her son and told him to take his time in getting up,

'Make the most of it son, it's all too short!'

Bill welcomed the solitude of his room and wrote to Alice before going to sleep.

It was the school holidays and Maggie brought breakfast to his room.

'Bloody hell, what time is it?' Maggie was shocked.

'Bill Proctor if Mum heard you swear she'd… ! Anyway, it's half-past nine and Mum said you needed to sleep, so here is your brekky.' As she watched him eat Maggie wasted no time before asking about Alice.

'That's why you're going back on Thursday isn't it!' It was half statement and half accusation, as Bill could see from her expression.

'Yes love, that's why. And only *you* know that little secret.' At this Maggie's expression changed to that of conspirator. 'Bill are you going to marry Alice? And why don't you tell Mum and Dad? Is she very pretty and do you think she will like me?'

Bill munched on a bacon sandwich, gasping at all the questions.

'Hey, steady on Maggie, but yes, of course, she likes you. I have told her all about you and she has even seen your photograph! But I don't want to tell Mum and Dad yet and certainly not Eileen…' Maggie nodded her head concerning her elder sister. 'We all know that it would be over the entire village if *someone* we know were to hear of it! You see Maggie, I really do like Alice enough to want to marry her – and we have an understanding about that – but we've only known each other a short while and I'm going to France as well. I just don't want anyone else to know yet…'

Maggie took his hand, 'And only I know – oh Bill isn't it lovely. Have you got a photo of Alice?'

Bill smiled, 'I'm so daft about her I forgot to ask, but I will when I next see her.'

Maggie looked about her, then whispered, 'Bill, did you know that

Jane Graham is sweet on you? She asked me to find out if you like her!'
Bill choked as she continued, 'Eileen thinks she's nice, but I don't like
her much, she thinks she's *so* grown up! Anyway you have to go and
fight a war.'

He laughed, 'She's only just out of school, and we've always been
friends. She's Eileen's friend really, in fact we're playing tennis later today.'

Maggie took his tray with a serious expression on her face, 'That
Eileen, she's trying to marry you off to her, but don't worry Bill I'll take
care of you!' As she left the room Bill chuckled to himself, what would
he do without Maggie!

Bill's first task was to the village shop/sub post office, where he
dropped Alice's letter into the open post-bag. Few of the villagers ever
received letters, or even sent them for that matter, and so delivery tended
to be irregular depending on the proximity of the addressee or the
possible urgency of the letter or parcel. The subjective nature of the
system was controlled by the postmistress, who knew most of the villagers personally and their business to boot. But for all that she was a
kindly soul and not given to gossip.

Bill made the usual greetings and after a while asked for six penny
stamps.

'I'm expecting a letter from Farnborough soon Mrs Bowden, I don't
suppose there's anything yet for me, but perhaps tomorrow? In fact
there could be a few later on, some friends will write to me here while
I'm in France, but Maggie will collect them. Don't bother to bring them
to the house – you know Maggie – she likes coming to the shop.' He
had already planned that Maggie should take care of his mail, and he
would leave her with sufficient money to re-post any letters he may get
from Alice, or from Gerry.

The rest of the day went well. Lunch at the garage took a good two
hours, with his father, Jack Henshaw and George Graham debating
the war, discussing engines and questioning Bill on his new-found knowledge of aero engines – particularly the rotaries. Jane and her mother
had brought two hampers of food then and after a few words to Bill,
had left the men to their discussions. Mindful of Maggie's words Bill
couldn't help noticing Jane's attention and realised he would have to
take care.

The tennis was pleasant and since Maggie had come to watch, the
machinations of Eileen and Jane came to little, despite Eileen's anger
and urgings that the 'little pest' should go home. And although Bill
found it impossible to refuse Jane's invitation to go boating on the Nidd

next afternoon, he noted that Eileen declined the invitation; a sorry ploy since Maggie invited herself along instead!

It was supper time, Maggie had gone to bed an hour ago and the family seated in the front room with all the doors and windows open. Kit Proctor continued the conversation of lunch-time and then left to smoke his pipe outside.

'How do you feel about Jane, Bill?' Eileen's question came as a surprise. Unlike Maggie she was never so direct, and he was quite unprepared and at a loss for a suitable answer.

'Well, I suppose she's a nice girl, but what do you want me to say? I mean … she's a good friend and…' It was obvious that Eileen was intent on getting a more conclusive answer.

'I know she likes you a lot Bill. Why don't you ask her to be your girl – now you are going to France?'

Muriel Proctor smiled. 'Now don't push the poor lad Eileen, I don't think Bill wants to have a steady girl at a time like this – so let him be. They write to each other and there's time enough…' She became quiet, then hurried from the room.

Kit Proctor found her in the outhouse, crying. 'Come on Mue, don't fret so, take each day as it comes luv, he'll be right.' He held her close until the sobbing died away, then kissed her gently on the forehead.

Bill and Maggie were seated by the river's edge, she eating the currant bun he'd bought her at the shop as he read, and re-read Alice's letter.

'Well, what does she say, tell me please.' Bill told her what little there was to tell, most of it being personal and intimate as only love letters can be. But she had also enclosed a photo of herself. It was almost a year old, and she had cut out the rest of the figures in the family group. 'Gosh Billy, isn't she lovely! I just know I'm going to like Alice lots and lots.' Bill was overjoyed, too happy to say more than a few words of caution as Maggie played on top of the logs piled by the riverside.

'Maggie! I told you before them logs can be dangerous! And the mill doesn't pile them there for you to play on, so come on down!'

'Now please Maggie, be nice to Jane, she's a good lass you know, and it should be fun on the river.' They were at the Graham's house where Jane was waiting for them with a picnic hamper.

'It's not long since we had dinner Jane – but it was nice of your Mum to make us a picnic.'

Jane smiled, 'I hope you like the apple and rhubarb pie Bill, I made it myself.' Maggie pinched Bill's arm, her eyes skyward as she mouthed unheard mimicries of Jane's conversation. It was Bill's intention to rent a punt, he was good on the river and knew every inch of the Nidd's fast and shallow waters. But to his surprise the girls voted for a rowing boat. He knew Maggie loved to steer, but it was only when they were in mid-stream and Jane asked to share the rowing that he understood her preference for a boat. 'Let's go to the island Bill. we can tie up there and have a picnic later.' She sat close, and taking one of the oars rowed with Bill, the water dripping onto her smock as she kept his pace and rhythm.

As Maggie splashed in the shallows of the island, her smock held high and the water above her knees, Bill lay on his back soaking up the late noon sun. Jane put her head on Bill's chest, content she had him to herself at last.

'You will write to me from France, Bill? I shall always write to you, I promise – wherever you are!'

'But sometimes I may not even have an address Jane, I've been warned about that, but of course I shall write.' He smiled at her; dear Jane, he could never hurt her. Turning towards him, and seeing the tenderness in his face she kissed him softly on the lips. In his response he had no thoughts of Alice as he returned her kiss, it was only a moment, a flash in time, then the guilt of it drew him back.

'Jane, I…'

'Come on you lazy things the water is lovely!' Maggie made good on her promise, pulling Bill into the water as Jane cursed the 'little pest'. Try as she might Jane failed to recapture the moment. The picnic, the return journey and 'goodbye' at her gate – even Bill's peck on her cheek left her unhappy – did he really care?

By Wednesday night Bill had said his farewells to the Graham family, there was some distance between Jane and himself mainly brought about by George, who insisted on walking him home as he had some matters to talk over with his father. Bill repeated his promise to write, as did Jane who, with tears in her eyes kissed him lightly on the cheek and gave him a small book of French phrases, duly inscribed with her love.

'Our Jane thinks a lot of you Bill – mind you write to her now and then or we'll never hear the last of it'. George was not going to press the matter – time would tell!

There were a few tears on Thursday morning, mainly from Maggie who, despite her solemn promise not to cry was overcome at the last moment. The family saw him off at the station where Bill was glad to see Jack Peables talking to his parents, it relieved him of having to make conversation; there was so little to say. At last the train came in, and after he put all his kit within the carriage, he came back to the platform to hug his sisters and kiss his mother. As the whistle blew, he shook his father's hand and re-boarded the train, waving out of the carriage window as it pulled out of the station. He doubted he had ever felt so sad in his life – it was almost unbearable this time!

Jack Peables had done well, his list of connections to King's Cross had been accurate and his journey quite comfortable. The busiest and most exciting part was now, and as he neared Farnborough Bill was reminded of his first introduction to the area, could it have been only three months ago? Yet here he was a trained airman going to France – and his girl only minutes away.

As he struggled through the volume of soldiers now crowding the platform, he took stock of the time as he pushed towards the ticket barrier. It was 5.20 pip-emma, just enough time to get some flowers for Mrs Webb and perhaps chocolates for Alice. Before he knew it, he was part of a queue – headed by a pair of MPs who were on duty at the barrier checking travel warrants and leave passes. That was all he needed – a military checkpoint!

'In a hurry to get to the front are we?' Bill looked surprised. 'You're not due in Dover for a couple of days yet; what is it, got your girl in the family way?' Before Bill could retort another voice was at his elbow.

'Not this girl corporal, she's not like that!' It was Alice.

The MPs saw the joke and pushed him through. There she was, at the side of the barrier waiting for him.

'How on earth … ?'

'Well I *can* read *Bradshaws* just as well as you can Billy – and you *did* tell me what time you were leaving Harrogate. The rest was simple my dear Watson!' He made to kiss her, 'By no means sir, I'll have nothing to do with people who discuss my 'condition' in such a public place!' She was enjoying herself immensely, 'And you can take that kitbag thing off my foot you Yorkshire oaf!'

They moved out of the throng to where she could kiss him.

'There, now you're forgiven. Pick up thee kitbag and we'll be off!' As they walked to the bus stop Bill remembered the flowers.

'Not a chance Bill all the shops are shut now. You can get mother a bunch tomorrow.' She never stopped talking all the way to her home.

Whereas Alfred Webb gave Bill a hearty welcome, his wife stayed back. As always, she was polite but reserved in that cold dispassionate way some people have. Perhaps that's the way she was with everybody he thought; surely Alice would say if her mother disliked him? He dismissed the thought, after all he only knew Yorkshire folk really, and the Webbs were of a different breed – southerners!

Alfred showed Bill his room, it was up two flights of stairs and shared space with an adjoining room which the Webbs used as extra space for second-hand books. Neat and well-furnished it was a bed-room such that Bill had never known before. It wasn't just the size either, the washbasin, curtains, coloured sheets on the bed and even a small balcony outside the French windows; it was very different to where he slept last night!

'I hope you will be comfortable here Bill. The lavatory is at the end, you passed it on your way up, and the bathroom is on the first floor.' He was shown where his towels were in the linen cupboard and he could take a bath now if he wished.

Feeling dirty after the journey Bill took a bath, then shaved with extra care. Putting on a clean white shirt, he wore a tie and pulled his blue and white cricket jumper over the high-backed RFC issue trou-sers. As he went downstairs Alice met him by her bedroom.

'Bill, dinner will be ready in about fifteen minutes and I think it best if you wear your uniform, mother tends to be rather formal I'm afraid – I hope you don't mind – never had the chance to tell you be-fore.' She kissed him and ran down stairs singing snatches from Chu-Chin-Chow.

Within ten minutes Bill presented himself in the dining room where Jean Webb was busy preparing places at the table.

'I hope you like mutton Bill? Do you eat that in Yorkshire?' He could hardly believe his ears, but recovered sufficiently to say,

'I live in a sheep farming district Mrs Webb and yes, we eat mutton quite a bit.'

She looked at him with interest. 'But I'm sure your mother must find it *terribly* expensive doesn't she? I mean it's all of a shilling a pound these days you know!'

Whereas Jean Webb's snobbery was understood by her husband and tolerated by her daughter, to Bill, who had neither experience or understanding of it, her comments were as 'water off a duck's back'.

'Matter of fact, Mum bought a good leg of mutton for only 10d this week, home-killed of course.' Jean was surprised at his knowledge of domestic matters and said so.

Bill laughed, 'When you live in a small village everything is com-mon knowledge Mrs Webb, and the price of food a daily conversation piece, particularly in our house.'

The dinner conversation continued with food and rising prices, and Bill was pleased to find that Mrs Webb was keen to talk to him on a number of matters, despite Alice's efforts to chatter on light-hearted nonsense.

'I suppose you will return to garage work after the war Bill'? I mean, you will continue as a motor mechanic, is that right?' Bill confirmed his intentions and his aim to help George Graham keep abreast of modern engineering developments. 'But surely, there can be little future for you in such a small village – I mean, wouldn't you rather have a white collar job in Harrogate or something like that?'

Although Bill had yet to understand the cruel intent behind these questions he did respond to Jean Webb's latest thrust with some spirit.

'White collar job! In an office ... not on your life Mrs Webb, my Dad would disown me!' As Bill laughed he realised his outburst was a direct affront to Alfred Webb, and as he looked across the table was relieved to see him joining in the joke.

'Stick with engineering Bill, I'm living proof of what happens to white collar workers.'

Alice touched her father's arm ,'I couldn't see you ever changing a car tyre Daddy.' But Jean Webb was not amused and with a stony glare at her husband made her position quite clear.

'Now that's silly Alfred, you are a respected businessman, and people look up to you. Why, if it wasn't for your office training, connections, and ... well ... education, where would you be today!'

After the sweet, Alice helped her mother clear away as the two men retired to the lounge.

'I wasn't fooling Bill. I could have wished for a more exciting career than the one I've had. Oh yes, the book business has given us a good living, but there much more to life than that. I envy you son, you have the future in those hands of yours.' At this point Alice ushered her mother into the room and beckoned to Bill with her little finger,

'Come on 4003, you can help me wash up while Mummy and Daddy rest.' Alice had taken charge once more and Bill was pleased to be alone with her in the spacious kitchen. Jean Webb seemed to be angry, perhaps more at her husband than anyone else, but it was now painfully obvious that Bill Proctor was not her first choice as a future son-in-law.

Their chores completed, Bill and Alice escaped to the park.

'Alice, I hope you won't mind me asking, but sometimes I get the feeling your mother doesn't approve of me?'

She squeezed his hand a little tighter, 'I know it looks that way, but that's mother! She's not at all like Daddy – as you can see. I think she's set her mind on a rich banker or someone similar for me – that's all.'

Bill had to laugh. 'Your Mum and my sister Eileen would get on fine.' They talked of his leave and his family, and the photo she had sent of herself; he showed her where he kept it – within his paybook.

'I'm so glad you don't take mother seriously Bill, I know how to handle her better than Daddy, and anyway I please myself! But tomorrow we shall spend all our time together, and I've borrowed Daddy's camera so I shall have my own photos of you.'

She was quiet for a while. Thinking something was wrong he turned her face towards him, it was wet with tears. 'Sorry Bill, sorry! It's just that here you are and we only have tomorrow and then you will be away to Dover on Saturday.' He took her in his arms and they were silent for a while.

'I've tried to avoid thinking about Saturday all week, but I'll have to face it Alice and tomorrow I must check my train to Dover, you know I have to be there for 5 pip-emma don't you love?'

She sniffed and searched her purse for a scrap of paper. 'No need, I checked at the station earlier this week. If you take the 1.15 train it goes direct to Dover, and gets you there about 3.30 pm, so don't worry. But in the morning we shall escape to Guildford, there's a bus about 9.30. I thought we would go shopping first, there is something I want to buy for you ... no I insist! Then we can have lunch in a lovely little place I know, and the afternoon can take care of itself!'

It was getting dark and in her summer frock Alice felt the chill. She cuddled closer, and as he felt the warmth of her thighs he became hard almost instantly.

'Oh Bill, I wish we had more time ... and I think nice girls like me shouldn't be thinking ... well I wish we were married.'

His emotions were in turmoil; he wanted her. But apart from the smutty jokes and comments from his pals, he knew nothing, not even the basic mechanics of how to make love. 'Fucking' that was the word everyone used in camp. He knew about love; what he needed to know now was much more basic and he felt ashamed of his ignorance.

His hand dropped to her thigh as she kissed him. 'I know my love, I know but I'm a little afraid.'

She sighed, thinking his touch an intended intimacy.

'I work in a bookshop and have read lots of books, love stories many of them, but I've never even seen a man – if you know what I mean?' She searched his face, it wasn't embarrassment she saw there but concern. 'You grew up with sisters but it's all a mystery to me, not

101

to know anything – only silly tales the girls talked about at school. Will you be honest, please don't be offended – but have you ever made love to a girl Billy?'

He knew there was no reason for her to believe him but he told her anyway. 'I have no experience. I've never done it before; the lads in the camp *say* they have but I don't believe them. The married chaps have of course, like Sam … He was out of his depth, half wishing the conversation could end, yet intrigued by their mutual frankness.

'It's so easy to talk to you Alice, I never thought we would talk like this though.' She moved her hand over his, keeping the intimacy of his touch.

'We have so much to learn about each other haven't we? Being married must be wonderful.' She giggled. 'But I suppose everybody has the same problems, I mean when they first make love? And yet it's not in any book – surely it should be?'

Bill laughed, relieved to break the tension, the tightness in his groin now unbearable. 'You and your books, you can hardly expect to find such things in a book for heaven's sake!' With his right arm about her shoulders, Bill attempted to adjust his trousers by removing his left hand from Alice's thigh. As he did, she moved to retrieve his hand and found his hardness to her touch. As Bill froze, embarrassed, she gently felt the warmth of him and closed his hand in hers. Neither spoke.

'Now I know you more! Do I really do that to you Bill?' He couldn't move and truth to tell didn't want to, despite the discomfort.

'Yes!' He thought of an expression, oft bandied about in camp, and he chuckled. 'Do you know what the lads in camp call girls like you?'

She joined in the humour, sensing the untold joke. 'Girls like *me* indeed! I'm not sure I care to hear what your uncouth friends have to say about the kind of girls *they* consort with but go on tell me!'

She was shameful Bill thought, yet so innocent as well. 'Prick teaser!' He had to repeat the term twice over as she considered the meaning of his remark. To his amazement she squeezed – hard, making him gasp out loud.

'So that's what you call it, I must admit I had always wondered. And Bill Proctor, you should be ashamed of yourself; I think you are quite disgusting.' As he protested she moved her hand, putting both arms around his neck, 'But I forgive you!' The episode was over just as quickly as it had started.

Bill had never talked to a girl in such a way, never. Yet it seemed so natural with Alice. He couldn't imagine a similar conversation with Jane, never in a million years! Although the boy was Christian in his beliefs, it wasn't the moral dimension that concerned him so much as the shocking frankness of it all.

Sensing his alarm she dropped her head and in a contrite voice murmured 'I think I have shocked you. But I don't talk like this to everyone Bill, just you. I know you go to church, and your family have brought you up in a religious way … and now I'm going to shock you again. You see, I have been brought up in quite a different kind of home to yours. Daddy doesn't believe in God, he's an atheist you see.' The subject had been worrying Alice all evening, listening to Bill talking about his family, their simple and uncomplicated life. She knew she could never believe as he did.

'I never gave it any thought lass. There are so many different religions, I know! I was living with about ten of them in camp. Methodists, Baptists, Catholics, C of E like me, Jews, Protestants and I don't know what. But I was told that it was very hard for an atheist in the army. You see we have to go Church Parade every Sunday and I'm told that those who don't have a recognised religion, like atheists, spend a lot of time doing fatigues, that's why we never meet any I suppose!'

'But does it worry you that some people don't believe in God Billy?'

He thought a moment. 'Well I have to admit I've never known anyone who didn't. I suppose it's the way you are brought up. I mean, I've never questioned it – too deep for the likes of me lass.' Seeing the concern on her face he went further. 'It doesn't matter you know. Sam was telling me his family never went to church, and the only time he ever went was in the army. Some of the lads back from the front have little time for the Padres either, talk a lot of rot most of the time, that's what they say. You see they tend to push it down your throat so to speak, and it doesn't seem right to stick a bayonet in someone you don't know, then go and pray!'

Like many young men Bill considered religion as something one conformed to, but never discussed. Yet since he had been in the RFC he couldn't help noticing that crude profanity often went hand-in-hand with sincere religious belief. And that many of the toughest characters would never use profane language particularly if they were Irish or Welsh.

'It doesn't matter to me love, but are you an atheist like your father?'

'No, but although he would never dream of influencing me … well, you know me! I've questioned the existence of God with him and I respect his views. So I think I must be an agnostic!' Seeing the question in his face she explained. 'By agnostic I simply mean I don't know. But

103

if I'm honest I think I mean I don't care! You see, my mother is ashamed of Daddy's views, so she goes to church just to be respectable … she is *such* a snob!'

As they walked arm in arm back to the house they agreed never to let religion influence their lives. Alice was relieved; she understood that her father's views were not popular, and although he never advertised his thoughts it had made a difference to his marriage. Her mother wanted him to engage in local church matters, not for any devout reasons but because it was a route into higher society – as she saw it. Alice loved her father and their time in the shop together was the best time of each day. Home life was a sterile affair, only made human by her own contrived attitude of being the 'silly young thing' and helping her father to cope with a loveless marriage.

She hugged him close. Bill was the man for her and she was more than content. 'I'm glad we can talk like this Billy, we shall never have secrets shall we?'

They returned to find Jean Webb making a supper of cocoa and biscuits. Alice announced their plans for the following day and asked her mother what she wanted from Guildford. Since Jean had agreed to stand in for her daughter later that morning, it was only fair that Alice should do the shopping . There was small talk for a while and Alice promised to give Bill a call about 8 o'clock.

It was close to 8.30 when he arrived downstairs to find Alice in the kitchen. He kissed her on the cheek and asked the whereabouts of her mother. 'Oh she's gone to the shop in a bit of a huff, all because Daddy agreed to give me tomorrow morning off! Poor Daddy – he's going to be in trouble again.'

Bill was concerned, 'You shouldn't cross your mother on my account love, I can look after myself tomorrow and can easily call in at the shop before I leave.' Alice concentrated on the bacon and eggs she was preparing for their breakfast.

'Come on lover it's feeding time; mother doesn't worry me at all, and Daddy always takes my side.'

Bill wore his uniform more out of deference to Jean Webb than his own preference and Alice, sensing his discomfort, suggested he should change into more casual wear, particularly since it looked like their day in Guildford was going to be a hot one,

'I will finish off here Bill, you go and change there's a dear.'

Although he had packed a lightweight pair of civilian trousers in his kitbag, their crumpled appearance brought a burst of merriment from Alice as he descended into the hall.

'Oh my gosh go and take them off – I'll iron them for you. You simply cannot go out in them like that!'

'Women!' Bill obeyed with good humour and returned to his bedroom. To his surprise Alice followed within a few moments, standing by the door and watching him as, with one hand supporting himself on the brass bedpost, he shook off the offending trousers.

In common with all the armed services, RFC underwear was designed for warmth and hard usage. The heavy wool and cotton combination being split into vest and 'long-john' underpants. She came forward and took the trousers.

'You look just like one of those prize fighters in those things.' Bill had got used to Alice, but she still shocked him, his face now a vivid hue. 'I know, I'm quite shameless but you do look grand.' The trousers dropped to the floor as she hugged him tight. Caught off guard he fell backwards, pulling her with him onto the bed as they laughed and played like children.

Her light summer frock had come slightly undone, showing a little more of her breasts through the wispy slip beneath. He roughly kissed her and she, pulling at his unruly hair tried to bite an ear. They stopped, breathless and unsure. Alice sat up, moving him at arms length to look squarely at the form of his pronounced erection.

'Really 4003 AM/1 Proctor! You should be ashamed of yourself.' Breathless, and childlike, they laughed as they eyed each other, unsure of the next move. ' I know what you are going to call me, but I'm not! It's not my fault you are such a … an *animal*!' She started laughing again, then stopped as he rolled on top of her, pinning her arms above her head.

'So I'm an animal am I? Well maybe I am and that's all your fault so you shall have to take the consequences young lady.' For a moment she really thought he would, perhaps even hoped he would… but then?

Suddenly the nature of their game changed. He kissed her passionately. Releasing her arms he rolled to one side a hand on her breast. It seemed so natural as, without discussion or jokes she loosened the three buttons of his long-johns to caress those parts totally unknown to her – until now.

They stayed in each others' arms not wishing to break the spell, not daring to take the next step. Then it happened! His ejaculation was a total surprise to them both. To Bill, the violence of his release was unexpected, to Alice it was a combination of shock and wonder. Flushed with embarrassment he choked on his shame.

'Sorry, Alice I'm so … sorry.' She still didn't understand what it was, not fully, but the sticky mess now flooding her hand was part of their love and, as she closed her hand on his penis – gently and with compassion she kissed him, tears of mixed emotions running down her cheeks.

It was minutes before they recovered. 'Bill my darling, I love you. Isn't this a wonder! This is baby stuff, isn't it?'

They laughed, more quietly now. 'Yes, I suppose it is – baby stuff.' He got up, to go to the bathroom. 'No, my love, wait here.' She returned with a face cloth, and lacking any inhibition wiped him down – overtly interested in his manhood. Bill relaxed, wondering at her interest as she inspected him, her giggles alternating with silent contemplation. To his surprise he found his embarrassment had gone. They discussed the event as she ironed his trousers, there were no secrets now and they were closer, more than just friends – as lovers should be, and they were satisfied.

They made a handsome pair as they walked through the streets of Guildford, she with her straw boater hat, ankle length boots and flowered frock, Bill with neatly pressed trousers and open necked shirt. Alice took them to the shop she wanted to visit – a jewellers, where she purchased a silver St. Christopher medallion and had it engraved: 'To Bill, from Alice. August 1915'. Despite his protestations she wouldn't allow him to buy any jewellery for herself.

'No Bill, the St. Christopher is special. You see it's my only concession to anything remotely religious and I want you to have it since you leave me to go in harm's way. It's to protect you, and remind you I shall always be with you!' It took but a few minutes for the medallion to be engraved, and as she placed it round his neck, among his service 'dog-tags' he told her it would stay there – with the never-to-be removed emblems of his identity.

They had lunch and talked as lovers do, rejoicing in their new found relationship. Their earlier fondling being accepted as promise of further intimacies to come.

The afternoon was filled with visits to a number of bookshops, and to stores. At one, there was a line of specially produced wooden dolls (effigies, according to the salesgirl) of fighting men, each dressed in the appropriate uniform. She implored him to buy her an airman.

'I shall take him to bed each night,' she said mischievously, 'He will have to be my Bill while you are in France.' Alice was very proficient with her father's Ensign camera, taking a number of photographs of Bill, and instructing him on its use. It was the first time he had handled

106

anything but his mother's Box Brownie, but soon became accustomed to the focus, aperture and shutter controls as he took snaps of Alice. With complete absence of shyness, Alice even managed to get a young boy to photograph them both as they stood arm in arm. Finally, before the shops closed, they handed the 620 spool of film into a photographic studio for printing. Wanting nothing more than their own company they had a quiet evening tea, then visited a pleasant pub for the rest of the evening before catching the last bus back to Farnborough.

Jean Webb appeared to be in a much better mood when they returned home. She had prepared a splendid fish supper, with white wine, and had even given him the latest edition of Conrad's *Heart of Darkness* to read on his journey to France. The rest of the evening was spent discussing the war effort and the continuing strikes which were now affecting munitions supplies. Eventually they all retired to bed, mindful of Bill's journey on the following day.

Alfred Webb joined Bill as he finished his morning shave. 'Well Bill, it's been very nice having you here, and remember – you're always welcome to stay. We shall no doubt hear all your news through Alice. Just look after yourself my boy, we can't have you breaking my girl's heart can we? Oh, by the way, I know Alice will be taking you down to the station, so I've arranged a taxi to call for you both at 12.45. God knows how you manage to struggle with all that kit!'

The train was on time. And although they had said little to each other she had managed to restrain her tears until now. Almost unnoticed, the platform had become full as hundreds of soldiers, wives, children and sweethearts swelled towards the Dover train. It was impossible to embrace, his bulky kit making it difficult to even kiss, and with a need to keep up with the milling throng it was all they could do to stay together as they pushed towards the waiting carriages.

They had managed only a few moments alone in the kitchen, as Alice quietly prepared sandwiches for his journey. But with her mother nearby, their embraces were few and constrained. And now, dressed in full marching order and surrounded by hundreds of soldiers, he couldn't find the words he wanted to say. She kissed him.

'I love you my darling – go now, I shall not wait!' She turned quickly and was lost to the crowd within seconds.

The carriage was full, but he'd found a good seat next to a window, and thankful for its relative seclusion pressed his cheek to the glass as the train headed for Dover.

Chapter Nine

It was his first time at sea, and after a hectic period of embarkation Bill was thankful for the comparative peace of the crowded B deck of *SS Chyebassa*, an old British India steam freighter now just an hour out of Dover and bound for Boulogne. With a clear and calm night ahead of them the painfully-slow freighter rolled slightly as she lagged behind the other transports and their flotilla of escorts.

Most of his companions were tired but thankful for the easy crossing; they said little, mostly engaged in their own thoughts. There were perhaps two hundred RFC ranks on B deck, some returning from leave but most, like Bill, were destined to entrain for St. Omer, the large RFC transit camp and servicing base some thirty miles east of Boulogne. From St. Omer his future was unknown, but the rumour was that riggers and fitters were in immediate demand for the new squadrons now being formed in France and it was unlikely that they would spend more than a day at St. Omer, unless they were posted to the aircraft park based there. If he had any serious thoughts about his immediate future Bill supposed he wouldn't mind being posted to the aircraft park. This would mean second-line servicing, looking after aircraft that required major repairs or replacement of parts; it would be mainstream engineering – and that was what he had joined up to do. Squadrons sounded exciting, and perhaps more important, but he wouldn't be at the heart of his trade!

By the time the RFC contingent reached St. Omer it was almost 2 ack-emma, and few of the tired and weary airmen took advantage of the hot meal awaiting them. Exhausted, Bill and most of his companions bedded down without delay, simply spreading the 'biscuits' over their allotted cots and sleeping almost immediately.

The hut was brought to attention at 8 ack-emma by the resident hut Corporal. They were given an hour for ablutions and breakfast, then were to return for further instructions. Half-expecting to be paraded and marched, the new arrivals were pleasantly surprised to find that discipline was more relaxed in this, their first camp in France.

Promptly at nine, the hut was brought to attention and then told to sit on their beds to be addressed by the 'Movement Control Officer'. As each name was called out they were given the number of the hut to which they should report, starting as soon as the MC Officer had departed.

Bill and three others found themselves at the door of hut 16 where a group of ten or more were already waiting in front of a long desk served by a Captain and two staff Sergeants. The interviews were brief and well-organised, each airman handed over his movement orders and paybook for inspection then received fresh orders and details of his postings. There was no discussion.

'4003 AM/1, W.C. Proctor, posted to 4 Squadron, 1st Wing RFC, 1st Army Group w.e.f. 10.00 hrs 05/08/1915'. The order of posting was read out to him by one of the Staff Sergeants. 'You understand these orders Proctor?'

Bill confirmed his understanding, so far as it went but...'Where is 4 Sqdn Staff?'

'You don't need to know son, just get on the Crossley outside your hut – it will have 4 Sqdn on its side and will take you there, all right.' With that he was dismissed, his immediate future already decided.

There were five of them detailed for 4 Sqdn, and as they waited for the tender they soon became good friends swapping names and details of their experience and trades. Three of them were engine fitters, one an electrician and one a cook. Bill chuckled to himself as, with good humour, they all took care to make good friends with Charlie Train. Cooks were important people and having one as a friend was a rare opportunity. From the driver they learned as much as they could before they arrived at the squadron. Evidently their C/O had been killed only yesterday, and 'A' Flight Commander was now acting C/O until he or a new officer was appointed. Based near Amiens the unit was mainly outfitted with BE2cs in 'A' and 'B' Flights, while 'C' Flight flew Avro 504Ks.

'Well I hope I go to either 'A' or 'B' because I'm not very interested in the rotaries.' said Bill. 'Let's face it, when this lot's over the rotary engine won't have much future.' The fitters were still discussing engines as they entered the airfield just north of Amiens.

The rest of the day was spent in 'arriving' at 4 Sqdn, and Bill was impressed by the relaxed climate at the base. With the rest of the new men he was billeted in one of the 'C' Flight huts, a temporary measure, they were told, until they had been interviewed by the C/O tomorrow morning. Discipline seemed to be slight, airmen walked everywhere rather than marched, and the air was filled with the constant roar of aero-engines. Most of the camp appeared to be either working or sleeping, with a few playing cricket outside one of the Bessoneau portable hangars. Nobody took much notice of them as they walked around the hangars and inspected the aircraft being serviced or prepared for flight.

'Oy, you airmen there!' In company with Ted Hamilton, Bill stopped dead. 'You wouldn't be fitters or riggers would you?' They turned to see a tubby middle-aged airman dressed in filthy overalls bearing down on them. Ted, who had been posted in with Bill that morning spoke first.

'Yes, we both are; just arrived this morning from St. Omer – who are you?' The large wrinkled face was covered in grime and sported a drooping 'Kaiser Bill' moustache below a pair of sharp blue eyes. But it was the wide open grin that put them at their ease.

'Flight Sergeant Owens, 'Dad Owens' when no officers are about. I look after 'A' Flight aeroplanes and am hoping you might be real mechanics for a change.'

Bill could now see the grubby arm band indicating his rank and came to attention. 'Relax laddie, we don't stand on any ceremony here – too bloody busy for that nonsense. But take care with some of the officers, they can get a bit huffy some of them – even on the flight lines! Anyway, have you been allocated to a Flight yet?' Ted explained they wouldn't know until the morning. 'Well I'm glad I found you before the other 'Chiefies' get their hands on you, we're very short of ack-emmas on 'A' Flight. Now what I need from you two is a bloody good story why you will be more valuable to me than to those useless buggers on 'B' and 'C' Flights.'

Bill and Ted needed no further bidding, they could hardly ignore such a welcome and Dad Owens suited them fine.

'Just say your training on rotaries was not complete, that should stop you going to 'C' Flight at least. Oh yes, and if you say you have some experience as riggers that should help with 'B' Flight since they are up to strength in that department - we are definitely not however!'

Bill sighed. 'But the problem is we don't know enough about airframes Flight Sergeant, I…'

Dad Owens put an oily hand on Bill's shoulder. 'God help us lad I know that, but by the time you've been with us for a couple of weeks you'll be enough of a rigger to do the work we need. For the last two months we've been employing some clerks and drivers for simple rigging jobs – under supervision of course and checked out by Sergeant

110

West, but with a couple of real mechanics like you, it will put us back on strength in no time.'

Ted Hamilton was cautious. 'What I don't understand Flight Sergeant is why are you so short of riggers and fitters. We were told that the squadrons had priority over the aircraft parks and they seem to have plenty of ack-emmas at St. Omer?'

Owens sighed a deep sigh. 'Look, just call me Dad when we're on the lines all right? But that's a good question and deserves an honest answer. You see, 4 Sqdn is a reconnaissance unit and needs someone in the back of the aeroplane to act as observer. Like all the other two-seater squadrons in France we are only just beginning to get qualified observers, officers mainly, trained in wireless, map reading and gunnery. But meantime we have to employ ack-emmas and I suppose riggers are an obvious choice! Anyhow, I must get along to the squadron office and get my bid in before the other buggers do. Let me have your names lads and I'll have you in 'A' Flight quick as that! The acting C/O is Captain Wells, he's 'A' Flight Commander, or was, so he knows our problem and will agree I'm sure.'

All five of the new squadron members were welcomed by Captain Tim Wells MC in the office of the recently deceased Commanding Officer. Giving them a brief history of the squadron and his own role as acting C/O, Tim Wells indicated that he intended to continue in the same fashion as Major Hunt who died only two days ago.

'Major Hunt was determined to further the reputation of 4 Sqdn as the best reconnaissance unit in France. We certainly are tops when it comes to photographic work and this is entirely due to the work of the late Major Hunt. You must know that we operate three flights: 'A' and 'B' have BE2cs and 'C' has Avro 504Ks. We are the only RFC Squadron on this field but there is also a Flight of French Moranes at the other side, they don't come under 1st Wing however and we have very little to do with them.'

'The first thing for you to get used to is the very temporary nature of things on a front-line unit. To begin with we live like gypsies! Our Bessonneau hangars are a living proof of that and you can expect to be taking them down and putting them up at another field at any time – twenty men can do it in a day. We all muck in together, officers too, and we all fly!' Seeing concern on some of the new faces he smiled. 'Yes, even you Mr Train! As far as I know we have never found it necessary to use cooks as air gunners, mainly because it might mean using fitters as cooks – perish the thought!' They could all laugh at the joke, and even Charlie Train smiled. 'But I think you know that regulations allow for everyone in the Corps to be ordered into the air. Nevertheless, those of you who work on the flight-lines will be required to fly from time to time and may even be impressed as observers. On this unit all of our observers are volunteers and we are very proud of that.' Captain Wells made a wry smile. 'The extra four bob a day flying pay may have something to do with it!'

Turning to their deployments Tim Wells pretended to consider their files as he gave his decisions. Bill and Ted were to go to 'A' Flight as expected, with the remaining fitter and electrician to 'B' Flight. Charlie Train was directed to the cookhouse which was under the control of a detachment of the Royal Army Service Corps. Once outside the Sqdn Office they were told to report to the appropriate Flight tent and, in Charlie's case, the RASC hut.

Known as RFC Bertangles, 4 Sqdn was no more than five Bessonneau type H hangars spread across one corner of the airfield and groups of tents allocated to each Flight. With the exception of 'C' Flight billets, the Squadron Office, medical centre and RASC huts, all accommodation was under tents. The perimeter of the field was backed by a forest to the west and cultivated land elsewhere. Fuel dumps were carefully camouflaged within the trees as were the ammunition dumps, each well separated from its neighbour with concealed paths leading onto the field.

Whereas 'A' and 'B' Flights were relatively close, 'C' Flight was about 800 yards away, its eight Avros well distributed about the perimeter.

'Well Ted, we made it! Thank God we're for the BEs and Dad Owens. I think we've done well eh?'

They found the 'A' Flight tents without difficulty and waited at the Flight Office for Dad Owens.

'There what did I tell you! Welcome to 'A' Flight lads. Did Mr Wells ask you any questions? No! Well I can see I did the trick yesterday then.' Dad Owens was delighted in procuring the new AMs, and had already allocated each of them to a machine. 'Right then, Proctor, you will be responsible for 988 and Hamilton you get 726. Normally there's a rigger and a fitter to each aeroplane. But… well I may as well tell you, you're bound to hear of it anyway. AM/2 Sayers was rigger on 988 until two weeks ago, but he was killed flying with Mr Kelly. So you have to share 726's rigger for the time being. Trevor Simpson is a damned good rigger and he can teach you all the ropes. He's also got asthma so he can't fly.'

The weather had steadily deteriorated since dawn and apart from a few local flights by 'C's Avros the squadron was grounded. Taking this opportunity to learn as much as they could, Ted and Bill put as many questions to Chiefy Owens as they could.

'It seems that 'C' have a different job to us Dad, what do they do then?'

'Well they are non-operational that's what. Mainly they are a training and experimental flight and since they only have clapped-out 110 hp Le Rhone engines it's just as well. You see they were clapped-out when we took them from St. Omer to form 'C' Flight. Glad to have 'em too, but by God we had to work on 'em. We use them for wireless training, observer training and even pilot training. Did you know that some of our observers even train to be pilots on those things? That mainly happens when an officer applies for pilot, and while he waits to return to Blighty to get his wings they give him dual instruction. Some have even gone solo here. There's a few units in France that even qualify their own pilots on the Squadron, just put their wings up when the C/O says they are pilots!'

'This chap Sayers, the rigger who got killed flying, did he volunteer to fly?'

'No, he was detailed at first, just as any of us can be at any time. As I remember, Mr Jones wanted an ack-emma to accompany him to St. Pol just north of here and after that he got keen on flying, *and* the extra four shillings a day flying pay of course. Nice lad, but you know the rules ... 'never volunteer'.' They all sang out the old soldiers' unwritten rule. 'After that he did a gunnery course on the Lewis over at 'C' Flight and that was that and why you two have to share Simpson as rigger.'

Flight Sergeant Owens was keen to talk about 4 Sqdn. 'You see, this Squadron has a bit of a fine reputation over at Wing HQ, not only in aerial photography but in wireless too. In fact 'C' Flight is the only unit in France with wireless. At present they're trying out the new Sterling set which is a great improvement over the earlier ones I'm told. The first ones weighed 75 pounds and would hardly fit into the cockpit, and the poor old Avro could only get off the ground with a jockey-sized observer and a limited amount of petrol. But the new ones are less than 20 pounds and from what I hear they will soon be fitted to all our BEs by the end of the year. So you see lads, you can be right proud to be on 4 Sqdn!'

After their introduction to 'A' Flight, Owens took them over the line of eight BE2cs to meet the rest of their comrades and NCOs. They had never been this close to a BE2c before and although they knew the 90 hp RAF 1A engine from their engine course, the aircraft was a new experience.

'I'm going to leave you with Sergeant West for the rest of the day. Dick West is Senior NCO i/c rigging and I've asked him to introduce you to the BE2c airframe. You will also meet AM/1 Simpson, your shared rigger. Then from tomorrow I will supervise your engine servicing on 988 and 726. We cannot expect any flying today so that's a blessing. But tomorrow you could find yourself preparing your machines for flight!'

After a brief lunch of bread and cheese, they spent the remaining afternoon and evening in the hands of the riggers. Sgt West was a quiet man and an ex-instructor, and in company with Trevor Simpson they were kept busy learning the rudiments of rigging. Although they knew a number of riggers at Farnborough there was a healthy and friendly 'them-and-us' attitude towards their respective trades. In general the 'engines' tended to look down on their 'airframe' brothers who, in turn, thought 'engines' to know nothing about aeroplanes and hardly fit to be near one. Their joint dismissal of all other 'gash' trades, such as electricians, armourers and photographers was their only source of common agreement.

Sergeant West was an excellent instructor and gave the new arrivals a thorough introduction to the BE2c.

'We call 'em 'quirks' in the RFC, mainly because that's how they fly – quirky-like! Mark you, the early types were much worse, they didn't have ailerons, just wing warping.' Ted wanted to know why this method wasn't still used to bank the aircraft. 'Well for starters it isn't very effective, but the main problem was for us poor bloody riggers. We had to re-trim the aircraft after each flight and sometimes you'd get a bloody driver that was always niggling that the aeroplane was out of trim, when truth be told it was 'im that couldn't bloody well fly straight!'

Trevor Simpson cut in. 'Yeah, things is better now we got rid of that old BE2c belonging to Mr Hamblyn. It was my machine for two bloody months and God it was a handful, mark you these bloody quirks ain't any easier now than they ever was.' He looked up at the darkening sky. 'If it rains later on, and it looks like it will, we'll have to drain these buggers before they fly again. Even after a shower quirks have difficulty getting off, the raindrops spoil the airflow, or so they say. But my guess is it's just the extra weight of the water.'

Dick West turned on the young rigger. 'A little knowledge is a dangerous thing Simpson, but with you it's a bloody disaster! I've told you dozens of times. Even with the smallest pilot up, a wet quirk can't always get into the air – so it can't be just weight can it! Like I told you at Farnborough you silly bugger, it's airflow!' The Sergeant grinned as

114

he turned to his new pupils. 'It was bad enough when Simpson was my worst bloody student at Farnborough, then some idiot had to post him here! But I'll give you this Simpson, with these old quirks most of the time our problems are with water leaking into the lower fabric. Once there it sloshes about in pools and *that* is where we get the extra weight my lad.'

Dick West took them to Bill's machine. 'There's a hundred and one things to learn Proctor, and talking about water within the wing canvas, your machine is the worst of the lot. Isn't it Simpson? You see 988 is usually piloted by Sgt Duffy who is far too kind to mention such things, right Simpson? As a consequence Bert Duffy often flies this death trap with constantly changing trim. So I want you to drain this quirk every day before flight and Simpson here will show you both how to do it right now!'

They visited the mess tent at 6 pip-emma for a welcome break of kippers and ginger cake. And their friend Charlie told them he would bring some 'extras' around later, since he had been put in the same tent as them. After tea Sqdn Sgt Major Keel found them and took them to their tent in 'A' lines, a new one from its appearance, then to the Sqdn Armoury to deposit their revolvers. Hidden under trees the Armoury was perhaps the most substantial building on camp. A large timber hut, filled with racks of .303 Lea-Enfield rifles, .455 Webley revolvers, Very (flare) pistols, Lewis guns, ammunition drums and workshop. Bill commented on a similar hut nearby.

'You two mechs will probably see quite a bit of that Proctor, its the 2nd line servicing workshop; coppersmiths, blacksmiths, welders and the like. Now we must get you to the clothing store for your overalls, Wellington boots and blankets. Come on, lively now!'

By the time they had finished with the stores and deposited their goods in the tent it was 7.30, but they still had to report to the flight-line for further instruction and orders for the following morning. It was past 9 before they returned to the tent, completely exhausted but strangely satisfied with their day.

As promised, Charlie Train had brought them some extras along with a dixie of tea. So what with getting to know their tent companions and the late evening supper, Bill realised his intentions to write to Alice would have to be postponed until tomorrow. Apart from Ted and Charlie there were three others, Ralph Downes a Sqdn clerk, John Taylor an instrument repairer and Keith Horton, storeman. It was all of 11 o'clock and 'lights out' before they went to bed.

Reveille was called at 6 ack-emma, and from the rush to the open ablutions and lack of exhortations Bill knew he was in the company of a front line unit.

'Where's Charlie?' said Ted.

Bill flipped his towel at him. 'Saw him getting up about an hour ago – he's getting our breakfast stupid!' There were no parades, straight down to the mess tent, porridge, fried bread, scrambled eggs. Wash their irons, back to the tent and down to the lines as soon as they could.

Even as they came to 'A' Flight they could see ack-emmas working on their respective aircraft. The day had started with a light drizzle but the clouds were now lifting with a watery sun just breaking through. They reported to the Flight Office where Dad Owens was busy talking to two pilots. He spotted them and broke off his discussion,

'Stand by your machines lads, I'll be with you shortly.'

As they walked to their aircraft they were called over by a tall Sergeant.

'Are you Hamilton and Proctor? Right then, Dad wants you to do complete plug changes on 726 and 988. Sign out your tool kits in the stores tent, get your overalls on and get a move on!'

Sweating under the humidity Bill found the plug change to be anything but easy. It was obvious that 988 had been neglected for some time and in his haste he skinned a few knuckles to boot, but eventually he fitted eight new plugs into the RAF 1A just before Dad Owens joined him.

'Not bad Proctor, not bad at all. Hamilton finished before you but he had an easier task with 726, it was flown three days ago whereas this one's not been flown for ten days. Best check there's no water in the bottom of the fuel tank; as you were! Let's go the whole hog and drain out what remains in the tank, it's been lying around too long. But save the old petrol in a bucket. Then do your normal daily inspection (DI) with a special check on the oil level, better change the filters too. I want a good check on the carb to make sure it's in good condition; if not change it. I'll send Simpson over in half an hour, he can help you refuel. When you're finished give me a shout and we'll have a go at starting her up.'

Bill was still repeating the instructions to himself when Dad returned,

'Oh yes, better use an air-line and blow out the fuel pipes as soon as Simpson gets here.'

Bill had never known two hours go so fast – but it was done! And as Simpson went to find Dad Owens he double-checked his work, including what he had learnt about rigging only yesterday.

116

'Simpson tells me the rigging is all right, and she's not waterlogged, so let's have a shot at the engine shall we!' Dad Owens took his time to go over the start-up procedure, making sure that Bill practised the cockpit drill and prop drill a couple of times before starting. 'I'll take the cockpit first lad, and Simpson can take the prop. You just watch, eh!' Relieved, Bill took careful note of Simpson's stance as he turned the four bladed prop in the opposite direction to its rotation – to prime the engine. Four turns to draw sufficient petrol into the engine. A check that the chocks were in position then, grasping one of the high blades...

'Petrol on, switches off... contact Sir.' Bill recalled the litany only too well, his eyes glazed as he remembered Doughy Baker – his severed head!

The engine took a few coughs and started, only to stop again. Dad Owens called from cockpit.

'Proctor! Oy Proctor!! Wake up lad! Take the prop from Simpson and see if you can get a better swing at it. Bill took over, scared stiff of the mighty four-bladed propeller.

'Petrol on...' It fired first time.

'Well lad, you'll do! You've made a good job of it and I can put this machine down as 'ready to fly'. Simpson tells me the rigging looks right so I'll arrange for an air test as soon as I can get a driver. But I want to see you in the cockpit now lad, I'll show you the magneto switches, fuel cock and throttle – it's on the joystick did you know?'

After Bill had seated himself in the roomy cockpit of the BE, Dad showed him the controls and the start-up procedure from the pilot's position. They fired up twice and satisfied that his new ack-emma was competent, Owens left to find a pilot.

Trevor Simpson helped Bill out of the cockpit.

'There's a right way and a wrong way Bill, and its ten days CB – confirmed to barracks – if you put a foot through the wing fabric! I ought to know, I got ten days of bloody 'jankers' when I first got here! Sergeant West wants me to show you and Ted wire splicing today, but I reckon we can do that after Dad gets a driver for this thing.'

Bill was pleased with himself, Ted had joined them now, and as the three of them discussed their aircraft he knew they made a good team. Most of all, his fears of prop-swinging seem to have disappeared and he had not disgraced himself so far. Indeed, he was even a step ahead of Ted, who still had to start up yet and was having some problems with an oil leak.

'Well I'll be blowed, it's Bert Duffy coming over; he was grounded last week with an infected hand. Silly bugger put it on a hot exhaust pipe.' Trevor obviously had a high regard for Sgt Duffy and seemed to be on good terms with the 25 year old pilot now approaching.

'As you know, 2cs have stove pipe exhausts pointing upwards from the engine! Well, Bert used to be a fitter on 2as which have exhausts running down the fuselage, so what happens? Just after he lands his quirk, he climbs up on a couple of ammo boxes to look at the engine and grabs what he thinks is an interplane strut to lean over the V-8. Unfortunately he grabbed a red-hot exhaust stack instead – God you should 'ave heard his language!'

'Watcha Bert, how's the hand?' Sergeant Duffy showed him a gloved hand,

'Not so bad Trev, the Doc's put me back on flying anyway. So, who's this then?' Trevor Simpson made the introductions. 'Pleased to meet you Bill, Dad just told me I've got an ace fitter!' Bill stammered out a modest denial, as Trevor exclaimed,

'Don't tell me they've actually *given* you 988 Bert?'

'Yep, its mine. The skipper told me I'm to put up my crown and I've got 988 – my own machine at last!' Seeing the questioning look on Bill's face Trevor explained. 'Ah, you probably don't know Bill, but on the squadrons NCO pilots hardly ever get their own machine. Officers do, along with a bloody servant and a high faluting voice, even when they first come to the squadron with fuck-all experience and...' Bert Duffy looked about him then shot a warning look at Trevor Simpson.

'Bloody hell Trev, pipe down! One day someone important – like a handsome Flight Sgt Pilot – will overhear you and have you shot!' The two ack-emmas laughed, congratulating their newly-promoted pilot, as he completed his pre-flight inspection.

'Have you ever flown before Bill? No! Well if you don't mind I would like you to accompany me on this flight. Just a couple of circuits round the field. I hear you are going to be doing the rigging on 988 so it would be useful if you had first hand experience of how she flies – what you think? Half-prepared for this eventuality Bill was happy to accept, his fears now drowned in a heady mixture of excitement and new-found comradeship. 'Better get yourself a flying helmet and goggles, you'll find a set in Dad's tent, on top of the engine record book. Oh yes, and put your tunic on over your overalls, it's cold up there!'

As Bill dashed to the Flight tent he wondered how quickly things seemed to happen. One moment he was happy and content with his morning's achievements and now...! As he entered the tent Dad held the flying helmet out to him and winked,

'Learn all you can while you can, eh son!'

Trevor helped him into the front cockpit which, although sparsely equipped was less exposed than that behind him. He could see almost nothing to the front, while above and below the almost transparent wings enclosed him in a world of fabric and wires. He copied his friend's grin as the rigger prepared to swing the prop,

'Petrol on...' the engine fired at once. Tightening the helmet about his chin Bill automatically looked for a convenient hand-hold within the cockpit, and finding none put his hands on his knees. Bert Duffy warmed the engine up to maximum revs then throttling back waved both arms across his head to signal removal of the wheel chocks. As the BE moved forward Bill looked behind to see Ted waving, Bert Duffy's face a mask behind the small deeply curved windscreen. To his right, Trevor was holding the lower wing, now trotting at a steady pace as he guided the quirk into wind.

Once into wind, Bert waved his rigger off, pushing the throttle forward as he did so. Within seconds the BE's tail had left the ground, rolling and bouncing on its main wheels as the biplane rushed across the hardened grass. Bill's first perceptions were the warmth flowing back from the V-8 engine, the blur of the grass and the rumbling shaking of the quirk as it sped to flight. Suddenly the vibrations stopped – they were flying! At only fifty feet or so Bert levelled off to increase his airspeed. Looking over the side Bill could only wonder at the event; he must write to Alice this evening, he had so much to tell her.

At 500 feet, Bert cleared the airfield and slightly reducing revs climbed at almost 70 mph. He levelled off at 2000 feet, turning slowly south to where he could see Amiens ahead. Removing his hands and feet from the controls Bert let the quirk fly itself, careful to note any tendency for it to depart from preset flight. Then, banging on the cowling separating the two cockpits he drew Bill's attention to their 'hands-off' state and using hand signals indicated that his passenger should also check on the quirk's trim.

As they flew towards the town, Bill kept a wary eye on the quirk's heading and noticed they were flying with a decided droop to port. He turned, attempting an explanation to his pilot but unsure if his signals would be understood when a sudden drop in engine noise startled him. Turning back he saw the propeller now turning slowly, each of the four blades clearly visible. The nose dropped sharply and the earth began to rotate, slowly at first then quickening as their descent became steeper. Although alarmed he was confident this was part of the test and he stayed put.

Bert Duffy pushed forward on the throttle lever and the engine sprung immediately to life. The nose came up and true to her nick-name *Stability Jane* flew straight and level once more. It was no more than a 'power-off stall' and 988 required little further attention other than a bit of lateral trim. Satisfied, Bert climbed back to 2000 feet and returned to Bertangles. As he approached the field he could see a number of the French Moranes and two of the 'C' Flight Avros in the area and was careful to approach downwind at 800 feet to establish his landing pattern. Turning into wind at 500 feet he throttled back and slowly descended onto the field. With the nose well down and the prop just turning over, Bill recalled that his forward view was almost unob-structed, and seeking to get a better view of the landing he stood up.

At about 45 mph and with only a slight headwind, the quirk was nicely set for a gentle approach to the field. But as Bill's upper body raised itself from the cockpit the sudden increase in drag produced a dramatic change to the quirk's legendary stability. Bert's reaction was immediate, and although the stall was totally unexpected he knew in-stinctively what had happened. Pushing the throttle wide open he let the quirk descend further, gaining essential air speed before lifting the nose and shouting to Bill to 'Get down!' knowing only too well he would be unheard.

The sudden blast of airstream pushed Bill back into the cockpit as the engine brought the propeller back to full revolutions. Still unsure of what and why, he stayed there, his eyes just above the level of the cockpit combing. The quirk was now at 200 feet and climbing. Bert looked about him taking care to check the surrounding airspace be-fore re-establishing a fresh landing circuit at 800 feet. He could see that his passenger had recognised his error and was duly crouched down in the forward cockpit – silly young bugger! But by the time he had crossed the outer boundary of the field and was on his (second) final approach he relaxed.

'Not his fault really, his very first flight and all. My fault for not telling him beforehand – silly bugger Duffy!'

As they taxied to the flight-line, Trevor and Ted came up on their wing tips, guiding them into their parking slot. Bert Duffy was first to dismount, humour written wide across his face.

'What kind of a landing was that then Duffy? Bloody pilots – I've shit 'em! My God Bert you need some more practice you do!'

Trevor's feigned annoyance stretching Bert's grin to even wider di-mensions. 'If that's the way you are going to treat our aeroplane I'm buggered if I'll look after it any more!' Bill had now joined the small group, excited and keen to tell Ted all about his experience.

'You'll make an aviator yet young Proctor! That was good think-ing – getting back into the cockpit when you did.' Bill didn't under-stand what Bert Duffy was talking about, but before he could ask for an explanation the pilot continued. 'All my fault really, I should have told you not to stand up when we're about to land, so how were you to know, eh?' Trevor Simpson looked at both of them in turn.

'Oh my God; he didn't, did he? Now it all makes sense!' They all stood about, discussing the near accident and its cause, Bill's face a ghastly grey.

'But what do you think needs adjusting Bill? Forget our little ex-citement for a moment and tell me what needs to be done to the trim.' Bill recollected the quirk's list to port just before the stall test and with Trevor's assistance made suggestions concerning 988's re-rigging. Bert Duffy was pleased. 'Right then, if you think it's only a couple of hour's job Trevor, I'll arrange for another test flight at 3 pip-emma. So hang on to that helmet Bill, you'll be going up again this afternoon.'

By six o'clock they had finished their day's work, Ted's machine was air-tested and ready for flight and Bill had made two flights with 988 before the trim was correct and the aircraft made ready for the next day. A dixie of tea had been brought down to the flight-line at 5 pip-emma and from what Dad told them 'A' Flight was ready with six ma-chines for tomorrow's flying. Bill's aircraft would be flying at 8 ack-emma, a contact patrol piloted by F/Sgt Duffy with AM/2 Armstrong as gunner. Ted's machine was in reserve.

By 8 o'clock, having eaten and cleaned up, Bill got down to writing letters. Fortunately Ralph Downes had a private store of notepaper and being in the Orderly Room gave Bill advice on the Sqdn mail sys-tem.

'Just give me your letter – open mind you cos it has to be censored, and I'll pop it on top of the adjutant's tray. That way it's likely to get read tomorrow. I've known some letters been at the bottom of his tray for two weeks before now! And here's a good tip Bill, never write more than a single page at a time. Captain Jackson, he's the adjutant by the way, well he gets a bit wobbly at times. He's a pilot, but I've never known him fly! Some say he's funky, but the M/O grounded him I know that for a fact, I know because I sneaked a look at his record sheet.'

'But why only one sheet of paper?' Bill had lots to write and didn't like this restriction at all.

'Well, if he gets in one of his 'rages' he'll just paint over half of it and say its censored – saves time! I've seen him do it many a time.'

Bill wrote one page to Alice, trying to tell her everything. It didn't work, and after three attempts he found he'd said little of importance – except his love for her. He mentioned his flying, unsure if this 'military secret' would get past Captain Jackson's paint brush. It was much easier to write single pages to his mother and to Maggie.

He turned in early. Such a day! And more to come tomorrow. He felt content with everything and happy beyond measure. He belonged to 4 Sqdn and was accepted by them. It was a completely different life and a million miles from Dacre, from Alice ... Turning over the day's events he was asleep in minutes.

Chapter Ten

By the last week of August, Bill could safely consider himself to be a reasonable rigger on the BE2c; not good enough to do major servicing perhaps but as far as 988 was concerned, he was confident he could keep her flying – short of any serious damage. Flying had been minimal during the past two weeks, mainly due to rain and very low cloud, and what flying there was had been restricted to servicing checks, training, and aborted attempts at photography. Nevertheless, Dad Owens was happy for the short respite granted by the weather and kept 'A' Flight busy with the various armament and camera modifications dictated by 1st Wing HQ.

A number of changes had occurred during the past few days, and it seemed that the squadron was growing in size. Not only had they gained a new C/O in Major Keith Fawcett MC, but a number of new ack-emmas had appeared as well, including four photographers, six riggers, three fitters, four armourers and an instrument repairer. Captain Wells now reverted back to 'A' Flight and brought two riggers and a fitter with him, much to the joy of Dad Owens. According to Dad, the photographers were to set up a squadron photographic section and had arrived in their own Leyland 3-ton truck converted as a darkroom. Evidently a number of changes were taking place to the RFC since Major General 'Boom' Trenchard had taken over as GOC RFC in France. Trenchard was a qualified pilot with the best interests of the RFC at heart, and although he only took up his new appointment a week ago the effects were already obvious. Those squadrons delegated for photographic work were now to have their own photographic sections, so rather than sending their work to Wing HQ for developing and printing they would now process their own photographs.

On learning of the new photographers, Dad appealed to his Flight Commander. 'Maybe we can get some of them photographers to go flying instead of my fitters and riggers, sir?' Tim Wells smiled ruefully, he was accustomed to his trusty F/Sgt's views and agreed with them entirely. But it wasn't just the pirating of valuable tradesmen that worried him; as a pilot he knew that the 'observer/gunner' in a BE2c was mainly wasted in the role. And although some gunners had managed to protect their machines very well, for the most part BE2cs were considered 'Fokker fodder' these days. It wasn't as though the Fokker El and E2 were particularly good aircraft either, in fact they were almost identical in design to the Morane monoplane which the French had on this very field. But for all its moderate performance as a fighter aircraft, the Eindekker had a machine gun synchronised to fire through its propeller and this made all the difference. Even with an experienced gunner the quirk's poorly-positioned Lewis gun gave little protection against a determined enemy, as Tim Wells knew only too well.

'You mirror my thoughts Flight, but if we are to press-gang some of those chaps we'll have to get ahead of 'B' Flight for I'm damned sure Captain Saul will have similar designs. However, if we *are* going to collar one or two photographer chaps for flying we shall have to emphasise our interest in the subject I think.'

Captain Tim Wells had been with 4 Sqdn from its earliest days in France and he was tired. A brave man, he'd gained a richly-deserved MC for conspicuous flying over Flanders when the squadron was based at St. Omer. During that time he'd experienced every job possible but the missions he hated most were contact patrols (CPs). Maintaining contact with allied forward troops was a dangerous task. Flying at about 100 feet above the trenches it required constant vigilance by observer and pilot as they looked for ground signal-panels and Morse coded signals from lamps and shutters. Once a signal had been put to paper it was then placed in a weighted bag and dropped on the appropriate battalion HQ. In this fashion commanders kept a limited check on their forward troops, but it was expensive on aircraft and their crews. Great promises were made concerning wireless contact, but until the existing sets were more reliable, most field commanders still insisted on contact patrols. The worst of it was that only experienced air-crews understood the danger, which was why so many young and eager pilots were lost within their first few days at the front. Ground fire was the problem. No good worrying about it, no good at all. But it only took one of the thousands of rounds of aimed rifle fire to hit a vital part. Tim Wells could hardly recall a single CP that didn't attract at least a couple of hits, and although he'd never suffered a scratch he had brought back two wounded observers, one of whom died.

Captain Hugh Porter was fully aware that his 'C' Flight Avros would bear the brunt of any future artillery shoots. For months they had been training observers and gunners of all flights on how to use the new Sterling wireless sets, so it was inconceivable they would be excluded from any future action. The problem was that their old Avros were incapable of defending themselves properly. They could only just manage a heavy wireless set – let alone a Lewis gun, but the squadron had been promised escorts of DH2 scouts for any future reconnaissance flights – maybe. Like most experienced pilots in France, Hugh Porter was alert to every rumour and fact concerning new aircraft, and was fully aware that DH2s were currently replacing the slow old FB5s on a number of squadrons. From what he'd heard, the DH2 was at least 20 mph faster than the 'Gun-bus' it was replacing and was a single-seater pusher with a forward firing Lewis gun and a ceiling at 14,000 feet. His fellow officers were constantly discussing it and stories of its success against the Fokkers were a major topic in the mess.

For Bill, Ted and Trevor their entire lives revolved about 988 and 726. They worked hard and long hours keeping their respective machines in top condition and were content to know they were respected within the flight. Bill had even acquired a proprietary feeling for 988, such that he only *loaned the* machine to its assigned pilot, and expected Flight Sergeant Bert Duffy to return it to him in good condition after each flight. But although he was on top of the work he enjoyed best, Bill felt mildly jealous of Tosh Armstrong who shared the flying with Bert Duffy. It wasn't as though Tosh actually worked on 988, he was only a fabric worker after all, and knew nothing about its rigging or engine. But his resentment went deeper than that, for he couldn't deny a feeling that it was he who should be flying in 988, it was his aircraft!

He had received three letters from Alice, two from Maggie and one from his mother during the past three weeks. Apart from his mother, the girls were very excited about his flying experiences. Maggie wanted to know every detail, how did it feel, was he scared? Whereas Alice seemed to consider it more romantic and a route to being an aviator, perhaps even an officer? He had to admit there was more to aeroplanes than just engines and was determined to have another flight with Bert Duffy.

'Gentlemen. I wanted to get you all together because it's time we discussed the role of 4 Sqdn and how we should pursue our orders in future.' Major Keith Fawcett MC, immaculate in his No 1 Field Service uniform stood up to receive his three Flight Commanders as they entered his tent. 'Please be seated. I have much to do and want to tell you what I expect from you and your flights in the coming weeks ahead of us. I'm aware that Mr Wells has been running things for the past few weeks, and from earlier discussions with him I know he is aware of the orders which just preceded my arrival here. It seems we can expect to have a busy time from now on, and it's apparent that things will have to be tightened up around here. For a start we now have Major General Trenchard in France, and I can tell you from personal experience he is an aggressive man – and so am I. The General likes to make spot checks on all his squadrons and we *shall* be ready for inspection when he comes here! A number of administrative changes have been made, and we now come under 3rd Wing of Army Group III. This will mean that along with 1, 2 and 3 squadrons we shall be totally responsible for all photography in our sector, which is why I have brought along a significant increase to our photo-mech strength.'

Major Fawcett stood up and tapped his swagger cane on the French map mounted on a wide wooden table. 'In two or three weeks time the Allied armies will attack in this region, the exact time is not known to me as yet, but we know that our front will be in this area, just north of Arras. You will keep this information to yourselves of course, but I want you and your flights to be prepared for this next push. Mr Wells tells me that 'A' Flight has the best photography crews and he suggested that 'A' should concentrate on this work. However, as he knows, the squadron also has CP and artillery duties to cover as well and I think it best if 'A' and 'B' Flights rotate this work on a weekly basis.'

Bernie Saul couldn't resist the jibe. 'At least your decision will provide fifty per cent success sir! I mean to say, 'A' Flight? They think f/8 is a new fighter aircraft!'

Tim Wells turned on his friend with condescension. 'I was only trying to save you further embarrassment Bernie, everyone on the squadron knows 'B' Flight have problems with navigation, even before they take off!'

Ignoring Hugh Porter's burst of laughter, the C/O banged his cane down hard on the table top. The sharp smack had immediate effect, and brought the three Captains to attention. 'This is not how I expect my Flight Commanders to behave! It may be the practice on some RFC units, but it will not be tolerated here. In future gentlemen, you will reserve your schoolboy humour for the mess. Now, to begin with; 'A' and 'B' will prepare their flights for photography, CP duties and infantry support. I have brought new 'C' type cameras and these will be distributed evenly between you. Bomb racks will also be issued and these will be fitted as appropriate.'

Tim Wells was aghast. 'I wasn't joking when I saw you earlier this morning sir. And I didn't say that 'A' had the best crews, just that we had more experience.' He turned to Bernie Saul, the unsaid apology clear from his expression. Bernie smiled.

'No apologies necessary old chap. Fact is sir, Tim is quite correct, 'A' have done far more than we have. Indeed, our late C/O 'bought the farm' on an 'A' Flight photo mission.'

Tim Wells took up his argument. 'With respect sir, I must argue the point further. You see it was Major Hunt's position that to retain our prominence with photo-reconnaissance we should concentrate our most proficient crews in one flight. Bernie, ah … Captain Saul and I always josh each other about our performance but the fact is that for over a month now we have located our most experienced photo crews in 'A' Flight. Which is why I requested support from the photo ack-emmas if this could be possible.'

Major Fawcett sat on the edge of the desk, whacking his cane against a highly polished cavalry boot.

'The late Major Hunt had his ideas, I have mine. More importantly, while I command 4 Sqdn I shall expect your full cooperation. It may interest you to know that before I came here I was interviewed by General Trenchard himself. He totally concurs with my plans for 4 Sqdn and agrees that all units should be prepared for a more offensive support of ground troops. If the weather precludes photography then all machines will be deployed on CP and artillery duties, surely that makes sense? And as for your suggestion that 'A' should be given some of the photographers for flying the answer must be no! I intend their section to be the heart of 3rd Wing's photography. They will be far too busy developing films, printing and compiling mosaics.'

Hugh Porter decided to enter into the discussions; their new C/O would be dealing with 'C' Flight next and he could see the man had no idea at all.

'When under 1st Wing 'C' Flight was essentially a training flight sir. Our area of expertise is therefore limited to that role, and in particular to wireless training with the new Sterling sets.'

Fawcett turned to the 'C' Flight Commander as though he had just realised he was there.

'Ah yes, Porter. We shall come to your Flight in a moment. But before we do, I want to talk about the four new pilots I have brought along. All of them are fresh out of flying school in Gosport, not many hours I'm afraid. Three are 2nd Lieutenants, direct entry RFC. And one, well one is a Corporal from the RAMC would you believe! Looking at each Flight's crew state I see that 'A' has only seven pilots, so I shall put Cpl Coats there with immediate effect. The officers will go to

'C' where, with Captain Porter, I shall evaluate their performance before Flight allocation.'

Tim Wells had already made his mind up concerning his new C/O and decided not to question his allocation of Cpl Coates. It was plain that Fawcett was not happy with his senior Flight Commander but worse, the man was a military snob of the worst kind. Seeing that Tim Wells was not inclined to question his intended insult, Fawcett pressed the matter. 'I suppose you are not too happy about me sending you a Cpl pilot Wells? But I notice you already have a F/Sgt pilot in 'A' so I imagine you know how to keep discipline with them, eh?'

Tim Wells had to exercise the greatest restraint in his answer, even so it came out as a bitter retort. 'Discipline is never a problem on 4 Sqdn sir. Not yet at least! But in our experience we find NCO pilots among the best. They have to work extra hard to gain their wings and that adds up to air experience in my book. If it's a question of choice, then you've already made it for me, thank you very much Sir.'

Major Fawcett breathed deeply. He knew, and he knew they all knew, he was being challenged. But there was danger here, and so he resorted to pomposity. 'Talking of discipline I am not convinced that it is good practice to have NCO pilots fly with officer observers. So between us, I want it understood that this will never happen, short of extenuating circumstances. I must confess that I am not very impressed with squadron discipline in general, that will shortly change. For example, I notice that quite a number of officers need to speak to their batmen and as for the men! I had occasion to talk to one of the clerks this morning, he was wearing long woollen socks in place of puttees, a practice no doubt copied from some officers.' As he glared at Bernie Saul's legs Tim Wells intervened.

'Captain Saul was flying this morning sir, he came over here only five minutes after landing. As you must know, all front-line aviators are allowed to choose their own mode of flying dress, in the best interests of comfort and protection. I can get the Adjutant to confirm if you wish.' No sooner had he opened his mouth he regretted his words.

'The Adjutant you say! As officer responsible for discipline he falls well below my standards and goes back to Wing tomorrow. His replacement is a fine officer, one who served with me in the 17th Hussars, matter of fact. He will tighten things up around here I promise you, and I shall expect you to give him every support. Captain James should be here within a day or two.'

Turning to Hugh Porter the C/O outlined his special plans for 'C' Flight. 'The reason I have left your flight until last Porter is because I

128

aim to take a very personal interest in its future work.' Tim Wells noticed that Fawcett even managed a smile as he spoke. I want 'C' to continue its training role during the next two weeks, but in anticipation of the future offensive I want all the Avros fitted with a Lewis gun in the observer's seat. Furthermore, and this goes for all flights – I want observers and gunners to practice with the new 97-round magazines.' The three Flight Commanders stole concerned looks at each other.

'Sir! Are we to assume the Avros are not to carry wireless?' Fawcett threw Hugh Porter a surprised look as he snapped.

'Good god man, of course they will carry wireless. It will be their major role in the coming battle to relay wireless messages from CP and artillery flights. Surely you of all people must know that?'

'We also know our Avros' limitations sir. Even with the latest, lightweight Sterling set and a normal 47-round drum on the Lewis, our Avros have difficulty in getting off the ground let alone trying to fight. I would also remind you sir that we have only two of the 20 lb Sterlings, all the rest are the old 78 lb types. The accepted strategy has been to provide scout cover, perhaps the new...'

Major Fawcett was in no mood to argue. 'The *accepted strategy*, Mr Porter, is that which I tell you! And for your information I have seen the Avro 504 working with wireless and Lewis gun on Salisbury Plain only three weeks ago and there are no problems!'

Hugh Porter couldn't disguise his disgust. 'A brand new Avro is one thing, ours were clapped out when we first came here and I must warn you sir, with our existing machines it's as much as we can do to use them even for training.'

Fawcett could see the danger of being trapped by technicalities and waived further argument by disclosing his other plans for 'C' Flight. 'We shall look into the suitability and servicing of the Avros later Porter. But this squadron is going to stand on its own legs; I'm not inclined to be wet-nursed with protective cover from other units. In the meantime, I shall fly with 'C' and evaluate the Avros myself. I shall also require the best wireless observer on the squadron in order to do some trials with Wing HQ. Now, who do we know as the best wireless officer?'

Hugh Porter spoke up. 'F/Sgt Williams is our best observer/telegraphist sir. Williams is an ex-wireless instructor with about 25 words a minute, and was specially posted to us for trials with the new Sterling sets.

'I specifically asked you who was our best wireless officer Captain! We cannot have an NCO evaluating message systems, *that* is an officer's duty.' Tim Wells wanted to smash his smug face, the bloody snob. Some of his best aviators were NCOs, the ack-emma gunners in particular. The pompous shit never got his MC flying that was certain, he was too old for one thing, and being ex-cavalry – where and when did *he* ever see action?

After a few minutes they were dismissed. Tim Wells was beside himself with anger.

'Jesus bloody Christ chaps – that's the worst excuse for an RFC officer I've ever met.

'You may be his particular hate Tim, but its me – Captain 'C' Porter that's going to get the worst of it. Did you hear what the bastard said? He and I are going to run 'C' Flight together! In a pig's arse we are. If he *can* fly an Avro, and I doubt it, he'll get his chance believe me!'

Bernie Saul was more philosophic. 'I can't make him out, he must be about what? Thirty six years or so? We've never heard of him before and a character like that? We would have heard of him I'm sure. I think I shall do a bit of finding out. Fawcett isn't the only one with friends at Wing,'

Tim Wells hung his head. 'I don't like it chaps and we'll have to do something about this new Adj too. See you in the mess later; I have an air test to do as soon as I get back to the Flight.'

Bill had finally decided to see F/Sgt Owens with regard to flying. 'If possible I would like to fly in 988 as gunner Dad, what do you think?'

'Well I suppose that's not a problem, son. But are you sure? It's a dangerous game you know, and the money isn't worth your life is it?' Bill assured him that it wasn't the flying pay, but found it more difficult to explain his real reasons – he didn't really understand them himself anyway.

'It's just that I feel I should you know, I mean, well 988 *is* my machine after all and now I can rig her as well as Trev…'

Dad laughed, 'You aren't the first lad, not by any means. Did you know Bert Duffy started as a gunner? You will have to apply through Mr Wells of course, and if it were anyone other than you I would stop it myself. Good ack-emmas are hard to find lad, but I know you will still work all hours to keep her flying, so it's up to him. Oh yes, and it's also up to Bert and Tosh. Mr Wells would never split up a good crew if they wanted to stay together you know. Anyway, I'll put in a good word if that's what you want. Stand by to see him later eh!'

Bill wondered if he was being stupid. It was the rigging that had done it, he knew that beyond question. Needing to know how and why the rigging affected flight had brought him to this state, 'stupid bugger Proctor!' But what if Tosh wanted to keep flying in 988? Did it matter? God knows what he was getting into now, anyway the extra four bob a day was worthwhile.

Dad Owens handed Bill a flying helmet. 'Quicker than you thought, eh? Nip down to 1021 and you'll find Mr Wells getting ready for flight. He wants to check you out first before he makes any decision. If you lose your breakfast don't let him know. He's going to ask you to fire the Lewis I imagine, so listen carefully to Tosh, he'll be there. Good luck lad!'

Forgetting to express his thanks, Bill ran down the line to where 1021 was being prepared. Captain Wells nodded to him as he continued with his pre-flight inspection of the quirk and Tosh Armstrong took him aside to explain the workings of the Lewis.

'I hear you might be joining us mad buggers Bill, and why not eh! Now the first thing you need to know for this flight is how to cock the Lewis, then how not to shoot the pilot's head off. That's all there is to it! Here's a tip, I know what he's going to do; he'll ask you to stand up and fire the gun over to one side of the quirk, he'll point to which side, see. Then he'll fly in ever-decreasing circles, try to make you sick or a bit woozy at least. He might also fly low and ask you to fire at that old wreck of a Morane at the other end of the aerodrome. One more thing, never ever fire bursts longer than five seconds. For one thing it shows you're nervous and for another the fuckin' gun will jam. Right, lets get you in the front cockpit.'

The Lewis was fitted to the starboard strut, pointing over the side of the cockpit. Tosh showed him how to move the gun and the care he must take with his firing arc.

'I've never heard of anyone blowing his pilot's head off – just make sure you're not going to make history, right!' Tosh showed him how to cock the weapon, and remove and replace the 47 round magazine. 'Right then. The gun is now ready for cocking, but don't do it until Mr Wells gives you the hand signal I showed you. Usually he will do this when you are about 500 feet up. Oh yes, and for take-off and landing don't forget to bring the muzzle inside the cockpit it affects the airflow you see. Put it on safety first though, don't want you shooting your sodding foot off do we?'

As Tim Wells climbed into the rear cockpit he checked to see that his gunner understood both the weapon and the few hand signals he would make during the flight. Then, after making sure Bill's safety strap was locked to the cockpit he settled back for starting up. Remembering his earlier flight, Bill settled down into the cockpit holding the muzzle of the Lewis to his side and keeping a running check on what was happening. The engine sounded rough, but then it wasn't 988, was it? He smiled at his own smugness, he could even make a good estimate of its revolutions at each stage of the taxiing and take-off. Tim Wells wasted no time, and after the usual rumbles and bumps they were aloft. Counting the minutes Bill gingerly lifted his head above the cockpit and turned to see the grinning face of his Flight commander.

It was hot, perhaps humid more than anything else, and as the quirk climbed to 1000 feet a cooler air impressed itself against the warm and oily slipstream. A veiled sun made little of the shadows cast by the scudding cumulus below them, lightly shading the undulating grasslands of Picardy. Tim Wells gave little attention to the flight, his thoughts still dominated by the frightful encounter with his new C/O earlier that morning. It was obvious that Major Fawcett was aiming to make a name for himself with GHQ, and intended to use Trenchard's well-known maxim 'aeroplanes are offensive weapons' to the full. Fair enough if he knows what he's doing he thought, but he doubted it. Meanwhile, he'd better see if this lad Proctor was a potential air gunner.

Catching Bill's attention the pilot motioned to his left, indicating that he should put the Lewis on the port strut. Bill had practised moving the Lewis before, but never in the air. Fortunately they were at 1200 feet and the thermals none too active, nevertheless it was no easy task to replace the heavy gun on its alternative spigot. Pumping his right hand backwards and forwards Tim Wells signalled his gunner to cock the Lewis, then nodded his head for the gun to be fired. Remembering Tosh's advice Bill fired two short busts, exploiting the limits of his narrow arc of fire. The exercise was repeated to starboard then Tim indicated he would like a burst over the tail. Moving his body to the right hand edge of the cockpit Bill could only just sight over his pilot's head to fire a series of short busts in a clear, but difficult arc of fire. At his pilot's command Bill applied the safety and brought the Lewis inboard. In an instant the quirk was banked to port and dived towards the distant aerodrome. At 200 feet Tim Wells circled the airfield perimeter and pointed to the Morane wreck lying in an adjacent field. Then, much to Bill's surprise, he signalled for the gun to be put on the port forward strut. It took him all of a minute to relocate the gun, a task made no easier by the climbing turn to starboard. At 500 feet Tim signalled for the gun to be made ready then put the quirk into a shallow dive towards the Morane. It was a highly skilled approach and at 200 feet he pointed to the direction for gunfire, but it was a difficult shot and before Bill knew it the target was below the port lower wing. Turning to his pilot he received the signal for a second approach. This time he would take his first opportunity, it would never got any better he knew that now! Tim kept the same approach, he knew the difficulty for his gunner and thought his approach should offer a reasonable chance of him hitting the target. As the quirk descended Tim kept it to the right of the Morane and as he flattened out Bill emptied the magazine in a path that walked up to and over the wreckage.

'Well done Proctor, you have a good eye and the makings of an excellent gunner.' They were walking back to the 'A' Flight crew tent as Tim Wells discussed the next step towards Bill's training as a gunner. 'It's not a difficult job, as you have shown on this, your first attempt. But it's not everyone who can do it! I'm not sure if I could!' He smiled; an engaging and modest man, Tim Wells was a natural leader who was completely unaware of the devotion accorded to him by his men. 'So what happens next is that I make arrangements with Mr Porter, and you will go to 'C' Flight for a few days for gunnery training. This will mean some ground training on the Lewis, 'immediate action' and that sort of thing, the armourers will have you field stripping the Lewis until you can do it in your sleep. Then as much air gunnery as possible – like we did this morning in fact.'

Bill nodded his head, dizzy with pride. 'I was hoping that I might be able to fly in my machine sir, in 988!' Tim Wells stopped and faced him. This was quite an unusual ack-emma, he was a first-class fitter and now, according to Dad, a skilled rigger. Furthermore, he really wanted to get married to *his* aeroplane and it was this, rather than the extra pay, that prompted his interest in flying.

'F/Sgt Owens mentioned this to me Proctor, and although I haven't spoken to F/Sgt Duffy and his usual gunner, I feel sure this could be arranged. Anyway, let's see how you get on in 'C' Flight first, then we'll see what can be done.'

Captain Julian James had no real desire to join the RFC, but when Keith Fawcett suggested that the 17th Hussars were not likely to see active service in France, he took his friend's advice and joined him for RFC pilot training. The regiment had only recently returned from India, where he had spent eight glorious years as a cavalry officer of the British Raj. But on the outbreak of hostilities in Europe the regiment was recalled to England only to find that by 1915 trench warfare had set in and cavalry units had no part to play, even in reconnaissance. At 30 years of age and with no private means it had been difficult enough to maintain a servant and two horses in India, but in England it was impossible. Yet without active service in the current conflict there was no chance of promotion, and so transfer to the new Corps seemed reasonable. In December 1914 all cavalry units had been circulated with requests for officers to apply for RFC pilot training. The general opinion being that if you could ride a horse then piloting a plane was a simple matter.

Whereas Keith Fawcett had managed to scrape through Farmans and Avros, his own efforts were crowned with a fatal crash that killed his Sergeant instructor and injured his collar bone. After four weeks in hospital and expectation of a 'return to unit' order, his prospects were bleak until Keith Fawcett turned up.

'Who's to say it was your fault old boy? After all, it was an insult to put an officer of your rank and experience in the hands of an incompetent Sergeant! I've had a few words with a friend of mine at the War Office and he suggests you remain in the RFC specialising in administrative work and retaining your current rank. Furthermore, we are to join the new 3rd Wing being formed in France. I've been posted to St Omer in the first instance, a kind of roving commission sorting out squadron requirements and priorities and have requested you for my administrative assistant! We are to have a department of two NCOs and team of ten clerks – how's that?'

Julian James was more than pleased, it could not have worked out better. He would now be on 'active service' with prospects for promotion and very likely a permanent commission in the RFC. But best of all, his disability could always be 'manipulated' to keep himself behind the lines and in the company of people who matter. Keith Fawcett had even greater ambitions.

'Oh yes, I didn't mention it but since I gained my wings, and with five years in my current rank, I've been promoted to Major on taking up the new post in France. Only temporary at present of course, but it will be substantive as soon as I get my hands on a squadron.' James was not impressed.

'Good heavens Keith, you're all of what, 35 or 36? Surely you can't take on such a job. Flying is a young chap's game and, well I don't want to be rude old boy but …'

Keith Fawcett smiled. 'In a two-seater squadron, a reconnaissance unit, the C/O is hardly expected to fly. Oh yes, the odd flight-test here and there, supervision of training, transit flights. Believe me I know laddie, I've not been wasting my time at the War Office I assure you.'

When Keith Fawcett took over 4 Sqdn his majority was made substantive, and with his pull at Wing he had little difficulty in getting Julian James as his new adjutant. By Friday 3rd September Captain James was busy making out Squadron Orders (SOs). One of them included the internal posting of 4003 AM/1, W.C. Proctor 'A' Flight to 'C' Flight for Air Gunner training, w.e.f. 4th September 1915.

During the following week Bill's course was all that Tim Wells said it would be. There were four of them all told. The other three being young 2nd Lts, each sporting a new badge on their RFC tunics. When Bill asked what the new badge represented he was told by one of the armourers that the letter 'O' with a single wing attached was the new Observer badge, but was reserved for officers. Evidently they are trained in map reading and morse code, but haven't done any gunnery yet. Bill could think of a number of ack-emmas and NCOs that had been doing these jobs for months – but had never received this kind of recognition.

The course went well and Bill came out top.

'Good lad Bill, that'll show those bloody officers up.' Ralph Downes had never been keen on officers, and after a week running after Captain James his opinion of them had not improved.

Bill laughed, 'I couldn't fail to be top Ralph, just couldn't fail.'

Ted Hamilton shook his head, 'That's what I like about you Bill, your bloody modesty!'

'You chaps don't understand, I could hardly fail to come top when I was the only one on the course!'

Ralph Downes couldn't accept that. 'What do you mean? I typed the bloody orders for Christ's sake, I remember it well cos that shit James made me type it twice: 'My fuckin' English left much to be desired,' cheeky sod! There was you and three sprog officers, four of you! I should know!'

Bill shook his finger at the squadron clerk. 'But what you don't know Ralphie is that when I was with 'C' Flight we were split up. Major Fawcett came over on the second day after we had done all the ground training and split us up. The officers flew in one Avro and I flew in the other. So I did three times as much gunnery with Sgt Wright as the sprogs did with their Avro. No wonder I came out top! I bet the results are never put on SOs though.'

Ralph laughed. 'Bloody typical! But from what I see every day in the office I would say that we're going for a hard time with our new C/O, he's an even bigger shit than James and that's saying something. I wrote up orders for weekly kit inspections today! Never mind Bill, as soon as I get the 'C' Flight report, Ralphie fills in the pay form and you'll be rich within a week! Four bob a day extra – if you live long enough to collect it of course.'

'I hear you did very well at 'C' Flight Proctor. Mr Porter tells me your gunnery is first-class and your deflection shooting is the best he's ever seen.'

Bill smiled 'I had very good instructors sir.'

Tim Wells drew him aside. 'You are now an 'A' Flight air gunner and I've made arrangements for you to draw flying clothing from stores. You are still ack-emma for 988 of course, but in addition I think you will be pleased to learn that you will also crew in her as well. I'm sorry that F/Sgt Duffy cannot be your pilot, he and Armstrong have been posted to 'C' Flight. You may as well know that all three flights are now going to do CPs, photography and wireless, eventually. So we lose Duffy's crew to 'C' and you will fly with our new pilot. Come with me and I'll introduce you to each other.'

Corporal Len Coats wore an RFC tunic with brand new pilot's wings over his left breast. He was a little smaller than Bill, dark haired and trying to grow a moustache. Tim Wells introduced them to each other over a mug of tea and told Len Coats that his gunner was also the fitter/rigger for his machine.

'You're a very lucky chap Coats. Young Proctor here has a first class servicing record on 988 and has recently come top in our local gunners course; I'd be happy to have him myself in fact. You are doubly fortunate to have your own machine too, it usually takes a few months before new pilots have such consideration. Major Fawcett has changed things a bit recently, and from now on all crews will be expected to take on every job the squadron is capable of doing. I see you only have eleven hours on quirks Corporal, and only six of them solo. I mean to alter that without delay, starting right now! New SOs stipulate that all crews will carry their sidearms while flying, so remember that. It's now 9.45 ack-emma, so both of you get your flying kit from stores, then pick up your revolvers. I have a note from the Adj saying you are to be NCO i/c Proctor's tent. So you can show him where you live eh Proctor! Be back here for 11 ack-emma then we'll go over your flying detail for today.'

Len Coats was a quiet-spoken 21 year old from Birmingham and the two of them were soon on the best of terms.

'I have to be honest with you Bill, I've only got a measly total of 23 hours so I hope that doesn't give you the wind-up. Mr Wells tells me you have just started flying, so I suppose that makes us even – but I've got lots to learn yet I'm afraid.'

Bill turned to his new friend. 'Not to worry Len, we shall learn together, and by the time we've finished we'll be the best damned crew in the RFC!' Laughing, the two young aviators talked away as they went to the stores.

They arrived back at 'A' Flight ten minutes early, only to find the tent filled with crews preparing for flight. Tim Wells called Len Coats over to his area map.

'Sorry about this Corporal, I intended to break you into our area slowly. But the C/O has just ordered 'A' Flight to put up all six aircraft over our lines facing the Vitry to Henin-Lietard road. Evidently there are reported troop movements along this area of the front, and Wing want us to cover it with photography and CPs. It's a rush job so you and Proctor will be doing CPs with Mr Wilson as section leader. Normally I would never let you go over the lines like this, but our pilot reserve has been depleted by internal flight movements.'

Unknown to the rest of the flight, Tim Wells had been as close to insubordination as he had ever been, arguing against the stupidity of ordering a novice crew into the air like this. Worse still, he blamed himself for putting his crews in harm's way, simply because Fawcett wanted to get back at him! 'As this is your first mission I've arranged with Lt. Wilson that you tuck yourselves about 100 feet above and behind his starboard wing. You will act as cover for him and Mr Crouch, so off you go!' As Len and Bill ran to the lines Tim Wells called after them. 'Now remember you two, do nothing heroic! Just stay with Mr Wilson and watch what he does! Keep formation Corporal, that's your job, and Proctor... keep good watch!'

As they approached 988 they saw an unknown fitter and rigger awaiting them. Bill went to the new ack-emmas to introduce himself when a bright cockney voice caught him off guard.

'Bit of a panic this is mate, we only knew about this half an hour back when your chiefy sent us over, are you Proctor?'

Bill was a little peeved. 'Yes that's me, I'm 988's regular fitter!'

'Well me and Taff here, we ran her up ten minutes ago and she's fine'. Bill was about to retort when he caught sight of Major Fawcett out of the corner of his eye. What he had to say could wait, but he didn't appreciate other mechs playing with *his* machine. Lieutenant Paul Wilson was already giving instructions to Len Coats and pointing out their flight plan on his map.

'I'm bloody pissed off about this Corp; this is no way to lead a section over the lines. Christ you haven't even taken off from Bertangles yet! But as Mr Wells has pointed out, just stick your arse above and behind mine and keep weaving best you can!' Paul Wilson was livid, and although he knew his voice could not be heard over the clattering engines now running up, he knew his anger would not go unnoticed. 'Just stay close Coats, we shall be flying at about 400 feet over the Boche so you keep to 500 eh! Good luck, follow me out.'

However Len Coats must have felt, Bill could only admire his young pilot for the professional manner of his take-off and formation discipline. Following Lt Wilson's lead he kept the quirk in good position and used the throttle wisely. Their route to Vitry was via Arras where, just inside the Allied lines, the two sections of three parted company. Whereas the photo section had to climb to 5000 feet for their photography, Lt Wilson kept his section at 400 feet as they crossed the front three miles south of Vitry. At their low altitude there was an element of surprise over the German trenches and no problems with archie. But as they progressed north they experienced concentrated machine gun fire which increased in intensity as they approached Henin-Lietard. Turning through 180 degrees, Paul Wilson signalled Len to maintain his height while he and Lt Crouch dropped to 200 feet, flying down a small tree-lined road leading to Douai eight miles to their south-east. It was Bill's task to watch for enemy aircraft with Len keeping position at 500 feet. But from what he could see they were alone, with no idea where the photo quirks were at all. As the section approached Douai, Paul Wilson climbed back to 400 feet bringing his three quirks around the south of Vitry to approach the British trenches west of this part of 'no man's land'. Bill recognised the German trench positions they had passed over only fifteen minutes before, and could see the tracers arcing towards them. The observers in the other machines were replying in short bursts, and seeing no enemy machines in the sky he happily joined in from the rear starboard strut. It was his first action, and for what it was worth no more than an exercise in pulling the trigger, but at least he had fired their gun in anger and that was something!

Paul Wilson used hand signals to indicate their CP was now complete and that he alone would drop low over the British lines to deliver his message bag. By prior agreement Lt Crouch and Len Coats were to fly back direct to Bertangles. Bill watched as Lt Wilson dropped to about fifty feet, flying towards a bright patch of canvas a few hundred yards inside their line of forward trenches. He was also aware that Len had stopped weaving, itself a difficult task in a quirk, but they were still receiving sporadic m/g and rifle fire from the German lines and they had yet to turn to the west. Ah, there it was! Lt Crouch made his turn to the west, and to safety, and Bill felt 988 lurch to port. He breathed a sigh of relief, it was over, his first flight over enemy lines and under fire too! He would have much to tell Alice he mused, someday.

Whereas the outward flight had only taken 35 minutes their return journey was noticeably longer. Bill closely watched the terrain below as the quirk rose and fell in the midday thermals. At 500 feet they were subject to every pocket of rising air they encountered and Bill noticed that although Lt Crouch had ascended to about 1500 feet, Len continued as before. Perhaps there was less wind higher up Bill thought, these dratted westerlies were a menace to fight against. He laughed at himself, 'Even thinking like a birdman now!' Fascinated by the flight he took stock of the land below, and vowed to bring a map next time out. After forty minutes he noticed they were passing to the south of Bellevue and that Len was flying much lower as he followed Mr Crouch now far ahead and dropping to their own level. In another fifteen minutes he could see the spire of Amiens Cathedral and from this easily recognised landmark realised that Mr Crouch must now be circling Bertangles field.

Bill watched as Lt Crouch's BE2c banked over the edge of the aerodrome and settled onto the grass. He turned to face Len Coats, his pilot's face masked and drawn under goggles and scarf. A weak smile and a nod being all that greeted his thumb's-up sign. Remembering the drill, he housed the gun inboard and settled down in his cockpit, feeling the quirk bank to port as it dropped to the downwind edge of the aerodrome. He clung to the muzzle of the Lewis. Yet another bank, steeper this time, and then the aircraft dropped like a stone only to bounce heavily as it reached the grass. Bill crouched even lower, he'd heard stories of how some pilots never mastered this part of flying, or more precisely the part when the machine stopped flying! He waited for the second bounce, it seemed a lifetime. God, he hoped Len wasn't going to smash 988... !

The final 'landing' put 988 on her nose, throwing Bill forward and knocking him cold as his head contacted the metal rim of the cockpit. Len had done a magnificent job, switching off petrol and ignition at the final moment just before 988 collapsed on its nose, and only a few moments before he fainted through loss of blood. Ted Hamilton was first on the scene. Having grabbed a ride on the 'blood wagon' he leapt off and ran to the wreck, there must be no fire! He checked the rear cockpit first and seeing that the switches were off, called for the medics.

Bill awoke as he was carried towards the Crossley tender, and as he was helped up the steps he looked for Len Coats. The medics had put the wounded pilot on a stretcher and were trying to stem the blood flowing from a massive wound above his right knee. He was semi-conscious and weak from loss of blood, Bill felt wretched – he never even knew! The tender was racing across the grass, bumping along towards the small field hospital they shared with the French squadron. Ted had organised the medics well, a tot of rum for them both which they gulped down, spilling much of it over their chins as the tender raced ahead.

'Len deserves a bloody medal Bill. Certainly saved your bacon old son! He's going to be touch and go so these lads say!'

After a check at the hospital Bill was released with no more than plaster stuck to his forehead. In fact he wouldn't even have had that, were it not for Ted's insistence to the pretty French nurse that Bill needed something to convince his comrades that he'd actually been in the crash!

On their return to the lines Bill was met by Lts. Wilson and Crouch who, with Tim Wells, were anxious to get his story before the C/O arrived.

'Never even knew sir, I admit I thought Len, that is Corporal Coats wasn't flying too well, but I never knew he'd been wounded.'

Paul Wilson cut in. 'It was a splendid show, really splendid; he flew according to my signals all the way and in my opinion Tim he should be up for a gong!' Tim Wells nodded sympathetically. Coats had done a wonderful job just staying awake and he would certainly recommend a DCM. It was at this point that Major Fawcett arrived in a motor cycle and side-car.

'Dreadful business this Wells. I shall signal Wing I want no more half-trained Corporals trying to be pilots on my squadron. I hear that Coats is going to survive, but it's a 'Blighty one' for him and one less pilot for us! Who was his gunner?'

Bill stepped forward. 'That was me sir, AM/1 Proctor.' Fawcett looked him over, slapping his cane against his boot.

'I don't think a written report is appropriate in this case Wells. But what can you tell me about this Proctor?' Bill told him, his Yorkshire bluntness coming out without fear or subtlety.

'Corporal Coats got me back alive sir. He must have been in terrible pain and his leg...'

Major Fawcett fumed. 'When I want a medical opinion Proctor I shall ask the MO, meanwhile you will confine yourself to describing those events that led to a perfectly good aeroplane make a normal approach, then flatten out about twenty feet from the field and stall! I know, I saw it happen. I suppose you stood up to get a good view did you?'

With difficulty Bill managed to keep his voice down. 'Corporal Coats must have been hit as we were coming over the lines ... Sir! There was considerable m/g fire from the Jerry lines as we returned from Vitry, I remember us returning fire into their trenches. But I never knew he was wounded. No I did not stand up... Sir, I know better... Sir. Corporal Coats was just weak from wounds, he's a bloody hero... Sir!' With that he turned and walked out of the tent.

The small group of 4 squadron officers were not happy, but neither were they unhappy – as the large collection of empty bottles would suggest. It had started with the humid conditions and resulting storms late that afternoon. All flying had been cancelled and the quirks picketed down, so Tim Wells decided to visit Cpl Coates at the hospital. As he went to his tent to change into best uniform, he heard Paul Wilson's voice coming from an adjacent tent. He was drunk, but worse, he was loud, profane and disturbingly frank in his appreciation of 4 squadron's Commanding Officer! Foregoing a change of uniform Tim resolved to get his drunken subordinate off camp as quickly as possible.

After Proctor's midday affair with the C/O, Wilson had retired to his tent and was drinking heavily. Although that in itself was nothing new, his comments regarding 'that Fawcett bastard' were becoming louder every minute. Erratic at the best of times, Paul Wilson was only tolerated because of his flying ability and his humour, but this was something else. Tim Wells decided to get him off camp before the fool did something drastic. Needing assistance, he called on his fellow Flight Commanders who arranged for a Crossley to be driven to the mess, from where they bundled Paul Wilson into the back and went off with Hugh Porter driving.

The four pilots were now to be found drinking in a sorry-looking estaminet some three miles west of the aerodrome on the northern banks of the Somme. They only used the place when they wanted to escape the mess and were desperate to avoid everything military. Certainly it was the right place to avoid anyone from Bertangles. There were no girls, the food was terrible and the crusty old *Madame* that ran it was as uncivil as she was ugly. Nevertheless, for all its faults *L'Echange* had a reasonable *vin rouge* and its unpopular reputation at least assured their privacy as they mutinously discussed Major Keith Fawcett and his equally abhorrent friend.

'God! Did you see me? I just had to bury my face in the area map when Proctor turned his back on old 'foreskin'. I really thought the old bastard was going to throw a fit!' Paul Wilson slopped wine over his tunic as he recollected earlier events. 'I only wish I had the guts to do what that young lad did today – he was bloody lucky though!'

Tim Wells had to laugh. 'You may remember what our Major fore-skin said Paul?' Tim continued in a passable mimicry of Major Fawcett's piping voice. 'Obviously that man is suffering from concussion Wells and must be taken off duties! Under the circumstances I cannot have him disciplined for insolence, but see to it that he sees the MO right away. When he's returned to duties you must warn and remind him that his behaviour was quite unacceptable! Yet another example of lax discipline in your Flight Captain, put it right or I'll have you removed!' Tim's performance was excellent and richly rewarded by appreciative laughter from his near drunk friends.

'Yes, but the big joke is that Proctor's head wound was no more than a small bump! Dad Owens told me that one of our ack-emmas got a nurse to put a plaster on Proctor's head, so he could elicit sympathy from his Flight Commander! But I agree with you Paul, our boy deserves a bloody medal, he just didn't give a damn he was so worked up! Nevertheless, I shall have to warn him, or dear old foreskin will have his guts for garters!'

Bernie Saul turned to Hugh Porter. 'Has Fawcett ever flown any-thing since he's been here Hugh?'

'Two days back he took his adjutant pal up for a couple of circuits in an Avro. Managed that quite well, then yesterday he went up with one of the new Sterling sets. Got one of those new observers to fly with him, trailed the aerial and had him send a message to the wireless hut. Never went further than the vicinity of the aerodrome however. Not even far enough to check the range of the transmitter, despite the fact that his observer particularly wanted to do that. If you ask me our C/O is scared shitless to go beyond our circuit.'

Tim Wells took an interest in Hugh's remarks. 'Strange eh! You remember when Cecil Hunt took over the squadron? His first flight? He came to you and requested a copy of our area map so he could familiarise himself with our part of the front! I remember it well be-cause he asked me for the best observer/gunner we had on the squad-ron. He wanted a reliable man who could recognise every feature of our front, so I gave him Andy Mills. I would say that was normal for any new reconnaissance C/O, wouldn't you agree?'

Hugh Porter considered the matter, nodding his head in agreement. 'Matter of fact his observer johnny *did* ask me for a map, so I gave him one of our usual French maps with an up-to-date overlay of the front. He told me, after the flight, that Fawcett never even looked at it! Seemed a bit peeved too, particularly since he was keen to establish transmission quality at extreme range. I forget the chap's name, but he made a rather interesting remark. Said he hoped he would be allocated a pilot that understood maps, but was cautious enough to say it was only *rumoured* that some pilots couldn't read them! An interesting observation, and one that deserves further thought. In fact I think these trained observers are going to be very useful Tim.'

Paul Wilson turned a bleary eye on 'C' Flight's commander. 'I take it dear C, you are referring to one of those new chaps with a 'flying arsehole' badge displayed on his jacket? Pray tell me (hic) what bloody use they are, I mean what are they supposed to do that our ack-emmas can't do?'

Hugh Porter put a friendly arm around Paul's shoulder. 'To begin with they can send morse, which is more than you can do you old sot! And can even receive it if we ever get round to having receivers in the air. But they also specialise in map reading, and the use of the 'clock-code' for archie spotting.'

Bernie Saul cut into the conversation. 'Steady on there Hugh, poor old Wilson here – he doesn't understand about maps. Last time I showed him one he used it for a napkin.'

Tim Wells ordered another two bottles. 'By the way Bernie, did your contacts at Wing give you any gossip about foreskin and co?'

Bernie Saul's eyes glowed large. 'Oh yes, came over to tell you about that, but got side-tracked when you were having trouble with this silly bugger Wilson. For starters, Fawcett has no war experience in airplanes! After getting his Wings he went to the War Office in London, collecting a staff promotion to Major en route. Spent some time in the Directorate of Military Aeronautics no less which, no doubt, is why he thinks he knows all about air reconnaissance! His MC was awarded in India, no citation in records so my clerical friend informs me! Probably stuck his lance up some poor bloody Pathan's arse on the north west frontier. More to the point though, his father is the late Lt General Sir Arnold Fawcett, so we can rightly assume that old foreskin has friends in high places. His friend, our illustrious adjutant, was with him in India. Failed his pilot's course evidently, and that's all we know about him.'

Tim Wells broke the silence. 'Fawcett is breaking up a damned good unit. Weekly kit inspections are unheard-of on front line squadrons, and I for one can see the effect it's having on the moral of our ack-emmas. Dad Owens was complaining to me today, evidently the first kit inspection was the father for two others because our Captain James wasn't satisfied! I never got to hear about it because Dad thought

I already knew and he didn't want to interfere! But it kept two quirks grounded for nearly seven hours!

When I saw James he said it was Fawcett's order that any time lost would be made up by that ack-emma having to work longer hours. Just imagine what that could mean if the Boche gave us any problems and we all had to move in a hurry!'

'Talking about map reading chaps, our beloved C/O passed an order to me only this morning.' Hugh Porter removed a crumpled message from his tunic. 'This comes direct from GHQ RFC and Fawcett told me to put it into effect immediately. As Flight Commander i/c training, it is my responsibility to draw up a local training programme that ensures that all personnel in receipt of flying pay, officers, NCOs and men, are to receive further instruction in map reading! This is to be done locally and such personnel are to be tested in navigation over a tringular, sorry, trangular – fuck-it, three-cornered course, with additional instruction on the use of the clock code!'

'Well that's interesting Hugh old boy! Because that *must* include foreskin as well!' Bernie Saul smacked his fist into his hand. 'Even if he doesn't fly much, he will have to be under your instruction, so fail the bugger!' They all banged on the table, spilling drinks, and yelling 'fail the foreskin!'

Hugh Porter was silent for a full minute before he spoke. 'I have plans for him don't worry, you'll see!'

Bill Proctor was thoroughly enjoying his three days in hospital. His 'injury' was a joke among the French nurses and even the Sqdn MO, who had heard the full story, made light of his condition. Bill had visited Len Coates, who was now starting to make a recovery of sorts, and read to him for short periods from letters he had received from home and from Alice. Only yesterday Captain Wells and Captain Porter, came to visit them both. His Flight Commander had joshed him about his head wound, but became serious concerning his 'insolence' to his Commanding Officer.

'I know you were not quite yourself Proctor, but let's face it – were it not for that bit of plaster on your head you could have been up on a serious charge!' Worse news was that the C/O didn't approve Captain Wells' recommendation for a medal for Len Coats.

'That stinks sir! I mean to say...'

'There you go again Proctor,' Captain Porter cut in, 'Just keep your big mouth shut... please!' Bill smiled as he recalled the grins on the faces of the two Flight Commanders.

During his visit to the hospital, Hugh Porter had given Bill a copy of his instructions and time-table relating to the new classes 'C' Flight were starting tomorrow. It appeared that GHQ wanted all its two-seater squadron aircrew to improve their map reading ability. The instruction and in-flight practical tests had to be completed within the next ten days and was to be considered as urgent. Each flight would send a number of its crews for 'C' Flight Instruction based on a daily and evening roster, starting tomorrow, 5th September. Bill was pleased, it was something he wanted to do anyway and since he was to be discharged fit for all duties in the morning, he wouldn't miss any classes. Studying the instructions he learned that the lessons would be (i) map reading from the air (ii) basic air navigation and (iii) the use of the 'clock code' for battery ranging.

Bill thought of his future a while. It looked like he was going to be spending most of his time flying if he wasn't careful, yet that was what he wanted – or was it? He enjoyed the comradeship, the greater sense of knowing his aircraft, but was this what he really wanted? Once again he felt life was running away with him, as though he was no longer in control. He had to admit he liked flying, with all its thrills and sense of adventure, and this is what surprised him most, it was so unexpected. Just as he relished the open admiration of his fellow ack-emmas, many of whom thought him crazy to volunteer for such a dangerous job. Strange, they never accorded him that same respect for his ability as a fitter *and* a rigger? Once again he felt events were taking over his life, a life he no longer controlled, but stranger still, he felt no fear of its uncertainty. Unknown to him, Bill Proctor was becoming a fatalist. 'Ah well it's four extra bob a day.' he thought.

Dad Owens was first to welcome Bill as he entered 'A' Flight's Daily Servicing Section (DSS).

'Good to see you Proctor. How's Cpl Coates?'

Bill gave him the latest news regarding his pilot. 'He's fine Dad, as fine as he's going to be with only half a leg. It's a 'Blighty one' for sure, but I still think he should have got a DCM at least!'

Dad nodded in sympathy, 'Not for us to say lad, but I agree with you for what it's worth. Anyway, you're well enough so that's a blessing. I'm sorry to say that 988 has to go back to the park at St. Omer, the engine was shock-loaded on impact and she needs a complete new engine runners and undercart.' It wasn't so much the damage report that came as a shock to Bill, but the fact that this was the first time in three days he'd ever given a thought about 988.

'So go help pack her away on the 3 tonners then report to 'C' Flight for 10 ack-emma. Since you no longer have an airplane you might as well spend all your time map reading.' Dad Owens shook his head. 'Looks like I've lost a good fitter Bill, I think you are going to be an observer from now on! Mr Wells tells me that he's arranged for you to do one week of concentrated training with Mr Porter, then you are to return here for full flying duties.'

Chapter Eleven

There were five ack-emmas receiving instruction on Bill's observer course, all of them with considerably more air experience than his own, and two even had experience in artillery ranging. In addition there was a Cpl gunner from 'B' Flight and six NCO pilots who seemed to come and go according to flying schedules. A similar course for officers was also conducted in much the same way they supposed. They would never know for sure however, since they never came together at any time, excepting now, when they came into the same tent for tea and biscuits. It was a large ridge tent, with a centre table on which two large tea urns rested along with tins of biscuits. At one end of the tent a small queue of officers lined up for tea, to be faced by a similar line of NCOs and men coming through the opposite tent flap. Their only common interest seemed to be the animated conversations within each group of airmen.

Bill's first map reading exercise was later that afternoon. He was given a 1:25,000 map of Picardy and told to plot his pilot's course on a tracing paper overlay. He never even met his pilot before the flight but after being helped into the rear seat of the Avro, he was instructed to plot the entire course using a crayon. Although it was a dual control Avro, the rear stick had been removed to a storage position, giving more room for the trainee observer in what was already a spacious cockpit. A Lewis gun, complete with one of the new 97-round magazines, was fitted to the upper wing and could be fired by the pilot. After reaching 4000 feet the Avro turned for Amiens and then went south-east. Bill found it relatively easy to follow the map, checking his position against the open cultivated fields south of the Somme, the low westerly sun providing sculptured relief of the low rolling hills. Using the compass as he went, Bill followed their course with ease. Crossing the river Luce he noticed their course was now due south and as they crossed the river Avre he knew the town ahead was Montdidier. The Avro turned left to a course of 40 degrees to cross the Avre again, this time over Roye.

147

Just as the young navigator's confidence was at maximum the aircraft spiralled down to 1500 feet. Picking up the position of the sun Bill tried to make sense out of the still-spinning compass as he looked in vain for a landmark. Bill recalled his instructor's words 'Find a landmark or two on the *ground first* then locate those landmarks on the map. Don't try it the other way round! Maps get out of date, and worse, farmers change the nature of their field boundaries all the time! This year it's fallow, next year it's wheat, probably spreading into the next field! What you see on the map is a cadastral boundary, a legal boundary, and bears little relationship to what you may see from the air. Look for the most permanent of features, large wooded areas, joining roads, river contours and villages. Very useful of course, except that over the front many of these features are blasted to hell!'

By the time the compass had stopped spinning he was lost. There were villages of course, but their identity was unknown. His compass indicated 300 degrees, and he checked his watch: 4.20 pip-emma. They crossed a river, the Luce? Fifteen minutes later another river, with marshes. Bill logged the time, 4.37, and noting the compass bearing hadn't changed plotted a line along that direction, mentioning the river as the Somme. Ten minutes later they turned due west and as they turned Bill caught sight of Amiens Cathedral. Resuming his plot he realised the exercise had not been a complete success, it was not a complete failure either, but he would certainly have to do better.

After landing Bill was introduced to his pilot, Sergeant Tom Bolton. 'Sorry about that Proctor, nasty trick to play on your first exercise. But Mr Porter suggested I should not make things too easy in case you had flown over here before!' Bill assured him it was his first trip over the area, and that he had become totally lost at 1500 feet. 'Right then, let's get rid of this flying clobber and have a cup of tea. Mr Porter will be attending our briefing.' As Bill and Tom Bolton entered the briefing tent they found Hugh Porter and Tim Wells awaiting them. Over cups of tea and biscuits Bill was made to feel at ease as he gave his plot to Sgt Bolton. Within a minute Tom Bolton handed the plot to the two Flight Commanders. 'Bloody good Mr Porter, damned good, considering. Young Proctor plotted our exact course up to Roye, then I cocked it up for him with a descending spiral. But at least he used the compass and noted the time, good thinking lad!' They discussed his errors and emphasised that lack of concentration was the problem.

'When something happens in the air, like a Fokker coming at you, or escaping some Hun's evil intentions by hiding in a cloud, you *will* get lost!' said Tim Wells . 'We all do, very frequently! The trick is to remember every bit of ground you fly over – and that takes practice. Never daydream, use every minute to establish your position. But I must agree with Sgt Bolton, you have done quite well Proctor, well done!'

Hugh Porter took over. 'I have to start allocating training crews as far as I can, difficult when most of them are flying on operations. But it will help if I can organise your exercises at least. So until further notice Proctor you will fly with Sgt Bolton. First thing tomorrow sergeant, at 7 ack-emma, I want you to fly east towards Albert, then north inside our lines to return via Aire. If possible fly at 3000 feet or so. Oh yes, and remove Proctor's compass, I want him to really map read this time! Go over your route together making use of railways, rivers and canals. Make a landing at either Bruay or St. Pol, and check Proctor's log at that point.' Tom Bolton was busy with his note pad, as Hugh Porter traced a rough outline on the map. 'Refuel if necessary then fly west for about twenty miles so that you return to Bertangles by crossing the Abbeville - Arras railway at a point close to Doullens.'

'Proctor! I want you to log every inch of the way, so make sure your watch agrees with Sgt Bolton's. This is quite a difficult task, because it's open country for most of the route. Remember! Roads have troops, trucks and horses, canals and railways don't! It can be very confusing, so take care when you plot a landmark – all villages look alike here. So if you are not totally confident about your position don't assume anything; try to pick up your course again. Nothing worse than making yourself believe you know where you are! Be back for the 1.30 pip-emma class and watch out for Fokkers; they are quite bold these days and not at all reluctant to pop over our lines if they see an easy Avro.'

As Bill and Tom Bolton left the tent, Hugh Porter resumed his conversation with the 'A' Flight Commander. 'Guess who I have for tomorrow's observer class Tim? None other than Captain Julian James! Evidently he is to become a qualified observer by special command of old foreskin himself. The C/O came in earlier to let me know that since James is an ex-pilot trainee he should have no difficulty in becoming an observer, and I am to get him through all the necessary ground instruction by the end of the week!'

Tim Wells made a face. 'Exactly what does he have to do to become a *qualified* observer, I don't think I've ever really known? It seems that each squadron just puts a chap in the air and they either sink or swim.'

Hugh Porter picked up his tunic, withdrew a sheet of paper and handed it to his friend. 'I don't think I ever showed you this did I? No reason to do so really, but it makes quite interesting reading in the light of what I've just told you!'

C.R.F.C. 1938 (G).

To/3 Wings.

Although it is undesirable to lay down any hard and fast rules, as regards the qualifications of observers, it is considered that the same general standard of proficiency should be maintained throughout the RFC.

Normally an officer should not be recommended for grading as a qualified observer unless:

(a) He knows the Lewis gun thoroughly.

(b) Can use the RFC camera successfully.

(c) Can send and receive by wireless at a rate of 6 words a minute with 98% accuracy.

(d) Knows the method of co-operation between aeroplanes and artillery thoroughly.

(e) Has carried out two reconnaissances or has ranged batteries successfully on two occasions.

In the Field.   *R. Brooke-Popham,*
1st August, 1915.   Lieut-Col. General Staff, RFC.

Tim Wells handed the signal back to his friend. 'No I cannot ever recall seeing that, but … ?'

Hugh Porter stopped him there. 'Fawcett says I'm to ensure that James completes items (a) through (d) as soon as possible, evidently he knows his Morse from his failed pilot's course. But this is the best part Tim, Major Foreskin will personally take Captain James on two reconnaissance flights to complete his qualifications.'

Tim Wells cursed, 'Jesus Christ! That's all we need, the two of them winning the war on this side of the lines!'

'You have it in one old son, that's exactly what they want. Then it's a couple of gongs each and up to Wing, hail the conquering heroes what!'

Tim Wells thought a moment. 'But why should we worry? At least we shall get rid of them eventually.'

Hugh Porter smiled, 'I have plans my friend, and the word *eventually* isn't included!'

As instructed, Tom Bolton flew due east from Bertangles to the small RFC aerodrome of Moislains some ten miles west of the British front line. Then, turning north he followed the British 3rd line of trenches to Arras, where he knew Proctor would be able to confirm his position. From Arras he turned slightly east bringing the Avro between the town of Vimy on his left and the front line to his right. From here it was simply a question of keeping the Arras–Bethune railway in sight as he flew north, constantly scanning the eastern sky for enemy machines. Tom Bolton knew the line well, but hated these early morning flights where the slim profile of a Fokker could hardly be seen against a sunlit eastern sky. It was now 7.35 ack-emma and a clear bright morning with at least 25 miles of visibility to the west. But to the threatening east, visibility was much less, being no more than 3 miles in those areas veiled with gunfire smoke.

Looking to the east Bill recorded the town of Vitry on the German side of the line and took care to log the exact time as it passed the starboard wing tip. Then to the left there was Vimy, and beneath them - the British first trenches. He'd been instructed to pay special attention to this area of the front, as this was to be his future workplace and had to be known with confidence. He could see why too, noting the white archie bursting high over the German trenches: he looked for the enemy machines that had attracted the British guns and was careful to scan every sector of the eastern sky. Encouraged by a flurry of black and sulphurous archie now searching for their range, Tom Bolton edged further inside the British lines as they continued north-west. Recognising the river Lys and the German-held town of Estaires some five miles or so to the right, Bill marked his position on the overlay and noted the time at that point. The Avro now followed the Lys until they circled Aire, then went south to pass Bethune and drop to 1000 feet, as Tom made to land at Bruay.

As the Avro was being refuelled the two aviators checked notes. 'Spot on young Proctor! Bloody good map reading that! But did you recognise anything else?'

Bill thought a while, 'Well we got fired at when we approached the Lys, Sergeant. And our own archie was firing at something, but I didn't see any Jerry machines!'

Tom Bolton shook his head very slowly. 'I didn't expect you to see anything lad, but there *was* a Jerry two-seater ahead of us, about 5000 feet, at 2 o'clock. Well, I think it was a Jerry cos it attracted a lot of our archie that's true. But that doesn't mean it was a Hun! Half the bloody time our gunners just fire at anything bigger than a crow. But the main thing is … you didn't report any activity did you! I mean, that's what you are here for isn't it?'

151

Tom Bolton was pleased with his young observer and knew he was going to do well with the rest of the flight to Bertangles. But perhaps it had been too easy for a trainee of Proctor's calibre? In which case he was sure he could justify a little extra exercise en route home. Sergeant Tom Bolton had the perfect flight plan in mind and could even add another out-landing for good measure. While flying with 5 Sqdn, Tom Bolton got to know the Pas-de-Calais region very well. And as a good-looking 25 year old he had made full use of his time when based at St. Pol. He liked his drink (too much it was said) and the attention of girls, but he was particular. Not for him the delights of a dubious red lamp brothel in Bethune, 'Tom Bolton *never* pays for a bit' was his constant boast! But in reality it wasn't the money that kept him from the brothels so much as the danger. He feared catching a dose more than anything, even if they did say a pilot only lasted about two months in France!

After a forced landing near Freyent earlier that year, his boast was finally made good. He had been test-flying an Avro at the time, and returning to St. Pol, when the engine cut without warning. Finding an open field just three miles south-west of Freyent he made an excellent 'dead-stick' landing close to a medium-sized farm. But his luck didn't stop there. After the brave *aviateur anglais* had been given a drink by the farmer, he was taken by horse and cart to Freyent, where the local military contacted his squadron at St. Pol, then returned him to his aircraft to await the squadron servicing unit. It was a full two hours before they arrived, and a further hour before the engine was repaired, during which time Tom had drunk a fair quantity of his host's *vin rouge* in company with the farmer and his pretty daughter.

Jean Louis Chenez had an excellent well-stocked cellar, but like all wine drinkers preferred drinking with friends. Unfortunately the war had taken many of these away, so when a French-speaking British aviator dropped in, he couldn't resist the opportunity to celebrate with his best selection. When it was finally time to go, and with a cockpit full of bottles, Tom managed to clip a low hedge as he waved a drunken *au revoir* to his hosts. Intoxicated he flew an erratic course back to St. Pol, happy with the memory of two beautiful green eyes and an open invitation to return whenever he wanted.

Jean Louis was a widower who lived on a successful farm with his twenty year old daughter. His only son had been killed fighting at the Marne and with his death Jean Louis had looked to his daughter Simone, to marry and bear the grandchildren he yearned for. A convivial and generous man, he had welcomed Tom with humour, and finding his guest to have reasonable fluency in French, as well as a capacity for drinking, he took an immediate liking to the young aviator. Since then Tom had visited them four times before he was posted to 4 Sqdn, making full use of a friend's motor cycle to journey the ten short miles that separated him from the farm. By this time Jean Louis already considered him as a possible son-in-law and even encouraged Simone in this respect. By the time he had left St. Pol for 4 Sqdn, Tom and Simone were lovers. Unsure if Jean Louis knew or not, he decided to leave matters as they were, safe in the knowledge that he would always be welcome. But since he had been at Bertangles he had only seen her twice. Once when the weather allowed him freedom to hitch-hike to Freyent, now almost twenty miles distant, and once ten days ago when his Avro had an 'engine failure' in that vicinity. Today would be another opportunity! He liked this young lad Proctor and decided that he could trust him with his secret. Who knows, if things turned out right he might even get him as his own observer!

'Now then lad, when flying it will be Tom and Bill right!' Bill grinned, he liked the happy-go-lucky pilot and confirmed his approval with a nod. 'Would you like to try your hand at flying her on the next leg of our tour? All we have to do is screw-in the rear stick and you can have a go if you like?'

Bill didn't hesitate, 'I think you'll have to show me how though Tom! I mean it's not like riding a bike is it?' Tom laughed as he screwed the dual-control stick into its rear cockpit socket.

'It's not all that much different come to think of it, the main difficulty is handling the power, particularly with a rotary engine. But hey! I'm teaching my grandmother to suck eggs here, you know all about them.'

Bill was quick to disabuse him on that score. 'I may know a little about the engine, but sod-all about controlling the aircraft with it, and that's quite a different matter I've been told!'

Tom smiled his appreciation. 'If you know *that* then you're streets ahead of many pilots who have never understood it! The first lesson you need to know is that to climb you apply extra power and to descend you reduce the power. To turn, keep the nose up slightly, improve the power and bank no more than twenty degrees in the direction of your rudder turn. With the Avro take care never to make a flat turn, always bank with the turn or else you'll spin for sure.'

With Bill seated in the rear cockpit Tom showed him the finer points of the controls.

'As you know, this bird has a 110 hp Le Rhone so you have to take

153

care with the fine adjustment. I'll take-off, but I want you to watch what I do. To start with I shall ease-off the fine adjustment as soon as we leave the ground, and fly straight and level for a bit to gain airspeed before I climb. I think you know that as we go higher she'll not need so much fuel?' Bill made notes as Tom explained the Avro's controls, taking care to question points he didn't understand and confirm those he did. He didn't feel too nervous he thought, but couldn't help wondering how on earth he could map read as well as concentrate on flying. 'Now, make sure you can touch the rudder pedals, but be light on them cos I want you to feel how I use them! You'll find I have a shade of right rudder on when we take-off, that's to counteract the rotary's twist to the left. In fact when you're on full throttle you can feel the engine pulling to the left all the time. So when you turn never use much rudder at any time, particularly if you make a left-hand turn. Just keep a light touch on the stick and follow me through from take-off to landing. When I waggle the wings you have her, another waggle and I'll take her back. As you know, we were briefed to fly west from here, then south past Doullens and home. We shall do that of course, but since we're doing some unofficial flying practice as well, I've decided to fly to a little field I know near Freyent where we can do a few bumps. Don't concern yourself about map reading until we leave Freyent.'

They left Bruay at 8.50 ack-emma and flew south west to Freyent with the main Bethune-Amiens road on their left. Bill took careful note of the flying, lightly holding the stick as it moved in sympathy with the one held by Tom in the front cockpit. Then, after a few minutes and at about 1000 feet, Tom moved the stick from side to side, waggling the wings to indicate that Bill was now in charge. The air was quite still, even at such a low altitude, and with no further inputs Bill found the Avro easy to fly. He experimented with turns, first right, then left, correcting his altitude on the second attempt and bringing the Avro back up to 1000 feet. Tom indicated they should climb, and with increased throttle he made a good ascent to 2000 feet where he flattened out and checked his position. After fifteen minutes of this, Tom indicated a descent, flattening out at 500 feet. Then with a waggle from the front cockpit Tom took over. He circled the farm twice, and finding the wind made a careful approach to the field, now kept clean and bare in anticipation of his visits.

As he taxied to the edge of the field Tom could see Simone, waving and running towards the Avro. He cut the engine and removing his helmet swung himself out of the cockpit before Bill had loosened his straps. Simone Chenez was deeply in love, and it showed. Flinging her

154

arms about him she covered Tom's oil-stained face with kisses, oblivious of Bill who could only look with wonder. Laughing and crying they pulled and tugged at each other, Tom's face now smeared with the mingled tears and kisses of the dark-haired beauty now pouting and talking without restraint. At last, breathless and laughing, Tom made the introductions as Bill dismounted from the cockpit.

'Bill! I want you to meet Simone; she is the love of my life but speaks hardly any English.' Tom gave Bill a short explanation of his story as the three of them walked up to the farmhouse then, turning to Simone, resumed his conversation in his halting French.

Simone had received her second letter from Tom only three days ago, and although it was difficult to read she was sure he hadn't mentioned a possible visit. She knew Tom could never say when he might come, which is why every passing machine could be him – and wishing had made it come true! They had agreed she should never write to him. A local letter could easily be spotted and opened by the censor, an open invitation to suspect his 'engine failures' should they ever be reported!

'We have but two hours my love, and I must pay my respects to your father, but perhaps we could...'

She put her fingers to his lips. 'First we see papa, we talk and have some wine, then your friend can keep him company while we have some moments together.'

Although Jean Louis had little English, he found it easy to talk to Bill and answer his pertinent questions concerning the farm. It was obvious that Tom's friend knew about farming and although Simone and Tom had been gone for over half an hour he hardly missed them as he and Bill made short work of another bottle of his best wine. Finally they had to go. Loaded with eggs, wine and brandy, they said farewell to Jean Louis as Simone escorted them to the plane.

'Bill! We shall leave these goodies with Simone while you and I do a practice landing how's that? Then after a couple of goes we'll remove the rear stick, load up our loot and get back to the squadron.' Giving Simone a final hug Tom climbed into the cockpit as Bill went to the propeller. 'Oh Bill, just follow me through on take-off and take close attention to my landing approach. You will do the second take-off, don't worry about it – it's dead easy! I will follow you through for the second landing. If you make a mistake don't worry, I'll waggle the stick and take over. One further thing,' At this point Tom smiled and winked. 'Don't forget to plot our journey all the way back from Bruay, via Hesdin to Bertangles. We never came near Freyent remember?'

Carefully positioning the Avro at the edge of the field Tom turned into wind with Bill straining on the port wing. When satisfied he signalled Bill to come aboard, making sure his trainee pilot was comfortable before opening the throttle. With the wind at about 15 mph the Avro took to the air with ease and climbed to 700 feet. Circling, Tom allowed Bill to take stock of their location then, with reduced power, made a slow turn downwind to position the Avro where he could just see his take-off point behind the starboard wing-tip – his touchdown point! Banking to the right, Tom turned 90 degrees onto the base leg and drew Bill's attention to the touch-down point some distance beyond their right wing-tip. Another drop of the right wing and he turned another 90 degrees onto his final approach, dropping, dropping until at 100 feet Bill could see the edge of the field rapidly approaching through the shimmering propeller disc.

Stealing a quick look at the air speed indicator (ASI) Bill noted they were approaching at 55 mph, then the engine was cut. Bill knew he had to be aware of the moment, but it was filled with events. Simultaneous with the drop in engine noise was the sight of a slowly rotating propeller. The grass was visible now, only a few feet below as the Avro drifted slightly to the right. A slight pressure under his left foot put the machine back on course, then the stick come back into his stomach and they were down. Bump, rumble, bump, the Avro slowed over the rough grass and came to a stop.

With the engine just ticking over, Tom issued further instructions to Bill who promptly got out and put his weight behind the port wing to assist turning the machine back to their take-off point. Within minutes they were lined up once more and ready for Bill's first take-off.

'There are some things I need to tell you before we go Bill. Nothing drastic, but important enough to require further explanation.' Bill gave the signal to cut the engine.

'I think you should switch off Tom. Not a good thing to keep a rotary running on the ground too long – as you know!'

Tom grinned and switched off. 'I bow to your superior wisdom old lad, you're quite right!'

Simone approached to listen, not that she could understand, but just to hear his voice. 'Good thing to start at the beginning anyway Bill. So, after you get us started, climb aboard then I'll let you do the rest. But to begin with, keep the stick well back into your tum and 'buzz' the engine on the thumb-switch until the oil begins to pulsate in the pulsator glass. Then increase the petrol by setting the fine adjustment to about one and a half inches. You should be able to read about

156

1,100 rpm on this bus. Taxi out a little to make sure you are into wind and before opening out the engine, pump pressure up to three and a half pounds. Keep the stick well back – and take off! As you know, the Avro will swing strongly left when the engine is opened up, so get the tail up immediately and counter the swing with right rudder.' Tom waited to let Bill catch up with his scribbled notes. 'Once you get going, lift the tail until the engine cowling is about level then, as the speed increases, pull back gently on the stick and climb straight at 55 mph to 500 feet. Level off then circuit twice before landing.'

Simone could see this was serious business and kept quiet.

'Now the Avro's rudder is very sensitive Bill, so take it easy. Turning procedure is very important! If you feel a draught on the inside of your turn then you have too much bank on for the amount of rudder – correct by lessening the bank and *slightly* increase the rudder. But if the breeze is felt on the outside then you have too much rudder, so you gently decrease the rudder pressure and increase the bank – got it? The next thing is landing. First off you should decrease revs until she's just ticking over; ah, I can see you remembered that! But remember, all the while you have been flying with an active engine you have needed right rudder pressure to counteract prop torque, yes? So don't forget to put the rudder neutral as you decrease revs. If you don't it can cause a spin, can that! Glide down at about 55 mph dead into the wind! Look for the flow of long grass, small trees and best of all, smoke, if there is any. The wind can change anytime, so don't take its direction for granted. When about 50 to 100 feet off the ground put the petrol lever to about one inch and hold the thumb-switch down, but don't buzz the engine. Flatten out gently, then hold the old girl about one foot off the ground by gently pulling back on the stick until all speed has been lost. From there she'll just settle down neatly. You taxi in by buzzing the engine, but if the wind is a bit too strong don't attempt to taxi, just bring her into wind and stop.'

They went over the procedures again and again until Bill was satisfied he understood everything. Then, after Simone had retired to the safety of the hedge, he took station at the propeller and started up.

Bill breathed deeply. He wasn't sure he wanted to do this, but knew he couldn't back out now. Collecting his thoughts he recalled Tom's instructions and when the stick waggled under his hand, took another deep breath and opened the throttle wide. As the tail came up he was ready for the usual swing to the left and put pressure on the right rudder pedal, only to find the Avro's left wing lifting and contrary to what he'd been told the machine was drifting to the right! Instinctively he reduced right rudder pressure and shifted the stick to his left to lower that wing. Before he knew it the Avro was at 100 feet and climbing steadily. As he reduced revs to maintain a climb of 55 mph, Bill remembered Tom commenting about possible gusts coming from the left – something to do with the high trees in that quarter.

Levelling off at 500 feet Bill reduced engine revs until he was at 60 mph. Circling the field he took special care not to lose altitude on the turns, all the while marvelling at the thought of anyone putting down on the tiny field below. Tom turned towards him, nodding his head downwards. It was now or never.

Bill made another turn and headed down-wind, keeping the edge of the field just beyond his wing-tip. Following the route taken by Tom only minutes before, he turned on base leg, but too high! He throttled back and looked for the touch-down point beyond and behind the starboard wing. There! But further away than last time. He turned again, lining up on the field ahead. A quick look at the altimeter – 170 feet. 'Too low? Better carry on ... Christ, what's the ASI? 65 mph, too fast! Throttle back, not too much, mustn't stall. Too far to the right – shit! Bank left, don't use rudder, God I'm over the field, there's Simone!' As he put the nose down to compensate he felt the stick waggle strongly under his hand at the same time as the throttle was opened up. Tom had taken over!

They climbed again, to level off at 500 feet. Tom positioned the Avro on base leg as Bill anticipated every move of his friend's landing. It was therefore a complete surprise when he felt the signal for him to take over. Quickly, he scanned the instruments, 400 feet plus, 60 mph ... good. He turned right, a steeper bank this time, and put the nose down as he reduced engine revs. A touch of left rudder, straighten-up ... not too much; 210 feet, and he could see Simone over the reduced shimmer of the prop. He must be bold, now! Bill cut back the throttle and saw the altimeter unwind swiftly, less than 100 feet, the ground coming up – frightening! He saw the boundary hedge from the corner of his eye, he still had her. Ease back on the stick; mustn't stall, what's the air speed? He dare not take his eyes from the ground ahead. He felt Tom's hand on the stick, a slight pumping back and forth until the machine settled. A large bump then the Avro ballooned into the air, the stick went forward, then back; another bounce, smaller this time and they were down!

He had done it! Certainly Tom had helped a bit in the end - but he knew what he had done. As the machine slowed to a stop Bill leapt out and swung the Avro around. Tom grinned from the cockpit and gunned

158

the machine forward as Bill ran alongside. As they reached Simone, they turned again, facing their machine into the prevailing wind. Tom cut the engine and climbed out of the cockpit only to fall into the arms of a rapturous Simone. Bill understood nothing of their conversation, but it was obvious that Tom was talking about him. Simone turned, and planted a sisterly kiss on his cheek, *'Bon chance Bill!'*

'I told her you were going to be a red hot pilot one of these days Bill. That was a really good landing you made, I would say you're a natural flyer and as soon as we have you as an observer we shall have to put you in for pilot training, what do you say?'

Bill's face mirrored his thoughts. Glowing with a sense of achievement he was quick to agree without further thought. 'Do you really think I could, be a pilot I mean? After all, you know that was a very bouncy landing and if you hadn't taken over...'

Tom made a dismissive gesture. 'Good grief Bill, you haven't even had training yet! The only problem you had was coming in a little too fast, which is a better mistake than coming in too slow, particularly with an Avro. Anyway, even if I hadn't given you a bit of help at the last moment, you would still have made a decent landing. Just a few more bumps that's all! Christ Bill! I know chaps with over a hundred hours who land like that all the time! But the main thing was how you anticipated that gust on takeoff, and I swear I never even touched the controls!'

It was 12.20 pip-emma when they finally landed at Bertangles and reported to Hugh Porter.

'Ah there you are sergeant! I was beginning to wonder when we would see you two again. How did it all go?'

Tom showed him Bill's map and overlay. 'Excellent sir, Proctor did very well. When I checked his map overlay at Bruay I found we hadn't really stretched him much. So, as you suggested, I flew him over my old area west of St. Pol. Even did an out-landing I know there to try and get him lost. Checked him again and he was spot-on!'

Hugh Porter was pleased. 'I think we're going to make a good observer out of you Proctor; do you like flying?'

Bill smiled with a boyish enthusiasm. 'Yes sir, very much sir.'

Tom decided to take a chance. 'I hope you may approve sir, but I took the opportunity to teach Proctor a bit of flying.'

Hugh Porter smiled ruefully. 'I thought you were a long time aloft Bolton. Let's put it this way shall we, *I* most certainly approve. I think you know my views on our role in 'C' Flight well enough. But I doubt that Major Foreskin would take the... what are you grinning at Sergeant?' Captain Porter could feel his colour rising as he realised his mistake. 'Jesus Christ if either of you two jokers ever repeat that slip I'll personally castrate the pair of you with rigging clippers!' Trying to keep his composure Hugh Porter did his best to maintain authority and discipline, then broke down into fits of uncontrollable laughter. 'Oh shit, what's the bloody use!' He looked squarely at Tom Bolton. 'How did young Proctor manage?'

Tom answered in a single sentence. 'I recommend he goes for pilot training sir.' Turning to Bill, Hugh Porter considered him further.

'If Tom Bolton says you're pilot material, then you are! He used to be a flying instructor in Blighty before he came to France, did he tell you that?' Not waiting for an answer he carried on. 'I can assume that since you volunteered for flying you'll not stop until you're a pilot, but let's see how you get on with being an observer first shall we?' The decision isn't mine of course, that belongs to Captain Wells. But I shall speak to him and see if we can't get you doing more flying with Sergeant Bolton in the Avro. So, off you both go, and remember, I'll have no hesitation in clipping your balls off if I ever hear a word about a certain person not a million miles from here!'

As they returned to the Avro they fell about laughing. 'Foreskin! that's really rich, but we had better be quiet about that Bill, good old 'C' will know for sure if we spread that about, and as you must know from this morning's little visit, I need my testimonials intact! Anyway Bill, I'll see you again for flying, maybe in a day or two. Mr Porter is on our side you can be sure.'

At the aeroplane they divided the spoils given to them by Jean Louis and Simone. Bill refused the wine and brandy, mentioning the difficulty of explaining their origin to a crowded tent. 'But I would welcome some of the eggs Tom. We have a cook in our tent, and Charlie Train could make us a few egg sandwiches for this evening. I'll tell him I bought them cheap in Bruay.'

Tom agreed. 'Don't forget Bill, not a word to a living soul – we'll be making another visit soon.'

By Friday Bill had made four more flights, all with Tom Bolton, and had been able to practice his flying on all but one of the flights, including another take-off and landing. He was quite confident he could control the Avro now, and according to Tom was a natural flyer.

Yesterday had been different. For the very first time he sensed the full importance of their work when he flew on a battery ranging exercise. But now it was to be the real thing. An order from Wing had broken into their training schedule and Tom Bolton was ordered to fly a battery shoot in the Loos area. Tom asked for Bill, and since this flight would allow him to complete the course today, Hugh Porter agreed.

They flew an Avro equipped with a new lightweight wireless in Tom's cockpit. Their task was to use 'clock code' and wireless to correct a British six inch Howitzer battery situated a mile behind the forward lines. Although Bill was just starting Morse lessons and hadn't even touched wireless training, he had shown good aptitude with the clock code and Hugh Porter could use that. There was pressure from Wing to train as many observers as possible before the 15th September. It was now the 10th, and with Fawcett constantly on his tail, he had to take chances. The advantages of gaining experience with a real shoot were obvious, but he also knew Tom Bolton would have to do the work of two men. Fortunately their target was well plotted and had already been ranged some months ago, but it would be heavily defended just the same.

Compared to his pilot, Bill had little to do except observe and make notes. Tom did all the real work: flying, observing, using the wireless, and if attacked fire the Lewis mounted on the upper wing. Bill was to practise artillery spotting, using the map and its celluloid overlay to plot shell strikes as Tom transmitted corrections to the guns. He felt like a passenger and was embarrassed.

Flying 4,000 feet above the enemy lines they had a good view of the German fortifications south of Lens, where Bill easily located the designated target on his map. It was a specially prepared map, squared-off so that a transparent clock-faced overlay could be centred on the target. Shell bursts could then be located within any of its eight concentric circles, each lettered to represent distances from the target. The first circle, Y, was close to the centre spot and indicated a strike within 10 yards, then there was Z, A, B, C, D, E, and F, representing distances with a radius of 25, 50, 100, 200, 300, 400 and 500 yards from the target. As a further guide there were twelve radial lines emanating from the centre spot each representing a clock position. In this fashion a shell bursting close to 100 yards due east of the target would be signalled to the battery as shot falling at B3.

Bill squeezed his memory for the appropriate Morse code, 'That would be 'dash, dot, dot, dot, then… dot, dot, dot, dash, dash, or was it?'

From his lectures Bill knew that Tom would now have wireless contact with the battery which, on receipt of his transmitted code letter 'G' would open fire on the target – a large open supply depot which occupied a field on the edge of a wood. The target was already marked on his map, making it a simple matter to position it under the centre spot of the celluloid. Within minutes he saw the first ranging shots fall into the general area of the target. Bill found it fascinating to apply his own estimate for corrected gunfire, and looking at his overlay estimated the first shells to have struck within 200 yards at about 10 o'clock. Looking at his notes he could see this would require transmitting the signal C10. Within twenty seconds the next shots came over, obviously Tom had corrected the battery for the shells were now falling within 50 yards of the target at 2 o'clock. Bill tried to remember his Morse as he pretended to send A2. The next salvo came dead on target!

Tom tapped out the code OK, 'direct hit'. He was more than pleased with his work, but it was time to go! They had been close to twenty minutes over the area and some Jerry 77mm appeared to have found their range. Tom sent his final messages; tapping out AA, CI, on his key, 'Anti-aircraft guns, am returning to landing ground' then, with the archie cordite thick and acrid in his nostrils he turned west.

Five minutes after leaving the target Tom could still hear the 6 inch shells bursting. The guns were now firing salvoes by the sound of things. Perhaps he should have stayed longer? But if Tom Bolton had any doubts concerning his turning away from the Jerry archie, they were dispelled as he felt, then heard the large explosions behind them. Bill was banging on the cockpit interspace, pointing to a large pall of white and yellow smoke, and numerous explosions over their target. The battery had scored a direct hit on the suspected, but now confirmed, ammunition dump.

Joyfully the two aviators punched air with their fists. It had been a good shoot, much better than expected. As Tom flew south-west past the battered town of Arras he noticed another Avro to the north, possibly one of theirs he thought. Not long now and he would be home, and he needed a drink!

On landing Tom checked his observations with those of his observer. 'Not bad at all Bill, your estimates are about the same as mine come to think of it. But I'm not used to flying the bird, checking the shell-bursts *and* tapping out Morse code all at the same time! I'm only the bloody driver usually, which is why we need observers! But we had an easy target – I think the battery had ranged it some time ago!'

Bill's attention was elsewhere. 'Crikey Tom, come and look at this!' He was staring at the starboard wings, the large ragged holes and flapping fabric. 'That Hun archie nearly got us, the bastards!'

'Bloody mice' said Tom, and walked off.

Hugh Porter greeted them as they entered 'C' Flight tent. 'Relax chaps and get yourselves a mug of tea. How did the shoot go?' Tom went to the tea urn and returned with two mugs before answering.

'Hot stuff sir, but we must have got it right cos the whole bloody target went up with a loud bang just after we left the area. The intelligence people must have got it right for once, it *was* an ammo dump!'

Hugh Porter made careful notes as he debriefed the two airmen. 'You say your wireless didn't give any trouble? And the battery response was good?

Tom thought for a moment. 'Well, until we can receive as well as transmit we'll never really know, shall we sir? But since they corrected their second and third fall of shots we can assume they received our signals without difficulty. Proctor did well sir! Here, you can see his observation report is much the same as my signalled transmissions.'

Captain Porter studied their scribbled reports and map sheets. 'Well done chaps, I'll make sure your reports are entered into the 'good book'. And Proctor! You are now a qualified gunner/observer and will find this entered on Squadron Standing Orders within a couple of days. As soon as you see your name on SSOs, report to the Orderly Room to get the new rating entered into your paybook.' Captain Porter came over and shook his hand. 'Congratulations lad, you did well on the course and I know Captain Wells is going to be as pleased as we are.' He then winked at Tom Bolton. 'I think we might need to borrow an observer from 'A' Flight now and then sergeant. If so, I think you'll find Proctor a willing volunteer eh! So buzz off, you can both stand down, and Proctor – you won't need to report to 'A' Flight until tomorrow morning.'

As they returned to their own lines Bill put a question to his friend. 'What exactly did 'C' mean when he talked about our reports going into the 'good book'?'

Tom laughed. 'The good book is correctly known as Army Form W.3343, the Squadron Record Book. I've only seen it once myself come to think of it. It's kept up to date by the adj and signed by the C/O as an official record of the squadron's activities. It's a very important document I suppose since it records all our missions, casualties, successes, failures, and I'm told it's used as a reference for commendations, medals and all that rot!'

Bill retired to his tent feeling pleasantly exhausted and found two letters on the squared-off blankets. One was from Alice, he would save that until later. The other was postmarked OHMS with an army box number.

Tom Bolton felt drained. He had been flying two, sometimes three flights a day for the past two weeks. It wasn't fun anymore, and all the signs indicated a heavy time ahead. He had seen the intensive troop movements surrounding Arras, the crowded communication trenches within the British lines, and knew an attack was being prepared. Opening his locker he found the brandy wrapped in an old shirt, it was three-quarters full. Within minutes it was less than half full. Tom re-corked the bottle and placed it under the straw pillow then, leaning over the bedside, was violently sick into the upturned German *Pickelhaube* helmet stuck under his cot.

Major Fawcett threw his flying helmet and gloves onto Hugh Porter's desk then sank deeply into one of the wicker chairs in the corner of 'C' Flight's large tent. He and captain James had been aloft for just over an hour and a half. They too had been on a training exercise, but further north than that flown by Tom Bolton.

'Quite busy over the lines today Porter! Lots going on, what! Was that sergeant Bolton that just landed before us?'

Hugh Porter confirmed and mentioned the successful shoot. 'They did well those two. Evidently put the guns onto an ammo dump – blasted it to hell they say!' Fawcett saw the report sheets lying on the desk and spent a silent minute looking them over.

'Humph! Now I don't want to mention this beyond these tent walls Porter, but our friend Bolton took to his heels as soon as the air got a bit choppy over the target area. In fact James and I were just discussing it a moment ago, before he went to change out of his flying clothes.'

Hugh Porter barely managed to keep his temper. 'I'm not sure what it is you are trying to say sir.'

Fawcett tapped the reports sheets in his hand. 'He even admits he left the shoot area before the dump went up! Good God man what do you think that means, eh? It means he had cold feet, that's what I'm saying!'

Hugh Porter couldn't let that pass. 'We teach a standard procedure set down by Wing HQ, 'pilots are not to hazard their machine once a battery ranging shoot has been completed'. Bolton did just that sir! You can see in his report, the third salvo was a direct hit, he then signalled OK, then, AA and CI to let them know he was going home.'

Major Fawcett took a condescending tone as he replied. 'What you don't know Captain, is what we saw happening. Bolton had turned west before the dump went up right?'

Hugh interrupted. 'No point in him staying when he'd signalled a direct hit, was there sir? He knew the salvoes would continue until the place went up or not. We have found many times that if nothing else happens, it's pointless to keep firing. Bolton knew that. The decision to continue on those coordinates belonged to the battery, not the pilot! The range was only five or six miles and the battery would know if it was an ammo dump or not from the noise let alone their observers in the forward lines. I repeat sir, it's the pilot's responsibility to bring his aircraft back intact, once his mission has been carried out successfully.'

'You were not there Porter we were! We were coming down from our exercise arc and just as I was about to signal James to wind in our aerial, I decided to give him a taste of the Hun's side of the lines. I saw the flack to the south of Lens and then saw one of our Avros leaving the area. Well I knew it was Bolton of course but saw some of our shells were not on target. So I signalled the battery as Bolton flew west. Which is how we got the direct hit – not Bolton!'

Hugh Porter knew a lie when he heard one. 'The bastard never went over the lines, let alone signalled the battery. From where he was he could never range guns correctly, too much parallax error'. But Hugh knew he could never prove different. Since their current sets only allowed a one-way transmission from the aircraft, and since both machines transmitted on the same frequency, who could say otherwise?

'So it was you that gave the final signal for a direct hit Major?'

Fawcett picked up the reports. 'That is so Captain, and although James and I witnessed what could be considered as dereliction of duty, I shall not pursue the matter further as it reflects badly on the squadron. In any case, all's well in the end, what! So don't mention this to Bolton, we'll give him the benefit of the doubt, eh. I shall get James to contact the battery and make sure there is no confusion at their end, don't want things getting too complicated at Wing do we? I shall give these reports to James, must keep the record book up to date, eh what!'

Hugh Porter took a couple of swigs from his flask. 'God all bloody mighty, the bastard will stop at nothing!' He knew he couldn't prove it, but was certain that Fawcett and James were never in touch with the 6-inch battery. 'Bloody opportunist – saw his chance and took it. Clever bastard! But not that clever'. Hugh could not speak to his friends about this, his plans were dangerous enough as it was. But it had to be soon, before James qualified as observer. Once that happened both of the bastards would retire to some HQ or other as 'honorary aviators'. *Their* war would be over, all but the promotions and decorations of course.

It was easy to see what Fawcett had in mind. Today, they had claimed Tom Bolton's shoot, a highly successful mission now duly recorded in the 'good book' as one completed by them. This left the obnoxious duo with one more mission to go! But they were impatient and he knew that. Very soon every one of 4 Sqdn's aircraft would be wanted for the big Allied attack now being prepared, and since Wing required all observer training to be completed by the 15th, he could assume the squadron would be heavily committed after that date. Hugh smiled as he reflected on Fawcett's obvious ploy. The man was predictable to a fault, and would surely want James qualified before the 15th. After that, every flight they did would be recorded under forthcoming battle orders, even if they were miles behind the lines. It would look good in their log books!

Hugh realised he would have to act without further delay. For although the C/O had decided to assist in 'C' Flight's training schedule, Fawcett couldn't alter the rules for qualifying observers. They still had to go over the lines one more time, either another shoot, reconnaissance or CP. That was it of course, a Contact Patrol!

He decided he would give them a helping hand by providing them with a choice of missions scheduled by Wing to be flown at 'first opportunity'. To begin with there was an outstanding photographic mission to be flown over the Jerry lines between Carvin and La Bassee, but so far the weather had not been favourable. Then there was an easy option – a CP over our own front line extending from the Somme marshes north to Arras, passing over the German salient at Bapaume en route. Hugh Porter took out the mission files and scoured the area map. Tomorrow! If the weather forecast would only hold, then tomorrow would be the day!

Bill put a foot on the edge of his cot and began the ritual of unrolling his puttees. He'd got used to them by now of course, but disliked them just the same and never felt relaxed until they were off. Then, slipping off his tunic he relaxed full length on the hard biscuits, eager to open Alice's letter. But first, there was this HMSO envelope. With a sense of foreboding he opened it with his thumbnail, anxious about its contents. The only other time he'd received an official 'On His Majesty's Service' letter was when he was called to the colours: whatever did this have in store?

It was from Gerry! Bill was puzzled, because they had agreed to correspond through each other's home address. How on earth did he know his RFC address? He read on:

England. 3rd August. 1915.

Dear Bill,

I suppose you will be wondering how I know where you are? Well your outfit is well known to us here at the wireless school. Yes, this is where Gerry Hardcastle now resides, I started my wireless course just over two weeks ago (9 Sqdn) and came here directly from my Gunner's Course, which I managed to pass, but cannot say I came out with the best of marks. Evidently I'm to be an observer/wireless specialist, selected on the basis of my school certificate physics marks – so I'm told.

Major Dowding (our C/O) tells me I'm to be commissioned if I get good enough marks on this course. So I'm 'burning the midnight oil' trying to improve my Morse. I can send and receive 12 words/minute at present. One of our chaps can do 15, but he's not the stuff for an officer all the same.

I wouldn't be too surprised if you didn't see me on your side of the water by late November. You people seem to have all the front-line experience with wireless, so it's possible I may be detached to 4 Sqdn for some flying. Evidently one has to 'qualify in the field' before you can be an observer, so I'm sure to be over shortly. They want me to be an officer instructor or something. Better start practising your saluting my lad! How are things with you? Still playing with oil cans? I was interested to learn you had been for a flight in the BE, I can't wait to start flying.

Hope to see you soon, best of luck.

Gerry

P.S. Don't bother to write back, better to leave things until I see you.

'Cheeky bugger!' Bill had to laugh, 'Playing with oil cans' indeed! But he was glad for his friend, and was sure he would make a fine officer. He thought awhile, but couldn't see himself as one. 'Not born to it I suppose', but he couldn't wait to tell Eileen. In fact he had lots to write home about, but now for Alice's letter.

By seven o'clock Bill was on his third letter. He had already written to his mother and father, one to Maggie, enclosing a short note for Eileen – mainly to tease her concerning Gerry's news of becoming an officer, and had just started writing to Alice when Ralph Downes came into the tent.

'I suppose you heard the news then Bill?' He looked up, striving to collect himself.

'Er, sorry, what news?'

Ralph tossed his cap onto the cot opposite. 'One of 'B' Flight's quirks copped it on a battery shoot up by Lens. We just heard about it in the office. Direct hit from archie, just blew up they said.'

Bill's thoughts took him back to the same area, where he and Tom had flown earlier in the day, 'Christ, that's where Tom and I were only a few hours ago! In fact *we* had to beat it out of there, cos of the archie, they had our range you see. Lots going on up there these days it seems. I wonder what they were ranging? I mean we put some six inch guns on a massive ammo dump this morning, left a hell of mess, maybe they were looking for another?'

Ralph bit his lip. 'It seems like everyone was in that area today. In fact I've only just finished typing out today's form W.3343. Did you know the C/O and Captain James followed you onto your ammo dump this morning?'

Bill laughed. 'More fool them! What on earth did they do that for? Christ the whole dump went up, I saw it as we were leaving.'

Ralph pressed on. 'According to the Major's account, it was him who put the guns onto the dump, after you had retired. He even 'phoned the battery to confirm it!'

Bill couldn't believe what he was hearing. 'But that was Tom Bolton's shoot – I know, I saw the corrections to the guns, the C/O was nowhere in sight! Christ almighty! I'm going to see Tom about this.'

Ralph had never seen his friend more angry. 'Forget it Bill, I mean that, forget it!'

'What are you saying? This isn't fair Ralph. That shoot belongs to Tom, what the bloody hell is the C/O thinking about?'

Ralph came over to sit on Bill's cot. 'For two bloody good reasons you say fuck-all about this, all right! First of all it's not only a question of Sgt Bolton not completing the shoot, which is what the Major has entered in the Record Book. It could go further than that. How about desertion in face of the enemy! Which could even include you!'

Bill's face was white with rage. 'But that's daft, bloody stupid in fact. I mean, good God man we did the fucking job we …'

Ralph stopped him short. 'Who's to say Bill? Who's to say eh? Best leave it my old mucker, for Tom's sake as well as your own And another thing, since you don't never get to see the good book, who told you eh? Little old me would be right in the shit, divulging official secrets no less! No Bill, don't you say a word to anyone, and certainly not to Tom Bolton. Certainly not him – he's a nice bloke, but when he's pissed I'm told he's none too careful.'

All the heart had gone out of his letter to Alice. Bill put his writing wallet away and left the tent. It was all too unfair, and there was no-body he could talk too. He walked down to the 'A' Flight lines, poor old 988 had gone, but Ted and Trevor were still working on 726, so he joined them.

Chapter Twelve

Saturday, 11th September, 1915

Immediately after breakfast Ted and Bill reported to Dad Owens.

'Pleased to see you back Proctor, got a lot of work for you to do! Mr Wells tells me you're a fully qualified observer now? Well done lad. But since you're not flying for a few days I'd like you to observe 1021 and do a plug change on her – so get your overalls on!'

Ted couldn't stop laughing. 'Very funny Dad, that'll bring him down a peg or two.'

Dad smiled. 'I'm glad you see the humour Hamilton! Because your first job is an engine change on our favourite 'hangar queen'. Mr Wells wants every one of his quirks in flying condition by Monday, and that includes 1005. So get those lazy buggers, Johnson and Bradley to help, you'll find her skulking in the far hangar. By God I'll have that bloody machine in the air if it kills me' Dad Owens turned back to Bill. 'That damned 1005 has only done fifteen hours since we've had her, and never a good word from anyone who's flown her. I hate to say this Proctor, she might well come under your care since we lost 988, but I'm blowed if I'd want to fly in the bitch!'

As he walked back to the servicing tent Dad turned about. 'You're improperly dressed Proctor! You should have that new 'O' badge up shouldn't you?'

Bill laughed, happy to continue with Dad's banter. 'Sorry Flight Sergeant, only officers are allowed to show themselves as 'flying arseholes', we ack-emmas are above that sort of thing!'

Dad shook his head from side-to-side. 'Bloody typical!' then put up a warning finger, 'Take care lad, better keep your feet on the ground. The C/O's inspecting this morning'.

Major Fawcett paced the lines of 'C' Flight considering his position. He'd just received orders from Wing that 4 Sqdn was to be at maximum readiness by the 14th with bomb racks fitted to the BEs and all the Avros made ready for reconnaissance and artillery shoots. The BEs would take the brunt of it, providing infantry support and CPs for the forthcoming offensive in the Arras area. It was going to be a bloody business, so it would be prudent to log as many flying hours as he could now! As soon as the offensive started he would be too busy to fly, and as Commanding Officer wasn't expected to anyway. But he would need to get Julian qualified first – only one more flight to go and then he could get on with his career. As he strode towards Hugh Porter's office he saw Julian James approaching for their arranged meeting. Weather permitting he would fly tomorrow!

Sergeant Bert Duffy and Tosh Armstrong were just leaving when Major Fawcett and Captain James entered 'C' Flight's tent. After nearly an hour's briefing by Hugh Porter and a gunner captain they were about to fly a difficult shoot over a small town 5 miles east of the lines. Collecting their maps and codes the two flyers saluted as they turned to leave. Fawcett greeted them jovially.

'Hello there! Where are you chaps going?'

Hugh Porter explained: 'Sgt Duffy has an archie shoot over Villerval this morning sir. You may remember we discussed it two days ago with Captain Saunders?'

Fawcett turned to acknowledge the young gunner officer's salute. 'Ah yes, you are from where?'

'The 213th Field Artillery Regiment, now part of the 54th Division sir.' Hugh certainly remembered the aftermath of those discussions, for Villerval was only four miles south of the German aerodrome at Douai and notorious in 3rd Wing. Its supply depot and troop concentrations were a constant target for artillery, but due to their mobility they required constant spotting. It was a costly business and the British squadrons had lost a number of machines in the process. Hugh recalled the heated argument he'd put up, trying to get Fawcett to ask for 5 Sqdn's scouts to give cover over the area. Their FE2bs could at least keep the Douai Fokkers busy while Duffy completed the shoot. But it was to no avail.

The gunner officer made his excuses and followed the two airmen out of the tent.

'Right Porter! What have we got for a suitable qualifying flight for James? As you know, we have to get all training out of the way within a few days, so I would like to get him polished off by tomorrow.' Hugh Porter was fully prepared and placed two urgent flight plans on the table.

'Wing want two jobs done as soon as possible sir. You can take your pick, both of them would qualify Captain James for his observer badge. First of all we have a photo-recce mission over the German lines between Carvin and La Bassée. As you know, this is within the forthcoming attack area and the weather looks good for about 11 ack-emma tomorrow. The details are all here; it's a line of eight miles which has to be photographed at 5000 feet.' James stole a glance at his pilot, but Fawcett made no comment. 'And what is the other mission Hugh?'

Taking his time Hugh Porter affected complete indifference, but he knew everything depended on the alternative appearing as a safe option.

'The other mission is not so direct, and requires more navigation. This requires a CP over our forward lines, with a short hop over the German salient west of Bapaume en route to Arras. Our lines have to be covered from the Somme marshes north to Arras.' He turned their attention to a large area map on his desk. 'If you prefer this job I would suggest an eight o'clock take-off, climbing to 5000 feet over the airfield. Then fly south-east towards Corbie where you can follow the Somme to Bray, which is a good seven miles inside our lines. Then turn north to Arras and descend to 400 feet so that you can observe our forward patrols within the Bapaume salient.'

Fawcett looked puzzled. Why do we fly at 5000 feet then descend? Why not simply fly at 500 feet then descend to 400 over the salient?'

Hugh crossed his fingers. 'As you know sir, early morning mists over the marshes will not allow you to map read easily on that leg of the mission. By flying at 5000 feet it will be easier to fly over the mist layer and use dead-reckoning. As soon as you fly south-east, at 65 mph, set your stop watch for fifteen minutes, then turn north and descend. From the time you turn north, the salient is eight miles distant, so you should come out of the mist at 400 feet just at the right time to look for any ground signals our forward troops may put out. In this way the Boche won't even see you coming and you will be across the seven mile stretch within five minutes.'

Hugh could see that James was worried, and had taken a ruler to the map. So now was the time for a little instruction. 'As you know Julian, we can always rely on a 10 mph westerly, so with 65 mph indicated air speed, plus a 10 mph tail wind you will be doing 75 mph right? And since Bray is 18 miles flying, that amounts to fifteen minutes before you turn north!'

Fawcett seemed pleased. 'Looks like a good approach Porter. I take it we are to read any ground displays, write down the message and drop it over our lines – if there are any messages of course, is that it?'

'Yes sir, in fact you will see our own trenches on your left. But if there is anything really urgent you are to wireless HQ 9th Brigade; their frequency is noted on the flight plan.'

Fawcett made a decision. 'Well I think we have it all wrapped up. Which aircraft do we have?'

'I shall have 1423 warmed up and armed with a Lewis and 97-ammo drum ready for take-off at 7.50 ack-emma, and in compliance with your instructions she will be fitted with wireless, and the Morse key will be in your cockpit Sir.'

As they left the tent Hugh Porter wore an evil grin. 'I knew you bastards would go for the easy one. And I'll bet a week's pay you don't even plan to go over the salient, let alone look for any troop signals!'

Going to the corner of the tent he picked up a six inch mahogany box and looked inside. He would wait until later before he made his daily inspection of 'C' Flight's aircraft. And since 1423 would be the first machine off the ground tomorrow, it made sense to inspect her last of all, late evening, after the men had finished work.

It didn't take Bill long to complete the plug change on 1021, and after he'd finished and completed the usual engine checks he joined Ted with 1005. Like most hangar queens she appeared to be in pristine condition, but in common with all queens, 1005 developed problems like a sickly child, and spent more time in the hangar than in service. By 2 o'clock the engine was run-in and she was ready for an air test. Dad Owens came over with Lt Wilson; it was to be a short flight, sufficient to see how she flew. Everyone knew 1005 would be trouble, but what?

'Get your flying clothes on Proctor, last time I flew this bugger it flew with a decided limp to port. God knows what she'll do this time, but it would help to have an expert along.' Bill dashed to the crew tent where his flying clothes were kept. He was elated, no one had ever called him an expert before. He didn't have to believe it – it was enough to be accepted and his work appreciated.

The new engine was rough, but easily tuned after their first flight. The main problem was going to be the rigging, and after various alterations to the landing wires it seemed possible that 1005 might join the rest of the squadron. After the third test they were satisfied, she flew as well as any other quirk, and Bill was content. He would be quite happy to look after her from now on! They landed and taxied into the line to find a less than enthusiastic group waiting for their report. Dad Owens was first to break the news.

'It's Bert Duffy and Tosh! Bought the farm about 11 ack-emma. Just had the news from Captain Porter, they were shot down during their shoot this morning.'

Ted Hamilton took up the story. 'Poor buggers, it was a flamer

173

from about 3000 feet, so they say. Both dead, burned to charcoal, it crashed behind our lines.' Lt Paul Wilson said nothing, he was deathly white.

Dad took over. 'Right Hamilton, enough of that! What do you think of her now Proctor? Is she operational?'

Paul Wilson had recovered his composure and joined in the discussions concerning 1005. 'She'll do, flies like all the other buggers now... like a pregnant sow! Bloody shame about Bert and Tosh. God, I hope they were killed instantly before she flamed.'

Dad Owens could offer no consolation there. 'Two Fokkers evidently sir, no chance at all. I know Mr Wells is cut up, and he was hoping to get them back into 'A' Flight soon.'

As predicted, the early morning mist was thick on the ground as Major Fawcett and Captain James completed their preflight inspection of Avro 1423. All was well, and as they were turned into the wind Fawcett could just see the glimmer of veiled sunshine rising in the east. By ten past eight they were 5000 feet above the airfield and ready for their fifteen minute flight towards the Somme marshes. As expected, the world below was covered in mist, thick in parts and totally obscuring the ground. Fawcett had to admit that Porter knew his stuff when it came to mission planning. He checked his compass and the pitot ASI, 150 degrees and 65 mph. Ten more minutes to go before turning north, and now and then he caught a faint glimmer from the Somme as they flew south-east towards the marshes. At 8.25 he turned north, there was nothing but mist below.

Julian James was trying to follow his map, but there was nothing to be seen. As the Avro turned north he checked his watch – bang on time! Checking the Pattern 200 compass he saw its card was strangely tilted and its movement sluggish, moving slowly then fast. Then it stuck, obviously its fluid had drained. But no matter, Keith Fawcett's compass would be fine or he would have turned back. The Avro was descending now, and as the altimeter unwound he searched for the ground. As soon as they could, it was essential to locate the British trenches – which should be on their left!

At 600 feet, Fawcett could make out the shell-pocked ground, now revealed below a thinning mist. He must find the British trenches, somewhere to the left ... and there they were! He moved the Avro towards the broken lines of upturned chalky earth. He would be near the salient now, possibly over it. Move closer to the trenches, no better still, fly over the trenches with no-man's-land to his right. Safer that way, if there is any archie he could easily swing further left to the safety of their own rear lines. As the Avro lurched to the left they were at 500 feet and a perfect target for the German machine gunners who, amazed at the audacity of the British aviators flying over their rear trenches, opened up with everything they had.

Julian James was horrified. He realised where they were and the knowledge froze in his brain. How could Fawcett come this far over the lines? These were not the forward British trenches but the German third line. They were too far to the east, and well behind the German lines!

Keith Fawcett would never know. Slumped over the controls he was already dead, and as the machine dropped from the sky a heavy burst of tracer cut into Julian James' stomach. In shock, he could only watch as the Avro dived towards the trenches, massed rifle and machine-gun fire continuing to stitch the stricken machine only seconds before it exploded between the third and second lines.

At half-past nine Ralph Downes took a telephone message from 3rd Wing. 'Did 4 Sqdn have an Avro in the Bapaume area about 8.30 this morning?' He took the message to Captain Porter who promptly called Wing HQ. Evidently a British forward balloon had observed an Avro fall to German guns in the area of their trenches west of Bapaume.

'Yes, it could be one of ours,' Hugh replied. 'Major Fawcett and Captain James were conducting the Bapaume salient CP, one of our outstanding missions for this area. No! I cannot see why they went behind the German lines, most strange, must be a navigational error. Captain James was not yet a qualified observer, and it was misty this morning – I fear the worst!'

Hugh Porter walked down to 'B' Flight to find Bernie Saul, and together they called on Tim Wells. 'It looks like you're back to being C/O Tim, and this time I think it will be permanent!' Hugh told the two Flight Commanders of his conversation with Wing HQ. 'You are acting C/O until Wing confirm your full appointment later today.'

Tim Wells gave a startled look. 'Don't tell me...'

'Yes, at 8.30 ack-emma, old foreskin and co went bust! One of our balloon observers saw an Avro explode *behind* Jerry lines. It must have been them, but Wing say we must wait three hours before their deaths are confirmed. But you are to be our new C/O with the rank of Major – congratulations old son!'

Bernie Saul danced a jig. 'Bloody marvellous – I mean I don't wish to speak ill of the dead – but it couldn't have happened to a nicer pair of bastards! Tonight, we celebrate! A double celebration, one to wet your crown Tim, and the other to ... to ... well you know well enough.

Sorry you lost an Avro Hugh' He stole a meaningful look at his friend. 'You'll have to tell us about it, won't you?'

Tim Wells had to think fast. As C/O he now had to pass 'A' Flight to Lt Paul Wilson, and reorganise the squadron. 'Right chaps, everything goes back to normal. But Hugh! You will have to stop all training in two days, then get 'C' Flight prepared for wireless, photography and artillery shoots. 'A' and 'B' will concentrate on army support, CPs and bombing. I'm sending Paul up with 'A' in a few minutes; they have a bombing job over Vimy scheduled for 10.15, no time to get 5 Sqdn scouts to support them, but I mean to get them or 6 Sqdn, or both, to cover all our jobs in the future. We lost two good men yesterday, all because of that arrogant... ah well.'

It was 4 Sqdn's first bombing mission, and as the six quirks climbed to 2000 feet Bill could only wonder at the ever-changing circumstances that pushed and pulled him every day. Only yesterday 1005 was a despised hangar queen and now, with a sceptical Lt Crouch as pilot, he was flying in her with a load of 25 lb Cooper bombs. So far so good, and 1005 seemed to be behaving herself. He couldn't see the extra load of four bombs making any difference anyway.

It was a day of creamy blue skies streaked with gold, a beautiful autumn day in fact. An ideal day for photography really but they were to be bombing this time. It was ideal for Fokkers too, so he'd been warned to keep a good look out! They were to dive down to 500 feet, drop their bombs on the Jerry trenches occupying Vimy ridge and then beat it back home. Talk about everything happening at once! Before they left Bertangles the entire flight was full of rumour that the C/O had bought it? Nobody appeared to be unhappy he decided.

Passing Arras, Lt Paul Wilson could easily make out the town of Vimy to the north-east. Signalling to the rest of 'A' Flight he descended to approach the German trenches from the south. In line astern, the six BEs made their bombing run so that each machine would bomb further up the trench line as they flew north, then break for home as they approached Lens. Bill could see Lt Wilson's quirk pull up as he dropped his bombs, to be followed by two others then themselves. His stomach churned as they climbed and he tried to observe the effects of their bombs. There was a lot of chalky dust but little else to see, but they were taking a lot of ground fire!

Nobody saw the four Fokker E1s until they pounced. By the time Paul Wilson had passed 1000 feet the first of them had closed within 200 feet in a near frontal approach. An opening burst caught his observer, Lt Randolph, in the chest and left shoulder, and chipped one of the rear interplane struts. Turning as swiftly as he could, he banked the quirk to lose height and made for the British lines.

Bill saw a quirk go down in flames before he saw any of the enemy machines then, searching for the enemy, he swung the Lewis towards a slim outline now approaching their tail. Lt Crouch kept turning his head, looking for the Fokker as it swiftly closed the space between them. Bill's first burst made the pilot duck his head, then the Fokker dived and within seconds was out of sight and below them. Too close, the Fokker pilot couldn't raise his nose to shoot at the vulnerable underside of the quirk. Frustrated, and in haste, he pulled to the right, breaking off his attack in order to climb and return onto his easy target. Bill had one moment of opportunity, his Lewis barked and flung a hail of .303 ball into the Fokker's wing. As far as he could see it was sufficient to have damaged the blighter since it never returned. He grinned to his pilot as that worthy swooped low over the British trenches and made for home.

'Fat lot of good that did us!' Paul Wilson was angry as he confronted Tim Wells back at the Squadron office. 'Those fucking Fokkers caught us napping, we never had a chance. Were it not for the proximity of our lines none of us would have got back! I tell you Tim, we must have scouts supporting us or we'll never survive at this rate. I lost Quinn and Barnes – went down in flames – not too far for them to go thank God! I got myself a crippled quirk and a badly-wounded observer, and all the machines have bullet holes in them. Now old foreskin has left us, you can tell Wing we need scout cover!' Tim Wells was worried, the squadron had lost two Avros and one quirk in a day, plus one grounded and four more requiring patching up. There was a paucity of spares, particularly for the Avros, and crews were being killed.

'Already been onto Wing Paul. We have their support, evidently other quirk squadrons have been hit even harder than us, so we will get support from scout squadrons, if available! We've been promised two more Avros and four more quirks for the big push coming up in the Loos area. Hugh Porter tells me that we'll have all the training finished by tomorrow, so have a word with Hugh, he'll fix you up with a new observer.'

Paul Wilson relaxed. 'As I'm now boss of 'A' Flight I can chose my own observer right? Well, during our little skirmish this morning Johnnie Crouch had a bit of a scare. One of the Fokkers got on his tail, then went underneath them...' Tim Wells sucked in his breath. 'Bit too close though, but when the Hun made a break for another go, young Proctor got him with a well-aimed burst – saw him off too! So he's my man. I want someone who can shoot and that lad's good. I've seen Hugh Porter's reports and they confirm he's done well.'

Tim Wells smiled in agreement. 'Hugh had a word in my ear about that lad. He's been doing a bit of driving with Sgt Bolton, on the quiet of course, and Bolton recommends him for pilot training. I'll send him back to Blighty as soon as we can, but there's a need for him here while we have this battle coming up. In the meanwhile Paul, he's all yours!'

By the end of the day 3rd Wing confirmed Tim Wells as Major, Commanding Officer of 4 Sqdn, and sent him sealed orders with regard to the squadron's role in the new push. It was to be a joint Anglo-French effort, with General Haig's 1st Army thrusting forward on a front stretching between Lens and La Bassée. The attack was scheduled to start on 25th September, but 4 Sqdn's work, like that of all 3rd Wing's squadrons, would begin on the 17th. The orders also confirmed Paul Wilson's promotion to Captain.

Although Bernie Saul wanted to celebrate in their favourite estaminet, he had to make do with the C/O's private tent since it was now impossible for Tim to be further than a few yards from the sqdn office. Bernie got Paul Wilson to help with the arrangements. They had sent Fawcett's personal effects back to Wing earlier that afternoon, in company with those of Captain James, Sgt Duffy and AM/2 Armstrong, and by evening had a table prepared for their celebrations.

After a three-course meal helped down by generous helpings of wine, discussions centred on the future work of the three flights. But after a second bottle of brandy had been finished the conversation turned to the recent demise of Major Fawcett.

'Come on Hugh, let's have the full story' Paul Wilson, and Bernie Saul were not going to let him escape. Tim Wells was uncertain. They had all heard Hugh Porter talk of his 'plan' but Tim couldn't hear it now.

'Look chaps, you go ahead with your evening, I *have* to leave you now, I have much to do. Many thanks for everything and Hugh, take care old son, and thanks!' With that he left his friends and went back to the squadron office.

'Fine bloody thing, gone to his head this C/O thing; here we are having a nice old party and…'

Bernie Saul tapped him on the head with an empty. 'Shut up you stupid sot, can't you see? Tim can't hear what Hugh has to say – not now!'

'Well it wasn't difficult chaps. A simple question of two idiots who can't navigate for toffee. Fawcett opted for the easy mission – a CP over the lines – as expected. They accepted my flight-plan, which was correct, more or less; but when it comes to dead-reckoning they should have known: a 10 mph wind at ground level is not a good basis for estimating your flight-time at 5000 feet! I would say they didn't allow for stronger tail winds at altitude – leading to faster ground speed – which sent them further up the salient.'

'And you call *that* a plan!' Bernie Saul snorted. 'Bloody hell Hugh, you were just hoping it would work out that way, you couldn't have been sure?' '

Aha, but if the pilot's compass had an eastern deviation of, say, twenty degrees? And if the observer's instrument had lost its liquid? Surely that would make life a bit difficult?' Paul Wilson said nothing. Opening a third bottle of brandy he filled Hugh's glass to the brim.

'Drink up 'C' you talk too much and besides , we didn't understand any of that horseshit did we Bernie?'

For the past three days Bill had worked long hours on the line. Bad weather had cancelled flying, so all three flights welcomed an opportunity to bring their machines up to scratch. Most of 'A' Flight's quirks had been damaged during the past week, and some required considerable attention, including the two new BEs, which had been badly rigged. Having patched up 1005, Dad gave him 1085.

'She's your new quirk Proctor. Captain Wilson wants you to fly with him, so I thought you may as well look after her.'

On the 16th the weather cleared sufficiently for Captain Wilson to take 1085 up on a test flight. To his delight she performed perfectly. There was a CP later that afternoon then, on the following morning, they flew an urgent photo-mission between Loos and La Bassée. Once again the Fokkers were there, but a flight of the new DH2s were waiting and soon chased them off. Bill was impressed when Paul Wilson invited him to see the product of their handiwork later that afternoon. The seventeen exposed plates had been developed and printed in the squadron's mobile darkroom and were now displayed, in an overlapping line, along a narrow trestle table. Captain Porter was there, and even showed him how to use a mirror stereoscope so that a pair of prints with overlapping detail could be viewed in three-dimensions! The effect was outstanding! With two sets of prints already on their way to Wing HQ by dispatch rider, the photographers were now making enlarged prints to create photo-maps for future artillery shoots. Bill could see how important their photographic work must be and resolved to take a greater interest in the photographers' work.

In the late afternoon of the 18th, Major Wells called a meeting of all aircrew, the three line chiefs and the SNCOs responsible for photography, wireless, instruments and armament. He told them of the 1st Army's coming attack in the Loos area and 4 Sqdn's supporting role. This was to be the first major British offensive since the war had started, and Tim Wells knew they could expect heavy casualties on the ground *and* in the air.

On the 21st September in good weather, the battle of Loos started with a preliminary bombardment. With other units, 4 Sqdn was busy with artillery co-operation then, on the 23rd, they switched to bombing. By the 24th it was raining and continued to rain on the 25th when the infantry went over the top. Bill was flying on an artillery shoot when the main attack started and could clearly see the British gas shells exploding. To his horror he saw the wind shift, returning the gas over our own trenches. God! What a mess – he knew nothing of gas except that it was a terrible and unpredictable weapon, and that their issue gas masks were not a complete protection, particularly against mustard gas. He silently thanked God he wasn't in the PBI.

After four days the offensive got stuck. The British troops dug in, and things were back to normal; trench warfare and shelling. Bombing continued as did CPs, shoots and photography. By the 20th October the offensive had all but petered out. The scout squadrons had covered them well enough and although they lost a number of crews and machines it was mercifully less than expected.

Bill got on well with Captain Wilson who, in turn, relied on his young observer and came to depend on him for many tasks. Now capable of sending at six words per minute and approaching this figure in receiving, Bill's Morse was getting better all the time. But his chief advantage, especially recognised by Paul Wilson, was his excellent eyesight. It was rare for them to be caught napping by the slim, almost invisible Eindekkers, and for this his pilot was duly grateful.

By mid-November Bill, in common with all other A/M and NCO observers, was granted authority to wear the 'O' badge. But more importantly, he was promoted to Corporal on the 19th November, with a pay increase of a shilling a day. With flying pay this now realised nine shillings a day, and Bill's thoughts turned to home leave and Alice.

'Sorry Proctor. No chance of any home leave for a while. Wing have a policy of allowing flyers ten days home leave only after they have served six months flying, so you have some time to go yet.' Although everything he said was true, Captain Paul Wilson would never have let Bill go at this time. With the Loos offensive now over, 4 Sqdn had been given a large section of the front for photographic work, and as the Fokkers were still about he was keen not to lose Bill until the DH2s had the cleared the skies of them. Bill hadn't really expected to get home leave, but he'd promised Alice he would apply, and he knew that only the flyers could expect it anyway. The AMs never got any leave, not even the married ones, except on compassionate grounds, even so he couldn't remember anyone grousing about it.

Bill wrote to Alice that night, telling her that there was no hope of getting leave for about three to four months. He didn't say much about the Loos battle, or his part in the offensive; it was in the newspapers anyway. But for the first time, he felt he could write freely. Paul Wilson had given him a 'green envelope' which meant that it wouldn't be opened or censored, so he made the most of it. They were of limited issue and only given sparingly, mostly to the married chaps. Bill felt free to express himself more clearly, and hinted strongly they could perhaps get engaged. In expressing his love, clearly and without inhibitions, he wrote with a passion and intimacy he could never express knowing his words would be seen by a stranger.

The following day he received his first parcel from home and although it had taken three weeks to reach him it was still intact and unspoilt. Eileen had baked him a large fruit cake which, thanks to its sealed tin, was still as fresh as the day it was made. There was a tin of toffees, and from Maggie a soggy ginger cake with a large hole in its centre. There was a tin of humbugs and some tins of fruit and a box of caramels from Jane. With each gift there was a letter – the longest from Jane. As usual, Maggie's was full of village gossip and in return she wanted to know everything Jane had said in her letter. As he read Maggie's letter Bill's eyes filled with tears. It was as though he had not seen his family for years and he missed them terribly. Then he was laughing as Maggie explained in fine detail every step of her ginger cake production – her own recipe! He was still trying to remove the sticky substance from his mouth and fingers as Ted entered the tent.

'Cake! Come on Bill let's have some! Charlie, get a billy of tea quick. Our Corporal's got cake – tons of it!'

To Bill's utter amazement they thought Maggie's ginger cake was some kind of Yorkshire delicacy – it was gone in no time. His mother's letter, with a note from Dad, was full of concern for him, he knew he would have to ease her fears. But this letter was earlier than the one he had from her last week and he'd answered that. She was knitting him a thick pullover, when would he home to try it on? She spoke much of the trenches and possibly imagined him there, he would have to tell her how beautiful it was to fly; it wouldn't be all lies he thought. Eileen's news was of Harrogate, where she worked, and how she could earn much more in a munition factory. But there were no munition factories, not in the posh Spa town at least. She would have to go to Leeds, or York, to make munition money. She had been to a dance in the Queen's Hotel and had danced most of the night with an Artillery Officer, but it came to nothing – he was posted to France. Bill smiled as he thought of the ribbing she must have received from Maggie.

As the humbugs were passed around the tent Bill started on Jane's letter. The back of the envelope had two large crosses – kisses, which didn't go unnoticed among the group.

'Who's the girl friend then Bill?' Charlie Train couldn't help commenting as he passed him his tea.

'That's from Yorkshire – I thought your Alice was in Farnborough?'

Bill was in too good a humour to be angered by the question. 'Oh Jane isn't a girl friend, she's just a friend of the family – known her since we were kids.'

Charlie Train winked, 'So that's why she sends kisses on the envelope, eh – come off it Proctor you're sparking two of 'em you randy bugger!'

Bill said nothing; he'd just got to the part where Jane said she loved him – always had, ever since they had left school. It wasn't the letter of a schoolgirl, although only sixteen she had written a mature and genuine love letter and he felt humbled. Had he led her on, that day on leave? Her letter moved him deeply, he couldn't reciprocate her love, he'd never felt that way about her – but her letter moved him just the same. Even Alice never wrote to him in such a way. As he went to another page a photograph dropped out. Ted picked it up.

'Boy oh boy! Our good corporal knows how to pick 'em look at this!' Charlie Train whistled, 'Pure jail bait this Bill – better take care my son!' Bill was the last to see it as the snapshot was passed around the tent. She had enclosed a photograph of herself, simple and honest, she looked a picture, smiling directly into the lens.

'You're a lucky fella Bill. She's lovely and I'm bloody envious!' He took the photo from Ted and put it his tunic pocket with hardly more than a glance. Later, he would look at it later, and finish her letter too. He would have to write something, but what? He knew he could never hurt her.

The month passed with little flying for 'A' ' Flight. The weather was against photography and 'B' Flight took most of the CPs delegated to 4 Sqdn. A fresh batch of lightweight wireless sets had arrived and all of A's quirks were being fitted with them. As a result both 'A' and 'C' Flights combined their efforts in fitting up the aircraft and training the crews. By the 10th December Bill was spending much of his time practising Morse, helping with the installations and flying with Tom Bolton.

'I'm sure you could handle a quirk Bill! If you can fly an Avro you can easily cope with a BE and you *can* handle the Avro my lad.' Tom Bolton was confident his young prodigy could fly a quirk without difficulty but, unlike the Avro, they were not fitted with dual controls and as he explained, 'Anything could happen in this game Bill and if we piled up with you in the rear cockpit we'd both be for the high jump!'

Bill could see Tom was hoping to see Simone, but as they were restricted to the circuit it wasn't possible. And although he wasn't unduly concerned about Tom's drinking, he was amazed Tom managed to hide it from Hugh Porter, despite the aura of strong peppermint surrounding him.

On the 19th, Bill was called to Hugh Porter's office. 'Now young Proctor, how are you getting along with the Morse code eh?'

Bill assured him he was making progress, 'Sgt Bolton says I'm sending at about 8 words per minute sir, but my receiving is still only around six.' The 'C' Flight Commander put an arm about his shoulder. 'That's good enough lad, but keep it up. I hope to be able to report you as fully capable with Morse by the end of the month, can you do that?' Bill was confident he could. 'You've completed a number of shoots now Proctor, so you must know the pilot has his hands full – yes? Mr Wells and I think the answer is for 'A' Flight to specialise in shoots, with all their observers up to scratch in tapping out messages. Naturally this will require some changes in crews, but I hope we shall have enough fully trained, that is wireless-qualified, observers by the end of January. Wing are letting us off lightly until we can achieve this status, then we shall move all of 'A' Flight's sets and keys to the front cockpit of their quirks. By the way, how do you like flying with Sgt Bolton?'

Bill showed his surprise. 'We get on fine sir, he's a great pilot and teaches me all the time.'

Hugh Porter nodded his head. 'Yes he is, but he's had a hard time you know, a lot of strain, been flying without a break far too long. Problem is he doesn't take home leave when he's offered it – keen type eh? Anyway, between ourselves I want you to look after an observer just arrived from Blighty. He's a wireless officer and will be here for a couple of months to qualify for his observer's badge. We get his help in exchange, good idea really. Come and meet him, he knows you I think.'

As they moved to the briefing tent Bill suspected who he was about to meet.

'Gerry! I mean Sir! Sir Gerry in fact!' Bill flung up a quivering salute as Hugh Porter laughed and left them alone. As they shook hands the two friends playfully punched each other in the chest.

'God a bloody officer – how could you stoop so bloody low!'

'And you, an observer no less. Whatever happened to the oil-stained devotee of engineering eh?' Gerry gazed at Bill's 'O' badge. *That* is why I'm here Bill, I need to qualify over here, then I can get a pilot's course.'

Bill assured him that it wasn't going to be difficult, and told Gerry of his flying experience with Tom Bolton. 'I can fly the Avro quite well, and maybe I'll go to England later next year for a pilot's course, might even beat you to it old son!' They discussed everything that had passed since they last saw each other, hardly believing so much could have happened in such a short time. Within twenty minutes they had caught up with each other's service life.

'I hear we are going to work together Gerry. You, Tom Bolton and me! You'll like Tom he's a great chap.'

Gerry frowned a little. 'We shall have to take care Bill, I mean me being an officer. It can't be like old times now. I'll be in the officers' mess too, so we won't see much of each other outside of office hours shall we?'

Bill thought a while. 'We can always meet here – you can keep me going with Morse and wireless, and photography for that matter. The C/O is a splendid type, all the Flight Commanders are too; we don't stand on ceremony much here Gerry.'

'From what Captain Porter has been saying I gather you are well thought of here Bill! He tells me you have done a splendid job over the lines too.' Gerry paused for a moment, there was a change in Bill that he couldn't really describe. He looked the same, a little older perhaps, but there was something else; a look of confidence about him. He'd grown somehow, and Gerry was jealous of his friend's experience. 'Are you ever scared Bill, over the lines I mean?'

Bill rubbed his chin, a thoughtful expression on his open face. 'Not been long enough at this game to get twitchy yet Gerry. But no, strange to tell, I've never been scared.' Bill laughed, 'My pals say I'm too stupid, but to be honest I think I get too interested in what I'm doing. Anyway, my drivers have always taken care of me.' Bill told the story of his crash with Len Coates. 'It's best not to know what's happening Gerry, like it was when Len and me crashed; we're all scared of going down in

184

a 'flamer' of course, but it doesn't help to dwell on things. I think how bad it is for the poor bloody infantry and realise how lucky I am – Loos was bloody murder for our PBI and all I did was watch them being mowed down!'

When Bill returned to his tent that evening he found a parcel from Alice. It was a Christmas parcel, containing a small iced cake decorated with the letters RFC surrounding an 'O' badge. There were biscuits, socks and a thick woollen scarf which Alice had been knitting for the past two months. But most of all there was a card, and a letter expressing her love and how much she missed him at this time. He wrote back to her without delay, telling her of Gerry's visit and hopes for leave in April of the following year.

On Christmas Eve Gerry took his first flight with Tom Bolton. Using the now standard lightweight set, his first task was to transmit signals at a rate of 8 words per minute while flying at four thousand feet in one of 'A' Flight's quirks. As part of this exercise Bill's task was to receive the signals in the sqdn wireless shed, and although he could only receive at 6 wpm, this rate was not uncommon among many of the new artillery gun crews and would indicate which parts of a message could be coded to improve its understanding at poor reception rates.

A significant part of 2nd Lt. G. Hardcastle's detachment was to find the useful limits of wireless aircraft transmissions, bearing in mind the known problems of interference, background noise and enemy jamming. Whereas the clock-code system was efficient, wireless telegraphy was still in its infancy and a single WT aircraft could only cover a few hundred yards of the front. It was Gerry's task to gain practical experience that could improve squadron signalling techniques.

By midday heavy clouds and sleet ended further operations. Nevertheless, Gerry was pleased with his first flight at the front, even though visibility had been too poor to see much of the terrain. The team then spent that afternoon analysing the messages Bill had recorded. Bill had done reasonably well, reception had been clear, and the content of each message was generally preserved.

'Not bad Corporal, not bad at all. I know my messages were very short, but you've managed very well. Some words are missing of course, and some are not exact, but the meaning is still there, and that's important! How did you do that?' Bill studied his notes, the ones that contained the actual words he'd jotted down from the received Morse, then turned to answer Gerry's question.

'Bit of a dog's dinner really, Gerry!' One look at his friend's face was warning enough. 'Sorry sir, I mean my reception wasn't accurate sir!' Hugh Porter took a sidelong glance at Tom Bolton, covering a smile with a hand, but his eyes were full of mirth. Embarrassed, Bill continued, pointing out the columns of Morse on the message pad. 'As you can see, I was ready for your stand-by 'A', then the DE before your call sign GH. Then I recorded the 'break sign' BT … here! And I waited for the text starting here! When I became confused with a letter, usually in the middle of a word, I just waited for the word space, you know, the dit dit, dit dit signal, then started again with the next word. I took special precautions to memorise the 'end of message' AR signal, to make sure I never confused individual messages. Sometimes I just guessed at a letter I was unsure about and substituted one that made sense.

It was a good start to the experiments and Hugh Porter was particularly pleased.

'Well gentlemen, I think we've got off to a good start. Unfortunately the weather looks like it could be set-in for Christmas thank God! So I'll leave further analysis to you and Cpl Proctor, Mr Hardcastle. But don't work too hard, it's Christmas Day tomorrow and in keeping with our new-found traditions, all officers and Senior NCOs will need to prepare for serving Christmas dinner tomorrow. Which reminds me Sergeant Bolton, could you inform all the 'C' Flight Senior NCOs that I would like to see them at 9.30 ack-emma. I'm sure you will have some ideas among you, but I want 'C' Flight to best those dull buggers in 'A' and 'B' when it comes to style! I have it from the C/O that we are not committed to anything from Wing tomorrow, and the Jerries like Christmas too, so what with the weather and all, I'm sure there will be no flying.'

As Tom Bolton turned to go, Bill reached for a box under the map table.

'Hold on there Tom, I thought we could have some tea and cake?' He looked at Hugh Porter. 'With your permission sir?'

Captain Porter reached for his mug. 'That's very good of you Bill, and a Christmas cake to boot! It seems a pity to spoil the RFC decoration though – from your mother?'

Bill couldn't disguise the pride in his voice, 'From my girl sir!' It wasn't a large cake, but it was sufficient for the four of them, and with a generous helping of whisky contributed by Hugh it made for a pleasant start to the festive season, their first in France.

The weather was kind to them that Christmas. It rained steadily for eight days and allowed the squadron a well-earned rest on a quiet front. Christmas Day was an eye opener for Bill; dinner in the airmen's mess was turkey, stuffing, bacon, sausages and greens, followed by the traditional pudding and mince pies. Two barrels of English beer were on hand as were numerous bottles of French wine. But best of all, the men were served by their Senior NCOs and all the officers, including the Flight Commanders and Major Wells. A great deal of planning had gone into the event, with all the 'servers' competing for first prize for the most outrageous costume. There were numerous 'ladies of the night', a Napoleon, three Kaisers, Lloyd George, an assortment of Arabs and numerous other characters, many of them well-known comedy artists such as Bernie Saul's 'Harry Tate'. The C/O came as an ack-emma, complete with oil rag, dirty face, tool bag and overalls. Without a doubt the most popular figure in the entire procession, Tim Wells received first prize – a bottle of whisky and a plaque contributed by all three flights. Second prize went to Tom Bolton dressed as a French waiter, complete with a long droopy moustache. He held onto his tray with admirable skill, particularly since he was very obviously drunk.

It was Ralph Downes who told them that the turkeys, beer and wine had come from contributions taken in both the Sgts' Mess and the Officers' Mess.

Bill saw little of Gerry except on those evenings when they worked together with the Morse code. Bill's Morse was getting better and with Gerry's help he could now send and receive at 8 wpm. In exchange Bill took Gerry over local maps and detailed aerial photographs of the front. On the 3rd January 1916 the squadron resumed flying in earnest. Although their sector was reasonably quiet, they were still required over the Lens area for photography and on shoots east of Arras. Bill did a photographic flight with Lt. Wilson on the 6th, then on the 10th he joined with Tom Bolton to do a shoot using one of 'A' Flight quirks. This time Bill was to work the wireless key from the front cockpit, while Gerry checked reception at the guns of the 49th Field Artillery regiment. This was both a normal shoot and an exercise, but it had a special significance which 4th Army were particularly concerned about.

During the recent Loos offensive, forward elements of British infantry made frequent complaints concerning supporting shellfire. Evidently a number of the 49th's shells had fallen short, with numerous casualties, many of them fatal. As a result the PBI of the 4th Army now called the 49th the 48½th, and something had to be done!

There were questions of dud ammunition, poor sighting, inaccurate spotting and inadequate corrections made from the spotting aircraft's signals, and it was the latter suggestion that had put Gerry into the 49th's wireless hut monitoring their reception.

Tom flew over the 49th's battery first, checking the large white panels which indicated their state of readiness, then spent some time getting the quirk into a suitable position over the target area. With a hundred feet of copper wire trailing behind them it was necessary to place themselves in such a position that they could see each shell burst with accuracy. But while they were doing this they were also attracting Jerry Archie.

This was Bill's first time with the wireless key in a quirk; he hoped the transmissions would be clear as he sent A, DE and his call sign BP – then waited for the first shell. It came within thirty seconds, but was easily F2. He sent BT... dah dit dit dit dah, then his message ... dit dit dah dit dit dit dah dah dah. The following shell came in at B5, Bill sent again. The shells were now undershooting at C7 when Tom signalled Bill to transmit a 'break'. He had to gain height, the Jerries were getting their range and he knew that with a cloud ceiling at 4500 feet, it wouldn't be long before they found him again. Levelling off and flying in the opposite direction Tom indicated to start again. Bill sent A, DE, BP and waited for the next shell. It took a minute or so, but was definitely an improvement, an A8!

A series of archie shells rocked the fragile BE, and ragged holes appeared in the upper plane above Bill's head as they flew into a stench of black oily bursts. Spent shrapnel rattled off metal and canvas as Tom chopped the throttle and dipped the nose of the quirk. Bill sent AA 'anti-aircraft guns' then CI, they were returning to base.

Tom landed at St. Pol. He needed to know the extent of damage inflicted by the Boche; that was an excuse – he knew the quirk was in good enough condition to reach Bertangles. But he also needed to telephone Gerry to confirm they had received the final shell observation, an A8. Gerry called it a day, he had enough to work on for the time being.

Bill scrounged some tape and fabric to patch the upper plane; there were numerous other holes, but they could be attended to back at Bertangles. He checked the engine, no obvious hits or oil leaks that he could see, they had been lucky. As soon as Tom returned they refuelled the quirk for their return to base.

'Go on! Surprise me, tell me you're not going to fly to some farm we know near here!' Tom took a swig from his flask before answering.

'It's been some time Bill, and little Tommy needs his new year breaking in! But it's also a chance for you to fly the quirk if you want?'

Bill raised his eyebrows. 'Christ Tom, I'm keen, but what if ... ?'

Tom slapped him on the back. 'One take-off and one landing –

solo. I'll wave you off if you don't get the landing pattern right, the quirk is easy Bill, it flies itself as you know. If you can fly an Avro you can piss a quirk! Anyhow, we have bags of time, your pal's finished for the day and no one knows how long it took us to check the quirk, even to an essential forced landing if necessary. Come to think of it, my little friend tells me it is *very* necessary!'

As they flew back to Bertangles, Bill could hardly believe how easy it was to fly the quirk. Certainly the take-off was very easy, the BE2c just lifted off by itself. And although Tom had waved-off his first landing approach he got it right the second time. He turned around to look at him, he was certainly very happy, the randy old bugger! Although Bill was perfectly at ease with his pilot's drinking, he couldn't help noticing it was getting heavier, but it never affected his flying ability, indeed he even flew better after a few drinks – or so it seemed. Sergeant Bolton was a natural pilot; everyone said so, and he knew he was in safe hands providing Tom never passed out!

By the end of the month, Gerry had completed three of his own shoots with Tom Bolton and was now wearing the 'O' badge. Hugh Porter was pleased with their results. Gerry had cleared the 49th battery from any wireless problems and it seemed that their shortfalls were due to a bad batch of shells. Bill saw even less of his friend as he flew CPs and shoots with Paul Wilson. On the tenth of February the skies cleared sufficiently for a maximum photographic effort. The entire wing was fully engaged in acquiring vertical and oblique photographs as 3rd Army prepared new maps of the front line. Since Gerry was the only photographic officer on the squadron Tim Wells made full use of him, and even sent him on two photo-flights with Tom Bolton.

By now the Fokkers were in considerable force, E2s and E3s, some with twin Spandaus. But General Trenchard had decreed that all recce aircraft were to be escorted by at least three fighting machines, and the underpowered Fokkers were beginning to lose to ever-increasing numbers of DH2 and FE2b scouts. Nevertheless, the BE observers still had to be on constant guard, and on Gerry's last mission with 4 Sqdn he and Tom had considerable difficulty in escaping the attention of two E3s intent on their destruction. Bill was waiting for them as their overdue quirk taxied into 'C' Flight's lines. Tom looked drawn and deadly tired as he dismounted, but managed to joke about their ordeal then, seeing Hugh Porter approach he swiftly departed 'for a warm bath' leaving a strong smell of brandy in his wake. Gerry was deathly white, even beneath the grime of cordite powder and oil, leaning against the tail he was violently sick, and dismissed Bill's attention with a wave.

189

On the following morning Bill was called into Hugh Porter's tent.

'Stand at ease Corporal. I'm afraid this has to be a bit official, but there it is!' Captain Porter looked decidedly uncomfortable as he asked: 'You have flown about 32 hours with Sergeant Bolton I think?' Bill said he had. 'During this time have you always felt Sgt Bolton to be in complete control of his machine?'

On this subject Bill was very confident. 'He is a magnificent pilot sir – I know of no one better,'

Hugh Porter found it difficult to say, but it had to be done. 'Have you ever known Sgt Bolton to drink alcohol while flying?' They both knew it was a serious military offence and they both knew it to be true!

Bill didn't even hesitate with his answer. 'Never Sir!'

'Sit down Corporal.' As Bill sat in the camp chair, Hugh Porter poured them both a drink of coffee from a thermos flask. About twenty per cent of the contents were brandy thought Bill, gasping as it caught in his throat. 'I won't have any of my crews drinking on duty. I'm very hot about that as everyone knows.' There wasn't a trace of humour on Captain Porter's face as Bill, tears streaming down his own, strained to keep himself from laughing. 'You see I've had a report, an official report, which suggests that Sgt Bolton has been drinking while flying! Now we know, that is you and I know, that Sgt Bolton is under a great strain – far too much flying! I've therefore grounded him for two weeks with a medical inspection to follow. So on your evidence Corporal we can safely say that the originator of this report was mistaken right?'

Bill stood up. 'Yes sir, the report is completely groundless, Sir!'

Hugh Porter returned the salute. 'Now, while you finish your coffee Corporal, I would like you to write those very words on the bottom of this report, sign it, then return to work!'

As Bill returned to 'A' Flight he was in little doubt who had informed on Tom. It wasn't difficult to recognise Gerry's writing after all! No doubt he considered it his duty, but it was obvious Captain Porter thought differently. No doubt the C/O knew about it as well. Poor old Gerry, he did get a fright on that last mission!

On the 27th of February, Gerry received orders to return to England. He was glad to be going, for it seemed that his report on Sergeant Bolton had fallen on stony ground, and worse, he was sure most of the pilots in the mess were intentionally avoiding him.

Since his last flight, with Bolton, Gerry had spent most of his time with the 49th FA and the 35th Heavy Battery. Whereas he wasn't fully accepted by 4 Squadron, he knew his work with the guns had been appreciated. Although the Signal Service of the Royal Engineers were doing excellent work he noticed that most of the field batteries' wireless aerials were badly positioned with respect to receiving signals from spotting aircraft. It was a constant problem. The range of the small airborne Sterling sets was never great, and even with aerials up to 150 feet in length reception was far from ideal. Gerry had written a report to 3rd Army HQ suggesting that an RFC wireless fitter should be attached to each battery with responsibility for aerial maintenance and positioning of aerials. Evidently his report had been accepted by 3rd Wing, and he'd been given to understand that Wing HQ had sent a commendation to his own unit in England. It could mean promotion of course, and now he had his flying badge, he had good reason to be pleased with himself and the hell with 4 Squadron!

Gerry called on Bill as he was working on 1085. 'Sorry I've not seen much of you Bill, but I know you must understand the difficulty. I go back to England tomorrow morning; I wish we could have some time together, say in Amiens but...' Bill had noticed his fellow ack-emmas moving away as Gerry Hardcastle approached. The entire squadron knew of his report concerning Tom Bolton.

'I quite understand Gerry, besides I imagine you won't have much time – packing and the like.'

'Thanks for all your help Bill, perhaps we shall see each other in Blighty when you get over on leave?'

Bill smiled. 'Providing the Jerries don't make a fuss – I'm due in April. Shall I reach you directly or send letters through your home address?' Gerry suggested the latter, but not the reason. He liked Bill, but was beginning to find his friendship an embarrassment, it was time to dissolve it - easy enough in wartime! 'Could you take a letter to England for me Gerry? It's for Alice. I'll have it ready for you by the morning. Letters are a bit slow at present and as this is rather private I would feel easier if it wasn't opened. I had a letter from her just this morning, it's my birthday on March 2nd, so it would be nice if she had my reply sooner than she would expect. If you could post it in London I'd be grateful.' Gerry agreed, and suggested they meet at the sqdn office at 10 ack-emma.

At 10 o'clock the following morning Bill presented himself at the sqdn office. His bulky letter to Alice also included a silk scarf he had purchased when he had visited Amiens some weeks ago. He chatted to Ralph Downes as he waited for Gerry who was now being interviewed by Major Wells.

'Thank you for your work with 'C' Flight Mr Hardcastle. I'm told you have made quite an impression up at Wing! For our part I can

191

assure you that your attachment has been most useful. I must also tell you that no further action has been taken concerning your report on Sergeant Bolton. Your evidence is not substantiated and we have no complaints from anyone else who flies with him. Rather than pursue this unpleasant business I have decided to let it go, do you have anything further to say?'

Gerry Hardcastle knew his own front-line experience was too shallow to allow him to press further. He also knew that Tom Bolton could report on his own poor defence of the quirk when attacked by the Fokkers. Best to forget it!

'I could have been mistaken sir!' Tim Wells was pleased, and dismissed Gerry with a smile and a handshake.

Bill walked with his friend to the tender waiting to take him to the Amiens railhead. 'Here's the letter Gerry. I'd better give you some money, it's a bit heavy.' Gerry felt a pang of sorrow for him, thanking God for his commission and a return to England.

'By no means Bill, anyway my orders are to go to Farnborough first. I have to report to the Wireless School at South camp and give a lecture; not sure how long I will be there, a day or two at least. So I can take it to your girl by hand – I'm sure she would like a full report on how you are.'

Bill was delighted. 'Are you sure Gerry? That's very good of you, I've spoken about you to Alice many times, so she will be very happy to see you. Naturally I would never have asked you to go out of your way, but Guildford isn't more than a few miles from Farnborough as you know.'

It was ten days later when Bill received his next letter from Alice. Gerry had called on the evening of the 3rd, the day after his birthday, and her mother had been deeply impressed. She thanked him for the scarf and hoped he would be able to get leave next month. Alice appeared to like Gerry, and said she was glad he had such a nice friend, she also said he looked very smart and what a pity he didn't have such a nice uniform as Gerry's, perhaps he should become an officer too! Bill laughed, he could just imagine how impressed Jean Webb would be when Gerry knocked on the door!

By the middle of the month Bill was flying with Tom Bolton again. They were taking an Avro for a wireless check with a battery near Lens, and Bill was to operate the key. Two weeks free of flying had certainly made a difference to Tom's appearance, he looked better and had even gained weight. Evidently his 'grounding' had been semi-official leave, and he'd made the most of it by spending a week with Simone.

'God, but it's great to be flying again Bill – I miss it when I'm not in the air. It's part of me now!'

He turned to face Bill as they prepared to enter the quirk. 'Give me a couple of days over the lines, then I'll be scared shitless again, like normal!'

Bill stared at him. 'Don't give me that you old bugger, I have *never* seen you scared! Pissed yes! But never scared.'

'I'm waiting for a 'Blighty one' Bill. One that'll ground me for good, but keep me fit enough to give Simone a houseful of kids. I've asked her to marry me and she said yes! But I've told her I won't, can't stop flying!' Bill was overjoyed, his pleasure obvious. 'You're to be best man Bill, Simone say's she's going to find you a French girl too.' They shook hands before Bill helped Tom into the rear cockpit.

'Nice of her Tom, but I've got my girl in Blighty, remember? But I'll try my best to get you in line for a bad ankle wound, something like that should do it, in fact if I just lower the sights a bit I could do it myself. Cost you a bit though!' They laughed, and as Bill made for the propeller Tom put a hand on his shoulder.

'You're wrong lad, I *am* scared you know. What I can never understand is *you*. I don't think you know what it is to be scared. You seem to enjoy the danger – like it was all a game!'

Bill pondered on the thought, 'I think I'm a bit odd Tom – either that or just bloody stupid. But I haven't had your experience either, there's time yet I suppose. The strange part is that I manage to keep quite cool as though I'm watching it all happen to somebody else. Sometimes I get the scare about an hour after we've landed – a kind of delayed reaction!'

As the months went by and the weather improved there was an increasing demand for photography. There were bombing raids too, some of them flown solo. When loaded with two 112 lb bombs the BE2c was overweight and the observer had to be left behind. As Flight Commander, Captain Wilson had to lead these flights and Bill either worked on the line or flew with Tom.

He had another letter from Alice on the 21st, she seemed to be in a hurry, only one page this time. She said she was very busy helping in the shop, and that Gerry had been round again – her mother had invited him for dinner, before he left for London. There was a letter from Maggie too, it made him miss the dales; he would have to see about leave in a week or two he thought.

On the fifth of April Bill applied for leave.

'Sorry Proctor, all of 3 Wing are denied leave until further notice.'

Paul Wilson was truly sorry; he remembered promising his observer leave as soon as he qualified with enough time at the front. That time had come and now here he was having to turn him down. 'If it's any consolation Proctor you are not alone, it's the same for everyone including me!'

From her last letter Alice seemed to be expecting him either this week or next. Now he would have to tell her he didn't even know when he would be home! He wrote to her that night, very concerned. Her last letter seemed a bit distant – there wasn't the same fun in her words and he was worried.

'Standbys! I'm bloody well fed up with them Bill. Do you know I've not seen my Simone for two weeks now; it's not as though were flying north anymore either. South of Bapaume that's us, the bloody Somme, swampy old Somme, that's all we see these days. Then this… this bloody standby nonsense, hanging about just in case some old fart at Wing wants us to fly!' They were waiting at the edge of the field, their Avro turned into wind and ready for take-off; waiting for a Very light signal that would send them over their designated sector of the Somme; waiting to fly a CP over a quiet area of the front.

Tom had already broken into his reserve flask of brandy and had even managed to get Bill to join him in a swig. 'Let's make a break into Amiens tonight Bill, what do you say? About time we threw a few down together!' Bill agreed; they were not due for duty until the following pip-emma anyway.

Already quite merry Bill and Tom took a tender into Amiens that night. 'Were it not for my great love for my gorgeous Simone I would let my evil little Tommy have his wicked way with that one Billy boy!' Tom pointed to a dark-haired, dark-eyed young girl sat on her own in the corner of the estaminet. Bill tried to focus on the designated target.

'Need my goggles on mon Sergeant! Must be all this gun smoke, can't see a bloody thing!' Tom picked his companion up and helped him over to the girl, where Bill promptly fell over a chair. 'Why don't you bloody well fly straight you drunken sot?' He put an arm around her as Tom went for another bottle. 'Alice! My Alice – sorry love, couldn't get leave … but you love me … don't you love?'

She was nineteen and her broken English good enough to ply her profession with the young aviators that came to the estaminet. 'I am Yvonne, what are you?'

Bill tried to keep her in focus. 'Yvonne? You are not Alice are you?' As Tom returned Bill fell aside and was violently sick. With great humour Tom cleaned up his friend as best he could while Yvonne went to the kitchen. She returned with a damp towel, a mop and a bucket, happy to help with the cleansing as they chatted in French. Tom apologising and shared his bottle with her while Bill dozed.

Still no word from Alice, Bill had written six letters to her in the last sixteen days and hadn't heard from her at all. Tom had started photographic work again, so Bill returned to flying with Lt. Wilson, mostly artillery shoots and CPs across the Bapaume salient. Tom was happier now and managed to see Simone by scrounging rides with a dispatch rider who did regular runs up the Amiens to St. Pol road. Bill had never known such depression, and while he suspected the usual army mail problem he had a nagging thought there could be something else. Change! It was always the same. Just as he thought he had everything settled the world seemed to change about him. Tom was a great help and the two of them managed to get into their favourite estaminet at least twice a week. Bill looked for the pretty young girl he'd met on his first visit, not sure if he would recognise her even if she was there and felt immediately guilty. Perhaps Alice was ill, maybe her mother didn't have his address. The pain wouldn't go away.

'Do you feel fit to fly Proctor?' Paul Wilson was a little concerned about his observer. If he didn't know better he could swear the young airman was suffering a hangover, most likely a cold or even the flu?

'No sir, I feel fine, just a bit of a cold coming on I think.' Bill's thoughts were elsewhere and his stomach was on another planet. He'd spent most of the night over a latrine and now there was nothing left to come up. But at least he'd found a solution, he would write to Sam! Good old Sam, he would ask him to visit Alice in the shop. Sam would find out, whatever it was.

'Did you see that Fokker above us Proctor? About two thousand above and behind us?' They had just landed and Paul Wilson was waiting as Bill climbed out of the quirk.

'No sir, I never saw any Hun machines. Not one!'

Captain Wilson wasn't worried, the Fokker was far enough away and his observer could easily miss the slim profile of an Eindekker in that position. 'He was there right enough. But I think you could be expecting a cold lad, better take the next two days off. Go sick if you need to, I'll fix things with Dad Owens.' Bill mumbled his thanks, maybe he *was* getting a cold!

Depressed and hung over, Bill slowly trekked back to his tent. He really hadn't seen the Fokker, but all he needed now was sleep. As he opened up the tent flap he could see it – lying on his blanket pile. The square blue envelope gave it away, it was from Alice!

Throwing his leathers on the cot he took the letter in both hands then, slipping his mess knife through the envelope, fell against the blankets to read her letter – at last!

Guildford,
18th April, 1916.

Dear Bill,

I'm so sorry you have not heard from me for the past two weeks and more. But I have had a terrible time these past weeks. I don't know how to say what I have to tell you. Dear Bill, I know you will hate me, but it's for the best, please believe me when I say that.

I cannot marry you Billy. I know you say you love me, and I have always been very fond of you. But, as my mother has often said, we do not really know each other well enough to consider marriage. I think it would have been impossible for me to turn you down if I had not met Gerry. But I did, and we are very much in love. Oh Bill, please, please do not blame Gerry. I know you will never forgive me, but please don't blame him. I love him, so help me, I love him so much.

I feel so wretched, it has taken all my courage to write this letter. I wish you all the luck in the world and I know you will meet a far better girl.

Please do not write to me – I couldn't bear that, and could never read another letter from you. Forgive me.

Alice.

He read the letter again and again. The world had changed once more, spinning this time. Would it never stop! Tears welled in his eyes, but they wouldn't come. He could hear his heart and was sweating cold. Voices at the door of the tent.

'Hey Bill! Got your letter I see.'

He dashed for the door, clutching the letter in one hand his heavy flying coat in the other.

'Bloody 'ell.' Ralph Downes gasped as Charlie Train joined him at the tent flap. 'Dose of the shits I think, either that or a 'Dear John'.'

Bill kept running. Finally he stopped at the far end of the field – exhausted. Strange aeroplanes surrounded him – monoplanes. He recognised the Morane scouts and knew he was in the lines of their French neighbours and another world! He turned and walked down the edge of the French camp – he was out of bounds.

'Hey, Tommy – Amiens?' Bill couldn't really remember getting on the French lorry, but when he recognised his surroundings in Amiens he signalled his companions to drop him off. He didn't have a pass, but he had his wallet and the estaminet was close. It was too early for the normal MP patrols anyway.

As he entered the door he felt naked. This was the first time he'd been here without Tom. He took three deep breaths. Fuck it! Corporal W.C. Proctor was going to get well and truly pissed tonight! As his eyes adapted to the dimly lit interior he could see there was only two others in the L-shaped room, and as he threw his coat onto an empty table he noticed the waiter approaching.

The wine helped. Bill had just ordered his second bottle of vin blanc and was starting another round of self-pity, recrimination and anger when Tom appeared at the table.

'Your pals told me! Did you know they followed you to the Moranes?' Bill didn't speak. 'They saw you get aboard the frog lorry to the city, then came to see me. I guessed you might be here.' Tom went to the bar and ordered his own bottle. 'Was it the letter from Alice?' As Bill's anger flared Tom quickly added, 'A squadron is a very small family, everybody knows everything about you – it's just that – like all families we tend to worry about each other; we care! Christ do you think I don't know everyone on the squadron knows I'm scared to fly over the lines? Of course I know. I know they take care of me too'

Bill's anger turned to tears, they came freely and he didn't care. Tom filled his glass for him.

'Jesus Bill, I'd cry too if I started drinking this piss!' Bill filled his glass again, drinking it down like beer. His tear-stained face convulsed with rapidly changing emotions.

'You! Christ you'd drink horse piss if it was bottled!' Bill choked as he laughed, the tears pouring down his cheeks. 'Bloody bitch! Why Tom? I knew something was wrong. I bloody knew it! I loved her Tom, just like you love Simone.'

Tom put an arm on his shoulder. 'It happened to me too, did I never tell you?' Bill searched his friend's face. He wanted to know.

'I'd been here about three months when I got *my* 'Dear John' letter. Come to think about it, much the same period of time as yours eh? Maybe that's as far as English girls can go before they change their stupid minds! It hit me pretty hard I can tell you. Oh, did I get pissed on that! Shortly afterwards I met Simone. I never think of Dorothy now, except to give thanks to God I wasn't saddled with her for the rest of my life.'

Tom went to the bar and talked to the Madame for a few minutes. When he returned he brought another bottle of white wine.

'Drink this Bill, it's far better for your liver!' Bill got up and lurched for the lavatory at the rear of the building. Ten minutes later he reappeared, looking pale but more in control.

'Read this Tom.' Bill handed over Alice's crumpled letter. 'You don't expect a friend to do that do you! It wasn't just the 'Dear John' but that bastard Gerry Hardcastle, a bloody officer he calls himself. Jesus, Tom, if I ever catch up with him I'll risk a Court Martial – I'll fucking kill him!'

'I never liked him. Oh I know he reported me for drinking on duty, but I never liked him way before that!' Bill listened intently. 'I didn't want to mention it to you, because he was your friend, or so you thought. But both Hugh Porter and I knew he was a snob! Captain Porter never said as much to me of course, but he used to pass the odd glance at me sometimes when Hardcastle spoke in the tent.' Bill had started on the third bottle, Tom had selected one of lower alcohol, but Bill didn't notice.

'I doubt there's no unit in all the armies in France, including the Jerries, that doesn't have its fair share of 'Dear Johns' Bill. And although I can't say how other units take care of them it's an RFC tradition to pin them up on the barrack room wall.' Bill looked alarmed.

'What! What the hell for?'

Tom smiled. 'It isn't nice for the girl in question when she gets a whole lot of nasty mail from your pals, telling her just what it is she has done to a serving soldier overseas.'

Bill thought on it for a while. 'I can imagine the effect. Did you do that with yours Tom?'

'No I didn't. I was pissed for a week and lost the letter. But certain people I won't mention had taken my letter and yes *they* did it.' Seeing the question on Bill's face he explained. 'I know because she wrote asking my forgiveness and implored me to stop the hate mail.'

Bill shook his head. 'No I couldn't do that, it's too private.'

By late evening the estaminet had become crowded and noisy and Bill was even laughing at Tom's jokes when Yvonne sat down beside him. Tom stayed for twenty minutes then made to take his leave.

'Bill, this lovely young lady has taken a fancy to you, did you know that? She's been asking after you for weeks since she first met you – remember when we first saw her? You know the old saying, so I won't say it! You have two days off I'm told. Make the most of it pal, so long!'

As Tom departed he signalled the Madame of the house and gave her a wad of notes. He knew Yvonne would look after him. She would help and she had been instructed not to ask for payment, Tom had already settled that.

As Tom left, Yvonne took Bill's hand and led him to her own room above the estaminet. Bill was drunk but not stumbling drunk. She said nothing – she'd been appraised of his problem. She also knew he was a virgin.

Yvonne's bedroom was speckless, with a pleasing blue and white decor of paint, wallpaper and matching curtains. There was a medium-sized double bed with quilted covers, an adjoining small lavatory with bidet, and a mahogany toilet stand with clean but cracked china basins and jugs.

Taking her time she uncovered a corner of the sheets and settled Bill on the edge of the bed where, without haste, she undressed him to his long-johns. She hung his uniform carefully across a wooden clothes horse then removed her boots and dress as Bill, half-dazed, rolled under the sheets. He watched, fascinated, as she removed her underclothes. Dressed only in short cambric drawers she washed her face and sprayed fresh perfume over her upper body. The girl turned to him, her naked breasts highlighted by dark aureoles exciting him to the point where he needed to go to the lavatory. Cursing the effects of the wine he leapt out of the bed covering his erection as she giggled at his modesty.

He had drunk a lot and it took all of three minutes before he finished. As he opened the door he found the gas mantle had been dimmed and Yvonne sat upright in bed – her small pert breasts inviting. Bill washed his face at the stand, no longer embarrassed. He turned and looked at her. It was to be his first time and he thought of Alice.

'Come! Quicky *mon cheri.*' She opened the sheets for him, never letting her eyes leave his face as he gazed at her nakedness. As he moved to join her she stopped him at the edge of the bed moving her mouth against his hardness. 'Slowly, slowly my love.' She was an expert and as Bill moved into the bed she raised her knees, legs apart.

It was the first time, and although he came too soon, she caressed him until a half hour later he entered her once more. 'Slowly, slowly my love.' There was no room for Alice as he grew inside her.

Yvonne awoke to a glorious spring morning. She had slept well, and as she studied her companion of the night a feeling close to motherhood almost overwhelmed her. The young aviator must be about the same age as herself, yet he was such a child. He had taken her three times through the night – the last as close to rape as she had ever known.

But he was a child for all that. Before he slept he had broken down, sobbing, calling out a name – Alice! Then he cried for her, apologising for his assumed brutality. She bent over and kissed his cheek. He even slept like a child and she felt something else; it could be called love – it was something she had never felt before. A child from a Paris orphanage she had been overtaken by the war, her first lover died at Ypres and then there were others, officers mainly, and then Amiens and Madame. She had a roof over her head, a pleasant room and her job in the estaminet. But she had no illusions, she was a whore just the same!

As he slept she withdrew from the bed, softly and quietly attending to her morning ablutions before putting on her dressing gown and going downstairs. Within ten minutes she returned, with a tray of coffee, croissants and jam. She tickled his cheek until he opened his eyes. His smile the only thanks she needed.

As Bill enjoyed the petit déjeuner, Yvonne joined him in bed. They laughed among the crumbs and, soon aroused, made love. Completely uninhibited Yvonne showed Bill how to use the bidet, an object of total mystery to Bill, and as she bestrode the china basin they laughed like children at his wonderment.

She never let him think, or reflect. There was more wine and more love making until the evening when a tap on the door brought Madame to enquire if Bill could come downstairs to see his friend. It was Tom.

'Had a good time Bill? No need to answer that, I can see you have!'

Bill was enthusiastic. 'She doesn't want any money Tom and she really does like me you know.'

Tom laughed. 'I told you she liked you didn't I? Anyway, I came because it isn't safe for you to try and get back to camp on your own. You don't have a pass, so I've brought a motor bike from the squadron MT pool. I'm going to have a couple of jars – see you in thirty minutes!'

With a mixture of feelings Bill said goodbye to Yvonne. 'I shall be back as soon as I can get a pass.' He kissed her quickly and left.

Yvonne cried. Her life could have been so different.

Chapter Thirteen

Sunday, 9th September, 1916

As the weather was unfit for flying, Major Wells took the opportunity to call a church parade. The Squadron Padre had pestered him for weeks, war or no war, a Sunday service was essential for morale! And today, 177 available officers and men gathered on the airfield under a bank of low stratus which threatened rain at any minute.

Bill felt ill at ease. It wasn't just the dull remains of his debauchery, or Alice's betrayal, or Gerry's treacherous behaviour, even though the hurt never left him for a moment. Yvonne had merely postponed the worst of it – the scars had yet to appear! But here and now at this service he wasn't ready for God. Since leaving home he'd remained a confirmed Christian, even the war itself couldn't shake his genuine faith, the faith of his family. He said his prayers secretly each night, and although it wasn't always possible to attend a service such as this he was content to share his thoughts with God. Until now!

He wasn't listening to the Padre's words – just his own thoughts, muddled and confused. And for no particular reason he thought of his family more than he had done for months. Perhaps because Alice was no longer there to push them into the background – but she *was* damn her – she just wouldn't retreat into the shadows! It was easy to dismiss Gerry Hardcastle, a bloody prig and a bastard! A bloody officer!

God! What God? He remembered arguing with his sister Eileen when they were about nine or ten. 'Who was most important? God; the King; or Father Christmas?' There were some doubts about the latter and the King was real enough, but God?

The spitting rain had now turned into a downpour. Bill's thoughts were swiftly nudged aside as the Padre looked up and then gave up! Commands were shouted and the squadron marched back to their tents; from which some went to the lines, the hangars and various workshops. There was always work to do wherever aeroplanes were concerned.

Rain squalls kept most of the aircraft grounded until the middle of the week. Bill flew once with Captain Wilson, a line patrol over the marshes, but spent most of his time doing sundry work in the 'A' Flight hangars. He was glad not to be flying, the weather matched his spirits and he relaxed a little as he worked with familiar tools, absorbed and quiet in his industry.

Friday started badly. Heavy rain persisted and the mud was unpleasant as Bill tramped to the latrines. He was experiencing an irritation in his loins and badly needed a piss. In the event it was no relief. A slight burning sensation that he had never known before. 'Too much wine I suppose' – Bill had heard that French wine could give liver problems, and he decided to drink less in future.

By mid-afternoon the need to relieve himself became increasingly urgent and the burning sensation much worse. By tea-time he felt a wetness in his pants and sneaking into the cockpit of an isolated quirk inspected himself. A pinkish-white fluid was seeping from the end of his penis which itself was swollen and inflamed. By supper time he was worried, very worried! Recalling the VD lectures, FFIs and, worst of all, Alan Butcher's gory Farnborough tales, he feared the worst.

It wasn't fair! Why me? Why does it have to happen to me? My first time, and Yvonne; dear sweet Yvonne, she couldn't be, could she? Maybe it wasn't? He'd heard of sexual strain giving the same effect as the 'clap', maybe that was all it was? He needed to talk to somebody, certainly not the MO, everyone on the squadron would know if he reported sick. In desperation he called at the Sergeants' Mess to see if he could find Tom. 'He wasn't there, sorry. No idea where he could be. He's not in his tent we know that!'

It was worse now! As he tried to sleep he knew he would have to go on sick parade first thing in the morning. Pain wasn't the problem. The prospect of facing the truth was!

Apart from his crash and a bump on the head, Bill had never been on sick parade before. There were only six of them, an assortment of boils, scalds, burns and minor breakages. Most of the ack-emmas were too asleep to inquire about his 'injury' and it wasn't until he confronted the Medical Orderly that the dreaded question arose.

'What's your problem then Corp?' Bill wasn't even prepared for the question.

'Stomach pains.' He even surprised himself with the suitability of his answer.

'What kind of stomach pains?'

Bill winced. 'Bad ones, or I wouldn't be here stupid!'

Lt. Brian Stanmore was new to the squadron, but had been a Junior Medical Officer at St. Omer for six months prior to this posting. He was young, but highly experienced as only military doctors can be when on active service. Bill was the fourth patient he saw.

'Stomach pains Corporal? Tell me about them.' Bill cleared his throat, he had to come right out with his problem he knew that.

'Sir, I was with a French girl in Amiens last Saturday. Yesterday I felt a burning sensation in my... my ... thing.' He was blushing and couldn't find the right words.

'In your penis, right? Very well then, remove your clothes Corporal. Let's take a look, shall we!'

The inspection was thorough and simple, with Bill answering numerous questions as they arose. 'Was the girl a prostitute? Where does she work?' Bill was reticent in his answers, not wishing to cause trouble for Yvonne.

'The MPs have to be told of all contacts you understand. She could give VD to many others if she's not listed you see. Did you report to the ETR when you came back to camp?' Bill gave a questioning look. 'The Early Treatment Room at the camp gates, did you sign in on your return?' As Bill hesitated further the MO snapped: 'It's not an offence to report sick with a dose, Corporal, but it *is* an offence to conceal it or to conceal the whereabouts of your contact. I must complete a contact report and you must provide the details, so let's have them!'

'Gonorrhoea!! You have a nice dose of the clap Corporal, congratulations!' He was breathing heavily, trying to come to terms with the horror of it all.

'I'm sorry sir!' The MO looked at him, he felt sorry for the young airman, as he did for so many youths he had treated for the same, and worse, conditions.

'I suppose you are lad. But you'll be much sorrier when you start the treatment I'm afraid. It's tough, but no great problem. We shall have to keep a check on you to make sure there is nothing else, like syphilis for instance, so that means you will have to attend the STC for about six months. About two to three days in the wards to start with, then a couple of visits in the second week and about once a fortnight after that.'

Bill was petrified. 'What is the STC sir?'

'The Special Treatment Centre. It's in Amiens Hospital, just outside actually. You go there this morning – right now in fact. You have your side-pack and personal effects?' Bill confirmed he was packed according to regulations, then dressed as the MO completed the necessary documentation.

'Will anyone know about this sir?'

'All medical matters are strictly confidential Proctor. They go on your records of course, but it's not general knowledge. Don't worry lad, you're not the first VD case on this or any other unit, and you certainly won't be the last. But a word of warning – keep it in your pants the next time you see a girl! I should also remind you that it was a breach of regulations not to have reported in at the ETR, but from what you have told me you didn't actually visit a brothel and your infection could hardly be anticipated, so I shall not refer to the matter any further. Now wait in the reception room. A tender will be taking you down to Amiens within the next half hour.'

Bill was feeling much better, the MO seemed a nice chap, and with luck no one on the squadron would ever know the nature of his sick call, particularly since the STC was in Amiens. He felt bitter and humiliated having to tell about Yvonne, poor girl. God if he'd only known! He would have to tell Tom however, just in case! As the Crossley jolted over the uneven road his affliction made him wince at every bump. Fortunately his three fellow patients were too concerned with their own problems to take notice.

At the British Medical Hospital in Amiens, Bill passed his sealed documents to the Medical Sergeant in charge of reception. Directed to wait on a bench with about twenty other soldiers he waited a full hour before being marched to the STC, a few hundred yards from the main building. Another long wait – then he was taken by an orderly to one of the clinics where he was examined by a RAMC Staff Sergeant.

Bill was told to strip and waited for ten minutes before a doctor arrived. Impatient and sharp-tongued he told Bill to roll back his foreskin. Using a gloved hand he made a thorough examination and briefly told him of his condition and the cure.

'I shall see you again a week from today. In the meantime, you will stay here for two nights and the Staff Sergeant will apply treatment today and tomorrow then, on Monday you will report back to your unit, reporting back here every other day until next Saturday when I shall examine you again. Your course of treatment will depend on the rate of cure. I must add it will be both painful and rather messy but it's a self-inflicted injury so don't expect any sympathy. Bloody fool!' He gave some instructions to the Staff Sergeant then left the room.

'Right! May as well get started Corporal. The treatment isn't as bad as the Captain says! It can be of course, particularly if the patient delays reporting sick. Then the infection spreads, the cock gets very swollen and inflamed and it really hurts when I remove the stick!' Bill tried to avoid looking at the array of stainless steel implements neatly displayed on a tray.

'What stick is that Staff?'

'I call it a stick, but 'umbrella' is the usual name. You've probably heard of it before?' Bill had, and he froze as he recalled stories told by Alan Butcher. 'This is the little fella! But while I tell you what I'm going to do, just dip your prick in this bowl of disinfectant.'

The umbrella was a slim tube of steel about three millimetres diameter with a small conical head. The Staff Sergeant held it in front of Bill to demonstrate its action.

'It's a simple procedure. I enter this tube up your prick, then I pull this little lever and the head expands radially, just like an umbrella. The painful part is when I withdraw the stick. It cleans the inside of your cock, perhaps scrapes is a better word, to remove the infecting pus. Then we syringe it out with various solutions until it's all gone. The treatment works well enough but it takes a few weeks, depending on the strength of infection.' Bill swallowed the bile surging in his mouth.

'My MO mentioned six months?'

'I've seen a few cock disasters in my time and I'm sure your problem will be cleared up in a few weeks lad. But we keep a check on you over six months just in case the treatment has to be continued and to make sure you don't have any other problems, such as a dose of syphilis. That means further treatment with sulphur drugs, mercury pills and such – *that,* my son is bad news!'

After the initial treatment, Bill collected his in-patient uniform of white shirt, blue trousers and a red arm-band and was directed to the sparse barrack room which acted as a ward. A corporal of the RAMC gave him instructions.

'STC don't feed with the other patients. Yer collect yer rations for each day and cook 'em yerself. Better take this chit and report to ration stores right away!' He found the stores and was given a grudging reception by the two FANY's working there.

'One half loaf of bread, one pat of butter, one cheese and two eggs, there!' Without looking at him the older woman threw the bread on the counter and Bill heard one of the eggs crack as she dropped them on his plate.

'I'll thank you for another egg, please take care next time!'

The woman glared at him. 'Don't you come that tone with me, if I had my way we wouldn't give you filthy STC people anything! Now get out!' Bill felt the shame - but how did she know?

The kitchen had a broken stone floor, a cold tap and a worn table.

The iron stove was ancient and the single pan had seen better days. Bill decided not to bother with the eggs and made the best of his bread and cheese. His companions were quite happy to accept the eggs however.

'Never seen the RFC in here before Corp' what was it you got?' Bill turned to face a merry-looking character with broken teeth.

'The clap!' Bill didn't feel disposed to talk.

'Me too, for the third time! Two sisters would you believe!' Bill nodded. 'I thought you couldn't get it from the same bint twice, but you can. So after the second dose I had a bash at her little sister, about thirteen I think. Fuck me if she hadn't got it as well!' Bill was still concerned about the two 'First Aid Nursing Yeomanry' women.

'How did they know I was from the STC?' The broken-toothed soldier laughed and pointed to his red arm-band.

'What do think that's for chum? It's to tell the world we're the unclean! By the way Corp make sure you watch your kit in here. Some of these lads are bad 'uns, and you know what the RAMC stands for don't you?'

Bill did: 'Rob All My Comrades' yes I know!'

There were three more applications of the 'stick', syringes and bandages before Bill left the STC ward for the squadron. The pus had cleared a little by now, but the inflammation seemed worse. Nevertheless, it was a relief to be rid of the place and the assortment of patients he'd been with these past two days and nights.

As he returned in the Crossley he tried not to think about future treatment. 'God almighty, it was enough to put you off girls for the rest of your life!' His two travelling companions were part of the group that had left Bertangles with him two days ago. More awake now, the inevitable questions regarding his condition had to answered. Yes! Further treatment was necessary, and yes, he was on light duties for a day or two! But he could see from their grinning faces – they knew!

His penis was encased with a lint bandage and he carried a small bottle of antiseptic solution in his side-pack. In addition he carried a letter for the squadron MO and an STC leaflet on hygiene instructions. But the worst part of it was the sense of shame. The treatment was bad enough in itself, but the nature of the disease put STC patients on the outer edges of normal medical care. They were the unclean – outcasts! Even so, the authorities had to be careful. Social diseases were a fact of life in all armies, so public humiliation and severe punishments had to be avoided, lest the afflicted never reported sick and created casualties worse than a major battle!

Reporting back to the squadron sick bay, he underwent another examination and was told to report sick in two days time for another visit to the STC. The MO said it looked like it would clear up soon, and put him back on full duties once more. Feeling a little better for that Bill went to his tent, more than ready to be flying again.

Things were much the same at 'A' Flight and nobody seemed to have missed him. Not unusual when he thought about it since half of his time was spent at 'C' Flight anyway. After reporting to Captain Wilson and finding there could be some flying the next day, he then went in search of Tom Bolton.

'What can I say Bill? I'm totally shot-down! I never had any idea she was infected, truth to tell I had her myself, but that was over six months ago and I'm clear, thank God. She must have caught it since then. She's only a part-time girl though, and the estaminet isn't a brothel which is why the MPs don't visit so often of course. I'm so sorry Bill, it's all my bloody fault, I just wanted to cheer you up!'

'Well Tom, it certainly took my mind off Alice so don't feel too bad. Anyway, it could be worse and I suppose I have to pay for my mistakes sometime!' Tom still felt responsible, even if it was all part of the lad's growing up. Nevertheless, he thought it strange that Bill, only 19 years old, should be so put out by women yet entirely without fear in the air. Maybe time would change that in due course.

'Let's have a drink this evening pal, I still have a few bottles of red from Jean Louis.'

Bill pulled a face. 'Not allowed I'm afraid, the MO says I have to stay off the drink until further notice!'

As Bill's Flight Commander, Paul Wilson had received the routine sick report concerning his men. But when he noticed Bill's name on the list he felt impelled to make further enquiries since his observer's health effected his own flying schedule. The Sqdn MO hesitated to say more than necessary until Paul told him it was a matter of operational necessity.

'Sorry to say this Paul but your lad has a dose of the clap! It doesn't look bad though, and you will have him back on full duties by next week, but please don't mention it to him or anyone else. He's a sensitive chap and quite cut up about anyone knowing. I haven't even told the C/O for that matter.'

Paul Wilson could see that Bill was looking a trifle grim, but apart from that his attention to his role of observer was quite normal. In fact he seemed to be extremely alert on this particular flight just north of the Somme marshes. They were flying inside their own lines, mainly showing a 'presence' to the troops moving in long columns below. Their orders were to keep a wary eye over their section of the front and to stay aloft for maximum duration. Bill was confident that 1085 could keep aloft for three hours and had even promised as much to his pilot. Unusually their orders had an aggressive tone to them. They were to patrol their sector for three hours and, also unusually, engage any and all enemy aircraft that should stray inside the British lines.

Aware of their orders Bill scanned the eastern sky while Paul Wilson flew the quirk in a regular weaving pattern, the more to extend their range of vision. As he looked below Bill could see thousands of troops, horses, artillery, trucks – all moving to positions behind the British rear trench system. It was obvious why 3rd Army didn't want any unwanted visitors from the east; this was a build up if ever he saw one, and an Allied attack was being prepared.

By the first week of May, Bill had conducted about fifteen similar flights in the same sector. The weather was fine with light fluffy cumulus scattered above and below their patrol altitude of 4000 feet. No enemy machines had come even close, although Bill thought he'd spotted a small single-seater biplane with a very small rudder, possibly one of the new Halberstadt D11s, said to be replacing the E3 Eindekkers. Fortunately it didn't attempt to approach – just as well since it was reputed to be very fast! Bill reconsidered his recent lapse of faith. 'Thank God there's sufficient cloud to hide in and thank God there *is* a God!' Left to his own thoughts he realised that he shared the same God with the Boche. None of it made any sense!

Although 'A' Flight's sector was very quiet, some of 'B' Flight's patrols, further north had been in spasmodic action with enemy reconnaissance machines escorted by the new Fokker Dls. Their reports claimed that when 11 Sqdn's FE2bs and DH2s came on the scene the Huns quickly turned tail. So it seemed the RFC had full command of the air for once!

The C/O had called all the crews together to discuss the situation. It seemed there were a number of new single-seater scouts about, and Wing required all squadrons to report any engagements with, or sightings of these new machines. Evidently the Eindekkers had now been replaced with the Fokker Dls, but from what they could see, it was no more a match for the DH2 or the new two-seater FE2Ds, than the Fokker E3 was.

Only two weeks ago, Wing HQ had sent rough diagrams of various new single, and two-seater enemy machines which had been reported through various sources. All observers had been instructed to familiarise themselves with these drawings and to report any information that could supplement the sparse details they had of them.

Bill had discussed his possible sighting of the Halberstadt D11 with Captain Wilson who, though not seeing the machine himself, had great confidence in Bill's keen eyesight. As a consequence the C/O asked Bill to supply details to the rest of the squadron. Somewhat embarrassed he explained what he saw,

'Not much I'm afraid. Too far off to get much detail but he must have seen us. As he turned I could see he was quite small, a conventional twin-bay biplane, and I could only see one person. Oh yes! It was very sleek looking and ... and I was glad it never came any closer!'

When the laughter subsided Tim Wells came up and punched him on the shoulder. 'Now that is what I call pure honesty gentlemen!' Then turning to the young and red-faced observer: 'God knows how many times I've wanted to say that in public Corporal, but I want to say well done! Your observations are just what we want. Your name will be mentioned in my report to Wing.'

That evening Bill decided to write home. Although his parents knew about Alice they had never known how serious he was about her. Only Maggie knew that and she had been sworn to secrecy before he left for France. It wasn't difficult to write to his mother, but his letter to Maggie required a great deal of care. Only she really knew what he felt for Alice, and it was proving difficult to explain how he felt now she was gone. In a sense he even felt guilty, as though it was all his own fault. Perhaps it was? But it was only after three attempts that he managed to write what he wanted to say – and felt better for it!

He had received another letter from Jane Graham, it was full of village news and contained cuttings from the *Harrogate Herald*. Much of her news was concerned with the January Conscription Act, now coming into force, and the various village men who were about to be called into the Army. There was also an interesting press cutting concerned with the new Summertime Act. Evidently people would have to put their clocks forward by one hour ahead of GMT – mainly to extend the working day, a device particularly useful for farmers.

It was Jane's 16th birthday in a week's time, an event that now made her a woman she was quick to point out! Bill had taken special pains to tell Maggie she was not to tell Jane about Alice. It was bad enough Jane constantly telling him of her love! So far he had managed to answer that by saying he had 'great affection and love for her as a close friend, but it wouldn't be fair to say more while he was on active service'. Jane seemed to be content with that, but still insisted in expressing her devotion to her 'brave aviator'. He removed her photograph from his wallet – she *was* a pretty little thing – but so young and innocent. In his present condition, and having slept with a prostitute, he could hardly look at her image any more, he felt ashamed. Nevertheless, he would have to get her a card and write within a day or two.

It was close to three weeks since his first treatment at the Amiens STC, and his attendance was now reduced to one visit per week. Although the pus was much less and the pain had completely gone, they still continued with the dreaded umbrella! But it was said that only one more week of this treatment would be necessary if recovery continued at the present rate.

On the 10th May, the squadron lost its well-respected Commanding Officer. Tim Wells had taken a new Lieutenant observer over no-man's land to give him experience when, according to witnesses at the front, the BE2c simply exploded in mid-air! It was generally thought that he flew into a British shell, always a possibility but generally ignored on statistical grounds. There was nothing left to say – or pick up!

Paul Wilson was given command and appointed Major with immediate effect. He was also grounded until further notice. Wing had seen too many changes in command of 4 Squadron in recent months, and in order to avoid further disruption the new C/O would be kept from flying for the time being.

Lt. Crouch was promoted Captain and took over as 'A' Flight Commander, taking his own observer with him. As Bill no longer had a pilot in 'A' Flight he was transferred to 'C' once more, where Hugh Porter allocated him to Tom Bolton and a new job.

'New wireless instructions have come through from Wing, and I have to send crews to various 3rd Army batteries where they are to learn, first-hand, the latest developments in RFC–Artillery cooperation.' Tom and Bill were seated in front of Captain Porter, drinking his special brand of coffee. 'The first crew, that's you two, are to report to 122 Battery RA. next Monday.' Hugh Porter went to the large scale map. 'The 122nd are positioned here, about five kilometres south-west of Arras. The plan is that you shall stay with them in one of their dugouts for a week and monitor all their incoming signals. There are a few new tricks you have to learn, new codes, procedures, positioning of aerials and most important of all help them with their ground signals, where to place them and that sort of thing.'

Bill was worried. 'I'm sorry sir, but I have to report sick on the 16th, that's the following Tuesday.'

Hugh Porter looked up – surprised. 'I didn't know that Corporal, I hope it's nothing serious? If it's just a routine thing I can get the MO to bring the date forward.' Bill hesitated, and seeing his discomfort Tom stepped in.

'Proctor's got a routine medical treatment that's all it is Sir. We'll go see the MO after this little session.'

The 'C' Flight Commander wasn't to be fobbed off that easily. 'If you have anything wrong with you Corporal, I must know! Anything that affects your flying efficiency must be known to me, and since I shall receive your medical records in due course you might just as well tell me now!'

'It's nothing sir, just that I had a small dose of the clap a few weeks ago.' Hugh Porter looked away then, unable to contain his mirth any longer, swung around to face him.

'God Proctor! I thought you said you had something wrong with you! Christ lad, who hasn't got the bloody clap around here!' All three of them joined in the laughter.

Tom couldn't resist a further observation. 'And that includes the officers too, but that's an official secret!'

Hugh Porter brought the meeting to a close. 'Right then, you two rascals, out of here now! Cut along to the MO Corporal and give him this note. He'll fix you up with an earlier appointment and don't worry. It happens to the best of us!'

Tom accompanied him to the Medical Unit. 'The only thing different about officers and us is that their blue lamp brothels have a better selection of whores. Better looking, younger and for the most part a lot cleaner. But don't think they don't get a dose now and then, they are just as likely to get unlucky as those who go to a red-lamp. I've been among them a lot longer than you have Bill and I know!'

There was no problem. The MO arranged for Bill to attend the STC on Sunday morning, and from what he said it looked as though he would be on fortnightly visits thereafter. The horror was beginning to fade a little.

Apart from flights arranged to test the wireless receiver of a 13-pounder gun battery, Tom and Bill had little to do for the remainder of the week except study the new RFC–Artillery wireless regulations. Much had been learnt since hostilities began and now, with improved equipment and greater experience, it was possible to regulate wireless procedure between aircraft and batteries.

As Bill left the STC compound he felt better than he had done for the past month. The pain had gone completely by now, and the pus had stopped running. He was still passing cloudy water, but that would clear up in time. The main thing was that the umbrella treatment was

211

over. The rest of the treatment was only a question of examinations and possible injections – he could almost breathe again!

Complete in full marching kit; big pack, haversack, webbing, water bottle, revolver and anti-gas helmet, the two airmen, armed with their detachment orders were transported to the 122nd battery in the early morning.

They were received by a young Captain, the Battery Commander himself, who was pleased to show them around his guns, dugouts and array of receiving aerials. They were allocated to separate dugouts, each with its own resident wireless operator. Tom's W/Op was an RFC ack-emma, whereas Bill had a Corporal of the Royal Engineers Signal Division.

'I must say your WOP dugouts are superb sir.' Tom had spent time in the trenches earlier in the year, assisting the infantry with their CP ground signals but even the rear HQ trenches were nothing in comparison to the relative luxury he saw here.

Captain Wright laughed. 'I can assure you we are not exercising any special consideration here Sergeant. The fact is, we *have* to be dry in order to earth the aerials and wireless sets. And we *have* to be dug deep, with heavy waterproof drapes to provide a quiet area. Receiving is difficult enough with poor signals, interference and jamming – we don't need the roar of our own guns as well.'

After a brief lunch Captain Wright took them round the aerials.

'As you can see, we suspend them on thirty foot poles. The wire, a single dipole 125 feet in length is lined up parallel to the guns. So the aerial is pointed in the same direction as the guns – at the target! And the wireless dugout is placed alongside one end of the aerial, we get better reception that way.' Bill thought he'd better say something.

'Excuse me sir! I really don't know anything about wireless, except for operating the Sterling Spark set in the aircraft, and having a go at receiving. But why is the aerial 125 feet long? I mean, couldn't it be any length?'

'Good question Corporal. It's all to do with wavelengths you see! For example, how much copper wire do you unreel from your aeroplane before you transmit?'

Bill had done this many times. 'Anything between 100 and 180 feet in my experience. I think the exact length is given to us by the particular battery we are sending to sir.' Captain Wright sat them down by one of the 60 pounder guns.

'This battery's guns have a range of about six miles, and our usual targets are along Jerry's main road of communication – the Lens to Perrone road actually! Usually we are much further forward than this, but we were pulled back to these earlier pits two weeks ago. I think we are to be moved further south shortly. But to continue answering your question Corporal, when you drop your aerial for say *this* battery, you will unwind something like 125 feet. And since you have a four pound weight on the end of the wire it goes out almost vertical, right?' Bill confirmed with a nod of his head. 'I think you may know that your transmissions are due to an electrical spark made by the Sterling set yes?' Another nod. 'Well, we make sure the squadron's wireless chaps set a spark-gap of about 6mm, which is about right for sending signals at a wavelength of 150 metres. Now! If you divide the wavelength by a factor of four what do you have?'

Tom looked worried. Bill guessed.

'One hundred and twenty five feet sir!'

Captain Wright was pleased. Evidently these aviator chaps were reasonably intelligent, so he would have little difficulty in explaining the receiving system.

'Right chaps! Lets take a look at the tuning sets.' Tom winked. He hadn't understood much of the Captain's discourse but Bill seemed to have grasped it all. Bill just shrugged his shoulders.

'What's a 'tuning set' sir?' Captain Wright stopped half way down the ladder leading to the bottom of the wireless dugout allocated to Bill.

'Sorry chaps! I suppose you call them 'receivers' in the RFC. Yes?' Tom concurred, but added.

'We don't know much about *them* either sir, we have wireless tradesmen who look after all the technical stuff. But we are very willing to learn!' Bill laughed to himself. The only interest Tom had in this detachment was the proximity of Simone Chenez, the farm was only ten miles west of the battery!

'The Short-Wave Tuner Mk III is our main type of wireless receiver, and this one is in the charge of Corporal Pickard. I shall leave you here for the rest of the day. Pickard will show you the ropes about tuning and our new procedure signals and codes. Everything you see here is duplicated in your dugout Sergeant Bolton, controlled by AM/1 Picton. Usually both installations are manned 24 hours a day. At night-time a second WOP takes over, but as we are not fully occupied at present, night duty is simply shifted from one dugout to the other.'

Bill could only wonder at the relative comfort of his allotted dugout. From what he had been told the average trench was water-logged, rat-infested, and uncomfortable in the extreme. But here there were two comfortable cots, a primus stove for cooking, clean water and most of all – peace and quiet!

Corporal Wally Pickard, a married regular soldier recently posted to France, was an amiable soul and more than pleased to act as mentor to the aviators.

'I'm dead pleased to meet you! Things are a bit quiet for the 122nd at present; until we move south we're only on standby. As the Captain said, we eat, sleep and work here all the time. During the day it can get quite crowded – there's usually a runner about the place – to deliver messages to the guns or the C/O. And an artillery officer is always present whenever a shoot is in progress.'

Tom looked around the dugout with interest. 'I bet this took some digging out, it's a work of art!'

Wally Pickard chuckled. 'Not really, our infantry support is a Company of the DLI.' Bill looked at Tom, who seemed similarly at a loss. 'The Durham Light Infantry, and every one a miner! When it comes to digging they are the best!'

From what Wally Pickard told them it was obvious that wireless communications were getting better all the time. It was now possible for a single aeroplane to cover 800 yards of the front, and by using a 'clapper-break' it was possible for two aircraft to signal on the same frequency, simply by changing the tone. Most of the other changes were concerned with wireless codes, ground signal strips and general procedures. There was much to learn, and both of the aviators were handed a bundle of papers filled with information to be learnt by heart!

On the second evening Tom managed to borrow a motor cycle and with Bill covering for him, he spent the night with Simone. On his early return that morning he brought back wine and brandy for both of the dugout crews. He could do no wrong from that moment and now had the full support of many in the 122nd RA. Tom repeated the exercise every evening of the detachment from then on, with the exception of the final night, which he spent with the battery.

Friday was their last day of detachment and Captain Wright was pleased with what they had accomplished.

'From what you have told us, it seems that closer cooperation between artillery spotting squadrons and the guns should be a regular feature. It's the little snippets of practical experience that count. Things like reception being better when the aeroplane is flying towards the guns with the aeroplane's aerial parallel to that of the battery. I think you have also confirmed my theory that spotting machines should work

214

within 3000 yards of their target, passing back and forth in lines parallel to the dugout aerial.'

Tom, looking rather tired, took great interest in the conclusions. 'I like your suggestion that while one of us does the ranging the other crew member should be watching out for new enemy batteries! There was a time when one of us was constantly scanning the sky for Huns, but now we have DH2 scouts giving us cover your suggestions make a lot of sense sir.' He turned to Bill. 'I propose you do the searches while I do the ranging, your eyesight is better than mine!'

Bill made a deal. 'That's fine by me providing you do the weather reporting as well.' The new procedures also included in-flight weather reports, mainly to help the squadrons deploy machines for photographic work and other duties, as well as to assist the heavy howitzers with the strength and direction of wind at various heights.

Tom laughed. 'I suppose I'll have to, since it's me that will be sending the signals anyway!'

On the Saturday morning they returned to the squadron, carrying a glowing report from Captain Wright, and a large canvas bag filled with bottles. By this time Bill had taken quite a liking to wine and was keen to drink with Tom glass for glass.

Hugh Porter was glad to see them back. 'Well, I hope you two enjoyed yourselves? Because I want you to write a full report about your new-found information. It seems that Captain Wright was very pleased with you anyway. So, you will be off flying for the next two days – your report is going to have top priority.

Two days later, their report completed, it was signed by the C/O, then typed to provide copies for each flight. The following day they were ordered to report to Major Wilson to discuss the new wireless procedures.

'Good work chaps. I had a call from Colonel Salmond at Wing this morning. He has seen Captain Wright's report, in which he refers to your contributions with high regard I might add, and with such a good introduction I asked him if I could get you both on home leave. I'm sorry to tell you it was refused!'

'Jesus!' Paul Wilson threw a sharp look at the young Corporal.

'I know Proctor, I know! It's a bloody poor show. But all leave is cancelled indefinitely, except for compassionate grounds. It's not official yet, but as you must have guessed, there's a big push coming up. From what little I know, it seems that a new British offensive, over the Somme, is only weeks away. You must have seen the signs as much as I have. Infantry movements, new artillery positions, fresh camouflage, ammo dumps. But unfortunately there are other signs! Such as the posting of key personnel – like you two!'

'Posted sir? From 4 Squadron?' Tom was shocked.

'I'm sorry Sergeant, you and Proctor are posted to 12 Squadron, as a specialist wireless crew. Just when we are going to need you like mad, the bastards have pinched you for another unit!' Paul Wilson looked at the Movement Order on his desk. 'With effect from 1st June 1916, Sgt Bolton and Corporal Proctor, posted to 12 Sqdn, with special duties to advise and instruct on artillery reconnaissance. That's what you get for being so bloody keen!'

'I shall be sorry to leave the squadron sir.' Tom didn't appear too worried thought Bill, but the last thing he wanted was to move now. Particularly since he hadn't completed his pox treatments yet. Tom continued, 'Are 12 still based at Avesnes-le-Comte sir?' Paul Wilson threw him a wry smile and went to the large scale map.

'I would say you are about half the distance, as the crow flies!' Seeing the shock now registered on Tom's face, and not understanding his Commanding Officer's remark, Bill could only ask.

'Half the distance sir?'

'You two bloody rascals! Did you think we never knew? All these air tests, forced landings, patrols that even went beyond the quirk's total endurance and always approaching our circuit from a north-west direction! Tim Wells spotted it first, then we took a further interest and simply put two and two together. Our main concern was to keep it from a certain ex-C/O who, we may assume, would not have been very happy about your secret romance Sgt Bolton, or about your unofficial flying lessons Cpl Proctor. But the biggest clue was the wine you so generously provided to all and sundry on this squadron!'

Tom Bolton actually blushed while Bill tried hard to keep his composure.

'In fact Sgt Bolton, Major Wells had to respond to an official report from the French police at Freyent.' Startled, Tom's face showed concern, worried that his visits could have harmed Jean Louis Chenez.

'No need to worry Sergeant. Tim Wells handled it in his usual manner. Evidently the frogs were concerned that the farm was designated as a future RFC aerodrome, so he simply said that 4 Squadron had permission to use the field for the odd 'forced landing' practice. As far as I'm concerned this approval by farmer Chenez is still valid? But take care when you get to 12 Sqdn Sergeant – not sure how their C/O may look at such arrangements.'

As Tom expressed his thanks, Paul Wilson told them how much

both he and the squadron would miss them. But the next time you visit farmer Chenez better thank him from me for his agreement to allow 4 Sqdn to use his field for outlandings. Furthermore, I hope you will both visit your old comrades here whenever you can – the odd spot of that fine red would always be appreciated, eh Tom?'

They flew only five times during the following week, mainly keeping track of various wireless communications between the squadron and its allocated gun batteries. A particularly welcome task was in testing communications with their friends in the 122nd RA who were now dug in at a position two miles east of Albert. There could be no doubt now; a massive assault against the German front was due very soon and Bill knew their posting to 12 Squadron couldn't have come at a worse time.

Having said goodbye to all their friends, Tom and Bill departed from Bertangles in a Crossley at 1000 hours on the 1st June. Tom had already informed Simone of their posting to Avesnes but even so, it took a lot of Bill's persuasion to keep the driver on track to their destination, particularly since the farm was only ten miles from their new aerodrome.

On arrival at 12 Sqdn's HQ, which was housed in a reasonably well-kept farm building, they were immediately taken to see their new C/O, Major Roger Kemp, MC.

'Welcome to 12 chaps. I see you are a well-experienced crew and have excellent reports from Major Wilson. I don't think you will have any trouble in settling down with us, indeed it looks as though we shall be relying on you two to help us out quite a bit with wireless and such like. We fly the same old quirks you did on 4 Sqdn, plus a flight of Avros, but I think you will find our crews lack your general experience. Most of our crews are officers, recently out of Blighty actually, a keen lot but have little experience with artillery and wireless. I want you to settle in first of all; Sgt Johnson is our chief clerk and he will fix you up with accommodation. The Sergeants' Mess is the old stone farmhouse you passed when you entered the gate and the airmen's tents are behind the three Bessonneau hangars. I'm putting you in 'B' Flight, so report to Captain Saxby at 0900 tomorrow morning and he will tell you what we have in store for you.'

Unlike 4 Sqdn Bill found 12 to be less well-organised and in some confusion. His tent companions were a motley lot of trades from various flights and few seemed to have been there longer than a week. Fortunately, one of his group, and the only other Corporal in the tent singled him out and introduced himself to the newcomer.

'Barry Chipping, welcome to 12 sqdn! I think we engine fitters should stick together don't you mate?'

Bill responded with a question. 'How do you know I'm an engine fitter?' Bill pointed to the Observer badge on his tunic breast. 'This flying arsehole says that Bill Proctor is an Observer, or an idiot whichever way you look at it!'

Barry Chipping held his hands up in front of his face. 'Your hands mate – like mine, enough grime and cuts to make 'em stand out like a dog's dick in a bowl of custard. You're a bloody engine man if ever I saw one.'

Barry was a typical Cockney, about thirty years of age, friendly and obviously in command of the tent. He had been with 12 since it was formed and was proud to boast that he had been with the squadron longer than anyone.

'But most of these lads are fresh out from Blighty, don't know their arse from their elbow I'm sorry to say. Anyway, wot's a decent young engine fitter doing flying around in these heavier-than-air machines?'

Bill tried to explain his irrational behaviour with a simple shrug of his shoulders. 'It all started with me doing air tests, then everything went blank.'

Barry Chipping nodded his head sagely, 'That's all right then. Jesus Christ I thought you might have been a volunteer!'

Reporting to 'B' Flight at 0900, Bill found Tom waiting for him in the crew tent. Then, some twenty minutes later Captain Robert Saxby arrived, spoke quickly to his line chief, and introduced himself to the pair.

'Right chaps, sit down. Major Kemp has already told you that you are in my flight eh? Well, from what he has told me, you two are experienced in gunnery, wireless and all that sort of stuff – yes?' Tom was about to speak. 'Now most of the chaps in my flight have only been active with photography and some CPs, in fact only a couple of our observers have any experience with archie spotting and I think they will all need to brush up their Morse a bit. So I want you two to give lectures and demonstrations to all the 'B' Flight crews starting, ah let me see, this afternoon. Check with Flight Sergeant Mailer about who will attend and where and that sort of thing.' With that, Captain Saxby, Welsh Guards, left the tent and two very dismayed aviators.

'So there you are Professor Proctor, you are now a bloody teacher!' Tom was furious. 'That man is a bloody idiot, I mean - what's the silly bugger want us to teach?' Bill managed to calm his friend down, and suggested they should see F/Sgt Mailer, 'whoever he is!'

Flight Sergeant Frank Mailer was the line chief they had met only briefly in the crew tent.

'I'm afraid Captain Saxby is a bit off-hand with everyone. Seems to think that details are best left to others. I've known him since he took over 'B' Flight two months ago. Never had what you might call a discussion with him at all! He usually scribbles notes to everyone, strange bloke really, doesn't fly much either. As a matter of fact he's written a note here about what he wants you two lads to do this pip-emma.'

The slow talking and friendly line chief unfolded a crumpled sheet of notepaper from his overalls and handed it to Tom. 'I'm to show you where your lectures are to be held and to say who will be coming. Depending on the weather like, it could be all the crews or maybe just one or two – it all depends on the weather.'

Three rows of chairs had been set out in front of an old blackboard to the rear of a Bessonneau hangar. This was to be their classroom.

'God almighty Bill, let's hope nobody turns up! I mean what the hell are we going to do?' Bill had more pressing concerns, still worried about his medical appointments he knew he would have to report to the squadron sick quarters before the MO sent for him.

'Well, how about just telling them what we do? Like what we have been doing? We can draw things on the blackboard and talk, and ask them if they want to ask us anything, can't we?'

Tom looked at his friend with disgust. 'Go on, piss off and see the pox doctor. I'll work something out but get back here quick as you can – we have a lot to prepare.'

Bill presented his Medical Attendance Card to the Medical Orderly and waited ten minutes before the doctor could see him.

'No further problems then Proctor? Right, let's have a look at the bloody thing.' The MO wrote a note, which Bill duly presented to the orderly. It seemed that everything was going well, his urine was almost clear and more of a natural colour. Unless further complications set in, he was to report in a month for final clearance. It was the best news he'd had in weeks. Delighted beyond measure he ran down to the hangar, eager to tell Tom his good news.

'That kind of news is worth a couple of bottles Bill. Let's hope we can hop into Avesnes tonight, with luck I could fix you up with a pretty French tart...' The blackboard rubber missed him by inches as Bill lunged towards his friend. 'Just a joke you arsehole. Anyway, we may not be able to get a pass this evening, we haven't been here five minutes have we! Anyhow, I think I have designed our strategy for teaching these morons all about artillery spotting and wireless transmissions.'

The afternoon lecture session went well. Tom had already contacted Captain Wright of the 122nd RA. and had suggested that he might be interested in allowing 'B' Flight to cooperate with his unit so that he would then be able to employ 12, as well as 4 Sqdn, in future shoots. All they would need was permission from his Brigade Commander and contact with 3rd Wing RFC, the rest could be done between himself and Captain Saxby. Addressing himself to Captain Saxby at the end of his lecture, Tom mentioned his conversation with the 122nd and suggested that if the 'B' Flight Commander wished it, he could contact the 122nd and make all the necessary arrangements.

'Not a bad idea Sergeant, I shall think on it. Just give me the fella's coordinates and we shall see. I suppose our plan would be to observe his shots and hope our chaps can make themselves understood what?'

Tom smiled, 'I'm sure you will come up with the right plan sir.'

'You crafty old sod Bolton!' Bill was beside himself. 'Of all the brown-nosed bastards I've ever known, you are the worst. 'I'm sure you will come up with the right plan sir." Bill mimicked his friend.

Tom smiled as he polished his finger nails. 'When you've been in the Corps as long as me old son, you will know that officers are a fucking useless lot who depend upon us Sergeants to tell them what to do; but you have to let the poor sods take the credit for your ideas, it's the only way it works I'm afraid. Besides, it's most likely I shall be doing all the flight planning, contact with our friends at the 122nd and so forth. We shall be dining at the farm everyday from now on – just you see! And another thing my lad you should keep up your piloting skills just leave everything to Professor Bolton.'

To Bill's surprise everything Tom predicted turned out just as he planned it. Within a week they were providing at least four shoots a day for the 122nd, much to the mutual advantage of the guns and 12 Sqdn. In addition, there were a number of flying visits to their old friends at Bertangles. Not only were the gifts of wine appreciated, but because of Tom's arrangements between the 122nd and 12 Sqdn, their old comrades were given a rest from ranging some of the guns now crowding the front. Tom managed the flight planning so that he and Bill made frequent flights over the guns, checking their ground signals, then helping to spot the falling shells over enemy territory. After a number of shoots they would land close to the 122nd's battery to check on 'B' Flight's overall progress. Bill had to admit they were doing a good job, and 'B' Flight were almost at operational efficiency, but it was obvious the Allies were massing more and more guns every day.

They had a flight of DH2s providing top cover for most of the time, and although there were a few enemy machines in the area their escorts were a source of great comfort. Nevertheless, the German archie was both intense and accurate and becoming more alarming every day.

Bill's main concern was Tom. He was drinking heavily again and was rarely sober at the end of each day. And although Bill was doing most of the piloting, including landings, Tom's work was strenuous since he did all the spotting, analysis and wireless communication. After a tense day of flying, a full meal and a couple of hours with Simone it was all Bill could do to get him into the Avro for the short flight back to the squadron. It wasn't that he minded doing most of the flying, indeed he welcomed every opportunity to increase his skills. But he feared that Tom would be found out one day, particularly since he was drinking raw brandy from a flask every time they went over the front! Although he couldn't mention Tom's drinking to Simone, he did at least manage to make himself understood to Jean Louis, who promised to hide away the rest of his brandy and put less wine on the table.

Nevertheless, Bill was happier now than he had been for weeks. Alice was fading into the background, the clap was almost gone, and he loved the flying for its own sake. They were glorious days, the summer sun, clear blue skies above and scattered white cumulus – almost idyllic. He could even ignore the acrid explosions that rocked the frail Avro every time they passed over the German lines. And that was the strangest thing of all – he still felt no fear!

Tom had even called him weird, perhaps he was, but for how long? It was strange but he never felt the gnawing fear as others knew it; as Tom knew it, and could describe it in fine detail and even taste it above the brandy that made each mission possible.

It was now the 23rd June, and 'B' Flight had been declared 'operational'. They were far from perfect, but were sufficiently practised to carry out wireless shoots with reasonable accuracy and were even being worked with other batteries within General Rawlinson's 4th Army.

As Bill left their target area – a strongly-held German line between Mametz and Fricourt – the sky seemed to be filled with Allied aircraft. Many of them were two-seater reconnaissance machines, mostly quirks, but there were a large number of scouts too, Niewports and Sopwiths, busy with the dangerous task of destroying enemy observation balloons. Without a doubt, the air above Picardy's rolling hills and marsh-filled valleys was owned by the Allies, and looking down inside his own lines he could see nothing but troops, lines of fresh tents, new dugouts and guns of all sizes. As far as he could see to the south, down to the

Somme, there were masses of red and blue, the French 6th Army, or so he'd been told. To the west were columns of cavalry and movement everywhere!

There was a strong tap on his flying helmet. Bill turned to follow Tom's gloved hand, now pointing to the 122nd's position, it was time to land and report on the day's shoot.

As Bill taxied back down the small field adjacent to the 122nd battery, they could see Captain Wright waiting for them, a cup of tea in each hand. They sat by the Avro drinking tea as the battery C/O gave them his serious news.

'I suppose you chaps must have known for weeks of the build-up along this front?'

Tom spoke quietly. 'Well, the truth is we didn't want to worry anyone sir, but we had a vague idea that an Allied offensive is being prepared.'

The officer smiled. 'Only days away I think. But I wanted to take this opportunity to thank you both for all your cooperation. All kinds of changes are now happening, and if we move up with the offensive it's quite likely we may not be working together in the future. Our ranging on Mametz Wood today has been excellent and we deeply appreciate your accurate spotting. But I think you had best be off now chaps, get an early night's sleep if you can. I think you will awake to a very noisy 'dawn chorus' in the morning!'

After Bill landed at the far end of the field, Tom took over and taxied back to 'B' Flight lines in the usual fashion.

'You know Bill I think Captain Wright was trying to tell us something don't you … ?' But before Bill could answer Chiefy Mailer ran to them.

'Major Kemp wants to see you two lads – right now!'

'Right! Stand easy chaps, I just wanted to say that your efforts have been highly commendable these past weeks. Captain Wright of the 122nd, and Captain Saxby think very highly of you both. Comments duly noted and placed in your record sheets. I know myself how hard you have been working. Two or three times I've been down to the lines this last week, only to find that even in the very late evening you were still at it… ? Are you ailing Corporal?'

Bill choked, his eyes streaming. 'Just something in my throat sir!'

'Your efforts have been appreciated for another reason. You could not have known of course, but Captain Saxby was wounded about three months ago, when flying with 5 Sqdn. He was posted to us for limited flying duties, but his wound was more serious than we knew.

He has now been grounded and will return to England next week. So you have my personal thanks for helping him out during this difficult time.'

Bill was still struggling to keep his face straight as Tom spoke.

'It's no more than we should be doing sir, and I know I speak for Cpl Proctor when I say we are very sorry to learn of Captain Saxby's wound.'

Major Kemp continued. 'I also wanted to tell you that your instruction has been a great success and that Wing HQ have just confirmed 'B' Flight to be at 'readiness' as of tomorrow. A job well done chaps, but we must move on! As you know, 'A' Flight have lost two machines and their crews this week, so Captain Booker is short of experienced crews. I know you are well-experienced with photographic work, so I'm sending both of you to 'A' Flight as of tomorrow.' Noticing the obvious dismay on Tom's face, Roger Kemp was quick to add; 'Naturally you stick together as crew of course!'

Tom made an effort. 'Thank you sir.' Filling his pipe the C/O continued, oblivious to the effect his words were having on Sgt Tom Bolton.

'Unlike your last unit, 12 is an Army Cooperation squadron and our main work is photographic reconnaissance. As a consequence, we take our orders direct from 3rd Brigade, Fourth Army. Captain Booker has instructions to provide deep reconnaissance behind the German lines, and he has his hands full now because, as you must be aware, there will be a massive Allied offensive within days from now. Fortunately the weather has been good, but it won't last for ever. In the next two days 'A' Flight will be flying around the clock – deep penetration. We have to photograph every road and railway track that can be a supply route to the German lines running from Serre in the north to Hem on the Somme. So please report to Captain Booker at 0800 tomorrow, he will have much need of you in the coming weeks. Thank you once again gentlemen.'

'Oh my word Bill. Just as I had everything planned for us. A nice cosy arrangement with 'B' Flight and that's all the thanks you get! Bloody hell, 'A' Flight are still losing machines, despite the fact they are escorted by DH2s. Photographic reconnaissance! The bloody Huns will be all over us.'

As hinted by Captain Wright, the dawn chorus of the 24th June 1916 proved to be extremely noisy. It seemed that every gun along the Allied front was in action from the moment the sun rose above the mist-filled landscape of Picardy. And by the time Tom met Bill at the

'A' Flight office, it was still going on albeit with a less concentrated barrage.

Captain Simon Booker looked tired. A small dark man with deep-set eyes, he gave Bill the impression that he had not slept in weeks.

'Welcome to 'A' Flight men. I know you two have good experience with photo-recce work so I won't try to tell you your job. We use the type C camera and a side sight for both the BE2c and the Avro 504. I think you have experience with both machines, yes?' Tom nodded in assurance as Simon Booker led them to a large photographic mosaic pinned to an old door. 'I have an urgent and highly important job for you this morning. The weather is going to hold good, so your take-off will be at 0915 for a journey to this area a couple of miles south-west of Marquion.' Tom Bolton whistled. 'Yes Sergeant, just so! But you will have an escort of six DH2s, all the way. You will take Avro 968 and two magazines of plates. Pilot up front, observer in the rear taking snaps. You will be unarmed in order to keep your overall weight down, in any event your task is photography and avoidance of fighting, leave that to the escorting scouts. I make the round trip something like sixty miles.'

Bill looked closely at the area pointed out to him. 'I'm afraid we cannot see much in this patch sir, it's mostly covered in cloud…

'Which is why you are going to get me some cloud-free pictures Proctor! You will take two overlapping runs here, and here. Everything has been worked out for you. Fly at 6600 feet, at about 75 mph ground speed. You know how to calculate your ground speed I suppose Sergeant?'

Tom gave a start. 'Oh, yes sir, of course. I will have that sorted out before I reach the target.' Captain Booker gave him a hard stare for a couple of seconds.

'You can expect a 25 mph westerly at that height, but remember, it's important to start camera at this point here, two miles due west of Marquion. And Corporal! You double-check on the ground speed! You expose twelve plates at intervals of 10 seconds, then as soon as they are finished, change magazines and tell your pilot to fly the adjacent run on a reciprocal path, with camera on here!' Booker pointed to their next run on the mosaic.

'Both runs are about two and a half miles long, and you will be receiving considerable archie all the way. A diversionary flight of quirks, from 6 Squadron will be in the area, that should help a bit. No need to touch any of the camera controls except changing plates, our photographers have set all the exposure controls, so leave them alone. You will climb to 6600 feet before reaching Arras, where you will find your escort waiting for you – good luck.' With that Captain Booker left them with their maps and a loose mosaic of their target area, complete with the designated flight-lines marked in blue crayon.

Avro 968 looked to be in good condition but, as usual Bill checked every inch himself as Tom looked over the cockpits and the camera installation.

'Not a bad machine Tom, how is the camera?' Tom was inspecting the type C and side-sight as Bill came around to the starboard side of the Avro.

'The camera has seen better days, but I imagine it works right enough. The side-sight is no different to those on 4 Sqdn, and the spare magazine is stowed carefully beside your control stick. Do you want to start up for an engine check?' As an engine fitter Bill never left the ground before checking his engine first - a safety precaution much appreciated by Tom.

'My pal Barry Chipping has come over to 'A' Flight with us, this is his machine, I don't want him to think I don't trust him. No we can let it go this time – he's a good chap!'

At 0900 they climbed aboard and started up. By 0910 they were flying over Arras and were happy to see their escort of DH2s waiting for them. As Tom flew on a heading of 110 degrees he checked his progress over the ground to assess his ground speed, adjusting the engine to make good a ground speed of 75 mph. Their escort soon divided, one flight of three making 10,000 feet or so, while the other three spread out slightly above. The German archie was sporadic as Tom weaved, then turned onto a heading of 170 degrees. Signalling to Bill the two aviators double-checked their ground speed on the heading that was to be used for photography. Keeping straight and level as they flew over two well-spaced landmarks they both made their calculations. Bill passed a note to his pilot: 'GS–81 mph'. Tom smiled as he punched the air twice, his own estimate was 78 mph. He compensated with the engine revs and flew on to his target. Bill noticed the archie had now stopped, it was time to scan the sky.

Tom saw them first. A flight of four Halberstadt DIII fighters, coming down in line astern from his one o'clock and slightly above. He knew them well, and like all RFC pilots treated them with the greatest respect. Fast and acrobatic, in good hands the DIII was a dangerous foe. Bill saw their escort move to intercept the approaching Huns and, for the first time, felt something akin to fear. Dry-mouthed, he could only watch as the DH2s broke up the oncoming flight, leaving them to continue to their target.

Tom checked his map and his watch. Another fifteen minutes to go. At least the archie had stopped, he couldn't see their escort and could only hope they couldn't see him! He took another swig from the flask, the brandy warming his guts as he filled his lungs with the sharp cold air. The smell of the rotary made him gag but he was never sick. Tom never ate before a flight, food never helped – only the brandy, and besides, it was said that a full stomach didn't help if you got a bullet in the gut!

Bill could see a DH2 in flames, spinning to the ground, and a speck growing larger, to take the form of a DIII fast approaching from their port quarter. They were helpless! He banged on Tom's helmet, pointing to the approaching threat. Without further thought Tom turned into the approaching machine, as if to make a head-on engagement. The young pilot of the DIII was trained in fighter tactics, it was what he would do when faced with a beam attack. He was not to know the Avro was unarmed. As the DIII flashed behind them Bill followed its path waiting for it to turn on them again as Tom slowly turned once more.

But their top cover had been watching, and within seconds the DIII was fighting for his life as two DH2s pounced on him.

Tom resumed his height and his course, it had been a close thing and it took another swig from the flask before he could settle down to the task in hand. He spotted his landmark just west of the town and turning onto 170 degrees signalled Bill to get ready. They were on their own again, or so it seemed, and the archie started once again, but was far too high. Bill turned on the camera as Tom flew a straight and level path down their first run.

Having removed his gloves, the better to handle the tricky plate-changing mechanism, Bill was glad when the first run was completed and he could rub his hands together. Carefully replacing the heavy magazine of exposed plates with a fresh load Bill made ready for the reciprocal run. The guns were getting their range now, and the black smelly explosions closer, three more exposures and they were done.

The Avro leapt a good fifty feet as a shell burst under their right wing. Wisely, Tom let the aircraft find its own level before reacting. A quick glance to the right confirmed his worst fears, the starboard aileron had gone along with most of the lower plane in the outer bay. Correcting the resulting wing drop he found he could keep a reasonable amount of control, but it took all his strength. Looking behind he saw Bill signalling to return to base, the camera work was over!

As Tom climbed, Bill noticed only four DH2s remained of their escort. They kept behind and a good thousand feet higher as the Avro flew a lop-sided course on 270 degrees. The wind was no help, it never was when flying from the east, and with a constant yaw to the right its correction made their progress even slower. Bill could see their escort had to keep circling to keep pace with the crippled Avro but they kept station, ever-watchful as Tom continued to 10,000 feet. The archie remained with them, feeling for their height, but fresh custom in the form of a flight of quirks kept their ugly attention divided.

Bill estimated their ground speed to be no more than 35 mph. God knows if the fuel will last he thought. He found he couldn't remove the camera magazine. The camera had most likely been damaged by the shell-burst – he only hoped the plates were still safe. Jesus it was cold! Then the starboard wing dropped in an alarming manner and the Avro lost height.

He could see Tom's body slump forward and his head roll to one side as the aircraft continued to drop and turn to the right. Thinking Tom was wounded, Bill reacted fast. Screwing his own stick into the socket between his feet he managed to level the wings and retain height at something just over 8000 feet. Their faithful escort dropped with them as he pointed his nose due west. It seemed like years before they gained the safety of their own lines, and once over Arras the DH2s waved goodbye, they too were now short on fuel. Bill could see no movement from the front cockpit and his worst fears were that he may be too late to save his friend if had lost much blood.

Dropping height dramatically, Bill approached Avesnes directly into wind. Keeping the Avro as level as possible he knew it would be a difficult landing. Bill kept a long float until the Avro touched down heavily and immediately dug its crippled wing into the sod. As the machine ground-looped at the far end of the field, the undercarriage gave way, swinging the occupants around like sacks of potatoes.

Somewhat dazed, Bill scrambled out of his straps and went to the forward cockpit. He could see no blood and Tom's face seemed almost serene under its mask of oil and grime. As he loosened Tom's leathers his flask fell onto the cockpit floor.

'Hello Billy boy – are we home yet?'

Bill dragged his pilot from the wreckage then retrieved his flask, filling it with petrol now seeping from the split tank. There was little chance of a fire, not enough fuel left, but he had sufficient to douse it over Tom's head who, vomiting with the smell, faced him in wonderment as Bill smashed a fist into his drunken friend's face. There was just enough time to hide the flask inside his flying suit before the medical and fire tenders arrived on the scene.

'Take care of him lads, I don't think he's badly hurt. Just a knock on the head but I think you should give him a sedative if he wakes up!'

Captain Booker was pleased. 'Good work chaps, my photographers don't think the second magazine was damaged. They are in the dark-room now, so we shall soon see. Had a call from 5 Sqdn just a minute ago they say you and Sergeant Bolton put up a good show when attacked by those blasted DIIIs. I suppose you know they lost two of their boys?'

Bill shook his head. 'They all deserve a bloody medal every one of them, never left us alone a single second bless 'em.'

Simon Booker took his arm. 'You are sure you and Sgt Bolton are not hurt?'

'No Sir, but I would like to see how Tom Bolton is getting on at the sick bay if I can?' Captain Booker called for his driver.

'Take Cpl Proctor over to sick bay, then report to the photography section. Let me know what's happening to those plates as soon as you can!'

Bill sat by Tom's bedside looking at his friend. From all accounts he was suffering from a slight case of concussion, and the MO had only given him a look and told his assistants to watch over him.

'Did you give him something to drink Corp?' Bill turned in his seat. One of the orderlies had arrived with a cup of tea for him.

'When I cleaned him up he smelled like a brewery! So I thought you had maybe given him something before we arrived.'

Bill thought fast. 'I usually carry a drop of brandy, just in case of any emergency. So when I pulled him out I gave him a snort – he was so cold you see! In fact I thought he might have hyperthermia or shock or something, it's bloody cold at 10,000 feet you know.'

The medic gave a short laugh. 'Christ man, I wouldn't go up in one of them things unless I was as drunk as a skunk!

But you did the right thing, probably saved his life, he was as cold as a fish when I undressed him.'

Tom was still asleep when Bill returned to 'A' Flight and a delighted Captain Booker.

'Splendid news Proctor, you will be pleased to know all your plates came out fine. They are printing them as we speak. I take it from your report that the last three missing shots were due to a jammed magazine when you were hit.' Not that they matter anyway. The essential infor-mation is there and Wing are going to be more than pleased I can tell you. How is Sergeant Bolton by the way?' Bill told him the pilot was asleep and looked as though he would recover in a day or two. 'Well I shall be along to see him on the morrow. Meanwhile you two are off flying for at least the next three days. For one thing, your Avro is now written-off-charge and Major Kemp insists you both get some rest – well done Proctor!'

It was eight pip-emma when Bill returned to sick quarters. The steady boom of the barrage was slightly less now, but rumour of the impending assault grew steadily.

'They are already talking of the battle of the Somme.' said one of the patients. 'Thank God for the RFC and a bed in sick bay; I pity those poor sods going over the top any day now.'

Bill smiled grimly. 'It's no joke two miles over the top either!' He could see Tom waving to him a few beds further down. He quickened his pace. Tom, looking grey-faced and sad came straight to the point.

'Sorry Bill, I just went under. It was the height and the cold. I just passed out. Thank God you can fly or we would never have made it. I remember the wing and how difficult it was to keep level, then it all went out.'

Bill smiled. 'Just as long as you never fill that bloody flask of yours again – *that* was the main problem! Christ almighty Tom, you were as pissed as a newt when I got you out of the cockpit. Had to smother you with petrol to cover up the smell. These medics think I gave you a tot to pull you round, so stick to that if anyone asks. Not that anyone will – we are heroes at present. Mr Booker's as pleased as punch with the photography, thank God. Anyway, we have at least three days off, so says Major Kemp.'

By the time Tom and Bill were back onto the flying roster the weather had clamped down preventing further photo-recce missions for the time being. Rumour had it that the assault had been delayed a couple of days, but the barrage went on even heavier than before.

'God! You could actually feel our own shells as they flew past. Couldn't hear 'em though – been bloody deaf these past few days.' Flight Sgt Andy Sawyer was a new replacement fresh from England. Even so, Captain Booker had him over the lines within two days of his arrival on 'A' Flight. It was his hard luck to arrive the day before the Somme barrage started.

'Corporal Proctor? Report to the C/O now!' Sharing a look with Tom, he left the tent, still afraid that his pilot's drinking had been discovered. They both knew it could mean a court martial.

Major Kemp invited him to sit down. 'Well then Proctor, it seems you are to be a pilot!' Seeing the surprise on Bill's open face he passed him the order from 3rd Wing HQ. 'As you see, you are to go to England for pilot training. Congratulations Proctor, I think you must have forgotten you put in for it when you were with 4 Squadron. Evidently you are to return immediately and report to Netheravon, Wiltshire, on the Monday 3rd of July. Today is the 29th, which means your first available boat is the 11 pip-emma from Dunkirk – tomorrow!'

Overcoming his surprise Bill had some questions. 'I should like to return to 12 Squadron if possible sir, is there any chance of that?' Roger Kemp liked the young airman, but he knew he could never promise his future.

'I would like you back Proctor, and this last mission of yours may strengthen my hand in getting you back, but you will have to do well on your course! No promises, but I will see what can be done. Now, off you go, see the clerk and get your pass, movement orders, back pay and so forth.' Major Kemp stood up and shook his hand. 'I'm sorry to lose you lad but right now it's a good time for you to be in England, so the best of luck and good flying.'

With mixed feelings Bill spent the rest of the morning clearing from the unit and getting orders for his posting to England. By the time he was back at 'A' Flight everyone congratulated him – good news always travels fast on an operational unit. Tom was sorry to see him go but happy for him just the same.

'You'll have to stop drinking Tom, or at least don't mix it with altitude!'

Tom hung his head. 'I could have killed us both Bill, and if you don't need it why should I? I shall manage without that damned flask from now on, besides, I'm getting hints from Simone and Jean Louis. I can't afford that!'

They shook hands. 'Write soon Bill, let me know how they treat you and remember, don't tell them you know how to fly; don't even give them a whisper. Flying instructors love to think they have a 'natural' on their hands. They get like mother hens then they want to tell the world how *they* and they alone brought you into the world of flying!' Bill laughed, but he knew Tom wasn't joking – he used to be an instructor before coming to France!

Tired and encumbered with kit bag, webbing and full marching order, Bill stepped ashore at Dover in the early hours of the 1st July. The Movement Control Officer, a testy WOI of the Military Police told him he could either go to London on the 0630 train, then take a train to Salisbury, or take pot luck on a coach to Winchester starting in

230

twenty minutes. Evidently the Army ran regular coaches between Winchester and Salisbury, so it was most likely the best route. Opting for the latter he received a chit from a sleepy MP and waited for the coach.

'Bloody MPs, about time them buggers did some fighting 'stead of fucking us PBI about!'

Bill turned to face his companion, a big East Lancs private. 'Can't say I'm fond of 'em myself. There's enough around here to make an entire Army I should think.'

They were joined by a small round Lance Corporal of the East Staffs. 'I nearly joined 'em myself you know! Problem was, they found out my Mum and Dad wus married!' As the laughter died away Bill realised that MPs did at least serve one important purpose, they were good for morale!

He slept most of the way to Winchester then, after an hour's waiting, boarded another coach for Salisbury. The local MCO, an elderly Captain of Engineers, was most helpful.

'RFC Netheravon! I think you are going to be lucky son. They usually have a tender coming into town about eleven o'clock. Why not leave your kitbag with me and get something to eat in the marketplace? Be back here for, say, half-past ten. Don't worry I'll make sure they don't go without you!'

As Bill took to the streets he could see the beautiful spire of Salisbury cathedral and, as a country lad, took interest in the market and the stallholders setting up their awnings. It was only 0750 but the city was alive with traders. It seemed a thousand miles and a thousand years from France. A strident west country voice and a milling crowd brought him to a newspaper stand.

'Big Allied push on the Somme – get your paper. British Army advances along a fourteen mile front! Get your early edition…'

Bill pushed his way to the voice and the slim edition was his for a penny. So it was true. Of course he knew it – he had actually been further than the Tommies now struggling in the shell-torn fields! He recalled Major Kemp's words…'Right now it's a good time for you to be in England'. His appetite had gone. A walk to the cathedral close – he could not enter, he still wore his revolver, then back to the town. Feeling a little better he had some fish and chips then returned to the coach station.

The friendly MCO was as good as his word; the Netheravon tender was waiting for him and his kitbag was already on board. Bill drew a deep breath. Would any of his friends still be alive in the event that he should he return to 12 Squadron?

231

The journey to Netheravon took almost an hour through rolling Wiltshire countryside. Then, without going through the village, the tender struggled up a long steep hill to the RFC camp at the top. Mostly comprised of huts, there were lines of tents, hangars of various types and a red-bricked headquarters. From the guardroom entrance he was taken to the station HQ and after waiting half an hour was seen by an RFC Warrant Officer who confirmed his orders and his posting to 'A' Flight Pilot Training Squadron. Allocated a billet, he was taken to the bedding stores where he collected his blankets, and since it was time for dinner, dropped off at the cookhouse. It reminded him of Farnborough and to thoughts of Sam and Alice too.

From the aircraft now flying he could see that training was conducted with Maurice Farnham 'Shorthorns' and Avro 504s, and from talks with members of his flight he was delighted to learn that the 'Shorthorn' was only used by 'C' Flight. Evidently Netheravon was now devoted entirely to NCO pilot training, whereas officer pilots were trained at Upavon a few miles distant. Direct intakes were sent to 'C' and trained on the old pusher-type Shorthorn. Army NCOs transferring to the RFC went to 'B' Flight and 'A' was reserved for qualified RFC observers converting to pilot.

Only half of his billet seemed to be present, and a total of fifteen were said to start the course on Monday. All were observers and all had seen service in France, most of them were corporals but there were a few AMs as well. Bill spent the weekend writing letters. There were letters home, he had neglected them of late, and one to Sam at Farnborough. It appeared that the course was likely to be anything from four to six months depending on the weather and also on ability. Leave was out of the question, but a 48-hour pass was possible after the first month. A number of observers boasted some piloting experience, but Bill kept quiet, he was going to follow Tom's advice to the letter.

Number 47 Observer Conversion Course started with sixteen pupils. There were two sergeants, three AMs and eleven corporals. They spent the first week with medical inspections, drill, physical training and lectures, and Bill could only wonder at his luck, since his discharge from the STC had occurred only days before his posting came through. He passed the medicals and the obligatory FFI without difficulty.

The second week started badly. One of the Sergeant pupils was killed and his instructor severely injured when their Avro crashed during an 'introduction to controls' flight. It was only at the end of the week that Bill flew on his first 'introduction to controls' with his Flight Instructor, Flight Sergeant Ron Wallace.

'Well done Proctor! You seem to have grasped the theory quite well. But one thing you must learn about the Avro 504 is coordination of controls. Next time we go up I'll show you what I mean but if you keep this up I cannot see any problems.'

By the end of the third week Bill had the complete confidence of his instructor who, just as Tom predicted, took a personal interest in *his* fledgling. He had now completed five hours of dual and were it not for a shower of rain Ron Wallace would have sent him solo.

Bill spent his Sunday answering all the letters he had received from Dacre, and from Sam. Jane Graham had sent him one of her silk stockings. Evidently she had read something somewhere that all pilots wore them around their necks, but they had to come from their girl! Maggie confirmed all of this and further informed him that Jane had even asked his mother if she could send it! His mother's letter was full of joy that he was out of the brutal fighting now bogged down on the Somme front. Bill had never even seen a newspaper since he had arrived at Netheravon, and was shocked to learn that the casualty lists now disclosed that over 20,000 infantry were killed on the first assault on the 1st July!

Sam was now an Acting Sergeant Instructor and urged Bill to visit him as soon as he got a pass. From what he said, it appeared there were a number of new machines and engines that would interest him! Bill resolved to make the visit as soon as he could, particularly since it was impossible to get home until the end of his course and even that was not certain.

At the start of the fourth week Bill went solo and continued to make excellent progress; by Friday he had a total of 14 hours in his log book and a 48-hour pass. But best of all, he managed a to get a lift in a Crossley that was going to Farnborough for some engine spares early on Saturday morning, and with luck would be returning late Sunday.

Sam was delighted to see him, particularly since it was a total surprise.

'Sorry I didn't have time to write Sam but I hoped you would be here.' Sam laughed as he took Bill to the accommodation he had found for him in one of the training huts.

'As a matter of fact I too got a 48-hour pass this weekend but as I was Orderly Sgt until 0800 this morning I managed to swop it for next weekend – talk about luck!' The two friends spent most of their time catching up with personal and technical matters. Sam being particularly proud of his young pal, took him to Farnborough for a meal on Saturday evening, where they discussed Alice for a short while.

'I'm over it now Sam, but I have to admit it hit me pretty hard at the time. I also know how lucky I am to have escaped the Somme offensive, so I can't complain; and I've had enough of girls thank you!'

Sam told him of the new machines and engines now being tested at Farnborough. 'If you go back to two-seaters, reconnaissance machines for example, you might well be flying the RE8. It's supposed to be much better than the BE2c and I've heard it will be in France this Autumn.'

Although they planned to have the rest of Sunday together it wasn't to be. Bill's Crossley was ready for return at 1000, so he had to say farewell to Sam earlier than expected. Filled with engine spares and two new Avro engines their progress was slow, finally arriving at Netheravon late in the afternoon. Although disappointed, Bill had to admit he needed the extra time since there were two days of 'principles of flight' examinations in front of him and he needed to study!

Wednesday morning found them all assembled for their first-phase examination results. These included theoretical studies as well as practical flight tests. The eliminations had begun! Three of the observers, two corporals and one AM had been scrubbed from the course and were to return to their units. They were now down to twelve, and two of them were put back one week for further flying.

Bill's theoretical work was average, but his flying was posted as 'above average' and Ron Wallace was even heard to claim, 'That lad's a natural if ever I saw one!'

By the end of August Bill had completed 32 hours of flying and was considered top of his course with respect to flying and engine handling. His cross-country flights were good, but poor weather had denied him his final test in navigation. Then a bad bout of flu kept him back for a further three weeks. It was only in the first week of September that he managed to catch up again, by which time he was actually one week behind the leaders of a course now reduced to ten. With improved weather and a further eight hours of cross-country practice Bill finally passed his navigation tests with 'above average' results. There followed further lectures on artillery spotting, oblique and vertical photography and more tests. Finally, there was ground gunnery. Each pilot had to qualify with the Lewis and Vickers using a simulator that resembled a pram and ran on a railway track. The track ran on a curve and the 'pram', complete with pilot and machine gun, was then pushed down a slope while the pilot trained his gun on a moving target running on an adjacent track. It was great fun!

As Len Howard, a comic Lancastrian put it. 'By 'eck if I could get this into Blackpool I'd make a million!' With bad weather limiting their flying they did extra work on the gunnery simulator, much to their general pleasure.

By Monday 16th October the remaining ten pupils of No 47 course were told they had all but passed, and that they could expect a 48-hour pass at the weekend. During the following week, depending on the weather, they would continue with formation flying. Then there would be a 'Wings Parade', a final flypast and notification of postings. The only leave allowed would be on compassionate grounds.

Bill wrote to Sam, telling him he would catch a train to Farnborough and could he meet him on Friday evening at the 'Saxon Inn'. It was nearly over! In the following days there were lectures and the start of formation flying, a tricky business with the Avro, but with light winds it was not too difficult. Then it was Friday.

'I thought you'd be wearing your pilot's wings by now Bill.' Sam was nursing a pint in the snug as Bill entered the 'Saxon' in his best uniform.

'Next week Sam, then it's all over. But we have to have a parade first, you should know that by now!' Bill had never felt so good for months, and relieved from much of the tension brought about by flying tests and examinations, his thirst knew no bounds. But fortunately Sam did, and took care to get him back to camp before he drank too much.

'Tomorrow I thought we might spend some time in Guildford, there's a good Charlie Chaplin film on at the Gaumont, what do you say?' Bill could agree to anything and insisted dinner would be his treat this time.

With a slight hangover to contend with, Sam was sure that Guildford would offer few bad memories for Bill, and indeed it didn't seem to. He couldn't help noticing that many a girl stole an interested glance in the young aviator's direction and that despite his earlier denial Bill was not totally unaware of their interest.

It was close to lunch-time, just as they were rounding a street corner that they bumped into her. Bill stopped dead in his tracks – his eyes fixed to her face. Sam spoke first, already taking in her obviously pregnant condition.

'Hello Alice.'

She was still looking at Bill as she replied. 'Hello Sam ... it's nice to see you again ... and a Sergeant now, congratulations.' Bill remained silent, his face a mask. She was too close for him to see her condition.

'Hello Bill.' She spoke softly and her voice made him churn inside. The old feeling – it was still there! 'I hope you are well ... you look just fine.' Tears were in her eyes as she looked at him.

235

As Alice stepped aside to allow passage for someone Bill saw her fully.

'I suppose you're married now then.' His voice was cold and tight. The tears were flooding down her cheeks as she searched for her handkerchief

'We were to have been married last week. Gerry was killed in a flying accident two weeks ago.' Sam sucked in his breath as Bill's anger gave voice to months of pent up emotion and despair.

'Serves him bloody right.' Alice put her hand to her mouth as Sam stood shocked at Bill's cold-blooded words.

'He didn't mean that Alice, that's not our Bill talking. He's just upset at seeing you…'

Bill walked off at marching pace, and by the time Sam had caught up with him he had recovered a little.

'I know Sam, I'm a bastard. It serves her right all the same! That's the end of it, that's the bloody end of it.'

They tried to forget the incident, but it was always there, even the Charlie Chaplin film couldn't change the atmosphere. There was still much to discuss, but it wasn't the same and the dinner didn't even help. Later that evening Bill told Sam he was sorry he had said what he did, but he meant it all the same!

Bill took the late morning train back to Salisbury and catching a local bus, was in camp by 5.30 pip-emma. He wrote an apology to Sam, posted it at the camp post office then returned to his bunk, to cry silently into the night before sleep gave him rest.

After two days of formation flying over the camp they practised their drill for the forthcoming 'Wings Parade' due to be held on Thursday. Cleaning the best uniforms they were reminded to remove their 'O' badge, they were getting 'full wings' tomorrow! They had also arranged for a party to be held in the village tomorrow night.

The parade went well, despite the low overcast that had already cancelled their planned flypast. But at least the rain held off long enough for the main event - as the Camp Commandant, a full Colonel, pinned Pilot's wings on the breast of ten brand new RFC pilots. There was the usual speech about duty, God, King and Country but nobody was listening. Then they marched off to the flight lecture room for their documentation and postings. The rain followed two minutes later!

As they filed into the lecture room the Flight Commander, Major Pearson, welcomed each of the new pilots with a glass of beer.

'Right chaps! Settle down at your usual desks and enjoy your beer as I tell you what is on the agenda. To begin with I want to congratu-

236

late you all! And I know I speak for all the instructors gathered here when I say that you've been one of the best flights we've had here, and it's been a pleasure to see you all come through with flying colours! Now I'm going to pass round an envelope to each of you. In it you will find your log-book, fully signed up with all your hours, your pilot certificate, your orders, and for some of you, notice of promotion. You all volunteered for pilot, so I'm sure you all expect your orders will lead you to France. Indeed this is true! And you are to report to the MCO at Dover by 1000 hours on Monday 30th October when you will sail for Dunkirk and all those nice French girls you've been dreaming about!'

As the envelopes were passed round Bill wondered if he was going to 12 Squadron – he hoped so. Tearing open the brown and bulky envelope the first thing he noticed was the stripes. Four sets of cloth Sergeant stripes each complete with its associated four-bladed propeller badge. He hadn't expected it at all.

'Well deserved Bill, welcome to the Sgts' Mess!' It was Ron Wallace his flying instructor. 'Thanks 'Flight' I suppose this is all your work?'

Ron laughed, 'Well only a small part, the C/O and the Flight Commander had the most to say. And it's Ron now – and you owe me a pint this lunchtime!' It was like opening a Christmas stocking. There was a pair of pilot's wings, travel warrants, his pay-book now completed with his new status, twenty five pounds of back pay in large five pound notes and two sealed envelopes. The first one he opened contained his pilot's certificate, with the rating 'Above Average'. The second one contained his orders: w.e.f. 30/10/1916. Sergeant William Proctor RFC is to proceed to 12 Squadron, Avesnes-le-Comte, 3rd Wing, RFC, France.

Bill was delighted, and since he couldn't go home he decided to stay in camp. He wasn't alone, and with three others in similar circumstances, he knew they could enjoy Netheravon as well as anywhere. With another new Sergeant, Bill spent some time in the Sgts' Mess, wrote letters home and enjoyed the late autumn sunshine watching the flying. There was lots of sewing to do as well!

It was a very tired and rather unshaven Sgt Pilot that reported to the Squadron Office at Avesnes on the 1st November, but he was greeted warmly by Major Kemp.

'Of course, I've been expecting you Sergeant. Things have changed a bit of course. Sorry to say, but Captain Booker was killed in the first week of the offensive, that's cooled off now as you probably know.' Bill said he knew about Captain Booker – he'd heard it from Tom. 'It's been a hard time for everyone Sergeant. We lost a lot of crews as well. I know you will be glad to hear that Sgt Bolton survived, got himself a decoration too. I tried to get you the same gong but Wing thought otherwise, sorry about that! But now you're a pilot it won't be long before you catch up. Oh yes! We are beginning to replace our quirks with the new RE8; not much better from reports I've been getting but there you are! Anyway, get yourself some sleep then report to your new 'A' Flight Commander tomorrow.' Bill saluted and left for the Sgts' Mess, leaving his kit bag in the care of the Mess Corporal.

He was about to walk down to the lines when a familiar figure stood in the doorway.

'Jesus Christ Bill you're a bloody Sergeant! I couldn't make it out when someone said they thought I might recognise the new pilot coming to 'A' Flight.' As they fell in each others arms there were tears of joy as they punched each other and sank into the broken arm chairs surrounding the bar. As they drank their beer, obtained from a friendly barman, Bill laughed as he spotted the oil-stained red, white and blue striped ribbon of the Military Medal.

'Where the fuck did you buy that you old sod!' Tom looked away, shaking his head from side to side.

'You earned it – I wear it! Christ Bill this is yours and you didn't get a fucking thing! I feel awful, but if I told them the truth…!' Bill thumped his friend on the shoulder.

'You earned that gong many times over Tom but the reason why you got it – I think it's the best joke of all!' Laughing loudly they ordered another round; it was going to be a long day!

Chapter Fourteen

The battle of the Somme was over, and both sides of the conflict were nursing their wounds. Over 400,000 British and 200,000 French were either killed or wounded over a sixteen mile battle front which, by mid-November had come to a standstill through attrition and mud. For all of 1,300 heavy guns, nearly two million shells, fifty tanks and 190 battalions, Rawling's army gained little ground – it was a disaster! The Germans had prepared their defences well, dugouts were forty feet deep and their machine gun nests were placed on hill crests, the better to shoot down on the advancing 'Tommies', who were instructed to walk since the enemy were not expected to survive eight days of continuous shelling.

Loaded up with ammunition and grenades, each advancing soldier carried 66 lb as well as his rifle and bayonet, and as the barrage lifted he walked into a hail of machine gun fire as the Germans crawled out of their protective dugouts and manned their machine guns. The barrage had not even flattened the enemy wire in many places – it was wholesale slaughter! The German Army of the Somme suffered too. Through deadly counter attacks and reluctance to yield ground, they lost no less than 500,000 dead and wounded.

Bill had reported to his new Flight Commander, Captain Brian Webster, and found him to be a quiet and distant man but a good officer for all that.

'He's all right; didn't spare himself during the offensive and always did the worst jobs himself, but he lost his wife only three days after joining us – childbirth they say, lost the kid too.' Tom had been telling him of the battle, and the role of the squadron during the early days, before the weather curtailed operations. 'I've never been so damned glad I was in the RFC! I tell you Bill, the ground was just a mass of shell holes and while we were flying there was as much chance of being shot down by one of our own shells flying over as there was from German archie! The lads went over the top at 0730, I saw them as I flew overhead. The whole lot of us were up, mainly doing bombing with

239

the quirks and CPs with the Avros; within minutes we couldn't see anything for smoke. What a mess! We lost three crews in the first week! When you next fly you won't even recognise the ground you used to know. Which reminds me, when do you get into the air Bill? Has the boss allocated you an observer yet?"

It was now the fourth of December and since the weather and the war were both at a low ebb, 12 Sqdn had not been very active. Nevertheless, after three days back on 'A' Flight, Bill was impatient to fly. He had only eighty minutes piloting time logged in a BE2c, a period experienced during his last month at Netheravon, when it must have been decided that he was to return to reconnaissance duties. And apart from his unofficial training with Tom he realised that his BE2c experience was very limited. It wasn't that the quirk was difficult to fly, far from it. But he would now have an observer to look after as well, and he felt painfully unsure of himself.

The bad weather got much worse, with blankets of low cloud scudding across Picardy and grounding everything on both sides of the front. Most of their time was spent on lectures, mainly concerning the new RE8 aircraft with which 12 Sqdn was to be re-equipped the following year.

Captain Webster was his own man and not the slightest bit worried about speaking his mind. 'The news, or should I say rumours, concerning the RE8 are not so good I'm afraid. I hear that it's just as stable as the old BE2c – too stable in other words. It has a maximum speed of 98 mph at 6500 feet, and slightly less than that at 10,000 feet. It takes all of 40 minutes to get there too! Its ceiling is only 11,000 feet but I never expected more; it's a ground-loving Army Cooperation machine after all. It has a good endurance it seems, some four hours or more and that with a full load of two 112lb bombs. Friends of mine on 59 squadron say they have had a lot of problems – deadly ones! The blasted thing spins easily they say, and if you let it drop below 50 mph it's goodnight! Like the quirk, but even more so. Do *not* stand up in the rear cockpit when landing! And pilots – use lots of bank when turning. Evidently flat turns can turn into flat spins with this beast. So far 59 have lost two crews and one pilot.'

Tom held up his hand. 'When do we get them sir? I hope I've got enough time to put in for a transfer to the infantry!'

Captain Webster saw the joke, but his reply was heavy with irony. 'Let's not be hasty Sergeant. All you need is faith, or failing that become pregnant!'

It wasn't until the 7th that Bill could fly. It was a humid cold morning with about four tenths cloud and a hint of rain but Bill's first solo flight was no more than two circuits and a landing. He knew that his Flight Commander was watching, so he was careful to make sure his landing was good; it was.

'I think we shall have to get you fixed up with an observer as soon as possible Proctor. And as we are to expect two new observers tomorrow I shall allocate him to you now. He is Second Lieutenant John Kenting, Green Howards. Evidently he has yet to qualify for his 'O' badge, but that won't be difficult since I see he did wireless training with 9 Squadron before he left for France. I'm going to put you down for artillery spotting to start with, mainly to get Lieutenant Kenting qualified with something he knows how to do. He looks pretty good with wireless – 15 words a minute!'

Tom saw him in the mess that evening. 'Heard the news Bill!' He looked up, Tom had brought over a couple of pints of beer. 'Lloyd George was made Prime Minister yesterday, he's leading a new coalition government.'

Bill sneered. 'Fat lot I care who's bloody prime minister, fucking politicians, they're all bloody crooks anyway.'

Tom looked at him. 'Why so glum, you did well this morning I thought...'

'I have to nurse a one pipper as my observer; he arrives tomorrow! I'll bet he's some public schoolboy who's never done a day's work in his bloody life.'

Tom laughed. 'Well you've flown with officers before so what's new? Except you are now the driver of course.'

Bill thought about his problem. 'Yes, but who's in charge when we're flying, me or him?'

'Good question Bill. In the Hun's flying corps it's the observer who's always in charge, but in our mob the driver is always boss of the aeroplane. Mind you, if you are doing a shoot or photography, then the observer is boss of the mission! I mean, *you* should remember that. How many times have you flown with officers when you were only a corporal? And who told the driver where to go? Then again, when attacked it's the driver who takes over! I suppose it's a question of co-operation and I cannot ever remember a difficult situation. I suppose that's because the observer has to rely on his driver more than the other way about.'

Bill met his observer the following afternoon. John Kenting was a pleasant-faced young man, about the same age but slightly taller than himself. Slim of build and level-eyed, he had light brown hair on top of what Bill liked to call 'aristocratic features'. Most certainly John Kenting was of the upper class and his long aquiline nose was proof enough of that.

Captain Webster made the introductions very simple. 'Sergeant Proctor is your pilot Kenting. You're a lucky chap too. He's rated as an 'above average' pilot and has seen lots of action as an observer on both 4 and 12 Squadrons. He's also a fitter – engines and airframes!' Bill was impressed. He'd never had his qualifications listed in public before; embarrassed, he could only smile shyly as they shook hands.

'I can see I shall be in good hands sir, thank you. I only hope I won't let you or Sergeant Proctor down as I learn the ropes.'

Brian Webster gave his new officer a hard stare. 'It's all a question of cooperation Kenting. Get to know each other, learn how to communicate when in the air, Proctor will show you. I want you operational in two day's time, so I want to see you flying as much as you can in the meantime. I shall allocate you a battery on Monday, but by that time I want you both comfortable as a crew. You know the ropes Proctor, see to it that Mr Kenting gets some air-to-air gunnery practice as well, eh!'

John Kenting felt like a new boy at school, but despite his nervousness he felt comfort in the thought that his pilot was more or less the same age as himself And although the Sergeant was much more experienced than he was, he looked a decent type and seemed rather shy if anything. Having introduced his observer to the BE2c, Bill did his usual pre-flight inspection with John Kenting following in his footsteps.

'You have no idea how reassuring it is to know my pilot has such a good knowledge of aircraft Sergeant!' It was the plummy tones that put Bill's teeth on edge.

'Well this is how I started sir,' he showed him his hands, 'This is what I do, and with luck – lots of luck – I'll get back to it when this lot's over.'

Sensing the distance that Bill was putting between them, John Kenting realised he would need to be careful with the young Yorkshireman. Bill had completed his inspection and after helping his observer to climb into the front cockpit he demonstrated the four pivot points for the Lewis gun. 'I suggest you try each point for firing the Lewis sir. I will give you the signal when we are at 5000 feet. Then, as an after thought he smiled and added, 'Please don't hit anything valuable, like me for instance!'

John Kenting laughed. 'Certainly not Sergeant, your wellbeing is my sincere concern, believe me!'

The flight went well, John Kenting managed to deploy the Lewis in all four positions and seemed to enjoy himself. Then, at a bumpy 2,000 feet, Bill took him up to the front. He was careful as he flew past Mametz Wood, remembering his last operational visit had almost been his last. As Tom had said, the terrain was now unrecognisable. And Mametz Wood remained as one in name only. He flew on as far as Flers then turned within a mile of the new front line to fly south towards the French lines at Rancourt, where they received a welcome from a German anti-aircraft battery. Bill looked at his map, Rancourt was just inside the new front – time to return! He looked at his observer crouching down within the cockpit. No doubt this was his first introduction to archie; he'd get used to it!

'Never expected that Hun archie sir, went a bit too close to the French front at Rancourt. Sorry about that!'

John Kenting had just climbed down from his cockpit. 'I think you must know that was my first experience of archie Sergeant. I have to admit I … well I got the wind-up, it was so unexpected I suppose.'

Bill felt sorry for the young officer. It took guts to admit to fear, just as Tom did. 'You and me too sir, it was as close as I've ever experienced.' Bill lied with ease – feeling much older than his nineteen years. As Bill inspected the aircraft before handing over to their ground crew he was impressed to see that 2nd Lt Kenting had removed the Lewis gun himself and had shouldered it for return to the armoury. It was true that all observers should take responsibility for their gun but many officers left it to the armourers. Perhaps he wasn't going to be so bad after all!

By the 12th December Bill was feeling more at ease with his flying and quite content with his observer. They had been given the 98th RFA battery for their shoot, and Bill was relieved to see that John Kenting had insisted on doing the observation as well as the wireless work. Overflying the guns just south of Le Sars they noticed the battery was at readiness for the first shoot at 1015 hours.

Flying at 4000 feet, Bill took the quirk in a wide sweep around their target, the town of Bapaume. A prime objective during the Somme battles, Bapaume remained a heavily defended position and as a frequent target for Allied guns was surrounded by a large number of archie batteries.

Following the road from Le Sars to Bapaume, Bill knew he could expect the worst as soon as he was sighted, and determined his best course of action was to keep altering his height as much as possible. By prior arrangement, John Kenting would transmit only when Bill flew the quirk on a heading towards Le Sars and so gain the best transmission quality.

The archie was intense and accurate but so were the 98th's guns. As the quirk buffeted along they could see their corrections were applied immediately, and Bill knew he had never seen a shoot as accurate as this before. He was now at 5000 feet and the archie was now drifting up to him, then stopped.

Bill looked around, thankful he had overcome his initial embarrassment and was now wearing Jane's silk stocking around his creaking neck. He couldn't see them yet, but he knew the Hun scouts would soon be on the scene and the promised escorts were nowhere in sight! As if mirroring his thoughts John Kenting was crossing his arms repeatedly – time to go home! Bill motioned for him to scan the tail, which was the only sector his observer could view easily anyway.

As Bill turned onto 225 degrees his banked turn was just sufficient for him to see the two E3s climbing up to them, almost within range. Cutting the throttle he pulled the stick right back and waited for the stall. As the nose dropped he flung the stick over to the left, precipitating a spin, directly into the approaching machines.

John Kenting had no idea of what was happening. Clinging onto the Lewis he tried to keep upright but failed. At the fourth spin he was violently sick and completely unaware of the fight now taking place as the two Eindekkers tried to shoot at the spinning quirk. The altimeter was unwinding fast and showed less than 2000 feet as Bill tried to see where the enemy were positioned. He caught sight of one as it passed his front but it told him nothing. There was no time left – he must straighten out now regardless of where the Huns might be stationed. Pushing the throttle and stick forward he waited half a turn then applied opposite rudder. The quirk responded slowly but readily returned to controlled flight as, in a shallow descent, it levelled off some 400 feet above the shattered ground.

Bill forced himself to scan the surrounding sky – nothing! He could hardly believe his luck, there was still no sign of his escort but where did the E3s go? He searched once more and looked to the front cockpit. A grey face hung over the cockpit edge then disappeared into the depths of the cockpit. Concerned for his observer Bill knew he must recover his position and land at the first safe opportunity. He could see khaki-clad figures waving below; at least they were over their own lines now. The compass was no use – still spinning. Taking stock he recognised Flers to the left and the stricken remains of High Wood ahead, but there was no place he could land. After five minutes he could see the only remaining landmark of Albert, the 'hanging virgin' of its Basilica. Toppled by gunfire during the fierce fighting of previous months, the Basilica's famous statue of the Virgin now hung precariously from the tower, a clear landmark for many aviators as it stood out against the flattened landscape.

Since his nearest field was Bertangles, Bill landed there and quickly gunned the quirk to his old lines. Mounting the lower plane beneath the front cockpit Bill hoisted up his observer. That he'd been violently sick was obvious but he could see no signs of blood.

'Are you hurt sir, were you hit?'

John Kenting turned his face upwards, smelling terrible. 'Just sick, frightfully sick – sorry!'

Bill dismounted as familiar faces appeared.

'Jesus Christ our Bill's been made a fucking pilot! And a hairy-arsed Sergeant to boot. God 'elp the RFC!' It was Trevor Simpson and Ted Hamilton. As they inspected the BE2c they chatted like monkeys, drawing the attention of many old friends on the squadron. Trevor Simpson frowned as he looked at the tailplane.

'Holy shit Bill! Your port elevator is only just hanging on. You're grounded old son until that gets fixed.'

Ted Hamilton joined in. 'Should take all of two days wouldn't you say Trev?' Bill laughed, knowing their intentions were for him to stay and indulge in some of 4 Sqdn's hospitality.

'Sorry lads, I'll have to get back to 12 as soon as possible, my observer is a bit out of sorts and needs to get back.' Seeing the concern now appearing on their faces Bill hastened to explain. 'He's been as sick as a dog and he's also an officer, so I don't want him embarrassed.' They were all looking at the front cockpit, apparently empty and where nothing stirred.

'Ted! Do you think you could get a bucket of water and some clean cloths? I'll get him and the cockpit cleaned up a bit first, then make my respects to … to?'

Ted helped him out. 'Best run over to see Captain Moore, he's our new 'A' Flight Commander, you wouldn't know anyone now Bill! Dead, wounded or posted – they've all gone, although Captain Saul is still here, he's acting C/O, but due home soon.'

Bill returned to the cockpit to find John Kenting busy cleaning off his flying suit with a handkerchief. 'While the AMs are getting some spares we might take this opportunity to clean you up sir, then we'll have a go at the cockpit.' Helping him down to the ground he took him to the other side of the quirk as Ted arrived with the bucket. Leaving

245

him to clean himself up, Bill left with Trevor and Ted to visit Captain Moore.

Having received permission to have the aircraft repaired, and a signal sent to his squadron, Bill returned to his machine to help Trevor Simpson with the elevator. Noticing some activity in the front cockpit he found John Kenting cleaning it up.

'I can get one of the ack-emmas to do that sir!'

John Kenting didn't bother to look up. 'No, it's my mess and I'll do it thank you!'

There were shell holes in the rear fuselage and in both lower planes, but it was the port elevator that was the main concern. Bill was helping Trevor to replace it when John Kenting joined them. Trevor made a face!

'Begging your pardon sir, but a drop of petrol on your suit might not be a bad idea!' Bill remained silent, embarrassed by his friend's impertinence.

John Kenting raised an eyebrow then broke into laughter. 'I couldn't agree more! And thank you for an excellent suggestion. I was even thinking of burying the damned thing.' They all joined in the laughter as Bill went to drain off some fuel from a nearby tank.

As Trevor continued with the elevator Bill explained his drastic manoeuvre to John Kenting. 'Sorry I had to spin the kite sir, it was the only thing I could think of – I never saw the two E3s until I started to return home and they were actually firing at us.' Smelling of petrol but looking a lot better the young officer shook his head.

'It's me that should apologise Sergeant. I was so taken aback by the spin I just lost my footing – then my breakfast! Couldn't even stand up, let alone man the gun.'

Bill sympathised. 'Nobody could sir, and I should know. I've spent enough time in the front cockpit of a quirk to know what it's like. That particular manoeuvre isn't unknown to me either. That's how I learnt it – the hard way! But strange to tell, when you are actually handling the controls you never feel the sickness so much.'

Within two hours they were airborne once more. The BE flew quite well, but Bill could see it would need trimming when they got back to the squadron. His thoughts turned to 2nd Lt. Kenting during the short flight home. He seemed a pretty nice chap, for an officer!

Captain Webster was waiting for them as they walked into 'A' Flight's office. 'Quite a busy day for you from all accounts! We were getting a bit concerned until I heard from Captain Moore on 4 Sqdn. We had a call from 2 Sqdn to say their scouts saw you spin down to the ground.

Oh yes, they also sent an apology, evidently they were intercepted by a group of Albatros DIIIs as they were covering you, which is why they were late in reaching those Huns that attacked you. So what happened Mr Kenting?'

'We had just completed the shoot; it seemed pretty accurate sir. Then I signalled Sergeant Proctor to return. The next thing I knew was being on the floor of the cockpit and we were in a spin.'

Bill decided to explain. 'It was either that or being hit by those E3s sir. I only just saw them as I banked to return home. I never saw their approach until they were right beneath, so I spun into them.'

They talked at length. 'Who taught you that particular tactic Proctor? I suppose it's something you picked up at Netheravon eh?'

Bill had to disabuse his Flight Commander of what seemed to be an official manoeuvre. 'I once experienced it myself when observing for Sgt Bolton sir, but I think I overdid it a bit.'

'We also had a call from the 98th RFA Mr Kenting. They were jolly pleased with your corrections and say you placed their guns bang on target. Well done the two of you, well done!'

Bill was pleased with his observer and it was obvious they worked well as a crew. There was little activity over the front as Christmas approached, and by the 23rd they had completed only three contact patrols before he went down with the flu. Sweating under his blankets he was isolated in a special medical ward for over three weeks, seeing nobody except his fellow patients and two orderlies. Fearing an epidemic, the Wing Senior MO had dispatched a signal to all squadrons indicating that each squadron must take every precaution to prevent the spread of infection and 12 Squadron's MO allowed no one near the isolated ward. Nevertheless, Bill enjoyed an excellent Christmas, with letters from home and notes from Tom and, to his surprise, John Kenting. Although he was not too surprised at the bottle of brandy that came with Tom's letter, he was touched by the gift of a large bottle of whisky that arrived with the note from his observer. Evidently John Kenting had been teamed up with another pilot, a 2nd Lt recently come to the squadron, but it seemed he had managed to extract a promise from Captain Webster that when Bill was released from the medics they should crew together again. 'You saved my life once, and I think I have the best pilot on the squadron. Always in your debt, John Kenting.'

True to his word, Captain Webster put them back together when Bill was returned fit for flying. It was mid-January and his first flight was no more than a one hour air test of 'A' Flight's one and only Avro

504. Well-wrapped up against the bitter cold, Bill knew it was no more than an excuse to ease him back into the air, but he was surprised to find Mr Kenting had joined him for this non-operational flight, particularly since it was the coldest winter on record, even the Lewis gun oil was frozen!

'It's only an air test sir, but you are most welcome to come along.' John Kenting had arrived only minutes before he was due to fly, and taking him aside, out of earshot of the ack-emmas, spoke softly.

'I'm sure we can get along without this Sir and Sergeant stuff. If, and only if you agree, I would prefer it if we addressed each other as John and Bill. Naturally our ranks have to be observed when in company, but surely *we* can be friends and address ourselves in a more civilised fashion – what do you say?'

'It could be a bit difficult sir. I mean ... yes, I would like that. Why not... John it is!' The air was crisp and clear and after a couple of landings Bill went up to 4000 feet to stall, recover, and make a few sharp turns. They landed, and after handing the Avro back to the ack-emmas the two frozen aviators returned to the crew tent for Bill to enter his report in the 'A' Flight record sheet. As expected, the tent was empty. The rest of the aircrew being either in a hangar or sensibly huddled around a stove in one of 'A' Flight's servicing huts. As Bill rubbed some warmth into his chilled hands he tried to write a legible report concerning the Avro's performance.

'Here you are Bill, get this down you!' John Kenting had two steaming hot mugs of cocoa in his gloved hands.

'Bless you sir ... sorry, John. Just what I need. But how did you manage to get this and where from?'

John pointed to the blacksmith's shop located in a nearby shed. 'Corporal Sands always has some hot water going, so I scrounged some cocoa from him.'

Bill showed his amazement. 'But he's the meanest bugger on the entire squadron – used to spend all his time with horses before he was transferred to the Corps. He's not known to speak to humans either; how on earth ... ?'

'John Kenting laughed with a schoolboy's enjoyment of his success. 'Well, for one thing I know he likes talking about horses, on which subject I happen to be an expert, and well... rank does have it's privileges you know.'

Bill burned his mouth on the hot cocoa. 'Bloody officers – biggest lot of scroungers in the Corps!'

'Tell me something about yourself Bill. I know you are from Yorkshire of course, tell me where?' Bill told his new friend about the dales and his home, his family and his work as an engine fitter.

'And the funny part of it is I never wanted to fly, just improve my skills as a fitter. But I have to admit it; I love flying now. What made you want to fly John?'

'I arrived at my battalion just after the battle of Loos. The officers were down by almost fifty per cent and I didn't think much of my chances of survival. So when they asked for volunteers to join the RFC, as pilots or observers, I put my hand up. I went to Upavon but was scrubbed from the pilots' course after two weeks. Then I went to 9 Squadron, the wireless school, and here I am. As you can see, I'm not exactly the stuff that heroes are made of Bill. I wish I could be more like you, but I'm not.'

Bill's face mirrored his puzzlement. 'I'm no bloody hero either. All I want to do is survive this lot, believe me John. I don't take any chances, and particularly with the life of my observer.'

John Kenting was quick to explain himself further. 'Please do not mistake what I am saying Bill. You see, while you were in hospital I spoke to your good friend, Tom Bolton. He told me you were entirely without fear, a sort of natural lack of the emotion, rather than some kind of cold courage that manages to overcome it. Tom also told me he wears a ribbon that rightly belongs to you; he wouldn't say more. It is also very likely that you exhibit pure courage, but both Tom and I know that whatever it is we do not share it!'

'What a load of cobblers! You and Tom Bolton both! How on earth do I manage to get such friends is a mystery to me. There's another explanation you know, it's called stupidity!' Realising he had embarrassed the young pilot, John Kenting relented and talked more about himself.

'My elder brother, Quentin, was severely wounded last year. Managed to get himself a DSO too. My family tends to place a lot of importance on that sort of thing, so I suppose I have a rather unhealthy interest in the subject and a lot of self-doubts too I'm afraid.' He opened up the top of his heavy flying leathers to remove a wallet from his breast pocket. Bill noticed the 'O' badge, bright and new on John's chest.

'Hey, you never mentioned the badge John! When did that come through?'

'While you were loafing in dock some of us had to carry on with the war you know. But I think they gave it to me because I managed to survive your flying.'

John showed photographs of his family. His mother and father standing against a tennis court, and a beautiful fair-haired girl standing by a horse. 'Don't have a snap of my brother and it's not likely I ever shall. He's a complete invalid now, poor chap hates his condition, lost both legs you see. Quentin refuses to be photographed.'

Bill was staring at the girl.

'That's my sister Mattie. She's a year younger than me, mad about horses too which is just as well since Quentin can't help now of course. Father used to breed hunters you see, but when our head groom joined up it was nigh impossible to replace him. Mattie left her finishing school a trifle early in order to take charge – she's doing a damned good job I'm told. I took that photo just before I left for France.' As John passed around the photographs Bill stopped short when he saw one of the house.

'Is *this* your house John? Where you were brought up?'

John took the photograph back, shaking his head from side-to-side. 'Yes and no. Yes it is the family home and no, I spent most of my youth at a school in Scotland.'

Bill gave a short laugh. 'Funny really. You and me, poles apart in class but ending up here. I mean, it's doubtful we would ever meet under normal conditions, would we?' Bill had only seen one other mansion in his life, and then only when he delivered a motor after it had been serviced in George Graham's garage. 'Bloody hell, this is a flaming mansion John. I grew up in a tiny terraced house. How much land do you have?'

John Kenting thought a while. 'I think it runs to over a hundred acres, we're farmers you see. It's good agricultural land too, but we have a few cattle as well.'

Bill nearly laughed, farmers indeed! 'It's a lovely house… and the grounds! I suppose you have a gardener?'

' Two actually, but they also work on the farm. Fortunately we are not too far from Norwich, so mother never had too much trouble getting domestics, but that was last year! Evidently all the local girls get better money in the munition factories these days.'

Their conversation was interrupted by the noise of a number of aeroplanes flying overhead. Going outside they found the lines becoming crowded with squadron personnel all looking upwards as a flight of four unfamiliar aircraft prepared to land.

'RE8s,' Bill recognised them from the photographs Captain Webster had showed them nearly two months ago. 'I suppose they are for us, the boss said something about our squadron getting them in the new year.' Now landed, the four RE8s taxied to the lines, their characteristic 'nose-up' attitude being accentuated by the air scoop on top of the 12 cylinder RAF 1A engine.

'Funny looking birds. I hope they are not as bad as rumour suggests.' Bill turned around, it was Tom.

'Well if I remember the facts Tom, the RAF 1A is a good engine, I saw something of it during my advanced fitters course.'

John Kenting commented on the large four-bladed propeller, looking at Bill for an explanation. 'Well it's a big engine John…sir, all of 150 hp and it needs a lot of propeller to absorb the power.'

Tom wasn't over-impressed by its appearance. 'I think those two exhaust stacks sticking up over the top plane make it look a bit like a steam engine, but the observer is at least seated behind the driver - that's an improvement on the old quirk!'

It wasn't until the first week in February that Bill flew the RE8. Tom had already flown it three times and was not too keen on its performance. 'Take care Bill. Everything that Captain Webster said about this machine is right. As you throttle back to land watch out for your airspeed, if it goes below 52 mph you are in deep trouble. The damned thing stalls too easily, right when you're levelling off. So keep your airspeed up when landing lad. All it takes is a gust of wind or a disturbance from your observer and the bloody thing stops flying! I haven't been in a spin yet and I certainly don't want to precipitate one, but when you turn make sure you put on plenty of bank and keep your speed up.'

Bill went over his allocated machine with a careful inspection. He didn't like the small fin and rudder, but he found the engine easy to service. Starting up required a team of three men – holding hands – to pull the big four-bladed propeller over, but it started easily enough. Although John suggested he should come with him, Bill preferred to make his first flight alone.

Since Bill was flying solo, the rear cockpit had to be filled with sandbags – up to 160 pounds of them in all.

John Kenting voiced his dismay. 'I think there is something wrong about an aeroplane that has to carry ballast like a ship.'

Bill laughed. 'You don't fool me. You just don't like being replaced by a load of sand that's all!'

Bill found his take-off quite normal, not too unlike that of the quirk except more powerful. Climbing to 3000 feet he made a few turns, remembering Tom's warnings, and then climbed to 6000 feet to check his maximum airspeed. It was true! The RE8 was just as stable as the BE2c, and apart from a slightly faster speed had little to recommend it

251

over that old worthy. It seemed that if the RE8 was like the quirk, then it would probably spin like a quirk. Bill thought about it for a minute. He knew he couldn't fly the RE8 on missions without knowing how to recover from a spin, especially a machine that had a bad reputation for spinning. One day it would happen to him and he would need to know how to recover.

Bill checked the aircraft's trim and looked about him – the air was clear of any other machine. Pulling his lap strap tighter he pulled the nose up and chopped the throttle. The nose dropped, he waited perhaps only a second, then the port wing dropped and the RE8 wound downwards into a spin. Unlike the quirk the spin turned vicious, becoming faster with each turn. After three turns Bill put the stick forward and his right boot to the rudder bar. He was close to 2400 feet before he recovered.

As Bill returned to the lines he could see a small knot of people waiting for him. Dismounting he was confronted by Captain Webster.

'Who told you to spin that machine Proctor! Of all the stupid things to do! Am I right in thinking you did it on purpose – because it looked like it to me!'

'With respect sir, I never received instructions saying I shouldn't spin and I had enough altitude. I thought...'

Tight-lipped the 'A' Flight Commander gave vent to his anger. 'You thought! No you bloody well did not think Sergeant. You didn't think at all. You know damned well the RE8 is a death trap for those who take liberties with her. You will report to me in half an hour, right!'

Tom helped him to remove his flying leathers. 'Bloody hell Bill, I sometimes think you really do go looking for trouble. Christ man, the idea is to avoid spinning the brute not invite it!'

John Kenting joined in. 'I'm glad you talked me out of that one Bill.'

Tom Bolton looked at the young officer, surprised at his familiarity. 'As I said sir, he's a fine pilot and you're lucky to have him, but he's a bloody idiot just the same.'

As Bill entered Captain Webster's office he pondered on his fate. Loss of pay? Loss of rank? Maybe he would get away with a reprimand. He'd intended to make a thorough inspection of the machine as soon as he landed, but there was only sufficient time to see there were no obvious structural failures. Nevertheless, he'd instructed the ack-emmas to leave the post-flight inspection to him when he returned.

'You're a bloody fool Proctor. God man! That was a risky thing you did up there. He came round his desk with a bottle of whisky and two glasses. 'Say 'when' Sergeant. Now sit down and tell me what you did and how you recovered.' Bill related his thoughts, actions and conclusions as Brian Webster took notes. 'You are probably the best pilot we have on the entire squadron Sergeant. But I had to bawl you out in front of everyone in case some other idiot tried what you did and came unstuck! Now for God's sake man, let's have no more of it. Thanks to you, we can tell our pilots that spin-recovery is possible, but not below 4000 feet. And we can also tell them more about its vicious characteristics. Thank you Proctor; now get out of my sight!'

By the end of February Bill and his observer had made five operational flights with the RE8, and John Kenting was much happier being behind, rather than in front of his pilot. Both cockpits were fitted with a Morse key but as before, it was John that did all the wireless work as they spotted for the 98th RFA.

Bill knew the RE8 was not much of an improvement over the quirk, but at least it provided a better platform for the observer. And although they never had to fight off any Huns, thanks to their escorts, they were confident the Lewis gun was in a better defensive position than that offered by the BE2c.

The weather was improving all the time and there were now six RE8s on 'A' Flight. It was said that a new, and improved version was to appear soon, one that included a fixed forward-firing Vickers for the pilot, and improved flying characteristics. But that was small comfort to the pilots now concerned with staying alive in what was a very inferior and dangerous machine.

John and Bill were close friends now. They saw each other only when flying and flight planning but their friendship was genuine and based on mutual respect. John knew he had the best and safest pilot on the squadron, all his fellow observers said so! But it was more than that – he felt safe with Bill at the controls and had lost much of his fear.

Bill saw Tom much less these days, he rarely came into the mess bar and had almost stopped drinking. In fact Bill thought his friend sank fewer pints than he did during mess nights. Tom's trips to see Simone were more frequent than before; he never flew to the farm but always used the motorbike purchased from one of the squadron's frequent auctions. It was common practice to auction off some of the less personal belongings of dead comrades, and the motorbike had come to Tom through the death of a Sgt observer.

Bill's last visit to the farm was on the 6th April, the day the USA declared war on Germany. Bill noticed that Tom drank very little, and although the usual hospitality was extended to him, he couldn't help noticing there was less wine than usual on the table. On their return, as Tom put the bike away, he told him the story.

'Simone and I are getting married Bill! But she only agreed if I proved to her I could stop drinking – so I did!'

Bill was overjoyed. 'Congratulations Tom, that's great news, when?'

'Saturday 14th of April. It's a civil ceremony in Freyent. So make sure you're free on the big day!'

Bill laughed. 'Try keep me away chum!'

Tom put his hand on Bill's shoulder. 'It's not a question of keeping away you stupid bugger, you're the best man, so get busy and clean your buttons. It's uniform I'm afraid; Simone's orders. Oh yes, and keep it dark eh! I'm not going through regulations. I know I should, but that's the way we want it.'

Bill was concerned. 'How do I arrange the day off Tom? It could prove to be a bit difficult, in fact the same goes for you surely?'

'It's easy for me, all arranged in fact. I told Mr Webster I wanted that day off in order to spend it with my girlfriend on her birthday and he agreed. I also said Sergeant Barber on 'B' Flight would stand-in for me if anything urgent cropped up. Maybe you could just say I had invited you along too? He's a good sort really and he knows we used to fly together. Better leave it until a few days before Saturday, with luck the weather will be our friend?'

As it turned out the weather was kind for them. Wet and overcast, it gave them no trouble at all and the happy pair were married in discreet circumstances with only a few of Simone's relatives and Bill in attendance.

On the following day, 12 Squadron were dismayed to learn that 59 Sqdn had lost an entire flight of six RE8s to Manfred Von Richthoven's Jasta 11, on Friday the 13th! Evidently they were bounced by up to twenty Albatros DIIIs; all six were shot down and only one crew survived.

Major Kemp addressed the squadron aircrew in the early afternoon. 'I think you should know that what happened to our unfortunate friends in 59 could also happen to us. I'm told that the Huns tend to move their units about by rail, mainly because they have a shortage of aircraft at the moment. Richthoven's Jasta 11 usually operate further north, over the Flanders front. But those six REs were caught over Vitry which means we shall have to be extra careful.'

One of the 'B' Flight pilots raised a hand. 'Where were their escorts sir?'

The C/O looked uncomfortable. 'The DH2s were there, eight of them to be exact. But they were decoyed away and kept busy while the rest of the Jasta made free with the RE8s. It appears that only five of our scouts returned after the fight. I'm sorry gentlemen, but it seems the RFC no longer has the superiority it enjoyed last year. The DH2 was fine against the E3s, but these new Albatros IIs and IIIs simply outclass our best scouts these days.' Major Kemp continued with a report concerning the current battle front. 'As you know, the so-called battle of Arras is very much our concern these days, and although it only started about a week ago, Wing tell me our scouts have a hard time keeping those blasted Halberstadts and Albatros off our backs. Their losses have been very heavy so I'm told. So escorts or no escorts, keep your eyes peeled and your guns ready – we still have a job to do!'

Saving his good news until last, Major Kemp gave news concerning the new RFC scouts due in France very soon. 'As you know, the French Spad is now on our front and is quite equal to anything the Huns have. Also, we have 54 Sqdn's Sopwith Pups and they have sufficient speed and manoeuvrability to give a good account of themselves. But the best news is that a squadron of SE5s has already landed in France. This is reputed to be the finest single-seat fighter ever produced and will re-equip many of our scout squadrons eventually. I'm told the SE5 has a top speed of about 120 mph, some 15 mph faster than the French Nieuport 17. But more important for us, it has a duration of two and a half hours, which is one hour longer than the Albatros can stay in the air!'

John Kenting asked a question. 'Can we still expect our usual DH2 escort in the meantime sir?'

Major Kemp gave a wry smile, 'Brigade regulations haven't changed Mr Kenting, and it's not much use sending a creaky old 'Harry Tate' over the lines without cover, so yes we shall still have them with us.' There was general laughter at the C/O's reference to a 'Harry Tate', a nickname brought about by the similarity of the RE8 to the name of a popular music hall artist. Nevertheless, it was a rather sober group of aviators that left the meeting that afternoon.

As they were leaving Major Kemp asked John and Bill to accompany him to his office. 'Sergeant, you are entitled to some leave I think, but it's still difficult for lowly squadron commanders like myself to authorise any leave at present. But I *can* order you, and your observer to attend a two week artillery spotting course in England. Wing HQ have asked me to send a crew, and I think you two should go.' Bill and John Kenting looked at each other then, with glowing faces expressed their gratitude. 'It will mean some hard work you know! You are to attend

255

the School of Artillery at Larkhill, Wiltshire and learn all about their new guns and techniques for spotting. They will also expect you to give a lecture on your front-line experience and make any suggestions you might consider valuable. Then, when you return you will be required to pass on your new information to the squadron.'

'When do we go sir?'

Major Kemp looked at the 3rd Wing signal. 'The course starts on Monday the 23rd, but there's another job for you as well. I want you to pick up a new RE8 at the Royal Aircraft Factory, Farnborough. I've spoken to Wing about it and they agree it's best if you go direct to the RAF, then fly your new RE8 to Netheravon, which is only a few miles from Larkhill, as I think you must know Sergeant? You see this is the latest version of the Harry Tate, and I would rather you got used to it before flying it back to France. Your orders will allow for some familiarisation flights while in England, but be back here on the 8th May. You will get the Dunkirk boat on Tuesday night. In the meantime, Mr Webster has taken you off his flying roster.'

Chapter Fifteen

Pamela Kenting was overjoyed to hear from her youngest son, and the more so to learn he was in England. Her husband had not been too happy to install a telephone in the house but as she passed the receiver to him she could see her insistence had won through.

'John my boy, where are you calling from?' Stewart Kenting hadn't seen his boy for months and although constantly worried for his safety, was extremely proud of him. John had managed to call from the RAF flight dispatch office as Bill inspected their new RE8.

'Hello father, I'm here with my pilot, we are to go on an Artillery Spotting Course on Monday, but are picking up a new RE8 here. We are authorised to do some flying in England before we return, in about a fortnight, but I was hoping we might be able to fly up and see you next weekend, that is on Saturday the 28th. I'm pretty sure we could land on high meadow, that is if the land is still lying fallow?'

Stewart Kenting was delighted at the suggestion. 'Well I'm not qualified to say what kind of a landing ground it would make John, but the grass has hardly started to grow after this bad winter, and its still very hard. Do you think there will be enough room to land? And naturally we hope you will stay overnight?'

'Look Dad, Bill Proctor is a first-class pilot as I've told you before. If anyone can get in and out of high meadow Bill can do it! I haven't mentioned anything to him yet, thought I'd better ask you first.' His mother came back on the 'phone.

'John, what a lovely idea, tell Bill he is more than welcome and I shall make sure he has our best guest room. I'll have Mary baking your favourite cakes immediately.'

John laughed. 'It's not certain we can come yet mother, and it's up to Bill really, he's in charge of the aeroplane…'

'It doesn't matter if you fly here or come by train John, I will expect both of you for that weekend and that's the end of the matter!'

John smiled. 'Yes mother, we shall be there, I promise. Please give my love to Mattie and Quentin, I will telephone later as soon as I can.'

As he left the telephone he found Bill waiting for him. 'Come and have a look at our new mount John. It's quite a bit different.' They went into the hangar where their new RE8 was waiting for them. 'As you can see, I've got a Vickers on the port side of the engine cowling. It's got Constantinesco interrupter gear and an Aldis ring-and-bead sight. Now I won't have to rely on your miserable gunnery to fend off those Albatros.'

'Cheeky blighter, you know damned well you rely on my eagle eye. Besides, we shall soon see how good your deflection shooting is next weekend!' John told him about the invitation home and his plans to fly there. 'I hope you can agree Bill, and we can take the guns out on Sunday, bound to be a bit of game around.'

Bill was quiet. 'I'm not sure John, perhaps it's not so good an idea.' Thinking Bill was worried about the flying John came up with the alternative. 'I can see you might be a bit worried about landing there Bill, but we can always go by train – take us a bit longer of course – but mother will be most upset if I turn up without you!'

Bill looked him directly in the eye. 'No, that's no problem John. But, you see I'm not from your world, and I think I would be out of place in your grand home. You are an officer John, I'm just a hairy-arsed Sergeant, I wouldn't want to be an embarrassment to you or your folks.'

John Kenting put on a serious face. 'So the man I know to have no fear of the Huns is scared stiff to meet my family, is that correct?' Bill avoided his gaze. 'You are not just a hairy-arsed Sergeant you're a hairy-arsed cretin! I want you at *Saddleworth*, my family want you there too. Don't be so bloody daft, you are coming and that's an order!'

Bill felt the sting of tears in his eyes as he looked away. 'Well don't bloody well blame me if I eat peas with a spoon. Thanks John, we shall fly there on one of our 'familiarisation flights' courtesy of the RFC and weather permitting of course. Be a lot better than you travelling first-class and me third-class anyway. One thing about flying, it's all third class! But before we plan anything let's see if I can fly the thing.'

After wheeling the RE8 out of the hangar Bill made an extensive pre-flight and ran the engine up before inviting John on board. 'I had thought of using sandbags but I'm told they are too valuable to risk so you'll have to do.'

The machine flew well, and although Bill had no intentions of trying a spin, he could feel the machine had been improved through the creation of a larger fin area. The RE8 had its front gun loaded and Bill had permission to fire the Vickers at 6000 feet. He had never fired a forward gun before, and although he knew the interrupter gear was sound, he was still apprehensive as he pulled the trigger, After three, four second bursts, the gun jammed but the propeller was still intact. Relieved, Bill made the usual flying tests then turned downwind of the Farnborough field to make his landing.

Unsure of the new machine's landing performance Bill flared the RE8 at 55 mph. It was a fair landing, and opening up the throttle he took off once more. The second landing was made at about 48 mph, and the machine handled well, despite an average crosswind. Content, Bill taxied back to the hangar feeling quite pleased with their new mount.

Having signed for the aircraft Bill now had sole charge of 892 and decided to seek out Sam before they left for Netheravon. 'You will like Sam, John and it will be very interesting to have his opinion of the new Harry Tate before we leave. I think it might be a good idea to take off early tomorrow morning, as soon as the mist has cleared, what do you think?'

'I'm totally in your hands and yes, let's wait until tomorrow. But have you contacted your family yet Bill? I think I have been terribly inconsiderate you know, after all I never asked if you wanted to fly up to Yorkshire and see your own family did I? Sorry old chap.'

Bill had already considered and dismissed the possibility. 'Nice of you to mention it John, but it's just not possible. Apart from the distance there is the problem of getting a suitable landing ground at Dacre, there's only the village sports field, and that has two lovely goalposts in it! It's very hilly in the West Riding of Yorkshire, not that you soft southerners would know of course. But I shall write them a letter tonight, it should get to them by Saturday with luck.'

They found Sam having a sandwich lunch in his workshop. More than surprised to see his old friend he was delighted to learn first hand news of the air war in France. 'Yes, we hear it's bad news over there, in fact the press called it 'Bloody April' what with the new German aircraft and all.' Bill talked about the their new RE8 as Sam provided each of them with a mug of hot sweet tea.

'Well you know more about its flying capabilities than I do Bill, but from what I hear it's going to be some time before its evil reputation will be overcome. The job you've got is one of a new batch designed to give better handling properties, same engine of course. I'm glad you seem pleased with it.'

They chatted on for a couple of hours, and John asked Sam what he knew about the SE5 now said to be arriving in France. 'They are exceptionally good scouts Sir. Designed and built here at the RAF, they say scout pilots think the world of them. The poor old RE8 was designed to be stable, just like the BEs. A pity they didn't get a better machine out of it, particularly since they are in full production now.'

John was silent for a while. 'So we are stuck with them is that it Sergeant?'

'Well Sir, you might get DH4s if you go on to a bombing squadron, but if you stay on Army Cooperation I think the RE8 is going to be your future, looking at the number they are turning out here.'

After leaving Sam they returned to the hangar where Bill made another inspection of 892 and ensured it was refuelled and oiled for the morning flight.

'Look Bill, what say we have dinner in town. I mean you must know a good place in Farnborough? I've brought my civvy suit so we are not likely to draw any undue attention.' Bill thought it a good plan, and before they departed, each to his respective Mess, they arranged to meet outside the main gate at 7 pip-emma.

Before leaving for the Sergeants' Mess Bill went into town to look for some road maps. He was not at all sure of his route from Wiltshire to Norfolk and needed some good maps to get there. He also purchased large scale sheets of Surrey, Sussex, Hampshire and Wiltshire – the latter just in case he had forgotten the route to Netheravon.

Friday morning found them waiting for a thick mist to clear before they could attempt an early start, but as there were a number of administrative tasks to complete before they could take off, their time was hardly wasted. John needed to make formal arrangements for their eventual departure to France, and it appeared they must land at Dover to get their final clearance papers before leaving England. If they were delayed for any reason, such as illness, weather or an unserviceable aircraft, they were to inform Dover immediately. Once over France they were to land at St. Omer, register the aircraft operational and install a Lewis gun in the rear cockpit before flying to 12 Squadron.

Although there was little room for their luggage Bill had checked its stowage before leaving France and he knew they could fly safely with the extra weight, particularly since they were not carrying a Lewis gun. The weather cleared up to give a fine morning and at 10.15 hours they took off for Netheravon. It was a pleasant journey and Bill made a small detour over Larkhill to give John a look at the School of Artillery before flying to their destination only ten miles or so further on.

They were expected, and received with some enthusiasm since none of the instructors had any experience of the 'devilish' RE8. Bill now found himself taking the part of an experienced aviator, despite the fact that some of his instructors could recall he had only finished his training with them some six months previously. Certainly he was impressed that none of the instructors asked him if they could try out the RE8!

During the weekend they flew for more than five hours over Salisbury Plain, making outlandings at Old Sarum, and Upavon where John still had friends. By Sunday evening Bill was very happy with his new machine and confident it was much superior to the earlier type he had flown in France.

On Monday the Motor Transport section provided them with a driver for their trip to Larkhill, and after booking in at the School joined the other 16 members of the course for a day full of lectures and demonstrations. Since they were resident in Officer's and Sergeant's Mess accommodation, the two 12 Squadron aviators saw little of each other apart from their daytime classes which, to a large extent, were rather boring and provided little which they did not already know about artillery spotting.

By Thursday the group got to know each other fairly well and since all, except one crew, were from squadrons in France they found their own experiences to be more interesting than the lecture programme. Then, on the Friday, they were asked to lecture on their own experiences of archie spotting, which turned out to be most revealing. The school instructors took copious notes and asked many questions; no doubt the course was more useful to them than to their students and they didn't even try to hide the fact.

Thanking them for their frankness the Chief Instructor, an RA Captain, told them that their talks had been most useful, and that the following week would be devoted to discussions relating to their own practical experiences with the guns. After which they would go out to the ranges and see the new guns in action.

Their Netheravon driver was waiting for them at 5.30 pip-emma, and with their luggage already for departure they climbed aboard the Crossley excited at the prospect of their weekend in Norfolk. Checking on the weekend's weather report, Bill found it very satisfactory then, going round to the hangar, had 892 brought outside for an engine run-up and refuelling. Knowing the prevailing wind and exposed positions at Netheravon, he picketed the aircraft down at a protected site; everything was ready for an early take off at 0800!

Bill was untying 892 at 0740 hours and had only just started to do his preflight when John turned up, a small haversack his only luggage.

'It's been a damp night John, but no more than we are used to at

Avesnes. Anyway, its pretty high and windy up here, so it won't be a long take off run.' With the help of an assisting ack-emma John took his place by the propeller and, after a couple of turns, shattered the morning air as they fired the twelve cylinder A1 at their third swing.

Taking a slow climb to 2000 feet, Bill brought 892 onto a heading of 50 degrees magnetic. With John he'd plotted a route that would take them just south of Oxford, past Luton and Bury St Edmunds then on to their destination near the village of Denton, some 12 miles due south of Norwich. The distance was about 167 miles and with a brisk westerly estimated at about 22 mph, Bill calculated they could make an average ground speed of around 100 mph at an airspeed of 78 mph on the ASI. At that rate they could expect to be over *Saddleworth* sometime close to 0945 hours.

As Bill identified Reading to the south, he made a few corrections and was pleased to find that Luton came up at about the right time. From there it was easy, and with Norwich clearly in sight, Bill left the final navigation to John who, excitedly, pointed out his family estate after a further six minutes of circuits about the villages of Denton and Alburgh. In accordance with John's signals Bill made a low pass over the house – fascinated by its size and grandeur. They were rewarded by the appearance of a small group, which became increasingly larger, now waving enthusiastically in front of the mansion. Climbing to 700 feet Bill followed John's directions to the high meadow, noting the wind direction as he did so.

There were two alternatives. He could land into wind and attempt a very short landing, or give himself more room with a significant cross-wind. Bill chose a compromise and reflected that this would be a good test of the new RE8's landing capability, but he had real fears he might ground-loop if he got it wrong.

His first approach was too high, the second too fast, but it did give him a better appreciation of the wind. The third approach was about right, and keeping 892 low as he approached the fence he dropped the Harry Tate into a good three-pointer. Keeping his right wing down to counteract the wind from that quarter, Bill had the stick firmly back into his tummy as the aircraft slowed to stop about 60 yards from the far fence.

'Dashed fine landing Bill, well done!' John was already on the ground and onto a wing tip as he helped Bill turn the aircraft into the wind-free protection of a clump of trees at the corner of high meadow.

Bill had switched off and was just dismounting as the Kenting family came upon them. He recognised Mattie immediately. She was first on the scene, hugging her brother as he swung her off her feet.

As Bill removed his flying helmet he was conscious that his face would, as usual, be covered in a film of oil and grime. He smiled a shy three-cornered smile as she approached on her brother's arm.

'Mattie I want you to meet my best friend, the man who makes all this possible, Sergeant Bill Proctor!'

To his great surprise she came straight up to his face and kissed him on the cheek. 'Welcome Bill, I've heard so much about you, and that was a wonderful bit of flying – just wonderful!' Bill's eyes danced in uncontrolled merriment, his smile breaking into laughter as he looked at her face, its beauty smudged by an oily stain from her kiss.

'I don't know about the flying, but by 'eck that's the nicest welcome I've ever had!' He didn't even know he'd lapsed into dialect as John joined in the laughter. Taking both their arms Mattie turned towards her approaching parents and the two large labradors bounding at their heels.

'Isn't this too wonderful mother!'

Bill tried to take it all in as he was introduced to John's parents and the two dogs. Trying to answer all their questions regarding the journey, he felt no embarrassment as the lovely blonde-haired girl clung on to him with both arms.

'Leave your luggage here Bill, Thomson will collect it later. Now, let's tie 892 down then we can get a drink.' As the happy group walked to the house Stewart Kenting directed one of the gardeners to pick up Bill's luggage as his wife squeezed Bill's free arm.

'We are truly very happy to meet you Bill. You have no idea just how pleased we are to meet you. After John's letters it's almost as though we have known you for years. And now, I want you to know that our home is your home – you are most welcome dear boy.'

As they entered the spacious hall Bill was assisted in removing his flying leathers by an oldish man who appeared to be a servant of some sort. He also noticed there were at least two servant girls in further attendance, one of them carrying a silver tray with cups of coffee.

'Drink this first Bill, I can see you must be frozen stiff!' Mattie handed him a cup of hot coffee as her father came over with a well-filled glass of brandy. John was smiling broadly, fully aware that his friend was quite overcome by it all.

'You are one of the family now Bill, better get used to it!'

After ten minutes or so John showed him to his room. A fire was already lit and a hot bath drawn in an adjoining room.

'We are about the same size Bill, so I'll drop in some of my old lounge clothes, I know you will appreciate getting out of uniform. Just take your time and enjoy a hot bath. I certainly shall. Mother says she expects us for sherry about 1200 hours.'

As Bill fell back in the deep bath, he felt it couldn't be happening to him. Bill Proctor from Dacre. He wanted all his family to see him here, to experience this wonderful place. How Eileen would love it, and Maggie; he knew she would laugh at everything. He felt sad too. That his parents would never know such luxury and worse, possibly ridicule him for being out of place in such surroundings. He felt a strange sense of being an impostor, it was all too unreal. Shrugging off an approaching sense of inferiority he leapt out of the bath. As he looked in the mirror he tried to sum himself up. Yes! He looked much older now, or was he just tired? There was a hardness about the eyes too, and he really did need a shave.

Clothed in John's casual wear, complete with slippers, he found John and his father in the smoking room, playing billiards.

'Hello there Bill – they look better on you than they do me! How about joining us in a game?'

Bill smiled and shrugged his shoulders. 'Never played before John, but you carry on!'

He was rescued by Mattie. 'Good for you Bill, it's a stupid game after all. Anyway, we are to gather in the lounge, mother is waiting with the sherry.'

It was a pleasant room, with a roaring fire, and walls decorated with paintings of horses and hunting scenes. Bill was fascinated by the paintings.

'Interested in horses Bill?' Mattie had joined him with a fresh glass of sherry. He looked at her flawless skin, clear blue eyes and light blonde hair. She was just about the most beautiful creature he'd ever seen. But it was her voice that made her so different. Quite unlike the usual haughty tones of upper-class women, more intimate than friendly, she never raised her voice to emphasise anything just simply changed its music.

'No, not really I'm afraid. Although born in the country my love has always been for mechanical things I have to confess, I've never even been on a horse in my life.'

She took his hands in hers. 'I am my father's daughter I suppose. And one of the first things we do in this house is look at hands. I knew you were not a horseman and it doesn't matter. But what is it like to fly an aeroplane?'

From his seat John Kenting raised his voice. 'Don't let that little pest worry you about horses Bill. I can see she's going to be a frightful bore if you are not careful.'

Bill turned to them. 'Not a bit John, anyway Mattie wants to know what it's like to fly an aeroplane.'

John Kenting joined them by the fire. 'Strange to tell, all my instructors at Upavon said I was bound to catch on pretty fast since I was a keen horseman. In fact I was selected for pilot on that premise come to think of it. But it didn't work for me as you know – kicked off training after two weeks. There seems to be a general opinion in the Corps that coordination in riding means the same thing with flying but I'm living proof that it doesn't work for everyone.'

John's father joined in the conversation. 'What matters is you are flying my boy, and doing an important job. It's enough for us to know you are in good hands with Bill. Here's to you both, and may you fly safely throughout the rest of this vile war.' As Stewart and Pamela Kenting raised their glasses, nobody saw Quentin come silently through the door, pushed in a wheelchair by one of the staff.

'Come father! What would dear old England do without a war? Let's face it, everyone seems to be having a jolly time with it.' He had a full glass of brandy in his hand, and took a large drink from it as he parked close to the window. Pamela Kenting left the room, a handkerchief at her cheek.

John went over to greet his brother. 'Hello Quentin, we have a guest. I would like you to meet Bill Proctor, my pilot.' Bill went over to the invalid with extended hand. 'Ah yes! We hear a lot about you Sergeant. Looking after my baby brother are you.' Bill's outstretched hand was ignored as Quentin sipped from his glass.

'I can assure you he's not considered a baby on 12 Squadron Sir. And it's more a question of him looking after me really.'

Once again Mattie appeared at Bill's elbow. 'Come on Bill I want to show you around.'

As they left the room Bill could hear Stewart Kenting swear at his eldest son.

'Sorry Bill. I know John has told you about Quentin. But you see, he was a fine horseman and all-round sportsman in the county. It's very very difficult for him now, and he compensates with drinking, too much sometimes,' A catch in her voice made him stop, and looking into her face he could see the tears now welling up in her eyes,

'There is no need to apologise, I fully understand. Please, forget it; I have.' She said no more and taking his hand, ran with him to the cloakroom where she handed him his leather flying jacket and boots, now cleaned. Putting a peaked cap on his head she put her fingers to her lips and enclosed her slim body with a large fur coat.

'Come on I'll show you my nags.'

They returned only a few minutes before the luncheon gong sounded. And after a brief wash in his room Bill presented himself for lunch. Quentin was nowhere in sight and no one mentioned him.

After coffee, John suggested they should check the aeroplane, knowing full well that Bill would not, in case he sounded rude. The sun was quite hot now and, with Mattie, the three of them enjoyed the walk to high meadow with only jackets and hats necessary against a warm west wind. The aircraft was quite safe and as Mattie climbed into Bill's cockpit she asked a million questions.

Eventually she ran out of questions and, with an appealing child-like expression turned to them both. 'Oh, could I go up with you Bill, please...please?'

Bill turned to her brother. 'I'm game John, what do you think?' John frowned, he knew it was against every RFC regulation, and if an accident occurred he would never be able to explain it away, or to his family for that matter.

'It could be very nasty for us if anyone found out Bill or if anything happened.'

Mattie pleaded. 'Nothing could happen John, and you said yourself that Bill is the finest pilot on the squadron, please!'

Bill made a suggestion, but he knew if John didn't agree he would have to resist her further pleas, even though he would love to take this adventurous and beautiful girl flying. 'What if I test out the flying with you first John. If I get in and out again without difficulty, then it's sure to be safe. I'm certain our new Harry Tate won't let us down.'

Reluctantly John agreed. 'But if the parents turn up, that's that! Mother would have a fit if she knew.'

Mattie had it all worked out. 'Look, while you get everything ready, I shall go back to the house for your flying helmets and tell mother we are going to test the engine. Father always dozes off in the afternoon anyway, and mother is hardly likely to come and watch you play with the engine.' As she turned to go Bill had a quick word with John.

'Oh Mattie! Bring Thomson back with you, he's in the greenhouse I think.'

Ten minutes later Mattie returned with the gardener who, keen to learn more about the aeroplane was a willing helper as he assisted John to turn over the big propeller. It took time, for although John knew how to swing the prop on an RE8, he had never done it with less than an experienced ack-emma to assist. But Thomson had strength and after six attempts it eventually fired. John kicked away their makeshift chocks of old fence posts, and straining on the port wing helped Bill turn the aircraft round to face the other side of the field. Running by the wing tip he raced down the field until, at the far fence he could help bring the RE8 into wind and ready for take off.

Shouting for Mattie and Thomson to join them, John made sure they were clear of the aeroplane before putting on his helmet and climbing aboard. After a short burst on the engine, Bill opened the throttle to its full extent and took off. The RE8 lifted off within half the available field and having settled at 800 feet Bill did two circuits before dropping to 400 feet for his approach. He had already noted a landmark that was into wind, and finding his approach accurate made a decent landing within two thirds of the available space.

As before, John got out to assist in turning the aircraft round. Putting both thumbs into the air and grinning, he shouted his approval. 'Well done Bill, I think we had better let the pest have a flight or we shall never hear the last of it!' Like most young men John wanted to impress, and allowing his sister to sample his manly world was too good to miss.

As they reached the take off point once more, John turned the aircraft and thanked Thomson for his assistance.

'Jolly good Thomson, thank's a million. We might do another flight in a few minutes, but now the engine's running we won't need your help. Better get along there's a good chap.'

As soon as Thomson was out of sight John helped Mattie into the cockpit and made her comfortable. Excited beyond measure she fastened John's helmet over her blonde hair, and wearing her brother's jacket, settled into the rear cockpit, sitting on her own jacket for extra height. Bill gave her a grin then pushed the throttle forward.

As they lifted over the fence Mattie could hardly believe she was flying. She found no fear in the experience, and with her goggles pulled firmly over her eyes marvelled at everything she saw. Although familiar with her own surrounds she soon realised how different things looked from above. Then, as they climbed higher, she could see Norwich in the distance and among the scudding clouds felt a thrill far deeper than anything she had experienced before. At 5000 feet the air was cold, so Bill went down to 3000, from which height his passenger could recognise many well-known landmarks. He turned in his seat catching a glance of her radiant face as she blew him an ecstatic kiss. He smiled to himself, thankful the turbulent air had caused her no sickness. Swooping low he flew over freshly ploughed fields, leaping over hedges, bridges and trees as they roared across the flat terrain. Conscious of his responsibility Bill climbed to 800 feet and turned for *Saddleworth*. He was used to the approach by now, and with a gentle side-slip dropped into high meadow to make a near perfect landing.

As John took the wing tip Bill turned the aircraft back to its protected position and switched off. With a shake of her flaxen hair Mattie climbed out of the cockpit chattering like a magpie.

'Oh you lucky things and to think you nearly stopped me from going!' Bill's feet no sooner touched the grass than she clung to him then, holding his face in her hands, kissed him full on the lips. 'Oh you darling man, that was so wonderful, just wonderful!'

John brought his sister down to earth. 'Now remember Mattie this never happened. You must never mention it to anyone, least of all the parents. If this escapade ever gets about you will be visiting a couple of jailbirds for the next 20 years, providing we don't get shot that is!' She never stopped talking.

After dinner Mattie took Bill out for a walk before it got too dark. 'Oh Bill, is it very dangerous in France? Everyone knows the RFC are having a hard time of things, it's all in the newspapers. And mother worries so.'

Bill tried to reassure her. 'Yes, it is dangerous of course, but all war is dangerous. But it's not so bad in the air, once you have sufficient experience it becomes safer. And it's far safer than 'the PBI.'

'The poor bloody infantry. Yes it must be terrible for them, but you will be careful Bill?'

Bill smiled at her. 'Now don't worry Mattie, I'll take good care of him.' She paused then holding his hand looked at him in the failing light.

'I mean you too Bill, not just John. We all feel he is so lucky to be in your hands. You see…' She hesitated a second or two. 'You see, John isn't as strong as you. It was Quentin who was the strong one, at games, riding, everything. John was bullied terribly at school, and although he tries to emulate Quentin he … he just isn't cut out to be brave.'

She kissed him lightly on the lips. 'Dear Bill, I feel I have known you all my life somehow. Yet I've only just met you, a few hours ago. And this afternoon, flying with you, it was too wonderful for words. You have to go back tomorrow?' Bill confirmed they would need to return in the early afternoon.

'But will I… will we see you again, before you leave for France?' They were returning to the house and on impulse he stopped. 'I hope

so Mattie I would love to see you again – if, if you would like me to …
but it depends on John.'

She laughed gaily. 'Oh no it doesn't. For one thing mother will
insist and for another I shall insist which means that Daddy will too.
As you have no doubt found out already I'm a spoilt brat and get my
own way around here.'

They spent the rest of the evening talking with the rest of the family. Quentin made a brief appearance then retired, making no conversation or even saying goodnight. Mattie brought up the question of
their next visit and looked at John.

'Well if Bill doesn't mind coming … what do you say Bill? You are
the driver after all!'

'He says yes , don't you Bill!'

Pamela Kenting feigned shock. 'Mattie! Let the poor boy answer
for himself, I really don't know where you have left your manners young
lady!'

Bill laughed as he joined a fleeting glance with Mattie. 'I would love
to come if I'm no trouble Mrs Kenting.' Then, turning to John he suggested they could fly up as they had done this weekend, and leave directly for Dover on Monday 7th May. 'As I remember we have to leave
Dover on the morning of the 8th and report to St.Omer that afternoon?'

John suggested they take the dogs and guns for a small shoot in the
morning. 'Let's say breakfast at 0730 and boots on at 0815. 'You will
be joining us father?'

Stewart Kenting agreed. 'Yes, mustn't miss that son, a good walk
will do me fine.'

Mattie gave them a warning. 'But no longer than two hours or we
shall come looking for you, won't we mother!'

It was getting late, and as they all said goodnight Bill stole a glance
at Mattie. She came close, and gave his arm a warm squeeze as she said
goodnight. 'Sleep well Bill – it's been a lovely day!'

Bill slept soundly, his last thought filled with the sight of a flaxen-
haired girl with cornflower blue eyes. Yes! It *had* been a lovely day!

Although Mattie had really wanted to join the men in their shoot,
she welcomed an opportunity to speak to her mother as she helped
arrange the freshly cut flowers brought in by Thomson.

'I think Bill is awfully nice don't you mother?' Pamela Kenting didn't
even pause to think 'Yes of course I do Mattie. He is everything John
said he was, and I think it's a blessing they get on so well together. And
he is so unlike most young men of his background, I mean he has such

good manners in his own way.' Looking up at her daughter she smiled and put her hand on he shoulder. 'I think you like him quite a lot don't you!'

Mattie blushed. 'Well, he is so... so different and so straightforward. Yes, I do like him Mummy, and I'm so glad for John because he will be very safe with Bill.' She dearly wanted to tell her about the flying she had done, to share the thrills with her, but remained silent as she re-lived the most exciting experience of her young life.

'Just don't get to liking him too much my dear. Bill is a nice boy. But he comes from a different world than ours and the war will end one day and all our lives will return to normal.' Mattie didn't hear a word, still absorbed with her thoughts she looked out of the window – they should be returning soon.

She heard their voices in the kitchen and rushed to join them. John and Bill were arguing about their shooting. 'You couldn't hit a barn door at ten paces Bill! That was my shot that got him, why you hadn't even raised your gun!' They were laughing and pushing each other like schoolboys over a large rabbit her father was handing to Mary, their cook.

She joined in the confusion. 'Well if that's all you got after two hours I wouldn't be so keen to boast who shot the poor thing; it looks like it's a hundred years old anyway!'

After they had washed and changed the menfolk returned for coffee and cake in the lounge where Mattie and her mother were waiting.

'Lunch is arranged for one o'clock John, I don't know what you have planned?'

John looked over at Bill. 'Is there anything we need to do about the aeroplane Bill?'

Before he could answer, Mattie spoke up. 'I haven't been to the stables yet and Bill can accompany me as soon as he's finished gorging himself on Mary's fruit cake!'

After they had visited each of the four horses in her care, Mattie took Bill into the tack room. 'I spend so much of my time here, cleaning and polishing. Rather like you do with your precious aeroplane and don't deny it because John told me so!'

Bill laughed. 'I suppose we both love our different means of transport, and it's natural to look after things you love.' They looked closely at each other, both eager to share the slightest thing that might bring them closer, yet each hesitant to make the first step that leads to further intimacy.

'It's been such a wonderful weekend Mattie! *Saddleworth*, your family… you! Already I'm impatient for us to return next week and… to see you again.'

She stepped closer. 'I wish you didn't have to go back to that dreary camp Bill, but I shall take you out riding next weekend, would you like that?'

He took her by the shoulders, wanting to kiss her, but still unsure. 'I'm sure John will have great fun at my expense, but yes I would like that, I think!' Mattie closed her eyes and shook her head. 'He won't be there silly!'

It seemed the most natural thing to do, so he kissed her full on the lips. And there was warmth in her lips as she responded to him. Then, with a shy smile she disengaged before he could embrace her.

'Perhaps we should go back now Bill. Mother will be expecting us for lunch – race you back!' He let her win, content to watch as he strolled behind, only his heart was racing.

After an excellent lunch, during which Bill refused all offers of wine, they were packed and ready to leave just after three o'clock. Although the general conversation was light-hearted and brisk throughout the meal, Mattie had little to say, and making her excuses left the table as soon as the meal was over.

It was a bright afternoon and the sky, stuffed with fair-weather cumulus, showed promise of an easy return to Wiltshire. Thomson had gathered another willing helper from the farm, and with a supply of petrol brought from a local garage helped supervise the refuelling as Bill took care to filter all the precious liquid through a tight mesh of linen.

Having mastered the art of prop-swinging, John fully enjoyed instructing his assistants, and was obviously keen to demonstrate his skills in front of his family. For Bill, leaning over the cockpit to control fuel, throttle and switches, he was delighted to know he could rely on his observer for such an important task, the more so since on this occasion the engine fired at the first throw.

With the exception of Quentin, the entire family was there to see them off, and as John kissed his mother goodbye, Bill shook hands with Stewart Kenting and received a brief kiss from Mattie as her mother approached the young pilot. Shaking her hand he thanked her and her husband for their kindness and hospitality, and for the invitation for the following weekend.

He looked about him, searching for Mattie. And disappointed in not finding her, mounted the lower plane to enter the front cockpit. Confused, and feeling strangely alone, he checked the starboard aileron and there she was, her blue eyes just below the level of his cockpit. He couldn't hear her voice over the engine, but he could see her outstretched hand and the envelope fluttering in the slipstream as she struggled to reach him. He smiled at her, and as she backed away to safety, Bill put the envelope in the top of his boot. It was time to go, and checking that John was ready, he made a final wave and gunned the RE8 across high meadow. The take-off was easy, and after a wide circle around the house, Bill swooped low over the waving group before climbing away on a heading of 230 degrees.

After checking his course and some scribbled calculations on his knee-pad, Bill was content with his estimates of wind and ground-speed, and settled down to a pleasant flight at 4000 feet. His map was already folded such that he could easily check their track, and by the time they were in sight of Newmarket he knew they would have little difficulty in maintaining a good course to Netheravon.

Finally he could wait no longer, and reached for Mattie's letter. Removing a glove he slit open the envelope with his thumb and removed the single sheet of pale blue notepaper. Placing the glove between his knees Bill unfolded the single sheet not knowing what to expect:

Dearest Bill,

I could hardly eat at lunchtime, I wanted to talk to you but could not find time or place...

Caught by turbulence the aircraft lurched, and as Bill's hand instinctively moved to the stick the note flew from his hand, cruelly snatched by the wind as he sought to right the machine. Bill could only curse and wonder as he flew on, his thoughts totally absorbed by questions he couldn't answer. Would a poor illiterate farmhand capture her letter? Would it be a source of great amusement for some small boy? Would it ever be found, or totally lost to the elements? What did she have to say? It must have been important, perhaps he should try to telephone her. Perhaps he should never have kissed her as he did? Maybe she would rather not see him again?

Miserable and undecided he flew on. A tap on the shoulder made him turn. John was indicating to port. Yes, of course, the railway line. Bill followed their prearranged route and within 40 minutes he picked out his destination against a setting sun. The journey had taken them much longer than originally anticipated, but he had taken little notice for the past two hours.

As they descended Bill rapidly found himself landing into the darkened world of Netheravon which, despite its height upon the plain, fell into the shadows of twilight. But there was light enough, and as his eyes adapted to the gloom he made a good landing.

'Well Bill, I hope you enjoyed yourself this weekend? You made quite a hit with my family I can tell you. All we have to do is stick out another week of this droll stuff and we shall be back home in a few days!' Bill could see that John had enjoyed himself and was happy for his friend. Indeed, he too had experienced a wonderful two days. But his own thoughts were mixed, if only he had waited until he landed before opening Mattie's note!

'It was wonderful John, many thanks for asking me up to see your lovely family.' He wasn't sure if he should ask John if he was going to telephone home, and if so...? 'Oh by the way John. Did you see a bit of paper fly past you when we had that turbulence near Newmarket?' John frowned a while as he helped to picket down the RE8.

'Cannot say I do old chap, what was it?' Unable to contain himself much longer Bill told him the story.

'What the dickens did she say then Bill?'

'I wish I knew, it was about something she wanted to say but didn't have time to, or something. That's all I managed to read then the damned note flew away!' John was still laughing as they trooped back to the domestic areas.

'Oh that's rich that is! Typically female old chap, if there isn't a mystery in their life, they'll soon make one! But I planned to telephone the parents this evening anyway, just to let them know we've arrived safely you understand. So I'll ask Mattie what was so damned important.' Bill felt uncomfortable, not sure of the contents of her note. 'But I hope you keep a better hold of your maps than a silly girl's letter; we could easily get lost that way. My word didn't it get dark quickly!'

The following morning saw the start of the promised 'experiences on the western front'. And although Bill sat next to John, the latter was too interested in the various experiences of other artillery spotters to discuss the trivia of his telephone conversation the night before. It was not until the lunch break that Bill managed to get an answer.

'Oh yes, Mattie's note. Well evidently she just said something about wishing us a pleasant journey back and hoped we would have good weather for this weekend, nothing important old boy!'

Somewhat relieved Bill still had reservations concerning her message, and recalled her sad face as he took the note. But he knew what was wrong. The last time he had a letter from a girl it was a 'Dear John' and he feared it could happen again unless he stopped falling for every girl he met.

The course ended in the early afternoon of Friday 4th May and John, anxious to start for home, made a call to Netheravon for their driver to collect them early. As before, Bill had pre-flighted their machine the previous evening, and all their luggage was stored in the rear cockpit. It was 3.50 pip-emma and the only problem now facing them was the weather!

'I'm afraid our weather man thinks we are going to be socked-in with stratus below 3000 this weekend, and we could be getting rain within the hour.' Bill's report, although gloomy, didn't seem to have any effect on John Kenting.

'Well, we've flown through rain squalls before Bill and have suffered Gerry archie at the same time, so what's a bit of good old English rain, eh. It's your decision of course, but it would be a shame to miss a good weekend what?' It was agreed they should go, and since they had paid their respective mess bills that morning, they took off without further ado.

Within the hour they ran into rain, and since the cloud base remained at 2800 feet, Bill flew just below the dark wispy stratus in reasonable visibility. By the time reached Newmarket they were considerably off course. The wind had shifted slightly and increased its strength. It was now pushing them slightly southwards, but as Bill altered course he was glad to see that his ground speed had not decreased any and was perhaps even faster. Visibility was now the main problem as he dropped height below the ever decreasing cloud base. By ten past six the ground was very dark and the rain was sweeping below them in sheets as they tossed about in frequent squalls. John was working hard and made frequent alterations to Bill's headings as they struggled to keep track of their course.

Now down to 800 feet, Bill was thankful for the flat open terrain below as he struggled to fly straight in the driving rain. If the cloud base got much lower he would have to land, somewhere! John passed him a wet and badly-smudged note held by an elastic band round the end of his swagger cane. The pencilled words hardly recognisable. 'We may have come too far. The village at our 10 o'clock is possibly Ringsfield. Turn onto 280 degrees, then as soon as we cross the main road we should be close to Denton. As Bill turned he felt the aircraft lift into the strong north-westerly. The airspeed was much higher, but they were making little headway against the oncoming blast.

Some ten minutes later Bill saw the main road and dropped down to 600 feet. Denton! Gleefully he turned into the circuit for high meadow, searching for a good approach. After buzzing the house he looked for his landmarks then dropped the Harry Tate into the centre of the field. Dead into wind they were soon down to walking speed, and as he slowed for John to dismount he noticed a burly figure coming to their assistance. It was Thomson.

Using the ropes, large tent pegs and tarpaulin left from last week, the three of them spent a good 15 minutes securing the machine against wind and rain. 'It should be safe here Bill, as you can see, most of the wind gets blocked by the large barn in the next field, and these oaks have been here for hundreds of years.' Satisfied, Bill nodded his approval before setting off for the house.

John's parents were waiting for them as they arrived at the door. 'We never expected you boys to come! It must have been a frightful journey!' Stewart Kenting helped Bill remove his flying clothes as his wife hugged her son,

'Your poor faces, they are like ice,' Pamela held Bill's face then kissed him. 'Bless you dear boy, bless you.' Bill looked about, there was no sign of Mattie.

'Thank you for sending Thomson over father, he's a brick – helped us cover up the kite and everything, bit of a bother in this wind too.'

Pamela Kenting laughed. 'He needed no prodding from us, he's been waiting all afternoon for your arrival.'

John's father appeared with two large whiskies. 'Get this down you first, then go and wash up. We told Peggy to get the hot water in your baths as soon as we heard you come over, they should be ready in about ten minutes or so. Now, in the meantime, let us know something of your flight.'

John's story kept his parents enthralled, but before he could complete the saga of their flight they were called to their baths. As Bill soaked in the hot bath he wondered about Mattie. No one had mentioned her in the flurry of excitement, and he could hardly ask, particularly if she had chosen to be away for this weekend. 'Bloody fool Proctor. Just like me to rush my fences, scared her off that's what!'

As he returned to the bedroom Bill noticed fresh clothes, John's, lying on the bed. Dressed in a comfortable white shirt, grey flannels and tie he thought he looked quite smart as he slipped into John's dark grey smoking jacket. Then, after checking himself in the long mirror he went downstairs.

Entering the lounge he noticed Mattie was there. Dressed in a tweed skirt and green roll-neck pullover she looked a picture. She hurried

275

over to him, both arms outstretched in greeting. 'Bill! I never thought you would be coming in this weather!' Taking both his hands she lifted herself onto her toes and gently kissed him on the cheek. 'So much so I spent the afternoon in the stables and never heard you arrive, I'm so sorry I wasn't here to greet you.'

At that moment John appeared. 'Ah, so there you are little sister! You didn't see us arrive then?' Still apologising Mattie asked them about their flight, wanting to know every detail. In the meantime her father came around with a tray of sherry as Pamela Kenting warned them that dinner was only five minutes away.

Served by their young maid Peggy, dinner took all of an hour during which time the conversation was dominated by discussions on flying. John loved to embellish the story of their flight to *Saddleworth*, the rain, turbulence, poor visibility and problems of navigation. So much so that even Bill was impressed by their accomplishments. Mattie looked at him across the table.

'I'm certain it was Bill that was doing all the work aren't you Daddy?' Before her father could open his mouth John replied heatedly.

'Of all the nerve! Pilots are just simple-minded drivers, it's us observers who get them there don't you know!' Their banter was kept up even into the lounge, where brandies and coffee were served, and where the family enjoyed a night rich with humour and happiness.

'Tomorrow I am taking Bill under my wing and shall start to teach him how to ride!' Mattie's announcement drew considerable comment from John.

'What! He will fall off for sure and you'll have to show him which end is which first, our Bill may have some slight knowledge about mechanical things, but horses! I shall have to come and see this!'

'No you will not! I'm not having you spoil my class and if you step anywhere near the paddock I'll tell Jean Matlock it was you who pushed her in the river last August!'

John laughed. 'Jean is still in Devon; anyway she would never believe you, that girl thinks very highly of me I can tell you.'

Closing one eye, Mattie lifted her chin to emphasise her point. 'If you dare come and spoil my lesson you will not be invited to accompany Bill, myself *and* Jean when I take them in the trap to Denton tomorrow afternoon.'

John's face lit up. 'Do you mean to say she's back home?'

Mattie smirked. 'Has been for the past three days brother dear. She was stupid enough to suggest she would like to see you, so I said we will pick her up at her house about two o'clock tomorrow.'

Pamela Kenting smiled at her daughter. 'Well, I hope the weather agrees with your plans my dear!'

Mattie stood up. 'Come rain or shine, Bill starts his first lesson tomorrow at … what is it, 0900 hours!'

'All right you militant little hussy. I won't give you the benefit of your brother's vast experience tomorrow! Poor old Bill – looks like you will be spending the rest of your weekend standing up!'

It wasn't until the following morning, as he walked with Mattie to the stables, that Bill had an opportunity to talk to her.

'I'm sorry about losing your note Mattie. I only managed to read the first line then it flew out of my hands!'

She laughed, 'So John told me, but it wasn't important. Just a note to say how much we enjoyed your stay!' Somewhat relieved, yet feeling strangely disappointed, Bill recalled his concern over the missing message and once more cursed his imagination.

'Who is Jean, Mattie?' They were saddling up as Bill asked the question.

'Oh she's a childhood sweetheart of John's. Our two families have always thought they would eventually marry, and they are still very close, even if John is a bit of a tease, but I think he's very fond of her. So that's why I thought we might all go out together this afternoon, if it's not too wet of course.'

Mattie had selected a benign old mare for Bill's first lesson. 'Mother rides her mainly, and her name is Cotton, she's an absolute dear – and very easy to ride.' The low overcast had now settled into a fine drizzle as they walked the two horses into the paddock where Bill found it very simple to mount his new charge. The lesson went well, and after half an hour Mattie left him alone as she took her own horse back to the stables. She returned ten minutes later to find the rain had increased and Bill trying to post as he brought Cotton to the trot. Clapping her hands she urged him on, then as the rain turned to a downpour she helped him back to the stables.

'Well done Bill, dismount here then we'll rub her down.' As he slipped out of the saddle Cotton pushed him into her,

'If I didn't know you better, I'd say you trained your horses to do that!' She giggled and planted a kiss on his mouth.

'Well you don't know me better, and even if you did, I wouldn't tell you all my seductive ploys,' They kissed for almost a minute then, leading Cotton to her stable, they kissed again before she spoke. 'I'm not just another girl am I Bill? I mean, I suppose you have met a number of girls in France, and in England, I suppose…' He stopped her.

'You suppose too much Mattie. For one thing we don't meet girls in our business and for another I don't go looking for them; anyway I'm hardly the kind of person girls look at twice!'

She looked at him, moving her head from side to side. 'No, I'm sure that's true, once would be quite sufficient I think!' Bill took a lunge at her as she deftly leapt aside. 'No, truce! We have to rub Cotton down now, then you can try and catch me. Truce?'

The Matlock home was completely hidden from the minor road which joined them and *Saddleworth* to the village of Denton, and although much smaller than John's home, Bill recognised that it too was a house of some stature. As Mattie drew up by the large frontage, Jean Matlock appeared within the porch.

She looked slightly taller than John, and seemed to wear a permanent expression of bored tolerance beneath a head of thick brown hair done in a chignon. John had dropped down from the rear step of the trap to help her aboard as Bill, somewhat awkwardly, came half to his feet for the introduction.

'Jean, I would like you to meet Bill, he's my pilot in France.' Taking his hand Jean Matlock took in the shy smile and mop of unruly hair at a single glance.

'Hello, pleased to meet you. Hello Mattie!' The two girls exchanged a friendly kiss before Mattie twitched the reins, 'Trot on Barny.'

Leaving the horse and trap in a relative's garden, Mattie took Bill's arm and led the four of them down the main street of the village. Although rain was still in the air, it had abated much since lunchtime, and since each pair had a large umbrella, they had little fear of getting wet. Jean and John were deep in their own conversation, and as they stepped out Mattie took the opportunity to lead Bill into a small arcade.

'I know that John wants her to himself for a while, and in any case we shall all end up in the same place by 4 o'clock – Hilda's Tea Rooms.' Seeing the surprise on his face she added. 'It's the only place for decent tea and cakes, and we always end up there anyway.'

They looked around the small arcade and at Bill's insistence walked into a shop which sold old and modern jewellery. A small silver brooch, a prancing horse, had caught his eye. Asking to see it closer he pinned it on her coat. 'No Bill, it must be very expensive!' It wasn't, and having paid for it they left the shop with her gift inside a small box. 'Thank you Bill, it was so sweet of you. I shall always treasure my little horse.' As they left the arcade it started to rain heavily once more.

'Hurry Bill, the tea shop is only just across the road from here.'

Bill ordered a pot of tea and a selection of cakes. 'Do you think

278

John and Jean will marry, Mattie? I mean, John has never said anything, and he usually shares important things with me.'

She wrinkled her brow before answering. 'I don't know. I asked Jean only yesterday, but she was not very helpful. Mother tells me that her father has offered John a good position in his business, should they marry. And father is very keen for John to marry into the Matlock's because they are filthy rich!' She looked directly at him. 'We are not you see!'

Bill couldn't refrain from laughing, and there was an element of irony in his voice. 'If you could come up to Dacre and see my home – as much as I love it and the family in it – I don't think you could say that.' There was a silence between them, broken only by the rain as it spattered heavily against the window.

'I sometimes think I'm very stupid Bill. No, I know I am. Please disregard what I just said.' Tears sprang into her eyes as she fumbled for her handkerchief. She put a hand over his and sobbed. 'Of course you must think me a spoilt child. I suppose I am. But you are the first real person I have ever known, and I am far from knowing anything about the world, or this war. I know our way of life is very different from yours Bill and many others for that matter. It's just that Daddy is concerned we may lose this place and that he won't be able to hand it down to his sons and me I suppose.'

'Look at me Mattie. I'm sorry my darling, I didn't mean that in the way it must have sounded.'

She looked across the table, a faint smile on her lips. 'What did you say?'

Deeply concerned, Bill repeated the apology. 'I said I didn't mean that the way it sounded.'

She shook her head. 'You said something before that!' Bill reflected on his words. 'I said I was sorry, my darling.'

She shook her head and wiped her eyes once more. 'Sergeant Bill Proctor! What gives you the right to call me your darling?'

Bill's face took on a serious expression as he feigned thought. 'Nothing I suppose, unless perhaps…' She looked at him with pursed lips. 'Yes!' Bill sighed as he poured her another cup. 'Unless I love you of course!'

It was Mattie's turn to think. There were things unsaid and she knew she had to address them, now!

'Jean came up to see me on Thursday, and although the parents were out, Quentin joined us for tea. I told her there was a chance you may be flying up the next day and that was when I arranged for us to

279

come out this afternoon. She was naturally quite interested in you, and that you would be staying over for the weekend. Then Quentin had to say something really nasty.' Bill lifted his eyebrows as she looked into his face. 'We forgive him and his bad manners, I think you can understand why?' Bill nodded. 'But he went too far this time. Saying he thought John was wrong to get too familiar with an NCO, and that the RFC must be a strange force if they allowed it – even if they did share an aeroplane in war. I called him a snob and he just wheeled away, as he does!'

Bill's face was like stone. 'Both John and I know the difficulties of our situation, and we are not alone believe me! Why even my Commanding Officer is pally, sometimes. But it was John's idea. I'm sorry to have been the cause of so much trouble.'

Mattie recognised the bitterness in his voice which she heard only moments ago. 'It's only Quentin! Mummy, Daddy, John – they don't concern themselves Bill. You see Quentin is all Army, whereas Daddy is just a gentleman farmer. Bill Proctor is what you are. That is what we see, not your rank. We are not snobs Bill.'

Bill sighed. 'And what does Mattie Kenting feel about this Sergeant of the RFC?' Mattie took his hand again. 'She wrote a love letter to a certain pilot in the RFC. But he's pretty stupid and let it fly away! In the final line she wrote: 'I love you Bill Proctor!''

Mattie got up and kissed him on the forehead. 'Idiot!' Bill was stunned. From the bitterness felt only moments ago to a love now shared – it was too much. Once again his world was changing; it was always changing, and the young flyer was beginning to understand it always would in time of war.

They never noticed the rain until the shop door opened. John and Jean swept into the shop shaking the wet from their bodies as John shook his umbrella in the open doorway. Catching sight of them Jean came over to their table, only to stop as John, looking rather grim, took her raincoat to hang up with his own. Rubbing his hands John signalled the waitress as he sat down. 'Thought you two might be here! Some weather eh Bill! I suppose we shall have to look at 892 when we get back.'

Jean Matlock spoke with her drawling voice. 'Be a dear and order some hot tea and crumpets would you John? Mattie could see that they had been arguing and she knew John's moods very well.

'John, be kind enough to order another pot of tea for us. You two seem to have brought a chill in with you!'

As they waited for their orders, Bill and Mattie resorted to foot engagements, while John and Jean generally ignored each other. The party were therefore quite happy when two well-dressed ladies stopped by their table, and relieved the tension somewhat. 'Shouldn't you two young men be in uniform?' Bill could only gape as a white feather dropped slowly onto his plate.

White-faced John Kenting stood up, reaching for his identity card. 'Madam! I happen to be a serving Officer of the Royal Flying Corps, currently with our Army in France!'

The other woman looked at his card. 'We must apologise Sir. But there are so many scoundrels about these days. Too many are dodging their duty!' Dismayed at having found no victims, she then cast her eyes upon Bill, 'And the other young gentleman, what does he do?'

Bill remained seated as he gave a passable rendition of Trevor Simpson's voice. 'Oh I'm not a gentleman ma'am I'm only the h'officer's driver, I goes where he goes!'

Jean Matlock went into convulsions as Mattie shed tears of laughter. Trying hard, John managed to keep a straight face. 'Pay no attention to these … ladies… ma'am, had too much to drink I'm afraid.'

From the smiles and laughter of other patrons it seemed that their comedy act went down well as the two elderly ladies hustled out of the shop.

'That was priceless Bill!' Jean Matlock was still trying to contain herself as she continued laughing. 'Do you often suffer from silly old birds like that John?'

John Kenting stopped laughing as he looked at Bill. 'It's my first experience of it but I have heard others saying they have known it in London. Ah well, it could have been worse!' The two girls looked at him. 'If Bill and I were in uniform for example.' Taking note of their questioning looks he continued.

'Civilians are worse than the military when it comes to concepts of military behaviour. On the squadron Bill and I fly together and it's acknowledged we could even die together. Everyone knows that and rules of rank are generally ignored. Bill can tell you! I know for a fact that when on 4 Squadron, he was on very friendly terms with his pilot, his Flight Commander no less!' Seeing Bill's questioning look he explained. 'Tom Bolton, he told me quite a lot when you were ill. Anyway, although I can accept military rules that separate ranks, I cannot accept civilians who use class prejudice to do the same thing!' Noticing Jean's interest in her empty plate, Mattie pressed the matter further.

'What do you mean John? I'm not sure I understand.' He was looking directly at Jean as he spoke.

'Would you believe that two men who fight for their country together, in a flimsy aeroplane or otherwise, are not even allowed to travel in the same railway carriage, or eat together when in this blasted country!'

Bill was embarrassed. 'It doesn't matter John really!'

John ignored him. 'Did Tom Bolton tell you of the time when he tried to get into a hotel dance in London, when he was on home leave?' He didn't wait for Bill's reply. 'Tom is a Sergeant pilot like Bill, and was on his way back to France, wearing his uniform. But it was 'Officers Only' despite the fact that his companion, his observer, was an officer. That rule was made by civilians not by the military. The Army have no authority over civilian establishments in England, and although the military may indicate they prefer it that way, the hotels can please themselves if they want to – some do!'

At last Mattie knew what it was all about. Jean must have mentioned Quentin's outburst, silly girl; she of all people should know her headstrong brother's views by now! Mattie smiled sweetly at Bill and kicked him viciously as he made to speak.

'Well I'm more interested in the tea, I think I see it coming.' Although the ride back was wet, at least it stopped them having to make conversation as the four huddled together under the large umbrellas. When they arrived at the Matlocks Jean shouted a brief goodbye and leapt into the porch. John said nothing, still in a brown study after his speech.

Later that evening Bill and Mattie managed to steal away to play table-tennis while John went to talk with Quentin. They were no sooner within the games room than they fell into each others arms. 'Bill, I do love you! I know it's totally impossible, but I knew it last weekend. Jean knows it too, and I didn't even have to tell her.' Bill kissed her with passion.

'Do you think John knows? I shall have to tell him of course.'

Mattie couldn't decide. 'Perhaps you should. I think he would be very pleased because he thinks so much about you. Indeed, you saw how passionate he was in defending his right to be your best friend, regardless of Quentin's snobbery.' She looked upwards. 'I do hope they are not having a fearful argument at this moment!'

Bill took her to a large leather settee in the corner and sat her across his knees. Mattie carried on talking. 'I'm very sure that Jean must have supported Quentin's point of view, for although she puts it on a bit, she really is a big snob that girl. And I have no doubt John was very upset.'

Bill hugged her tight. 'I love you very much Mattie Kenting. And

I've come to think of John like a brother. That was quite a speech he made in the tea rooms, and it settles a lot of things for me.' Sensing his remark had a deeper meaning Mattie turned his face up and kissed him.

'In what way?'

'When I first met John he was just another officer to me. And although I've flown with some really fine gentlemen, John was right, I have, I think it was his toffee-nosed voice that...'

Mattie shook him vigorously and ruffled his hair. 'His what!' Bill struggled with her, deeply conscious of her firm breasts under the fine wool jumper.

'Toffee-nosed, like yours!' It was some minutes before they recovered, each happy for the excuse to fondle and cuddle.

'You see, even posh people talk Yorkshire where I come from, dosta know that lass!'

Mattie giggled and asked for more of his strange dialect. 'I'm not a bloody side show thar knows.Anyway I was telling you I wasn't too impressed with John at first; for one thing he had no experience, and in our work the observer is also your gunner and possible life-saver. And for another, I thought he was a bit, how shall I say, a bit patronising! Well, after a few missions I found he was very reliable and good at his job. And now I also know him to be an honest and true friend.'

Mattie snuggled up closer. 'I'm so glad Bill, because he needs you, he needs you very much.' They were huddled in each others arms when the door opened – it was John.

'Fine thing! I bring home this...this driver and now I find him seducing my poor innocent sister as soon as my back is turned!' Red-faced Bill sat open-mouthed as John strode into the room.

Mattie was quick to recover. 'John Kenting, why don't you knock before disturbing people;and another thing, if you had any eyes in that dumb head you could see that I am the one doing all the seducing!'

John could hardly keep a straight face, but made a brave attempt. 'Oh, well, in that case, carry on Sergeant!' He was about to go when Mattie leapt upon him.

'Oh John, you just wouldn't believe it's true but...'

He looked fondly at his sister. 'I'm not totally blind sis, I had a pretty good idea what was going on, perhaps before you did – or either of you for that matter.'

They talked for a full hour and at the end, agreed that as far as the rest of the family were concerned Mattie and Bill were just very good friends. It was John that put their situation into perspective.

'I think we are a damned sight older than the parents in some respects; the war and that. And love at first sight is not easily understood by our aged and respected – particularly when father once told me that he courted mother for five years before popping the question.' John hesitated. Bill and Mattie looked at each other, they hadn't even thought of marriage or discussed it yet. Bill knew it should be discussed in some way, and now.

'Mattie and I have just fallen in love John! We haven't even thought about marriage yet.' He looked at her and took both her hands. 'Mattie darling, I want to marry you more than anything in this world. And if you want to marry me then...'

With tears in her eyes Mattie flung her arms around him. 'Yes Bill. Yes I want to marry you, of course I do.'

Bill continued as she clung to him. 'But I think John would agree with me; we should wait until this war is over. It will help with your parents, to get to know more about me. And anything can happen in a war!'

Mattie sobbed, heaving with emotion. 'Oh Bill you must come back. Oh please God keep you safe!' She broke away and put her arms around her brother's waist. 'Both of you!'

All three played some table-tennis, then returned to the lounge for a nightcap and discussions concerning the Sunday church service. Evidently their parish church was halfway between *Saddleworth* and Alburgh, and John had been invited to read the first lesson of the late morning service. Bill could see that his parents were terribly proud of their son and that the church was as important to the Kentings as it was to his own family in Dacre. Pamela Kenting didn't request, but took for granted that Bill would also attend, in uniform.

'You will both look absolutely splendid with your wings and all, so if you let Peggy have your uniform in the morning Bill, she will press it for you.'

Mattie had other ideas. 'No Mummy, I shall do that. I think Peggy might get quite confused if we ask her to press a 'maternity jacket' for one of our brave aviators!' John smiled to himself, fully recognising Mattie's claim to Bill's domestic affairs.

John's lesson went well, and although the morning had been reasonably free of rain the weather turned nasty soon after lunch. Mattie and Bill made every excuse – short of rudeness – to be alone, with John helping them whenever he could. On inspecting high meadow they found it quite soggy, and although capable of a take-off, Bill was hardly concerned if it got worse, a few days more would be fine!

On Monday morning John telephoned the dispatch centre at Dover. Evidently no flights to France were authorised until Tuesday, and they suggested that weather permitting, he should fly down to Dover on Tuesday, then proceed to France on Wednesday. Dover would signal 12 Squadron to inform them of the delay.

Delighted beyond measure, John told the family they had at least another day before they had to return. Mattie made the most of it, and took Bill down to the stables.

The rain stopped about five o'clock to give them clearing skies with patches of blue, so John suggested they should take a look at high meadow. As the three of them walked up to the field the sun broke through.

'Oh blast!' Bill felt the ground then frowned, 'Bang goes our excuse John, unless it rains later we shall have to fly-off tomorrow!' Mattie gripped his arm tightly. 'But we did get an extra day Bill, let's be thankful for that.'

Mattie kept a brave face throughout the rest of the day, and although they managed to get some time alone together, they dare not leave the family group too long, particularly since this was their last day. Pamela and Stewart Kenting, already aware their daughter was attracted to Bill, exchanged smiles as the two entered the lounge later that evening. Pamela got up and greeted them both.

'Hello you two, did you have a good game?' Bill blushed, they hadn't even played table-tennis.

Mattie took the initiative. 'Oh yes, I won every match as usual!'

Her mother smiled. 'You are going to miss Bill I can see that!'

Tactfully the family retired to bed first, leaving Bill and Mattie alone.

'Don't keep Bill talking too long dear, he has to fly in the morning don't forget!' She tried hard to keep the tears back, and as they held each other in a long embrace Bill felt the moisture in his own eyes.

'Bill! Have you a photograph of yourself, in uniform?' He told her he hadn't one, but would get one made when he was in France. 'Please Bill, please say you will send me one as soon as you can.' She got up and presented him with a leather photo-case. 'Mummy took me to the photographers in Norwich on my 18th birthday'. Bill opened up the case, there were two photographs of her, both hand-coloured portraits. 'Please take them Bill, just in case you should forget what your girl looks like!' He grabbed her close. 'I could never forget, how you look my love, never!'

At 1000 hours the next morning high meadow was almost dry, and with the exception of Quentin, the entire family and Thomson were present to see them off. With the aircraft positioned into wind, chocked, and with the engine ticking over, they said their farewells. Bill had thanked the Kentings and was now with Mattie as her mother kissed John a tearful goodbye.

Not caring who saw them, Mattie held Bill close and kissed him with passion. As they broke free they could see they held the attention of everyone. Stewart and Pamela joined them, smiling a sad approval. Amidst her tears Pamela took charge.

'Come on you two, it's time to go!'

After the take-off and fly-past, Bill set a course due south for Ipswich. The wind was favourable and as the day drew on they found the visibility improved all the time. Passing Ipswich he changed course slightly by following the river Orwell down to Harwich. From there he flew due south, over the sea until sighting Margate. Not far off course he made a slight correction then, on reaching the channel coast at Dover spent ten minutes finding their airfield.

They landed at 1125 hours and taxied up to the hangars, where they were received by the duty ground crew. The following day they crossed the Channel to land at St. Omer without any difficulty. Having crossed the Channel Bill now felt himself to be an experienced flyer. Most pilots were conscious that the Channel was first flown only a few years ago, and it still remained a milestone in a pilot's log-book.

Since they were now in an active theatre of war they had to be fitted up with ammunition and the new Lewis gun. Later, at 1530 hours, they flew to Avesnes and returned to 12 Squadron where everyone was anxious to inspect the new Harry Tate.

Chapter Sixteen

After reporting to the squadron orderly room, Bill and John were directed to see Captain Webster at the 'A' Flight office.

'Right chaps, how was the flight over?'

Bill gave the 'A' Flight Commander a full report on 892 in a few words. 'It's a better machine than our existing ones sir. It lands at a slower air speed for a start, and although I haven't flown any drastic manoeuvres such as spinning I think she can be turned much tighter than the earlier types.'

Brian Webster studied the young pilot closely. 'Since you are the only pilot on the squadron to have any experience with 892 I want you to demonstrate and inform the C/O, myself and Lieutenants Compton and Anderson on the aircraft. She has been allocated to 'A' Flight and we five pilots will be the only ones allowed to fly her. Two more new RE8s are due here from St. Omer next week. By the end of the month we can expect 'A' to be completely equipped with the new types, then 'B' will follow. It seems that 'C' Flight is to retain the BE2cs and the two Avro 504s. Did you fire the Vicker's gun Proctor?'

Bill mentioned the few bursts he had fired at Farnborough. 'Well Proctor, as soon as you have given us the benefit of your experience tomorrow morning, I want you to do some more Vickers practice, air to ground, and check with the armourers regards performance. Then, as soon as possible I want to know how effective that front gun is; air-to-air.' Seeing John Kenting's unspoken question Captain Webster explained. 'I shall arrange with 5 Sqdn to send a DH2 over to play the enemy. Spend about an hour at 5000 feet to see if you can bring your Vickers to bear on him. I doubt it of course, but if it's possible I want to know. The Hun has brought more squadrons of those blasted Albatros to our sector these past two weeks and it's making life quite difficult. I shall have a go myself as soon as I can get the chance.'

Within an hour of entering the Sergeants' Mess, Tom Bolton found Bill and invited him for a drink.

'Nice to see you back Bill, you must come over to the farm for dinner one evening. How was the leave?' Bill related all his news including his love for Mattie. 'Bloody hell Bill! You don't waste any time do you! But I think you're playing with fire just the same. Anyway, best of luck old son, she sounds a really nice girl.' They discussed the new RE8 for a while then Tom brought him up-to-date with the latest news of the air war.

'It seems the Huns have finally realised their Fokker monoplanes just can't beat the DH2s, not that they haven't tried of course! Like us, they know that when it comes to dog-fighting it's the lightly loaded biplane scouts that provide better manoeuvrability. As you and I know only too well from our experience with quirks, manoeuvrability is everything, and if it wasn't for DH2 cover we wouldn't be having this conversation right now!' Tom took a long draught from his tankard before continuing, and Bill could see he was concerned.

'The EII and EIII Eindekkers are only used against our observation balloons these days, so we are now facing biplanes like the Fokker DI and DII. It's not just those Fokkers either!'

Bill could no longer resist the well-worn joke common to the RFC. 'Or any other fucker for that matter Tom!'

Tom Bolton pulled a face and continued. 'We now have Halberstadt DIIIs, and Albatros DIIs in our sector. I had a bit of a run-in with a Halberstadt DII only last week – it wasn't pleasant Bill! They are so bloody quick in the turn, and our DH2 escorts had great difficulty protecting themselves let alone us. Then one got on to us and although they have only one Spandau, a single gun can be very effective when they get very close below your tail. I managed to spin out of it – your technique Bill – and we got away, but the quirk was riddled with bullets. Quirks are death these days Bill. Thank God we are getting the new Harry Tates!'

Bill was not so sure. 'I wouldn't get your hopes up too much Tom. Although I have only a few hours in the latest version of the RE8, I'm not sure it's any better than a BE2c, but at least an improvement on the earlier RE8 I flew. We are going to do some trials against a DR2 soon, to see if we can bring the forward firing gun to bear on an enemy scout. But as you say, it's manoeuvrability that counts these days and from what I can see the new RE8 is just as stubborn as the quirk!'

Tom looked downcast. 'Jesus Christ, Bill! We do all the bloody work – photography, spotting, bombing, contact-patrols – you name it, and the Corps can't even give us a new machine that's any better than a quirk! I think I'll desert, become a farmer, and you know where!'

From the tone of his voice Bill knew that Tom's outburst had more than a hint of intent behind it. Married life had changed him from the carefree aviator of yesterday to a cautious pilot and potential future deserter. But his chief concern was for Tom's attitude in the air. An over-cautious pilot had little chance of survival against a determined enemy at any time but now, with the odds so much against them, only experience and boldness could provide that small advantage necessary for survival.

'Not to worry Tom, there is some good news too! I hear from my pal at Farnborough that a new version of the SE5 scout is coming over to France soon. The RAF SE5a to be exact.'

Tom gave a wry smile. 'So long as they come here, that's the point! We know 85 Squadron have SE5s, but they are up north at present. In the meantime we have DH2s and that's all. It's not just Fokker and Halberstadts either, there are a number of Hun squadrons, Jastas they call them, operating with Albatros DIIs in our sector, and at least one of them, Jasta 11, operates Albatros DIIIs from Roucourt!'

Bill looked shocked. 'Roucourt! Isn't that the field near Douai, in our sector?'

Tom called out to a F/Sgt Pilot recently transferred from 8 Sqdn. 'Hey, Pat! What do they call that group of Huns flying from Roucourt?'

Pat Scully came over sipping his beer. 'You mean the 'flying circus' mob?'

Tom raised a finger in assent. 'That's the one, they paint all their machines in the most gory set of colours you ever saw, which is why we call them the flying circus.'

Pat Scally took a long pull of his beer. 'But that's as far as the joke goes I can tell you. The chap in charge is a bloody Hun hero. Christ! He's even in our newspapers let alone being the idol of the Fräuleins. Hauptmann Manfred Von Richthoven no less, and his current score is over fifty Allied machines! It's said you can always pick him out from the rest of the colourful bastards. His machine is painted red, all over! Which is why he's called the 'Red Baron' would you believe. Anyway, the important thing is that he eats two-seaters like us for breakfast, and the red bastard is in our sector, with the German sixth Army. They also work with a similar unit, Jasta 10, and I'm told these two units put up about twenty Albatros DIIIs at a time. So if we don't get those SE5s soon it's going to be bye-bye 12 Squadron!'

'Thanks Tom! I just love listening to your cheerful friends!' Bill lifted his glass as Pat Scully went to the bar.

'Well it's the truth Bill and everyone is on edge I can tell you. It's no sin to sneak back over our own lines if you see one of those V-Strutters.' Bill creased his brow with an unsaid question. 'You will recognise a DIII from earlier Albatros by its V-shaped interplane struts – sufficient reason to return as soon as you see one, young Bill!'

Tom discussed recent Allied movements during the past month, bringing Bill up-to-date with the war on the western front. 'Most of the action is now in Flanders with the battle of Ypres, where our lads are fighting the Jerry 4th Army. I suppose that's why the SE5s are up on the Belgian coast. But the Jerry Arras Corps are still down here at Douai and while you were away we lost three crews through those bloody Albatros.' Bill was tired and after making arrangements to go to the farm for dinner on either the Friday or Saturday night, he left his morose friend and turned in for the night, too tired even to write to Mattie.

Bill awoke to a warm and fresh morning and felt pleasantly alive as he walked to the mess for breakfast. Tom would most likely have gone to the farm for the night, as he usually did unless there was a dawn operation, but sometimes he would breakfast in the mess simply to give the appearance that he had been in camp all night. Avoiding Military Police patrols was second nature to him by now, and even if he was pulled up, the motor bike was his own, and there were no restrictions on movements out of RFC airfields mainly because there was nowhere to go, and due to their temporary nature they had no official boundaries!

Walking to 'A' Flight's hangar Bill could see it would be a fine day for flying, with the sun shining softly through a thin layer of high cirrus. The noise and smell of the aircraft took him back to his trade, and as he drew close he felt hungry for the feel of a spanner in his hand, oil soaked overalls and even the bruised knuckles of an engine fitter.

John Kenting was waiting for him by the 'A' Flight office. 'Had a good night's rest Bill? I slept as soon as my head touched the pillow.' Turning around to make sure they were out of earshot Bill replied.

'Bloody hell John! Only sodding officers have pillows, we poor sergeants have to make do with sandbags.' John laughed. 'You slept well I can see that. Still the same cheeky bugger I knew yesterday. Now, do we both fly today or what?'

Captain Webster waited until all the aircrews had gathered before addressing them. 'Right chaps, you will notice that we have three crews tabled for… ah good morning Sergeant Bolton, thank you for joining us!'

Tom Bolton flushed. 'Sorry sir, took the bike out for an early morning spin; won't happen again sir!'

'As I was about to say. Three crews are detailed for artillery work this morning, Mr Browning, Mr Larkin and Sgt Bolton. Your mission details are on the flight board. But before we start work I just want to say that, as you know, we now have a new type of RE8 here. Sgt Proctor will be giving myself, Major Kemp, and Lieutenants Anderson and Compton some tips on its performance this morning. We shall have to get up to speed on the new RE8s very quickly because 'A' Flight will be operating the type exclusively within a couple of weeks. In the meantime we shall carry on with the two remaining RE8s we received a few months ago, and our beloved quirks. Right! Those on operations stay with me. Mr Anderson and Mr Compton please join Sgt Proctor and Mr Kenting. Major Kemp and I shall be with you with in about 20 minutes Sergeant!

After Bill and John collected their flying clothes they departed to the lines and made for 892. As they walked, ahead of the others, John was quick to mention a matter they had been discussing while at St. Omer.

'Thought you would like to know Bill, I've fixed that little problem about your letters to Mattie!' Bill's eyes widened. They had recognised possible difficulties if one of Bill's letters should be intercepted by a squadron censor. It would be only too obvious that Bill's relationship to his observer was more intimate than that allowed between a senior NCO and an officer, and such a revelation would undoubtably result in one or even both of them being posted from the squadron. John continued to explain.

'I was lucky. One of the chaps in the mess started to talk about the heavy chore of censoring the ack-emmas' and NCOs' letters. Evidently it's a job distributed among the squadron's junior officers. And since it would be my turn soon I simply volunteered to do all of 'A' Flight's Senior NCOs. So I am now your official censor! Naturally I shall not read your letters to Mattie Bill, but just hand them to me unopened in the normal way. Then I will seal and stamp them as usual – and off it goes!'

Bill was overjoyed. 'Thanks John you deserve a medal. In fact I will make sure you get one by volunteering us for the most dangerous missions the squadron can offer…' John's retort was swallowed by the roar of 892's engine as its engine fitter started up their machine.

The morning's test flights went well. All five pilots, including the C/O, did at least 30 minutes in the air, always with a passenger in the rear cockpit. John Kenting occupied the rear seat on four flights, but Bill took this position when Captain Webster flew the new RE8.

After they had all flown 892 the group retired to Brian Webster's office to consider their experiences. Major Kemp was first to talk.

'Well, as you know I do very little flying these days, particularly since General Trenchard stopped Commanding Officers from flying over the lines. But I did fly the earlier of RE8 and I must say this one handles much better, particularly as one flares to a landing. Rudder control seems to be much more positive too.'

Peter Anderson and Robin Compton's comments were much the same, and both agreed it seemed that the new Harry Tate was an improvement in overall performance, but little better than a quirk in terms of manoeuvrability. Peter Anderson brought up the most important point.

'We all know the nasty habits of our earlier RE8s. The blasted thing spins as soon as you try a steep turn and one needs lots of height to recover. I should like to try out its spin characteristics if I may?' As he spoke he looked at Bill. 'I think we are all very grateful to Sgt Proctor for his … ah… unofficial testing of the earlier RE8's spin, and if I may sir I should like to test out 892 in this respect?'

Major Kemp nodded to Brian Webster who, as 'A' Flight Commander had responsibility of 892.

'Thank you Mr Anderson, but I have already considered this and shall do that job myself. My own feelings are that this is a far better machine than the previous one, but as you say can we get a safer manoeuvre from it? I totally agree with all the comments made here this morning and the next step is to determine the combat limits of 892. This means general manoeuvrability with respect to bearing the rear gun and the pilot's Vickers gun on an approaching enemy. This is an immediate priority before the other new machines arrive and Sergeant Proctor and I will spend the next few days on this task, assisted by our friends on 5 Sqdn.'

Captain Webster made a wry grin before making a final comment. 'The question of spin characteristics may well be opened up during these trials Mr Anderson! But if it doesn't then you may go ahead, as soon as we receive our new RE8s next week.'

During the following afternoon Bill and John did low level flying at a ground target, testing out both guns and various manoeuvres in order to establish optimal flight attitudes for bearing their guns on ground targets. Whereas Bill's main concern was to safely handle 892 at various heights, he also had to consider the angle of bank and the degree of turn necessary for John to lay his gun on the target. After a while they found most of the solutions they were after but on two occasions

292

Bill nearly lost control.

It was nearly 6 pip-emma when they finally landed. They had expended over 700 rounds with the Vickers and nearly eight drums from the Lewis gun. A total close to 1500 rounds of .303 ball ammunition. It had been a very busy day, involving three landings and only one stoppage from the Lewis.

Bill had learnt a lot about the new machine, much of it by accident rather than design. For one thing it gave no warning of a stall! There was no pre-stall buffet, just a severe drop in airspeed and the nose went down. Providing there was sufficient height to recover this was hardly a problem but it was certainly fatal for the unwary at low altitude. As he discussed their flights with Captain Webster he noticed that his Flight Commander made careful notes of everything he said, often asking him to repeat fine details.

'Mr Kenting and I found it quite easy to bear the Lewis onto a ground position at all heights from 600 down to about 100 feet sir. Flying around the target with about 30 degrees of bank is best, but one has to be careful. I found the machine could stall below 50 mph and if you have less than 30 degrees of bank during a turn, the tail swings about. I'm not sure yet, but I imagine this could be the first signs of a spin. However, if the machine does start to 'fishtail' the important thing is to take off the rudder and increase the bank. Oh, one other thing Sir. As the fishtailing starts the rudder becomes very still; in fact it can be very difficult to centre. I imagine this will also be a problem if the aircraft spins!'

Brian Webster was impressed. 'I've inspected your targets gentlemen, there can be no doubt you hit them very well. Congratulations to you both, you make an excellent team.'

Talking about the rudder reminded Bill of an earlier incident when approaching the airfield at St. Omer. 'As a matter of fact sir, there is something else that should be mentioned. I forgot all about it until now, but as I made an engine-off approach to St. Omer yesterday, I turned onto the field with a glide approach of about 60 mph. I do this quite often with the quirk sir, I like to practice engine-off landings. Anyway, as I turned we stalled, without warning. Fortunately the engine picked up immediately and I could land normally. It was the rudder application that did it I'm sure. As rudder is applied it offers resistance and drops the air speed to a stall.'

'Well done Sergeant. Tomorrow I shall check out all you have told me. Mr Kenting will fly with me and we shall make sure the aircraft is loaded exactly the same as when you landed at St. Omer. I think we are getting closer to spin tests at this rate. Well done chaps, report here at 0900 tomorrow.'

'I must say Bill, I never realised we were close to an accident at St. Omer yesterday.' John's voice gave a hint of concern as they walked to the domestic sites.

'Not really John, I gunned the engine and all was well. In any case I could still counter a spin at 800 feet I think!'

John looked horrified. 'You mean you don't know!'

Bill made a play of deep thought. 'Well until we've tried it we shall never know, but don't you concern yourself John. I've a sneaking suspicion you and Mr Webster are going to find the answers tomorrow morning.'

By 10 ack-emma Bill's suspicions were confirmed. 'Dead right young Proctor, we had the very same problems!' Brian Webster was jubilant. 'We shall have this up to Wing HQ as soon as we have put our findings in the squadron log book. From this morning's tests I can say that the engine-on stall is 55 mph, and engine-off stalls can appear at anything less than 65 mph. And you were right about the rudder dropping the airspeed Proctor. I can see I'm going to have a busy day writing all this up.'

Bill spent the rest of the morning servicing the engine on 892, he had little enough experience with the RAF4a engine and was determined to know it better. By midday John came over to say they were to fly at 2 pip-emma. They were detailed to fly simulated air-to-air gunnery with a DH2 from 5 Sqdn. The main intention was to avoid being shot down but in the process they were to evaluate their best firing positions with respect to an approaching enemy scout.

Bill took off at 1410 hours with a full load of ammunition for each gun. The simulation required that each aircraft should be at normal operational weight, but more importantly all RFC aircraft had to fly armed while in France. All guns were to remain uncocked however.

Starting at 5000 feet they first met the DH2 as it approached with a beam attack, followed by tail attacks from above and below. Their 'enemy' was good, and he provided John with very few opportunities to return defensive fire. The next attack was frontal. Coming from a high one o'clock position the DH2 swung into a sweeping attack well out of John's arc of fire. Bill turned his machine steeply to the left, hoping the DH2 would slide into John's sights but it didn't work. Seeing the manoeuvre the DH2 pilot gave them a second chance and made an identical attack from the same position. The one o'clock attack was an established approach against two-seaters, and took advantage of the gunner's blind-spot. Bill wondered… could he use the Vickers?

The DH2 was about 120 yards away when Bill pushed the throttle forward and rolled to the right. As he did so he pulled the stick back and applied a little right rudder. For a fleeting moment he could see the DH2 within the ring and bead sights of the Vickers. But he'd pulled too far, and as the DH2 slipped below him, he relaxed the stick, only to fall into a vicious right spin!

Bill pushed the stick forward. Then reducing the throttle he applied left rudder, but the spin continued getting tighter with each turn. Then, as the nose dropped deeper he found the rudder almost impossible to move. Reducing the throttle more, Bill pulled the stick back and found he could move the rudder more easily. Eventually they came out of the spin at just under 1000 feet!

As he climbed, Bill saw that the DH2 had come all the way down with him. He waved a greeting to his opponent then indicated they should return to 5000 to start again with another one o'clock attack. Turning to face John in order to make his intentions clear, he noticed his friend bravely clinging to the Scarff gun-mounting, his face deadly white – obviously sick!

Correcting earlier mistakes, Bill managed to bring his Vickers to bear on the DH2 on two passes. On the second he even managed to simulate a three second burst. Then as his opponent waved goodbye Bill returned to land making an uneventful glide approach.

Bill taxied to the edge of the field before returning to the 'A' Flight lines then, turning to face John, took stock of his friend's condition.

'Oh my God, I'm not sure if I'm cut out for this sort of show!' John had recovered somewhat and his face had a better colour.

'I'm so sorry John. I didn't spin on purpose, but I now know how to get out of one, even a vicious one like that! Shall we go straight back to our lines?' John Kenting smiled as he nodded his assent.

After eight days, Bill and five other pilots had demonstrated anti-spin techniques in all three of the new RE8s on 'A' Flight's strength. Bill could now recover within three turns and with only a loss of about 1000 feet, and John, who had now learnt to eat very little before flying, experienced a further two test spins with only slight discomfort. They also completed further simulated gunnery trials with the same DH2 pilot, after which Captain Webster arranged for all his crews to experience the same training.

By the 18th of May, Major Kemp was able to forward a very encouraging report to 3rd Wing HQ, and included a list of names responsible for the success of 12 Squadron's RE8 training. Heading the list of names, underneath that of Major R. L. Kemp, was that of Captain B. Webster. Then followed all the officers, pilots and observers of 'A' Flight, involved in the trials. At the bottom of the list, Bill's name was included as:

Sergeant Pilot W.C. Proctor, RFC.
This SNCO Pilot has accomplished excellent work in establishing the general and operational performance of the improved RE8 and is recommended to be Mentioned in Dispatches concerning these trials.

Bill had written three letters to Mattie since his return, and received her first letter seven days after they arrived at the squadron. Since then he had read her letter every night before going to sleep, and looking at her photograph he knew he was the luckiest man on earth.

Bad weather precluded further operational flights until the 24th, and Bill only flew 892 on two tasks during this time. One was a weather check and the last one was to test the installation of a new compass and tail trim wheel. It seemed as though there were modifications to the RE8 every week, and the cockpits were getting more complicated with every addition. With a new compass by his left elbow and a tail trim wheel on his right, just under the Morse key, the RE8 didn't lack for instruments and controls. Then there was the new air camera installation to be fitted next week. Instead of the external fixtures he was used to on the Avro and BE2c, the camera was to be placed inside the fuselage behind the observer. But most important of all these modifications was the tail trim facility. The RE8 was sensitive to weight distribution, and the weight of the observer, camera, extra ammunition pans, etc., were variables that could now be compensated by trimming the tailplane from the pilot's cockpit, while in flight.

Bill was thankful for the rest from flying. For one thing he wanted to be involved in every modification and installation the ack-emmas were fitting to 892, and for another he was behind with his letters. He had now received three letters from Mattie and had yet to reply to her last one. There were also two from Maggie, one from Jane and one from his father – the latter also enclosed a note from his mother.

Although the news from home was much the same, he read each one twice, anxious not to miss a single detail of his family's news. According to Maggie, Eileen was seeing a boy in Harrogate but she was upset because he'd just been called up for the Navy. But the whole family were well, and his father seemed to be busier than ever at the garage. Indeed, according to his father there were many more cars on the roads now, and he'd even been servicing one of the new Model 'T' Fords, now seen in ever increasing numbers in Harrogate. The family also received a daily paper for the first time. The *Daily Herald*, a paper which gave slightly less emphasis to war news than other papers, and seemed to concentrate more on social matters, strikes and suchlike, but at least it didn't publish page after page of casualty reports. His mother could never face that.

One of the letters disturbed him slightly. Jane seemed to assume she was his girl, and even called herself such. He was glad she didn't know about Mattie, and although he'd mentioned John's sister in a letter he sent from Netheravon, he'd not mentioned any close attachments. Certainly Maggie wanted to know more about 'this sister of your friend John' and it was very likely she had even guessed of a romantic attachment. Bill also knew he would tell her everything, he always did! But Jane must never know, not yet at least. Only Maggie would know for the present and time would do the rest.

Mattie's last letter had been filled with her deepest feelings and she wrote passionately of her love for him. So much so, that Bill even mentioned the fact to John, always worried that he might not approve. But John had dismissed his concern with a breezy

'Well I know that old son! The brat is always going on about you – not sure why, but they do say there is a strain of madness in our family!' He then looked squarely at the young blond-headed pilot and said 'I also wrote and told her that she couldn't have made a better choice for a future husband and I'm happy for both of you.' They had little time to discuss the future, a subject that was hardly ever discussed on the squadrons anyway, but Bill assured his friend that any question of marriage would have to wait until the end of the war. Just as his future career could only be faced when his survival was certain. But he was an experienced pilot and aircraft engineer, and there would be no turning back. Aviation had passed its uncertain infancy, and in peace would expand into a developing industry. Bill Proctor had a good future in aviation, and was confident he could support a future Mattie Proctor well enough.

It took three nights to complete his letter writing and now, on the 26th of the month, he was back to the war as he and John prepared 892 for a morning sortie over the lines.

Captain Webster outlined a contact patrol made up of three new RE8s. 'Mr Compton will be the flight leader, accompanied by Mr Read and Sgt Proctor. You will arm up with four 65-pound bombs and carry a full complement of ammunition for both guns.' He then drew their attention to the map outlining the current position of Allied troops in their sector. 'As you can see from this map, which is as accurate as anything Wing knows about today, our front extends about five miles east of Loos, then south past our front line just this side of Vimy. It then extends about ten miles further south until we meet the French line here.'

'Now remember! British and Canadian troops only captured Vimy Ridge after some pretty bloody fighting last month. They had hoped to capture Douai and Cambrai, but got stuck here, about one mile in front of Douai, and what 3rd Army needs is the exact position of our forward troops facing Douai. *That* gentlemen is your task this morning. Bombs? That is 3rd Wing's idea The C/O tried to talk them out of it, but they insist it will cause confusion. The plan is that you should fly in opposite directions releasing your eggs en route. This, our lords and masters say, will confound the enemy and give you a better chance to observe our forward positions! Naturally, they expect you to use the forward gun as you go!'

It required no imagination to realise the danger involved in such a mission. The Germans were very well-established with anti-aircraft batteries, and surrounded by numerous aerodromes, all of them equipped with superior biplane fighters. Bill could see anxiety among the crews and John had gone as white as a sheet.

'It is essential you use your wireless to relay whatever information you can back to 3rd Wing. The frequencies have already been set on your transmitters. I know you will be flying the forward edge of our lines but make no mistake, the Boche will have every gun firing at you. Our front line battalions are spread out in company strength along the front and have been instructed to put out their usual position markers at 1000 hours. Observers will note their position on the maps which I shall distribute in a few minutes. It is very important that you are seen to be acting as a CP, so you are to fly at 100 feet over our front lines first of all. These will be indicated in the usual manner with white markers. Then you are to go over no-man's land and spot the forward positions. Once the forward troops have seen you they will be very happy to let you know where they are mainly because we, and other two-seater units will be dropping ammunition and food to them in the coming weeks. That is why we must know exactly where they are! Any questions?'

Colin Read spoke up. 'If we are doing a CP why do we need to use wireless sir? I mean, normally we just drop a message on our own rear positions.' It was a good question, and one that the Flight Commander would have preferred to avoid if he could.

'As I said Mr Read. The Boche will be very intent on shooting you down and an opportunity to drop a message behind our lines might well be compromised by that intention! So please use the wireless; I know Wing will be very pleased to hear from you.' At this there was general laughter at the expense of the young officer.

Lieutenant Compton's question was on everyone's lips. 'Do we get top-cover sir?'

'Yes, you do but don't expect to see the DH2s or the SE5s – yes they will be around too. They will be busy with the Huns and keeping them off your tails and those of Sgt Bolton and myself.'

Bill looked over the group until he spotted Tom who, seeing his friend, shrugged his shoulders with an expression of complete surprise.

'Sgt Bolton and myself shall be taking photographs at 2000 feet while Mr Compton's flight is busy below us. Now, while the observers are being briefed by Mr Anderson I want to go over our flight strategy and timing with the pilots. Take off will be at 0930 hours!'

Tom Bolton said a few words to his observer, a young Corporal called Danny Price, then joined Bill with the rest of the pilots.

'Hello Tom, haven't seen much of you recently, how's Simone?'

Tom grinned, 'She's blooming Bill, and I'm sorry I've not seen you since we had you over for dinner last Saturday. But you see… she's having a baby! And I've been as busy as hell with all manner of things.'

Keeping his voice and enthusiasm as low as possible Bill shook his friend's hand with vigour. 'Oh that's splendid Tom, when does the little fella land?'

'From some very serious calculations we can expect it in late November, or early December – we think.'

'Look Bill, one of the things I've been busy with is writing home to my sister. I've told her all about it, she was the only one who knew I was married to Simone anyway. If anything happens to me – no wait a minute Bill – you know the score as well as I do. If anything should happen to me, here is my sister's address in Blighty. I want you to write to her. She will look after Simone and the baby. You see, my parents will get any official notification and well …I don't really get on with them…'

Bill nodded his head. 'Don't worry you old bugger.'

'And Bill, I want you to be godfather if that's fine with you?' Bill just nodded again, not daring to speak as his mouth choked up and his eyes brimmed with tears.

By 0915, all five REs were puffing out oily brown smoke from their vertical exhaust stacks while the ack-emmas made last minute inspections to rigging, engines, armaments and instruments. Bill knew only too well the effort that must have kept the ground crews busy all night, and was stirred by the concern they showed for the aircrews as they pre-flighted their machines. Even they knew this was a dangerous one he thought.

Captain Webster and Tom took off first. Their mounts were the two remaining early versions of the RE8, easily distinguished by their small fin and rudder. Then, as the two photographic machines gained height, Lieutenant Compton signalled his flight to taxi out and take off.

Flying at 200 feet Robin Compton led his flight in a loose V formation as far as Arras. Then, as they had arranged, Bill led Colin Read up to Loos while Lieutenant Compton flew to the 3rd Army's front line east of Arras. As soon as he reached the shattered township Bill turned south at exactly 0950, and noted that Colin Read's machine was following some 300 yards behind and slightly higher. He soon found the Allied lines and flew within them; the German lines clearly in view to his left. As they approached Vimy they received a considerable barrage of archie and machine-gun fire, and no doubt every German rifle in the vicinity, but the range was great and their height too low for accuracy. Just as they passed Vimy they saw Robin Compton's machine approaching from the south. It too was taking archie bursts but the shooting was poor.

John Kenting was making notes, and had already made an initial transmission to Wing HQ, mainly to confirm their first run and to report on some of the obvious Allied concentrations. At 1010 hours Bill turned north and made his reciprocal run closer to the German lines. It seemed that the Boche never stopped firing, and the air was filled with filthy acrid smoke. After two or three miles he turned left and ran inside their own lines, mainly to disturb the enemy's range but also to give John an opportunity to see a different area of the front line. As he approached no-man's land once again he saw a bright yellow explosion ahead. It was at his own height and slightly to his right. Bill knew almost immediately that it was Robin Compton's machine, and as they passed it by he could see remnants of the RE8 fluttering to the earth below.

They were taking hits themselves now, mostly random shots from rifle and MG fire, but the lighter archie was beginning to feel them out as well. An archie shell exploded in front them, and as they flew through the dark cloud of evil-smelling smoke Bill could feel the shrapnel hammering on the upper wings. Waiting no more, Bill rolled the aircraft to port and dropped the nose. Skimming over the rear positions he could see British Tommies waving. 'Obviously enjoying the show' he thought as he flew lower than 50 feet before climbing once more towards Loos.

Once he was safely out of range and well behind their own lines Bill turned to see if John was safe. He could see his huddled figure well down in the cockpit, no doubt using the Morse key. But looking beyond his tail he could see no sign of Colin Read.

While he circled the area west of Loos he tried to see if they had sustained any damage. There were numerous tears in the upper planes, and one of the lower planes had a few holes, but 892 seemed to fly well enough for all that. A tap on his shoulder made him turn to see John's face and receive the note he passed to him.

'Make another run south, at about 400 feet and past Vimy. Think we have some forward troops on the edge of the town's western perimeter. Then go home – please!'

Bill smiled, he had much the same idea himself. But he would drop his bombs first, then dive on the German trenches with his Vickers. As they turned south Bill took the RE up to 500 feet then made a shallow dive over the first line of Boche trenches. Most of their MGs were sited there, and firing directly upwards would be difficult he thought. The bombs were wired to drop in pairs, and as he reached 400 feet Bill released the first pair. Not knowing, or even seeing their effect he continued his shallow dive firing the Vickers into the German trenches. Then, rolling right, he dived down to 200 feet and dropped the final pair before turning for home at 50 feet.

As he turned west, the RE lurched to an explosion which threw them onto their starboard wing. Bill pushed hard on the throttle, and with stick and rudder managed to gain height for a moment before he levelled off to prevent a stall. Only seconds later there was a loud clatter as the engine stopped, and a cylinder-head flew off – narrowly missing his cockpit before bouncing off the Lewis gun positioned on the port side of John's cockpit.

There was no height and no time for a suitable manoeuvre, and as Bill pushed the stick forward he was surprised to find how calm he was. There was no real control but as they skimmed over a gun-limber he was aware that his approaching crash could be fatal! Cutting the fuel cocks and switching off the magnetos was a mechanical reaction, just as his application of stick and rudder, which brought them onto an open track. Bill pulled hard on the stick and 892 flopped fully stalled onto the dusty path before bouncing back into the air – only to drop even harder onto the rim of a large shell crater.

The impact threw Bill forward, breaking his lap strap at its mooring point and catapulting him over the windscreen to land on the petrol tank. Striking his head on a forward fuselage strut Bill was slightly stunned, and as the nose tipped down into the shell hole he grabbed blindly at the first thing he could find. Unfortunately it was the port exhaust pipe!

Bill's scream brought John out of his stupor. He had prepared himself well for the inevitable crash, and by holding on to the Scarff ring as he crouched low in the cockpit he suffered no injury.

'Jesus! That was fucking hot!' As John carefully looked over the side he could see Bill standing up to his waist in a pit of water and mud, and cursing loudly as he leant over the lower plane. By now a number of soldiers had arrived and, under John's instructions rescued Bill from the pit while others held on to the tail of the wrecked aircraft.

Bill's right hand was seriously burnt, much of the palm being left on the exhaust pipe and he was in severe pain. The medics had been called and by the time they arrived he had fainted.

They had been more than lucky! As John surveyed the remains of 892 he knew they had survived one of the worst problems associated with the Harry Tate. All crews knew that almost every 'nose-over' with an RE8 resulted in the engine being pushed back through the two fuel tanks pinning the pilot in his seat while the petrol ignited to flame him to death. As John retrieved his notes, maps and codes he had time to think more clearly. It wasn't just luck! Bill was a superb pilot, everybody said so. His crash landing was carefully manipulated to pancake onto the edge of the crater, which allowed the nose to drop into the mud and so absorb the impact!

As John entered the medical tent he could see a small group of white coated figures attending to Bill's hand. The Medical Officer turned as John approached.

'We shall have to send him to BMH Arras. It's a very bad burn and infection could set in. What a landing! I actually saw it myself. You were damned lucky old chap, I'd hang on to this young fella if I were you!'

Bill was in considerable pain but managed a weak smile as John sat beside him in the Leyland Ambulance.

'It's not far to Arras Bill, and you will soon be in good hands. My God but what a landing! You planned it just right, all the way up to that shell crater, you're a bloody terrific pilot Sergeant Proctor!'

Bill could easily have disabused his friend from such illusions, but he was too tired and anyway if it made John feel more comfortable to think he was such a good pilot then perhaps it was best to let him think so.

'Promise me you won't mention my injury to Mattie, John she might get worried!' John said he wouldn't.

'But perhaps I should mention that you committed crashery with one of his majesty's RE8s? And that you are likely to have to postpone marriage too until you have paid it off.'

Bill grimaced with pain as he tried to raise his right hand. 'Piss off – Sir!'

Leaving Bill at the BMH in Arras, he had the ambulance take him to the squadron where he reported immediately to 'A' Flight. Captain Webster was talking to the C/O as he walked in to the office.

'God man where the hell have you been?'

John looked at his watch, it was 2.30 pip-emma. 'Sorry sir, I'm afraid we were brought down just inside our lines west of Vimy. I had to get Sergeant Proctor to the BMH at Arras...' John told them the whole story.

Major Kemp was more concerned about their observations. 'Wing HQ told us you managed to get some information to them by wireless Kenting, good chap. But did you manage to get any further observations concerning our forward posts?' John showed them his notes and map annotations.

'Splendid stuff, some of this also supports Mr Compton's wireless reports too.'

John looked at his C/O. 'Don't you know sir? Robin Compton was hit, we saw them explode in the air!'

Roger Kemp nodded. 'Yes, we knew. Lieutenant Read's observer sent a message to that effect, his last one evidently!'

Captain Webster explained. 'They too were hit. I actually saw it from above. In fact their crash is possibly recorded on one of our photographs. They were hit just after you turned north, a flamer I'm afraid, I saw them crash just in front of our lines – no chance anyone survived.'

John steadied himself against the map table. 'So we were all shot down, all three of us!' Brian Webster put a hand on his shoulder. 'It's worse I'm afraid. My own observer, W/O Stanley, is seriously wounded in the chest, and we lost Sgt Bolton and his chap. In fact within a period of 40 minutes, 'A' Flight lost half its aircraft and seven of its aviators this morning. That could be eight if Stanley dies!'

The following morning John and Brian Webster made an official visit to see Bill. Major Kemp had sent a note congratulating him on a successful mission and for his airmanship, and hoped he would be soon well enough to return to the squadron.

Bill was sat up in bed drinking orange juice when they arrived. They had treated his hand and fresh dressings were applied every two hours.

'How are they treating you Sergeant?' Bill grinned, knowing that his Flight Commander really wanted to know how soon he would be fit to fly again.

'The doc says my hand has some infection and I will be at least another day or two here. Then I can return to light duties on the squadron, but no flying until my hand is better. He thinks it will take a month sir.'

Brian Webster wasn't concerned. He needed four new REs and four new crews, until then 'B' Flight were to take the load.

'I'm sorry to be the bearer of sad news Proctor. Yesterday was a bad day for us – yes we got the information, thanks to you and your comrades. But we had to pay a high price. As you know, we lost Mr Compton's crew. But we also lost Mr Read and his observer as well; and we also lost Tom Bolton and Cpl Price!'

Bill said nothing. He was thinking of Simone and her baby. 'We all know that Tom Bolton was your best friend, you flew together with 4 Sqdn as well as with us. He was a fine pilot and we shall all miss him terribly of course, but you most of all... I'm sorry Bill.'

Bill looked at both of them. 'How did it happen ?'

'As you know, Tom and I were flying at 2000 feet, taking photos. I started first, then Tom flew a parallel track a few minutes later. We could see you chaps trying to dodge the archie as we went along. Warrant Officer Stanley then drew my attention to some activity about 5000 feet above us. The Huns were busy with a squadron of SE5s. Then another group of Huns, Albatros IIIs I think, came down to us. They were all brightly-coloured chaps, and although the SE5s came down among them we were their main attention. I kept straight on and I could hear Stanley's Lewis going like mad. Then we were hit in the tail. It was impossible to fly straight so I turned for home. I looked round and saw Tom was still flying straight ahead – but he had an all over red Albatros on his beam. They stood no chance at all, it was Richthoven for sure. It was a flamer, but I'm pretty sure Tom and Cpl Price were dead before they caught fire.'

Tears were streaming down Bill's face as dropped his head, his shoulders heaving. 'Anyway Sergeant, if there is anything you need... Mr Kenting will stay with you a while, I have to see the MO and W/O Stanley before I leave.'

After a couple of minutes Bill lifted his pained and tear-stained face to ask John a favour. 'John I want your help. See if you can get the MO to release me tomorrow – no listen! I'm the only one on the squadron that knows this and no one else must know, promise?' John nodded, knowing it must be very important to affect his friend so much. 'Tom Bolton married a French girl, Simone. She has to be told, and since the marriage was not through official channels she never will know unless I tell her. What is worse, Simone is having Tom's baby. He told me less than two hours before he was killed!'

John Kenting knew he would have to help. If he didn't, Bill would find other ways to see Tom Bolton's widow.

'I will do my best, but you had better convince me that you are fit enough to be released tomorrow. Then if the MO agrees I shall drive you there. Where does she live by the way?'

True to his word, John managed to convince the MO that he needed to confer with his pilot concerning their recent mission and since Bill was to be under medical care at the camp it would not affect his treatment. The MO agreed, and Tom got a Crossley to pick him up the next morning. As they approached the farm Bill asked John if he would mind waiting in the tender as he broke the news.

Simone answered his knock on the door. 'Ah Bill, I was expecting Tom and…' It suddenly came to her and Bill's face did the rest. 'No, Bill it cannot be so – please tell me my Tom is not hurt – please!' John heard her cries as he stayed in the tender. It was the first time this side of the war had crossed his path, poor Bill.

Jean Louis had joined them now, each trying to comfort her. After ten minutes or so she got up and made a pot of coffee.

'Did you know we have a baby Bill? Did he tell you?' Bill told her that Tom wanted him to be godfather to the child, and to inform his sister in the event of his death.

'Simone, he was my very best friend. Please let me help you in anyway I can. I shall visit you when I can and I want to be the godfather to your baby.' He was crying now and Simone came over to him.

'I think perhaps we both loved him, and yes, please be godfather Bill.' Jean Louis touched him on the shoulder and they left her with her grief.

'What do we do now Bill? She is a brave girl, but what can we do? Please visit us soon eh!' Bill told him of Tom's wish to contact his sister.

'You see Jean, Tom had already made plans – just in case – and his sister knows all about Simone and their marriage and the baby. He told me his sister would look after them both.'

During the journey back to camp, Bill told John the full story and Tom's plans for Simone and the baby. John looked at him.

'You're a good man Bill Proctor and you will make a good godfather!' There was nothing else to say.

Although he was grounded for a full five weeks Bill's 'light duties' kept him very busy working with the squadron equipment officer, W/O Larry Barnes. Bill had spoken to him a few times in the mess, but he was a quiet man and not easy to get to know. Mostly Bill's work involved checking the spares inventories and ordering fresh items against priorities. He was bored stiff within a week and made every excuse to visit 'A' Flight lines whenever he could. He had written a letter to Tom's sister, the hardest task he had ever undertaken in his life, but had not mentioned anything to Mattie. There was little to raffle from Tom's effects, since most of his personal belongings were kept at the farm. In any case there was no question of doing this since he was known to be Bill's friend.

The President of the Mess Committee happened to be Larry Barnes, and as PMC it was his decision that Bill should look after his friend's effects including Tom's motor bike. Bill had wrapped up Tom's spare flying helmet and gloves, and took his best uniform for Simone. Most precious of all was his Military Medal. Still boxed with its red white and blue striped ribbon, Bill took care to make sure Simone received the medal rather than Tom's parents.

As his duties required constant checks on the spares requirements for all three flights, Bill had a Crossley and a driver to take him round the lines. His driver was easily bribed to silence, and visits to the farm could be made without difficulty. On his second visit, Simone insisted he should have Tom's bike, since it would help him to come to the farm later, as soon as his hand was healed.

By June the 10th, Brian Webster had six new RE8s on strength and four new crews, all fresh from England. He saw John at odd times and was concerned that his usual light humour was absent these days. 'Truth to tell I'm not happy with the pilots I have to fly with Bill. I mean, I don't want to talk ill of my fellow officers but they can't fly for toffee! At first it was Trevor Browning, and my first sortie with him got us well shot up I can tell you. Then he force-landed us into a ploughed field, removing the damned undercarriage in the process. Brian Webster has sent him to 'C' Flight for further instruction I'm glad to say.' Bill laughed at his friend's tale of woe.

'It's not funny Bill! I'm scared stiff with some of these chaps. Peter Anderson is fine, but I'm not his regular observer. My current pilot is

Lieutenant Don Larkin, and he is neither proficient or experienced. His chief aim in life is to get me killed and himself the VC, particularly when we fly CPs. For God's sake Bill, get back soon!'

Bill didn't see John for a full 12 days after this conversation, and had to leave two letters for Mattie with the Officers' Mess Sergeant. He had put them in an official brown envelope with firm instructions. 'Make sure they get to Lieutenant Kenting, he's expecting this report from me!'

His hand was much better now, and he could grasp things quite well. His palm was very stiff, and quite painful when he tried to hold things, but most of his fingers were flexible and the MO seemed to think he would be fit to fly within another week or so. It was on one of his regular visits for a fresh dressing that he bumped into John, who quickly steered him out of the medical room. Bill noticed his drawn features and was quite shocked to see the dark lines around his eyes.

'Those damned Albatros shot us up again yesterday. Even got myself a flesh wound in the thigh, which is why I'm here. Unfortunately it won't keep me grounded. Christ Bill, when do we get you back? Brian Webster promised me we shall crew together, just as before, as soon as you are fit.' Bill told him it would be about a week. They mentioned the letters, and news from *Saddleworth* but Bill could see that his friend was very distracted about the flying.

On the 5th of July Bill was cleared for flying, and reported to Captain Webster for duties. 'Good to see you back Proctor, how's the hand?' Bill told him it was good enough to fly with, and getting better every day. 'I promised Mr Kenting you two would crew together once you returned. But he's now doing a lot of photo work with Mr Anderson, and I don't want to take him off that yet because they are the only crew who know the area well enough to complete the job. However, I want you to break-in a new observer this morning. Sergeant Nettles is fresh from England and he seems to be an excellent gunner too. Show him our sector for an hour or two; stay out of trouble and get yourself back into the picture eh!'

Bill found he hadn't lost any ability through a five week absence from flying, and delighted in showing his new observer the boundaries of their sector. The sun was warm and even at 5000 feet the air was not too cold. He found the RE8 required trimming however, and despite applications to the trim wheel it still flew nose heavy. Bill determined to have this corrected as soon as they landed. As it turned out the problem was really very basic. Peter Nettles only weighed 118 pounds and two weeks ago, Wing HQ recommended that in the absence of an observer, the rear cockpit should be sandbagged to a total of 160 pounds! Bill reminded himself – the RE8 collected new orders every day it seemed.

Four days later Bill and John were given their own aircraft, and they started their first mission in RE8 C 989, on the afternoon of the 9th. It was a conventional artillery shoot for a heavy 9.2 inch Howitzer which just been moved to a position close to Vimy. Their targets were a railhead and two supply dumps some nine miles behind the German lines and south- west of Douai.

'Our old patch, eh John!' Bill was happy to be flying with John once more, but his observer was deadly serious.

'This is the area I hate most. You realise of course that this is where Mr Richthoven killed Tom Bolton? And the bastard is still out there with his flock of peacocks! Look Bill, we go in at 3000 feet and at exactly 3 pip-emma the 9.2 will open up. Circle the target around here!' John drew a crayon around the target area on his map. Do three circuits then it's back behind our lines. We have DH2 cover today, which means no cover at all against those bloody Albatrosses.'

In the event it was a quiet afternoon. They saw some aerial activity thousands of feet above them, and there was plenty of Boche archie, but of the Albatross they saw none. The shoot went well however and they were delighted to see a direct hit on one of the dumps, which exploded in a terrific flash of orange flame and gave them a thorough shaking as the blast reached them seconds later. After they had landed John was quite different.

'There you are Bill! What did I tell you? As soon as the old team is together nothing can go wrong eh!'

The following three days saw them in an entirely different role as they flew 'Counter Attack Patrols' along the enemy front line. The CAPs were a new idea, and 12 Squadron were the first unit to try them within 3rd Wing, RFC. They were designed to provide infantry support for allied attacking troops. Each CAP crew had first to identify ground signals put out by the front line infantry. These signals then indicated where they wanted the CAP to attack enemy positions immediately ahead of them. Fitted with eight 20 pound Cooper bombs and a full load of ammunition, CAPs gave considerable support to attacking infantry, but were highly dangerous for the flyers.

On every CAP they flew, 989 received numerous hits from small arms fire, but Bill found he liked the job. He loved the low flying, and although most pilots flew at the recommended height of 500 feet, first dropping their bombs then following up with shallow dives for machine gunning the trenches, Bill preferred to fly at 100 feet or even lower when using the Vickers gun. As he flew down the Jerry trenches he knew they were reducing the casualties which would otherwise be inflicted upon their attacking infantry. The Vickers was a deadly weapon at this height, and John's Lewis gun gave additional fire power from behind.

After the first CAP John was furious. 'What the hell are you trying do? No one flies *that* low and lives to tell the tale. Just look at all these bullet holes! You were lucky this time, but in future I would appreciate you flying at the approved height!' Bill remained calm, he knew he had to expect this from John.

'Yes we were lucky John. There were no Albatros around today. But tomorrow there will be, you can bet on it! Those poor sods in the Jerry trenches will have complained like hell they were given no air protection today – so we can expect the Huns to be down to 500 feet tomorrow.' John waited, he knew Bill would probably have some reason or other.

'Certainly we are going to get hit from rifle fire, every now and then one is sure to hit us. But the closer we are the safer we are! At 500 feet even their machine guns can get time to find you, but not at 50 feet! The main thing to remember is that the Albatros can easily get on your tail, and under it for that matter, at 500 feet. But if we are lower than that their dives will take them straight into the ground!'

John was far from convinced. 'All right smart Alec! Then if that is so obvious why do Wing HQ recommend CAPs at 500 feet?' Bill grinned, he loved to tease John when he got like this.

'Just like a bloody officer! Think John, when did you ever see a bloody RFC Colonel flying a CAP? Those chairborne flyers at Wing might be good at thinking up these schemes but the bastards never fly them. You just see, six months from now and I bet all CAPs will be flown at 100 feet!'

John Kenting said no more. He was scared stiff and he recognised that, but these CAPs were almost suicidal. Bill's explanation made sense all the same. 'I don't know why I put up with you Proctor I really don't. But if we get killed tomorrow I'm putting in an official complaint!'

On the following day they found that British infantry had occupied the first line of Jerry trenches, and their ground signals now indicated new positions opposing their front. The CAP flight comprised a total of three RE8s, flown by Lieutenants Anderson, Larkin and Bill. Each aircraft approached its own part of the front line and took stock of the ground signals laid out. Then, as prearranged, they climbed to 800 feet before splitting up to make their ground attacks. While Anderson and Larkin took evasive action before diving down to straddle their bombs along the trenches, Bill flew south, dropping height as he turned back towards his own lines before turning to approach his target tangentially. At about 100 feet he lined up along his line of the German trench system and dropped their bombs in sequence as he gunned the Jerry infantry now clearly in his sights.

John was busy raking the third line of trenches as the bombs burst. At only 100 feet there was some danger of being hit by their own bomb shrapnel, but as far as he could see they never received any hurt. Then they climbed higher as Bill turned once more for their own lines. Replacing the drum on his Lewis, John chanced to look up and stiffened when he saw the five Albatros scouts diving in line astern. Although the turn was not steep it was impossible to fit the heavy 97-round drum on the Lewis until 989 returned to straight and level flight. Keeping a wary eye on the approaching scouts John eventually got the gun loaded, and as Bill began an opposite turn to the German lines leant forward and hit him hard on the shoulder with his fist.

Turning round, Bill took in John's agitated look and followed his pointing finger to the approaching Albatros fighters. With a nod of his head he dropped the nose and flew only 10 to 20 feet above the heads of crouching infantry now massed in the British trenches. There was an entire battalion of Black Watch strung out along the trench line, six companies strong – 900 men in all. And as the leading fighter fired at the RE8, ten heavy machine guns opened up among the massed rifle fire of the battalion. Two of the leading scouts fell away, one with smoke streaming out behind, while the other flew straight into the ground, its pilot stone dead. The remaining three Albatros broke away, climbing steeply out of the hail of ground fire.

John saw it all while Bill turned once more to approach the enemy trenches from the north. Keeping low he raked the trenches with the Vickers until his ammunition ran out, then climbing slightly made a cautious turn towards their own lines and safety.

Looking upwards John searched the sky for the Albatros. He could see what might be a dog fight some 3000 feet above them, but that was all.

As he turned from the Jerry lines Bill saw the Black Watch going over the top. They were a splendid sight, wearing khaki aprons over their kilts, their bayonets gleaming in the soft sunlight. He could almost hear their battle cries as they rushed the 100 yards of open ground separating them from the horror yet to come. He only hoped he had played his part, that the German resistance was crushed by their air attack but he knew the Jerries would recover and stand firm in the hand-to-hand fighting of steel against steel. He silently thanked God he was not among the brave men down below.

They were first back, and while waiting for their comrades were pleased to note only six holes in the wing fabric.

'There you are Sir, what did I tell you! Hardly a scratch thanks to Professor Proctor's brilliant flying!' John threw his gloves at him as their two ack-emmas joined in the fun.

'I wonder you can bear flying with 'im sir and just look at what he's done to our lovely aeroplane!' Cpl 'Smokey' Black drew their attention to the starboard aileron post that was nearly severed in two. 'Oh my God!'

Bill looked directly at his engine fitter. 'Bloody hell Smokey. If that had gone I hate to think what would have happened!'

Their rigger, A/M Percy Parsons joined them. 'Nowt much Sarge, unless you were turning at time, but that thar couldn't harm thee if tha flew straight – unless it busted them thar airlyrons.'

Bill looked at him seriously, then turned to Smokey Black. 'I don't talk like that do I?'

John Kenting was bent over, laughing. 'You two Yorkshire tykes should go on the stage, really you should.'

Their merriment subsided as they heard the sound of an aircraft approaching. Smokey Black came to Bill's side.

'Doesn't sound too good Sarge, who is it do you know?' Bill knew, he could spot the large black patch under Peter Anderson's wing - a hasty repair undertaken after yesterday's mission. John came round to join the small group as Anderson's machine coughed its way into the circuit. 'Who is it Sergeant, do you know yet?' Bill was about to answer when the coughing stopped.

The RE8 was about 100 feet above the field when it stalled. Its pilot was quick to drop the nose and as the machine fell he managed to keep the glide for the next 70 feet before it fell onto one wing to collapse in the middle of the field. The fire tender was already racing to the wreck before the ambulance truck managed to get started, but as the watchers joined the race they could see there was no smoke, fire or movement. They arrived in time to see the fire crew lift the observer out of the rear cockpit, riddled with bullets, covered in blood and very dead.

Peter Anderson was alive, but badly hurt with bullet wounds across his chest and legs. It looked very bad, and as the medics took him to their ambulance they didn't appear too hopeful. Brian Webster arrived in a Crossley and took them back to his office.

'What a bloody mess! Larkin shot down and now Anderson. God knows how you two survived!'

John looked at his pilot before speaking. 'You say Larkin was shot down sir?'

Brian Webster stopped pacing and sat down. 'They were lucky. Tangled with a couple of Albatros then as they turned west, one of them chased them over the lines, got in a good burst wounded the observer and knocked up the prop. Evidently Larkin kept his head, switched off and coasted on. He crashed E 1002 a couple of miles east of Aubigny.'

Bill was puzzled. 'How on earth did he get as far as Aubigny sir? That's only ten miles north of us, and with a dead engine?'

Brian Webster looked at some written notes. 'Larkin telephoned me direct from the crash area. Fortunately there was a mobile medical unit near there and they soon took care of his observer, a shoulder wound evidently. But it seems that they were shot up on our side of the lines, which means the Huns are getting confident enough to trespass over our own skies – something they never dared to do before. I tell you gentlemen, I'm fed up with filling in 3347s these days!'

From his five weeks in the equipment section Bill knew that an Army Form W.3347 was a report on casualties to personnel and machines. He also knew that if they continued with these CAPs, his squadron would be needing a new stack of forms at this rate.

On the following day Bill was made Flight Leader with two machines from 'B' Flight. Their CAP was to support any assault the Black Watch may indicate between 0800 and 1100 hours, after which time they would be relieved by Captain Webster and two more machines from 'B' Flight.

Flying mostly between the original lines and the newly-held trenches Bill kept a visual watch on the Scottish battalion's front, but there were no ground signals requiring further action. At last, after three hours of flying in circles, they were relieved by Captain Webster.

Later that day Brian Webster's flight returned without seeing any action.

'It seems the front is being held where it is at the moment, thank God! And 'A' Flight is stood down from further CAPs until we are re-equipped with more machines and crews.'

John Kenting breathed a sigh of relief. 'Best news I've heard in weeks Bill!'

Bill and John flew a few artillery shoots to the end of the month and on the 2nd of August made a photographic survey of the front line between Loos and a position 20 miles east of Peronne. With a top cover of nine SE5s at 10,000 feet and a flight of six SE5s at 8000 feet John knew their mission was of great importance. He was to keep the camera running for a distance of 22 miles as Bill flew straight and level at 6000 feet. They were perhaps halfway down their run when the archie stopped. The two flyers knew what to expect, but the enemy fighters were not their concern, they had 15 SE5s to look after them.

The RE8 was made for such work, and for all its faults Bill had to admit the machine's stability made it easy to fly straight photography lines. John was out of sight, buried in the fuselage where the camera was located behind his seat. His task was to keep the camera loaded with fresh plates and ensure that used magazines were safely housed in the slots provided. He saw nothing of the dog-fights now being fought around them.

But for Bill, intent as he was on following the trench line below, he could hardly miss the drama being enacted within his airspace. There must have been about 20 of them, Albatros and some other shark-like forms with large black crosses. Each Hun was engaged with an SE5, but it was obvious the RE8 was their prime target. Escaping his opponent for a while, one of the Huns made a beam attack on them, his twin Spandau clearly firing as he approached. Bill pulled the stick back, his intention being to spin their way out of the problem. As he did so a dark brown shape with a flat nose passed in front of him. Instinctively he dropped the nose and levelled off. Looking to port he could see his saviour, an SE5a, seeking the tail of his attacker.

Regaining their correct height, Bill turned to see John's worried face. He threw up a thumb and they resumed photography.

It was a good mission. They had commendations from Wing HQ, and Major Kemp even brought a loose mosaic for them to see.

'Jolly good work you two, our masters are very pleased with your recent photographic stunt. Incidentally, I heard those Huns you encountered were Jasta 11. The old Red Baron himself!'

Bill had a question. 'Do they have some new machines sir? I could swear there were some new ones out there, V strutters like the Albatros, but sharper looking.'

Roger Kemp made a grim smile. 'Yes Sergeant, you are quite correct. The new Pfalz DIII scouts, supposed to be replacing the Albatros, they are good too. Very manoeuvrable so they say, but not as fast as our SE5s and the Sopwith Camel now coming into service.'

Two days later John went sick with catarrh, headaches and diarrhoea. Bill tried to visit him in the medical hut, but was told that he was in isolation – gastric flu!

Brian Webster called Bill into his office. 'Mr Kenting is out of action, and I cannot break up crews just to provide you with an Observer, so I'm lending you to 'C' Flight for a while. As you know they use our old quirks and Avros for communication work and gunnery training, but since I needed some more observers, Major Kemp thought we should give them one of our experienced pilots for a while, a kind of *quid pro quo* you see.' Noting Bill's lack of enthusiasm, the Flight Commander sympathised. 'Don't look so glum Proctor! You'll be back with us soon.'

Bill smiled. 'That's all right sir, it will be nice to fly the old quirk once again.' As he left to report to 'C' Flight he smiled to himself, what the hell was a *quid pro quo* anyway?'

The work was boring, but so long as he was flying Bill was happy. He trained a number of ack-emmas, in air-to-ground gunnery, and flew some budding observer NCOs on map reading exercises. It was a relatively peaceful occupation, but they always had to fly with a loaded Lewis, particularly since the Huns now ventured considerable distances inside their lines. He wrote nearly every other day to Mattie and was able to pass the letters to John by handing them to the medics. On the 12th of the month he learned that his friend had been discharged fit and was now back to flying.

Visiting 'A' Flight some days later he looked for John but found he was back in the sick bay. He asked Lieutenant Larkin what was wrong.

'Not sure Proctor, not sure at all. Seems his gastric problems returned from what I hear.' Visiting the medical centre he found John was again in isolation.

'Surely you can tell me what's wrong, I need to discuss some flying matters with him!'

The medic was unconcerned. 'Sorry Sergeant, you'd better see the MO if you want to know more.' Bill left his letters and returned to 'C' Flight.

It was early in September before he saw him again. 'How are you John? I've been quite worried. I had a letter from Mattie yesterday and she said you were in hospital with tummy problems? I hope you are well again; it sounds serious.'

John put his mind to rest. 'Oh I'm all right really, it's just that I never got rid of the blasted bug. The Doc says it may recur from time to time.'

Bill changed his tone. 'That's as maybe but I felt quite daft. There's Mattie telling me you are in hospital and me not telling her! You had better explain that to her or she'll think I don't care!'

John apologised. 'I shall explain don't worry, but did you know I'm to fly with another pilot? Brian tells me that you have to stay on 'C' for another two weeks yet.' Bill already knew.

It was September the 17th before he returned to his own flight. John looked very strained, but was delighted to see him back.

'Am I glad to see you! That stupid bugger I've been flying with is hopeless. He flew us to the wrong target yesterday, then climbed to get a better look at the terrain and we were bounced by a couple of Pfaltz. Fortunately, after two passes and a number of heart attacks our escort came to the rescue.'

Bill was more concerned about his aircraft. 'I've just seen Smokey Black. He says that 989 needs a lot of attention. You're damned right John, it's time I was back!'

Rain and more rain kept them grounded for almost a week, but Bill was happy to spend time working on their aircraft. He managed to fly an air-test beneath the clouds but the air was too turbulent to check the trim correctly.

On the 24th they were detailed for an artillery shoot east of Vimy. John checked the wireless transmitter, then used the telephone to get map references and wireless frequencies from the 126th battery RA who were located near Vimy Ridge. 'The whole sortie should take no more than an hour,' he thought.

They had three DH2s as cover, and as Bill scanned the sky he knew their escort would be totally outclassed if any Albatros or Pfaltz turned up. Fortunately there was about five tenths of scattered cumulus at 3,500 feet, and as this was about their height for ranging the guns, he knew he could make full use of the larger clouds if any Huns should appear. After half an hour, John signalled their work was completed and as they turned for home he saw three specks about 2000 above them. They were coming down from the east, getting larger all the time, and as he looked for their DH2 escorts he noticed the Jerry archie had stopped.

The three DH2s hadn't a chance. While two of the Pfaltz broke them up, a third came directly onto the RE8. John was now shouting unheard warnings as he brought the Scarff ring round to face the rapidly approaching threat. Bill entered the first large cloud he could find. It wasn't large enough to hide in for long, but it took the Pfaltz by surprise. As he flew into sunshine once more, Bill searched for their highly manoeuvrable enemy. As expected, the enemy scout had climbed, and had turned to come back on their tail. He heard the clatter of John's gun behind him, and realising his gunner wouldn't open up until the Pfaltz was getting close. He knew it was time to duck for cover.

Climbing at full throttle Bill managed to fly into a cloud considerably larger than the first. He knew the Pfaltz wouldn't risk getting too close, not with a cloud stuffed full of RE8! But he had to attempt something; they had been lucky so far but it couldn't last for ever! Pulling his airspeed back, Bill turned as tightly as he dared, then carefully watching his ASI and slip-bubble, applied a coordinated turn to the right. Returning into the bright sunlight he scanned the sky above him – and there he was!

Vizefeldwbel Carl Weischer was an experienced pilot, and although he had completed two years of active service, it was mainly in two-seaters. Nevertheless, Weischer was a good pilot and had done well on his conversion to the new fighter. Joining Jasta 9 only two weeks ago he was being gently introduced to air fighting, and so the easy kill was to be his, while his comrades fought the more difficult escorts. He'd throttled back, waiting for the Tommy two-seater to reappear, but could hardly believe his eyes when it approached him so closely. Whereas an experienced fighter would be wary of such a manoeuvre Weischer was impatient, and as he nosed down to face the lumbering Harry Tate, his Pfaltz was instantly stitched by the RE8's forward-facing gun. It was pure luck, but twelve rounds of .303 also included two tracer bullets – it was enough! Even Bill never expected such a drastic encounter. At best he thought he might buy some time, or even scare his opponent off. But at nearly 100 yards his two-second burst caught the Pfaltz in its fuel tank, igniting it immediately. Instinctively Carl Weischer banked his machine into a steep side-slip as he tried to keep the flames away from the cockpit. The crew of the Harry Tate watched in horror as the Pfaltz pilot placed his arms over his head, it was the worst of deaths, a flamer! Bill looked about him, there was no sign of the other machines. He could look no more and headed for home.

'I cannot be certain Sergeant, but I think you may well be the first pilot to shoot down an enemy fighter from a Harry Tate!' Major Kemp was delighted with their report and even had Bill sketch diagrams of their battle with the Pfaltz. 'I shall recommend you both for appropriate awards in my report, but as you know I cannot guarantee anything.'

Bill could only see a fellow pilot dying an agonising death, nobody deserved a medal for that! He looked squarely at his Commanding Officer.

'I don't want any medal sir. But a spot of leave would come in handy.' He looked at John. 'I believe we are due for leave are we not sir?'

Roger Kemp was a bit put out. Damn the man, at least he could be grateful for the recommendation. Keeping his composure he managed a smile.

'Well I'll see what can be done Sergeant... Mr Kenting. But it may take a few weeks before we can manage something.'

'I don't think the C/O was all that pleased when you turned down his offer of a gong.'

Bill looked at his friend. 'I love flying John, but there is something horrible about a flamer, no medal can compensate for that! Anyway, a spot of leave, now very much overdue, that's different!'

They continued to fly a mixture of contact patrols, shoots, and photo-flights for the next five weeks, and although the Albatros and Pfaltz were an ever present threat, the SE5s were now supported by the Sopwith Camel, a highly efficient twin gun scout that could better anything the Huns had to offer. As a consequence they were now heavily escorted on every mission, and best of all, the Camels had taken over the dreaded CAPs. Nevertheless, for all that their sorties were becoming safer, John's fear was becoming more and more evident with every flight. Bill knew his friend needed a rest. He was an excellent observer and they worked well together, but John made no attempt to conceal his frequent headaches and gastric complaints. At one point Brian Webster even joked about it openly in the crewroom.

'If you take any more of those damned pills John, you'll rattle more than a Lewis gun.' But it was the confidential wink between Lieutenant Larkin and his observer that worried Bill.

On the 20th of October John received his promotion to 1st Lieutenant. There was the usual party in the Officers' Mess, but the two friends could only settle for a future celebration. On the 28th they were notified of home leave. Promulgated for a period extending from the 5th to the 21st of November they were to receive 14 days leave with two days travelling time tacked on. They could hardly believe it true. As a crew their leave period had to be a joint one for operational reasons, but for John and Bill it meant more than just dates on a calendar.

'I shall have to go up to Dacre of course John, and I would like you to come too for a few days perhaps? It's your big chance to see just how uncivilised we are in Yorkshire, what do you think?'

John laughed, it was like old times. 'I would love to come, but will your folks be able to put me up? I think you said it was only a small

317

cottage.' He hadn't really thought about it until now, but the solution was already to hand.

'The *Royal Oak* is a fine country pub John, I can make arrangements if you like.' It was settled. They would have to travel independently of course, their travel warrants made sure of that, but they would both meet in Norwich, spend some days at *Saddleworth*, then Bill would go to Dacre. John could then join him there for a few days. After which they would then travel back to Norfolk together to spend the rest of their leave at *Saddleworth*.

Bill wasted no time before writing to Mattie and his mother, and could hardly sleep for excitement. John too couldn't sleep – there was yet another week of flying before they could go home!

Chapter Seventeen

Saturday 3rd November 1917

Bill was already packed and ready to go on leave. Brian Webster had taken them off operations after their last sortie yesterday afternoon, a relatively easy shoot near Vimy, and already Bill could see the relief on John's face. He was to spend today with Simone and Jean Louis, and as he started up Tom's bike he could only wonder at Simone's courage. He had collected cigarettes for her father, just as Tom used to do, and had with him a letter which Tom's sister, Gertrude, had sent to him – to read to Simone.

'You see Simone, Gertie says she would like you to know she will help in any way she can. She has two young children of her own and a friend who can read and write French. She cannot come over to see you of course, but after the war she says she will. Meanwhile she asks you to write to her, and then you can write to each other in French of course. She asks me to say she is now *your sister* and she loves you very much.' Simone cried and left the room. Later, as she called them into lunch, she gave Bill a note.

'Please Bill, please send this to … to Gertie, and tell her I thank you, and that I write her a long letter very soon.' She was very close to her time and looking forward to the baby. 'Perhaps very soon I have Tom's baby, when you come back to France we celebrate eh Bill! And you will be godfather; I want that.' Bill left them later that night. She was happier than he had seen her for the past few months and he knew that Gertie's letter had helped. He would have liked to visit Tom's sister while in England but she lived in Bristol, and he had too many visits to make – but later he promised himself he would.

On the 5th they set off home and while travelling to Dunkirk made all their plans for meeting in Norwich.

'I shall wait for you on Norwich station, and if you are not on the 1415 from Peterborough all you have to do is 'phone from the station and we shall come and pick you up. See you soon Bill.'

At Dunkirk they had to separate, and although they boarded the same troop ship, they spent the night crossing on different decks.

From Dover, Bill took the London train and was in good time to catch the first train from King's Cross to Peterborough. Although his 3rd class travel warrant entitled him a journey all the way to Dacre, he got off at Peterborough where he was to catch the 1415 to Norwich. Hopefully he would be able to use the warrant for the rest of his journey to Dacre, but it wasn't a problem. He'd managed to save quite a sum while in France and was not short of money for this leave. He knew that John had taken a more direct route home and would have arrive at Norwich some two hours earlier, but he was still unsure of their route to Denton.

On arrival at Norwich main line station Bill alighted onto a crowded platform to be greeted by Mattie and John, with Thomson bringing up the rear.

'Oh my darling Bill, isn't this wonderful!' Dropping his kitbag he lifted Mattie off her feet as she ran into his arms. Oblivious to the fact that her heavy long coat was caught in his webbing they kissed a long kiss as he held her off the ground. John was still in uniform, and to the wonder of many onlookers, helped release his excited sister from the blond-haired Sergeant who, totally unaware of their attachment, continued to hold her as with tears and kisses she clung to him. As Bill put her down, John tried to speak above the general hubbub of the platform, but there was little point. Not caring for the crowd that pushed past them, the two had neither eyes or ears for anyone but each other. Thomson had already picked up the kitbag and was leading them to the exit as John steered the happy pair down the platform.

It was cold, and the east wind cut into them as they followed Thomson out of the station to a short line of cars.

'Now let's have a little order here shall we! I would have you know Sergeant Proctor that we have been waiting patiently here for the last two hours, and I have no intention of dawdling in this chill wind while you dally with my sister!'

Bill shook his friend's hand as he managed to release himself from Mattie's grasp. 'So you've not been home yet John?' Thomson had now stopped by a fabric-topped, highly polished automobile, and was busy placing his kitbag on the rear seats.

'How do you like the Kenting family's new transport Bill? I was just as surprised as you are! When I arrived here some two hours ago Thomson was here with the brat and our new toy! Evidently father thought if I can fly in aeroplanes he can at least drive in a car!'

Bill was overwhelmed as he inspected the immaculate Ford Model T.

'My Dad had written to me only a few weeks ago about these, he says they are wonderful. All of 20 horse power too. Just look at those lamps, the brass and the leather, phew!'

Mattie brought him down to earth. 'Just as I'm thinking that I am the only love in your life! Now I find I have to share you with an automobile – men!' She bundled him into the soft leather upholstery as Thomson swung the starting handle. The Ford started immediately, and as John joined Thomson in the front seat she pushed Bill against his kitbag and kissed him.

'You need a shave my darling but I don't mind. You're home at last and I love you – just love you like anything.'

Their reception at *Saddleworth* was memorable as Pamela Kenting hugged them both. Stewart Kenting was there too, as were Mary and Peggy who helped to remove their coats as they welcomed them into the house. Pamela was smiling at her man-son come home, and with damp eyes drew him close as her husband waited patiently to greet them both.

There was no secrecy now. Mattie had taken Bill's hand and placed him beside her as they sat on the large settee. It was plain he was accepted by the family, and generally understood that he and Mattie were to be married at the end of the war. The content of their letters had obviously been discussed and he could see that her father held him in no small regard. Bill felt comfortable and was extremely happy as the family included him in their plans.

'You have a birthday coming up soon John, and your mother and I thought a car would be the most useful gift we could give you! But we give it to you now, so that you and Bill, and Mattie of course, can go places while you are on leave.' John was delighted and kissed his mother warmly after thanking his father. 'I'm sure you won't mind if we use it sometimes John? Particularly when Thomson takes us to see Quentin.' John was puzzled, not understanding what his father had said. But he hadn't asked about his brother yet. 'How is he father, any improvement?'

'The doctors hold out little hope John. It's not his physical condition anymore – he needs special care. You see it's his mind that's gone, and under advice your mother and I have reluctantly agreed to put him in a home where he can get appropriate treatment. These past months, well, the burden has just been too much for your mother and last week he left us. Quentin doesn't mind, in fact I think he even prefers to be with his fellow officers – you see it's a military home.'

Later, when they were alone, Mattie told him more about Quentin's state of mind.

'I'm afraid he was getting violent Bill, and Doctor Wilson had him under constant sedation. It is for the best, and mother is far happier now he's gone. It's very sad but in some way I think you have taken his place, you see they recall Quentin's courage, something they see in you my darling.'

Mattie knew of the plans made by Bill and her brother, and although she fully understood the necessity for Bill to visit his family she was secretly jealous to lose him for nearly a week. Even so she was very careful not to show it!

The next two days were wonderful. They went riding and Bill found he did quite well, even though he fell off when attempting a low hedge. But the Ford was his delight, and within an hour of driving it round the estate he had the bonnet up to tinker with its ignition and carburettor.

'I suppose we could go to Dacre in this.' John said.

Bill shook his head. 'We could, but I think it would take longer than the train, and if anything went wrong we might find it difficult to get spare parts. It's not as though we can spare time for such things either – besides I think we might find it rather cold!'

On Thursday morning Bill took Mattie to Norwich. Well-wrapped up against the cold east wind they enjoyed the drive in the Ford, and were in the city by 10.30. Proud to show her airman to the world she insisted he wore uniform which, in the event, proved to be a sensible choice as they walked about the cold and windy streets. Mattie showed him round the shopping centre where they welcomed the warmth of the shops and the hospitality of the young girl assistants who, as Mattie could easily see, found Bill a romantic figure in his uniform and pilot's wings. Basking in their love it was sufficient just to be alone, the more so as they purchased inexpensive gifts for each other.

Mattie took him to a cosy restaurant where they had a fish lunch with white wine. Then, seeing an advertisement for a Buster Keaton comedy they visited a film theatre for the matinee. Still laughing they left the theatre to find it was nearly dark outside, and as they walked to the car Bill took her hand, turning her round to kiss her in the privacy of approaching night.

'I love you Mattie Kenting and I want you for my wife!' She kissed him back. They felt no cold, only their own warmth.

'I love you too Bill Proctor and I want nothing more than to be your wife, for ever and ever!'

They walked on. As they reached the car Mattie turned to him.

'Bill, when you next come home shall I see your family? I should dearly love to meet them all.'

He hugged her close. 'And so you shall Mattie. But I haven't seen them since I went to France. Only Maggie knows about us, but I want to see them all first. I don't think I should take you to meet them until my next leave. You see they all know about John, and he will be staying at the *Royal Oak* in Dacre. If I were to appear with you, Mum would have us married in a week!'

Mattie feigned extreme hurt. 'And what would be wrong with that I'd like to know. Didn't you say we were going to get married? I think you are insincere Bill Proctor and not to be trusted!'

Bill laughed. 'And you don't know my Mum! Yorkshire women-folk rule the roost where I come from! I tell you Mattie, once she claps eyes on you she will never let you go and I would have very little time with you alone. Time is very precious my love and I don't want to share you with anyone, not even my family.'

They arrived at *Saddleworth* cold but very happy, and as Pamela Kenting brought them to the fire she smiled as she saw how they were together.

'Now, what did you two love birds do in Norwich all day?' They recited the events of the day – it seemed there was so much to tell and Pamela almost cried as she realised the true depth of their feelings for each other. 'So tomorrow you are leaving for home are you Bill? What time do you leave?' Bill was about to explain when Mattie took over.

'He is deserting me mother, but I forgive him and shall even take him to Norwich myself.' John had just entered the room and looking at his watch poured sherry for everyone.

'I heard that young lady and you will do no such thing. I might just let you come with us as I drive Bill to Norwich, but if you think I'm going to let a ham-fisted brat like you drive my precious car you are sadly mistaken!'

Mattie threw him a look of pure malice. 'Mother! Will you tell this… this son of yours that he is only a year or so older than me and to stop calling me a brat!' Bill found the whole charade highly amusing. 'And you can stop laughing Bill Proctor! If you were any sort of man you would defend me and not laugh at my discomfort.' Bill always had a ready answer as far as John was concerned.

'I'm very sorry Mattie. But you see John is an officer, and sergeants are not allowed to argue or remonstrate with officers – it's against regu-lations!'

Stewart Kenting laughed. 'I think our Bill is going to be able to handle this brat of ours, don't you mother?'

Although Bill had never seriously thought of her in a sexual way, he was pleasantly surprised to find that his past embarrassments with Alice no longer arose when he was close to Mattie. They were alone in the lounge, sitting on the floor in front of a dying log fire, and as he pulled her close the thought of such a happening gave him concern. But she was different to Alice, and he knew he'd grown up in the past year. Alice was his first and he realised he'd never really experienced the love he now felt for the beautiful girl now resting on his shoulder.

Bill's train left at 1105, and they were in good time. Mattie had prepared a thermos and sandwiches for his journey, and a similar bag carried much the same, from which the three of them now ate as they sat in the cold waiting room before a small coal fire. Mattie clung to him for warmth and comfort while John laced their coffee with brandy.

'I'm not sure I should be encouraging you to drink little sister but if you promise not to keep worrying me about driving home I shall give you a small drop, just to keep you from freezing to death. God, will they never manage to keep these places warm!'

The train came in on time and after confirming John's arrangements to come to Dacre the two airmen said their farewells. Mattie said very little, struggling all the while to keep her tears back as Bill threw his kitbag into the carriage. There was little time left, and as he kissed her goodbye he began to wonder if it was fair to leave her so. Interrupted by the guard's whistle they drew apart. He hated farewells, but as the train pulled away he leaned out to see her standing alone on the wind-swept platform, waving her hat until he was out of sight.

To his surprise the MCO at Peterborough initialled his warrant and stamped it. There was no problem and he could use it all the way to Dacre.

By the time he arrived in Harrogate all the shops were closed, spoiling his intentions to buy presents for the family. But as the train to Dacre pulled out he planned to bring his mother to Harrogate the following day, and Maggie too, if she could get time off school. In that way they could choose their own presents, and he would be able to take them to Betty's Cafe for lunch; Eileen too if she could get off work.

Bill felt a lifetime had passed since he'd last stood on the tiny platform at Dacre Banks. It was dark and the two gas lamps that illuminated the station were barely sufficient to make out the slim figure now running towards him.

'Bill! Is it really you?' It was Eileen. 'I don't believe it, we must have caught the same train! Oh Bill, and here I was thinking you would already be here!' He caught her in his outstretched arms as she dropped

324

her handbag to kiss him. Tears of joy streaming down her face. 'My, oh my, you look so well. We've all been counting the days and here you are!'

Eileen ran ahead and opened the front door shouting excitedly of their arrival. Bill could smell his mother's cooking, and although it was more than a year, he felt at home immediately. Maggie rushed to him clinging and hugging as his mother quietly came into the front parlour. It was all too much, and with tears streaming down his face he was laughing and crying in sobs of joy.

They were all crying now, and Bill could never remember his mother's face being more beautiful than it was at this moment. He grasped her in both arms as she sobbed, and held her for a full minute while his father clasped an arm over his shoulder.

'My word thee looks grand son! It's bin a long time but tha's home at last. Let me have thee coat.' As he shed the heavy greatcoat there was a clamour from the girls as they saw the wings on his chest.

'Oh Bill you do look wonderful – a proper hero and no mistake!' He lifted Maggie up the better to see her.

'Not a bit kitten - whenever did you see a hero with tears on his face eh?' While his mother dabbed her eyes Maggie winked at him. They both waited, knowing what she was about to say.

'You must be starved lad, your dinner will be ready in a few minutes. Just you wash up first!' Maggie burst into laughter as she threw her arms around her brother.

'There you see! Didn't I tell you so; now you owe me sixpence.' In her last letter she'd made a bet with him that her mother would say exactly that within five minutes of him coming through the door. Laughing and shaking his head, Bill searched for a sixpenny piece as Maggie told her story to the rest of the family.

His room was just as he left it. And he was reminded that here in his home nothing ever changed. A warm coal fire burned brightly in the hearth, with a large iron fireguard for protection. There were even flowers in a vase and his old heavy dressing gown warming over a clothes horse. As he emptied his kitbag, looking for the canvas 'housewife' which enclosed his shaving kit, there was a knock on the door. Pushing it open with her foot Maggie brought him large china jugs of hot and cold water for his ablutions.

'Can I watch you shave Bill?' Entranced, she watched as he stripped off his woollen vest and proceeded to shave, using the open razor his father had given him before he left for France.

'Maggie! Just you come down here, let the poor lad have some peace, do you hear!' His mother knew she would never leave him for a minute, besides the table had to be prepared and Eileen was changing out of her working clothes.

Putting the dressing gown over his shoulders, Bill let himself out of the back door to go to the privy. It felt strange to sit on the old wooden seat of the earth closet. Much better than the facilities provided by the Army of course, but still primitive when he considered the indoor water closets at *Saddleworth*. He knew his reluctance to bring Mattie was partly a concern that she would be uneasy in such conditions and he felt ashamed. But there it was; in a way he'd tried to explain things to her, only he didn't know how. Whereas John could stay at the *Royal Oak*, he knew his mother would insist on Mattie staying at the house. Eileen and Maggie in their own room, and Mattie in his – just as on previous occasions, when Auntie Netty came to stay and Bill would sleep in the attic. But how could he bring Mattie to this! He loved his home, and his family were used to such country life. Their water came from the village pump, they had no electricity, no telephone, no car, no horses, or servants! Yes, he had to admit he was ashamed, not of his home or his family, but of himself.

Rising up from the seat he looked about and smiled. At least the *Daily Herald* had some uses! Letting himself back into the house he went to his room, and locking the door washed himself all over with the rest of the water. Towelling himself dry he resolved the problem. Mattie loved him and she was not a snob. She would cope he knew that, and John would tell her what to expect anyway.

It was roast pork, roast potatoes, brussels sprouts, carrots and apple sauce. His father had made a short prayer before the meal and as he did so, Bill noticed his mother looking at him.

'You look well son, a bit tired, and definitely older perhaps; you're a grown man now, a soldier. We are all so very proud of you!' She handed him the sprouts and as Bill reached for the bowl it dropped from her hand, spilling its contents onto the table.

'Oh dear God, what happened to your hand?' He had quite forgotten. Even though he'd found it necessary to explain everything to Mattie and her parents only a few days ago. It no longer pained him and was rarely visible, but as he turned the palm of his hand uppermost the scarred tissue was an ugly sight. He laughed it off.

'Don't worry Mum. I did a stupid thing, Dad can tell you just how stupid! I put my hand on a hot exhaust pipe. It hurt a bit at the time but I won't do that again!' Amid his mother's concern, Bill noticed his father's look, he wasn't convinced he could see that.

326

'Dids't tha know our Eileen's got a new job Bill?' His father was quick to change the subject as Eileen spooned up the spilt vegetables.

'Yes, I'm now working at a posh shop down Parliament Street. It's a much nicer job and better pay too, dressmaking for the high and mighty!'

Bill told them of his plans to go to Harrogate the next morning.

'Oh yes Mummy, can I go, please.'

Muriel Proctor demurred. 'Well I can't have you missing lessons Maggie...'

Her father intervened. 'It's not every day her brother comes home Mue, let the lass go.'

Eileen was confident she could get out to meet them at 12.30. 'After all, Betty's is only at the top of Parliament Street. You will be wearing your uniform won't you Bill!'

After they had all gone to bed, Chris Proctor stayed up with his son. 'Tell me how it is lad. Is it as bad as them papers say? I want thee to tell me all about it.' They stayed up for two hours while Bill talked about the war, and his part in it. His father rarely drank, but he brought out four bottles of Stout to go with the bread and cheese as Bill told his story. 'And that hand of thine, how did that come about!' So he told him about the crash and about John, and Tom's death.

'It's all very strange thar knows. Here I am, never bin to war, know nowt about killing folk and here is my lad – flying and shooting and getting shot at! We're all very proud of thee Bill. Now just make sure tha comes out safe, your poor mother, she worries so! When dids't tha say this friend o'yourns coming?'

Bill told him. 'In a couple of days Dad; he's staying in the *Royal Oak* if you remember.' Bill then talked more about *Saddleworth*. As Chris Proctor listened, smoking his pipe and taking in every word, he could see his son had a very special relationship with the Kentings. But class was class and he doubted it would ever change in England. It wasn't an easy matter to discuss so he kept his own counsel. Just so long as he survived the war, that was all that counted.

Setting off early, Bill, Maggie and his mother joined Eileen on the early morning train to Harrogate. The sun was out, and for Harrogate it was a warm and almost wind-free day. The three of them enjoyed their shopping, and Bill insisted on buying quite expensive presents.

'Well Mum, it won't be long before it's Christmas and it's my only chance to get your presents. At least I know they are things you want.'

Muriel Proctor smiled up at him and took his arm. 'I have my Christmas box here and now son, but thanks for my new coat pet, it was very generous of you.' Maggie held Bill's swagger cane as he helped his mother with the parcels.

'We haven't got anything for Dad yet! Shall we look now?' By 12.15 they had bought a large tin of his father's rough cut tobacco, a winter dress for Maggie and a new handbag for Eileen. Then, with time to spare, they walked down to Eileen's posh shop.

Spotting her family waiting outside she called them into the shop. 'Why don't you leave all the shopping here. I'll place the parcels under the counter then you can pick them up later this afternoon. Why not leave your greatcoat too Bill.' Looking around he could see it was a high quality woman's shop, and as usual he felt uncomfortable among all the finery and displayed underclothes. To further his embarrassment Eileen insisted on introducing him to her friends now leaving for their lunch break. 'I think you've heard me talk of my brother Bill, he's on leave from France!' As Eileen introduced him to her friends Muriel stepped back, pleased and proud of her only son, now the brave aviator and obviously very attractive to the girls.

Eileen took his arm as they walked into the cafe. It was Saturday and as usual there was a large queue for seats. The head waitress drew them aside.

'We like to give our brave boys special consideration, so come on!' Bill was about to protest, but a well-aimed kick in the ankle from Maggie stopped him short. As they were taken to a reserved table by the window Muriel gave a questioning look at their guide. 'Don't worry – just the usual couple of rich old dears who have it on a permanent booking. They can wait like everyone else today!' She looked at Bill's wings. 'My husband is a flyer too, are you in France?' Bill said he was. 'So is Terry, I'll serve you myself.'

It was a wonderful meal and as they left Bill asked where they should pay.

'It's on the house love; the old dears never arrived and they'll never know the difference. Good luck lad!' On impulse he kissed her on the cheek.

'Thank you lass, what's your husband's name and squadron? I hope to meet him one day.' That evening, after they had dinner, the family sat down to talk about his adventures in France. It was about eight o'clock when there was a knock on the front door.

'By gum, I nearly forget to tell thee lass. George Graham and his lass said they might pop ower about this time.' Muriel shot her husband a hard look as she went to the door, while Eileen and Maggie leapt to put the kettle on.

As George and Jane entered Bill got up to greet his old employer. 'I think the RFC suits you Bill, how are thee lad?'

Jane stood on tiptoe and kissed him full on the mouth. 'Hello Bill it's lovely to have you back.' As the family readjusted their seating Maggie swiftly sat next to her brother, much to the annoyance of Jane who could see she had done it on purpose.

They carried on talking, and after a light supper with the family, Jane managed to extract a promise that Bill would come to see her the following afternoon. He said he would. 'If it's a nice day we could take a walk together Bill, just the two of us!' As she spoke she took care to give Maggie a hard look, the message was plain to everybody.

At the door Jane kissed him again and squeezed his hand. His mother missed nothing.

'Are you serious about Jane son? I know she's in love with you, or thinks she is, and I know she's been writing to you. What do you feel about her?' He knew it had to be faced, and John would be here in two days. It was no longer possible to let Jane go on this way. Despite the promise he'd made to himself, he couldn't avoid hurting her. He would have to tell her it was no more than friendship.

It was obvious the whole family had discussed the possibility of marriage, or an engagement at least. Only Maggie knew about Mattie, and that was very little. She'd not even spoken to Bill about her yet.

'Maggie, it's time you were in bed love, tomorrow is Church so it's an early breakfast.'

Bill asked if his little sister could stay. 'It's only fair if she stays to hear this Mum. I've known Jane since childhood, and Maggie is her friend. Yes, Jane and I are close, but I've never led her to believe I wanted to marry her. And yes, we have been writing to each other. But recently her letters gave me the impression she thinks she's my girl, my intended if you like. It's just that I don't want to hurt her Mum. She's too nice and I've been dreading having to tell her – I'm not sure I even know how to!'

'Oh Jane Graham – she's been after our Bill for years...'

Muriel Proctor turned on her youngest. 'No more of that our Maggie or it's straight up them stairs; now be quiet,'

'I shall see her tomorrow Mum. Although I have no intention of marrying anyone while the war is still on, I can't keep using that as an excuse. I shall have to tell her it's just not on between us.' He looked at his father. 'I hope George Graham won't be upset Dad?'

Chris Proctor relighted his pipe. 'I think he knows well enough lad. After all, that lass is a bit young for thee. She's what, 16 or summat like that? Only a couple a weeks ago he wus telling us she was taking too much on hersen. Nay lad, thar don't need to worry, but thee needs to tell her.'

Before Maggie went to bed she whispered in Bill's ear. 'Is it Mattie Bill, you must tell me, you must!' As she kissed his cheek he told her.

'Yes love, it's Mattie and we intend to marry after the war is over, but that's our secret for the present.' She dashed off to bed, happy with their secret.

They had eaten breakfast and Bill was helping Eileen with the washing up.

'What's your John like Bill?'

'Well he's an officer of course, a full Lieutenant now; a bit taller than me, dark hair and I like him! He's a nice chap, comes from a very well off family, has a lovely sister and his parents are nice not at all snobbish...'

She stopped him there. 'His sister, that's Mattie isn't it?' She looked at him closely. 'Is there anything between you Bill?'

He took his time answering. 'Yes, we're in love.'

She considered his words a while. 'But you haven't mentioned anything to Mum yet?'

'It's all too fast Eileen. I don't get much opportunity to think these days, things just happen. But yes, this is very serious, and please don't say anything to Mum or Dad. When John arrives something just might slip out, but I shall say something before I leave of course. You'll like John and it would be nice if you and I go out with him one night, perhaps to Harrogate, we could meet you there after work if you like, or down at the *Royal Oak*.'

Eileen thought a while. 'That would be nice Bill, I shall look forward to it – does John have a girl?'

Bill told her about Jean Matlock and laughed. 'He has the same problems I have, a childhood sweetheart, but that's not the same thing as a girlfriend is it?'

'You said in one of your letters that they lived in a very grand house, with servants and all. Do you think he will– do you think he will mind being here?' As she spoke Eileen looked about the small scullery, a tight smile about her lips.

'To be honest love the same thing crossed my mind a few months ago. When I came back to France with him, after we had been to *Saddleworth*, I suddenly realised his life on the squadron must be very difficult after coming from such a home. But John seems to settle into each life without difficulty – as though it was perfectly natural. Perhaps that's why they give office⌐ ⌐⌐vants, we call them batmen in the Army, just to help them get along in rough places. So I don't think John will worry about our little home.' He held her wet hands in his own. 'I've never wanted better anyway!'

It was a bright wintry day, highly suitable for walking, and after church Bill changed out of uniform in preparation for his afternoon walk with Jane. Having broken up his mother's routine, mainly the baking she usually did each Saturday, it was decided to break a further tradition and have dinner at six o'clock. As a consequence their mid-day meal was soup and apple pie.

When Bill arrived at the Grahams he found Jane almost ready for their walk, and as he waited for her he chatted to her parents. Mrs Graham was a quiet woman, not given to either gossip or conversation, but she was a kindly person and very concerned about the war.

'I hope you look after theesen young Bill, it must be terrible in them trenches.'

Jane was now ready, and hearing her mother's last remark couldn't resist correcting her. 'Mother! Bill's a pilot; he doesn't fight in the trenches.' Then looking at him with disappointment added. 'You should have worn your uniform Bill!'

They walked across the cricket field towards the mill, then down the river bank. She stopped and looked at him, removing her arm from his.

'Bill Proctor! You haven't kissed me today!' He kissed her lightly on the tip of her nose.

'And you have a cold little nose, did you know?'

She shook his arm in mock anger. 'I sometimes think you don't love me at all!' He stopped, and putting both arms on her shoulders, came right out with it.

'I've always loved you as a very close friend Jane, ever since we were little kids, and that will never stop. But it has never been more than that, has it?' She dropped her head and was silent a few moments before she answered.

'I have always loved you, ever since I can remember. And I thought you loved me, but were to shy to show it. Then with our letters...' Jane wept silently, then clinging to him with both arms broke down completely. Bill had feared this, and would rather have faced a CAP than suffer the torments of her distress.

'Jane...Jane. Please don't cry! I just cannot stand to see you hurt, and I never intended to lead you on. My letters were to ... a best friend. A friend of my childhood. That's how I see you, how I have always loved you – as a friend. Maybe, perhaps if it wasn't for this war, perhaps we might have known each other better. You are only seventeen Jane and…'

She lifted her tear-stained face. Soft and appealing, she nearly broke his heart. 'But I'm only two or three years younger than you Bill, that is all!'

He stroked her hair, trying to comfort her. 'I'm much older than my years Jane. My best friend killed in action, and many others too. And even I could be killed at any time. Jane, listen to me! I never *said* I loved you. Not in the way you mean. You see, I'm already in love with a girl, she lives in Norfolk.'

They turned around. She was calmer now as they retraced their steps. 'You never told me, you could have told me Bill, I feel such a fool!'

He put an arm around her. 'Yes, I could, but it all happened so fast and I never realised she felt the same until recently.'

Biting her lip, Jane gave a deep sigh. 'Is it your officer friend's sister?' Bill looked at her in surprise. 'Eileen once mentioned her to me, and she said you had been to Norfolk.'

She turned round once more, to walk back along the river. 'I cannot go back to the house looking like this. Let's walk on as far as the woods.' She broke away from him and ran ahead, crying bitterly. Feeling more miserable than ever, Bill caught her up and put an arm about her.

'I want us to be friends Jane, as before. You are very dear to me and always shall be.' As they reached the woods she stopped again, drying her swollen eyes. Then, putting on a brave smile she turned to walk back home, taking his arm as before.

'We shall always be friends Bill. I suppose I must grow up too, it's just that… it doesn't matter.' Jane squeezed his hand. 'I would like to keep writing Bill, if you don't mind that is?'

Bill smiled. 'I would like you to Jane ; as good friends I would like that!'

She had recovered herself by the time they reached home. And as they entered the garden gate she kissed him tenderly. 'I think we can remain as we've always been Bill. I shall always love you, and write to you. Please see me before you go?'

He said he would. 'I'm sorry my dear, it's just that…'

Putting her fingers to his lips she shook her head. 'Don't worry love, we can tell everyone we are what we are, just good friends. I'll be fine – go now!'

'Did you manage to speak to Jane, son?'

Bill told his mother what happened. 'She took it well Mum, and wants us to remain as we are, just good friends, and we'll keep on writing. It's a relief I can tell you.' He considered for a moment then decided to tell them about Mattie. 'I have told Jane too, so she understands how it is. Mattie and I hope to be married you see.' As expected his mother wanted to know everything, not least being when she would see her prospective daughter-in-law, and the rest of the evening was almost dominated by questions concerning the Kenting family.

'But son! We are just country folk, I fear they are all too grand for the likes of us!'

Bill laughed. 'No such thing Mum, as you will find when John arrives tomorrow.'

John had taken the first train out of Norwich and was in Harrogate by two o'clock. Had there been time he would have loved to looked at the famous spa town, but as the next Dacre train was in 20 minutes he decided to catch it straight away. At ten minutes to three he was on the small Dacre platform, and immediately recognised by Maggie, who had gone to meet the first afternoon train from Harrogate.

Dressed in uniform and carrying a leather suitcase she half ran towards him, then stopped in his path.

'Are you Mr Kenting, come to see our Bill?'

John smiled. 'And you must be Maggie, am I right?' Maggie blushed, he was so handsome.

'I'm Maggie Proctor, I'm nearly 12 years old, and I've come to take you home.' John picked up his case and held her extended hand. 'Thank you Maggie, I'm very lucky to be received by such a lovely young lady.' Smitten, she kept hold of his hand and led him out of the station.

'Bill didn't think you would be here until later but I told him you might be early and so you are!' Chattering all the while she took him home.

Muriel Proctor greeted them at he door, an apron over her best frock. 'Oh my goodness, Maggie!' Taking John's hand she hastened to undo her apron and pat her hair. 'Oh, Mr Kenting, I … we were not expecting to see you until the later train. Bill went down to the garage, to see a friend, he should be back soon.' As she led him into the front parlour she helped him off with his coat. 'Maggie, go and hang Mr Kenting's coat up.'

'John, Mrs Proctor, please call me John.'

They were having tea and cake when Bill arrived 20 minutes later. 'Sorry John! How did you manage to get here so early?' As the two

333

friends shook hands Muriel Proctor relaxed. It was clearly obvious the two friends were very close. 'I see Mum and Maggie have been looking after you. I just popped down to the garage to see my old friend Jack Henshaw. He was with the BEF in the early days, but was badly wounded. Since then he's been working in the garage.'

It was dark when Chris Proctor came home. Bill had difficulty in keeping himself from laughing as he watched John trying to follow his father's dialect. Then, taking charge of things he broke the spell.

'Dad! I have to tell you, this idiot makes fun of my Yorkshire accent all the time! And he once told me he had been flying with me for two months before he understood anything I said! So if you think he's a bit of a clod please excuse him, he'll larn in time!' They all joined in the laughter as John did his best to protest.

At 6.30 Eileen arrived home. Bill noticed John's interest in her and had to admit, his sister was a good-looking girl. Funny, he hadn't seen her in that way before. but he was pleased to see the effect on his friend. After an hour or so Bill took John to the *Royal Oak*. The old inn was only across the road, almost opposite the railway station.

'As you can see John, our home is very small compared to yours, which is why you are staying in the *Oak*. But as you already heard, Mum expects you for dinner, we call it supper, at about half eight. I thought we might look around the village tomorrow morning. Then go to Harrogate about lunch-time. We could meet Eileen out of work in the evening and perhaps go for a drink or two before coming back, what do you think?'

John was delighted, 'I say Bill, you never told me about Eileen – she's a perfect smasher I must say!'

After supper, John retired early and Bill took him back to the inn. On his return Eileen lost no time in taking him aside.

'So we're going out tomorrow, after I finish work?' Bill confirmed the arrangements already made. 'He *is* very nice Bill, I like him!' She was giggling like a schoolgirl.

'Now you keep your claws off him girl. I don't want him under your evil spell, it's taken me months to train my observer just how I want him and I don't want him disturbed. We all know you've set your sights on snaring an officer. One word to Maggie and she'll soon warn him off!'

Eileen laughed, 'A lot you know Bill Proctor, our Maggie is head over heels in love with him already!'

The following day went well. Bill could see that John was quite taken with Eileen, and although Maggie had been upset when she heard they were having a night out in Harrogate, Bill made it up to her with the promise of a special present he had in mind.

John loved Harrogate; it was his first visit to the spa town and they were fortunate in having a warm day to explore the shops and the valley gardens. While shopping with his mother, Bill had noticed a rather novel brooch in one of the less expensive jewellers, and took John with him to look further.

'See? There in the left corner, about ten o'clock. Pilot's wings in silver, or what looks like silver. And there are observer wing brooches too. They look expensive though!' To his surprise the brooches were very reasonable. Recognising the two flyers by their uniforms the jeweller gave them a good discount.

'We only got them in a week ago, and since you are our first customers I can reduce the price a bit.'

Bill took two. 'One for Mattie of course, the smaller one for our Maggie.' John purchased an observer brooch. Leaving the shop Bill suggested they have tea before they met Eileen. As they started out Bill stopped in his tracks. 'Hang on a minute, something I forgot.' John watched as Bill returned to the jewellers. Within minutes he'd returned. 'Just another little gift I forgot.'

The two airmen walked into Eileen's shop a few minutes before closing time, and Bill couldn't help noticing the stir of interest they caused as Eileen made a fuss of them. A rather saucy red-haired girl called out as Eileen made to leave.

'It's not fair Eileen, you could at least leave one of the Flying Corps behind for us!' Laughing, she left for the door – arm in arm with her two escorts.

Despite the war, Harrogate still had much to offer, and to Bill's complete surprise John took over the rest of the evening. The Majestic Hotel was only a short walk from Eileen's shop, and neither Bill or any of his family had ever set foot in its grounds.

'Wait a minute John, this is far too expensive!' John had only seen the large hotel that afternoon.

'The rest of the evening is mine Sergeant so shut up!' Eileen giggled with anticipation.

'I think the *Prospect* would be better John. It's a pound to a penny the *Majestic* will have some objections, we're in uniform remember!' It was all above Eileen, and not understanding the problems associated with their ranks she was happy to go wherever they chose. John understood perfectly.

'Where's the *Prospect* then Bill?'

They were in luck. Tuesday was a regular dance evening, and the *Prospect's* ballroom was filled to capacity. After a splendid dinner and brandies, John took Eileen onto the floor. Bill watched in envy as they danced together. No matter how he tried, he could never dance. True, he'd never had much time for dancing in the past, but seeing the two of them on the floor he knew he would have to learn.

Breathless, they just made the last train home, and settling into an empty carriage all of them agreed it had been a wonderful evening. Leaving the station at Dacre, Bill decided to go on ahead. Knowing that John would appreciate some time alone with Eileen. Saying goodnight, he arranged to see him for coffee the following morning.

Some 15 minutes later Eileen came through the door. 'Oh Bill, what an evening! John is such a lovely dancer and what a lovely meal. Wait until I tell the girls tomorrow.' She came over to sit by him. 'John said he would like to take me out tomorrow, for dinner. But he didn't know if you or Mum had made any other plans for him?' Bill smiled at her. 'You like him I can see that, and no we haven't made any plans. I think that would be nice for you both.' She kissed him goodnight. 'I'll mention it to Mum in the morning.'

Although breakfast was usually no later than 7 o'clock, Bill was pampered, and allowed a late meal while he was on leave. As usual, Maggie brought him a mug of tea before she left for school. Sitting on the edge of his bed she came straight to the point.

'Bill, did you get me a present yesterday?' Disregarding his surprise and sleepy disclaimers of such a promise, she persisted – knowing her brother well. 'You didn't forget did you! You promised me!'

At last he relented. 'Pest, I was going to give it to you later this evening. But you can have it now I suppose; look on the dresser.' Rushing to the old oak dresser she found a small box.

'Is this for me?' Bill nodded as he sipped his tea. Bringing the box over she asked him to open it for her.

'Oh Bill this can't be for me?' Wide-eyed she gazed at the silver wings. 'Oh Bill it's the most beautiful thing I have ever seen!' Smothering him with wet kisses she leapt from the bed and dashed downstairs.

'She wanted to wear it for school but I said no. It's far too valuable and you know what kids are.' Bill finished off his porridge while waiting for the bacon his mother was preparing. 'It was far too expensive a present Bill, really you are too generous. We had a few tears, but I told her it's only for best!' Bill had wanted to buy one for his mother, but she would never wear jewellery, only her wedding ring.

'I bought one for Mattie and for Jane too.' Placing his breakfast on the table she kissed him on the top of his unruly hair.

'Bless you son, that was a kind thought, and I know the poor lass will treasure it.' Bill knew his mother had expected them to marry one day, and although she remained silent on the matter he knew she was sad that Jane wasn't going to be part of the family.

They talked about John and Eileen. 'She tells me John is taking her out to dinner again tonight! Do you think this is serious son?'

Bill chuckled. 'Oh Mum, how would I know? Eileen enjoys going out with John – well he *is* an officer after all! Besides, John thinks she's a real smasher.'

His mother echoed his words. 'A real smasher. My, the things you boys say these days!'

An hour later Bill put on his uniform and walked to the *Royal Oak*. Over coffee they made plans for their departure the following morning.

'If we take the 0930 to Harrogate I think we can get a train to York, then down to Peterborough. Maybe you could check the rest while you are in Harrogate later today John? I know you are picking up at Eileen after work, and I have a few visits to make, mainly to say goodbye to the Grahams and some other folk in the village.' John agreed and said he intended to take Eileen out for dinner at the *Majestic*, but hoped they could be back for around ten o'clock, to say goodbye to his father. 'The *Majestic*! Eileen will never let us hear the last of it! I gather the two of you like each other John?'

'She's a very sweet girl Bill and yes, I think she likes me a bit.'

Bill walked his friend to the station then went home. After lunch he walked down to the garage where he spent most of the afternoon talking about the cars and new motorcycles now in the workshop. George Graham had taken on a new apprentice, but was afraid he would lose him to the Army within a year if the war didn't finish before then. 'We've much more work on nowadays Bill, more than thee Dad and I can handle. So we'll be glad when you can get back here. I was telling thee Dad only last week, we need someone with a wider experience of engines, not so much here but in Harrogate.' Seeing the look on his face George explained. 'Aye lad! I hope to set up shop in Harrogate, and want you to run it!'

Bill was shocked and looked to his father. 'There's a lot o' trade in't town son, and me and George have enough on here, so think on't eh!' Bill said he would like to, but there was a war to finish first. Secretly he knew there were a number of things to settle, not least would be what

Mattie wanted. Then there was the flying; he wanted to continue with that more than anything.

Saying goodbye to George and Jack Henshaw, Bill went to see Mrs Graham and Jane. Bracing himself, he knocked on the door, when it opened suddenly.

'Ah Bill, was it Jane you wanted to see?' Dressed against the cold Mrs Graham was obviously going out. She seemed pleasant enough he thought. No doubt Jane had said nothing to her parents.

'I have to leave in the morning Mrs Graham. So I'll say goodbye to you now since I see you're going out.' She wished him luck and told him to step inside.

'Jane's only doing some needlework, so she'll be glad to see thee lad.'

Jane led him into the house, and kissed him lightly on the cheek. 'Thank you for coming Bill. When do you have to go back?' He told her of his plans. 'Did Dad tell you about his ideas for Harrogate? About the new garage I mean?' He told her of the conversation they had in the garage, and that he would think about it very seriously.

'I would like to do it Jane, but I have aviation to consider too. And I want to continue flying if possible, they say I'm a good pilot.' They chatted on as Jane told him she had now taken charge of the garage books, and was starting night school in accountancy.

'Please let me know how you are Bill, I shall worry about you.'

He took the box out of his pocket. 'I got this for you yesterday, I hope you like it.' Jane took the brooch and holding back her tears thanked him.

'It's so beautiful Bill, I've never seen anything like this before.' She put it on her blouse as he got up to go. 'I gave a smaller one to Maggie, I hope you don't mind.'

Jane shook her head. 'Thank you Bill, I shall always wear it and be thinking of you – please take care love.' They kissed and he was gone.

Looking at his watch he walked to the village school. Maggie's class would be leaving in five minutes so he thought he would wait for her. It was a mistake. By the time Maggie appeared he was surrounded by her classmates who, seeing his uniform, wanted to know how many Jerries he'd shot down! Eventually his proud young sister took his hand and marched him away.

'Oh Bill, why can't Mum let me wear my brooch to school?' He promised he would speak to their mother.

It was just after ten when John and Eileen arrived at the cottage. Eileen never stopped talking. Full of her night at the *Majestic* she'd

338

captured every detail for her mother's interest. John had purchased small gifts for the family and Eileen was proudly wearing her brooch. Thanking him for the gifts Muriel said she would keep them until Christmas. 'Though I imagine we'll have trouble keeping Maggie's present unopened! I hope you'll be able to see Maggie before you go John, she'll be that disappointed if she misses you.'

John reassured her. 'I shall be here about 7.30 if that's convenient. Then I can say goodbye to everyone before they go to work. Naturally we'll have to kick Bill out of bed!'

Eileen saw him to the *Royal Oak* and thanked him for the evening. 'I shall miss you John, but I hope we'll see you before long.' He promised he would come back on his next leave, and would write to her when he got to France. They cuddled against the cold, as with genuine concern Eileen pressed him to take care ... and look after Bill. Then with a final kiss she ran home.

Before retiring to his room John asked for a brandy. Eileen was a nice girl, but who was he to consider anything further than tomorrow? Soon he would be back on the squadron, and the fear was already eating at him.

True to his word, John came to the cottage at 7.30. Eileen was almost ready to catch her train and Bill said he would see her off. Chris Proctor shook John's hand and wished him luck.

'Take care of theesen lad, it's bin grand to know Bill's friend.' John gave Maggie her gift, then kissed her goodbye as Bill hastened him to the door.

'We'd better walk Eileen to the train John, she doesn't have much time.'

Early morning was the only time Dacre station had more than a handful of people on the platform, and as she kissed the two airmen goodbye Eileen became the subject of much conjecture among the villagers. Blushing proudly she entered the carriage waving her farewells, fully aware of the gossip John's kiss would encourage.

Bill returned home, leaving John to complete his packing at the inn.

'Don't forget Bill, wear your civvies. That way we can travel together.'

Bill had a better idea. 'If you travel in civvies I'll travel in uniform and use my warrant. I can get as far as Peterborough on that! If anyone gives you a white feather I'll simply tell them you're a conscientious objector and I'm escorting you to jail!' John shook his head, as he laughed.

'I'll call for you in about half an hour and think yourself lucky I haven't told your mother about your true nature Sergeant!'

Muriel Proctor was determined to be brave and managed to smile as the two left her cottage for the train. 'Bless you both, take care and come home safely.' She kissed John and wished him well then, hugging her son, kissed him on both cheeks. 'Now be off with you and try not break any more hearts before you get back to France.'

By 4.30 pm they were in Norwich. John telephoned home and came back laughing. 'Mattie said she is going to drive up for us, or we can wait here indefinitely! If she puts one scratch on my car I'll kill her!' It was nearly 40 minutes later when she appeared.

Ignoring her brother completely she dashed for Bill and threw her arms about him. 'Oh I've missed you my love!'

John tapped her on the shoulder. 'Don't I get a kiss, at least for letting you drive my car!'

Mattie gave him a peck on the cheek. 'Of all the cheek! Here am I acting as unpaid chauffeur and you have the nerve to complain. I think we'll leave him to walk don't you Bill?'

After greeting John's parents, Bill and John washed and shaved before coming down to dinner. They spent most of the evening talking and joking about their visit to Dacre and Harrogate then, after a nightcap, they all went to bed early.

Much refreshed, Bill started the morning with a hearty breakfast before going for a long walk with Mattie. The air was fresh and as the sky appeared to promise a nice afternoon, they decided to go riding soon after lunch. By evening Bill complained he was a bit saddle sore and much to Mattie's amusement suggested they turn back to the stables. Laughing at his discomfort she sympathised as she saw him walking to the tack room.

'I have some good horse liniment here Bill, shall I rub you down?' Sitting down gingerly he winced at the thought.

'Stay away girl, I swear I'm seriously injured. It's easy for you, you're used to these beasts. I'm better suited to the wicker baskets they call seats in an RE8.'

She came over to ruffle his hair. 'Oh my poor brave pilot, did the nasty horse hurt your bottom then!' Bill caught her off balance and pitched her into a pile of hay. Picking up a convenient brush he put her over his knee.

'Now miss clever. Maybe I should give you a good tanning?' Mattie screamed as he gave her a good whack. 'No please Bill, I'm sorry, sorry … no don't, you rotter!' In a moment they were in each others arms.

Pressing her into the hay Bill could feel himself becoming excited and rolled her over to one side. Kissing her passionately he felt her pert breasts beneath the tight jacket and knew he wanted her. Looking into her powder blue eyes he saw encouragement as she held him close. Perhaps not, she was so innocent after all. On impulse he let her go.

'So that's your game, you wicked woman! Plying your female charms won't help – a good spanking is what you deserve.' Wriggling away she escaped to taunt him once more. Bill relaxed, the moment was over and he was glad he'd not taken advantage of it.

For the rest of the evening Mattie teased him unmercifully, 'I read the other day the RFC fly Camels, is that true Bill?' Unsuspecting Bill explained the nature of the new British Scout. 'John said it was very difficult to fly, why is that?' He was about to go into technical details when she released the trap. 'So I doubt if they will ever let you ride a Camel my love, if you are not comfortable on a horse...'

They played cards for a couple of hours then retired. 'Goodnight Bill. I'm sorry I teased you so. If we were married I could comfort you...'

Shocked, Bill took his time in answering. 'As much as I love you my dear, as much as I want you, in that way, right now I think such comforts would have to be restricted.'

She kissed him and swept herself away. 'Sleep well my love!' Bill climbed the stairs slowly, amazed how the other sex could manipulate him so.

On Saturday Pamela and Mattie joined them in a drive around the countryside. They stopped for lunch at a thatched inn, and after a detour to Norwich did some shopping. On the return journey John let Bill drive them home. After dinner that evening Mattie signalled for Bill to join her in the billiard room. As soon as he entered she handed him a parcel.

'Open it Bill, I hope you like it.' To his surprise it was a pair of blue silk pyjamas. 'I think you will find them more comfortable when you go riding!' He burst out laughing. 'Oh bless you, you wonderful girl. Shall I put them on to show you!'

He made as though to strip off his clothes. 'Bill Proctor, you are shameless.' She kissed him just the same.

They started Sunday with church, then relaxed for a settled day in the house.

'You are both to wear uniform for dinner tonight – mother's instructions!' They looked at Mattie in surprise. 'No questions or peeping into the kitchen to ask Mary what's for dinner, mother would be most upset!'

The dinner gong answered all their questions. The whole family were dressed in their finest and as they were seated Pamela explained.

'It's not often we dress for dinner, only a couple of times since the war started I think. But if we cannot have Christmas dinner on the 25th of December we can at least have it on the 18th of November, and in style.' It was a magnificent feast and Bill knew the wine was of the very best. The turkey was magnificent, followed by Christmas pudding and mince pies. As Bill got up he thanked his hosts for the splendid meal.

'Yesterday I couldn't walk for horse riding, tonight you've made sure I won't be able to walk at all!'

Bill decided to overhaul John's Model T Ford on the Monday, and having expert advice from his father looked forward to the task. '

At least it will be checked out before we leave John. They're pretty safe of course, but I need to fill-up with oil and grease some of the bearings at the very least. Having checked over the car Bill went to the nearest garage for oil, grease and a couple of spanners. Mattie was a willing pupil, and took great interest in the servicing schedule as well as keeping them warm with hot cocoa.

Bill enjoyed tinkering with the car and was pleasantly surprised to find Mattie was of a similar mind.

'I might not make a good horseman love, but you would make a good mechanic. Remind me to buy you a pair of overalls next time I come.' Tomorrow was Tuesday. No one had mentioned it yet, but they all knew this was the last day of their leave. Bill's remarks brought it home to her, and with a sob Mattie slowly came to him.

'I'm sorry Bill, but we have such a short time left to us.' She left them to clear up and dashed to the house.

After lunch they made arrangements for leaving the following day. John was very quiet throughout, and although Mattie did her best, it was difficult to get him out of a deep depression.

That afternoon Bill, Mattie and John went for a spin in car. John had to pay his respects to the Matlocks before leaving and so they dropped him off before driving on to Denton. Curious, Bill asked about John and Jean Matlock.

'Do they intend to marry one day Mattie?' She thought a moment. 'I think it's possible, but I know John isn't in love with her. You see, John has been used to having everything on a plate and I suppose you could say there is no reason why they shouldn't get married! After all, he would become part of the Matlock business, and he's known Jean all his life. He's not adventurous like you Bill, in fact I think that's why he relies on you so much. After the war is over he will need someone else to prop him up a little. You've met Jean and you can see how she would dominate him!'

They each took turns in driving then had tea in Denton.

'What are your plans for after the war Bill, apart from flying I mean?' He told her of George Graham's offer in Harrogate. 'It would be a good opportunity Mattie, and we could live in Harrogate if you liked, but I think I would rather seek my fortune in aviation.' He took her hand across the table. 'I can offer you a decent life Mattie, but not the one you are used to, not at first anyway.'

She squeezed his hand, her eyes smiling. 'This isn't my life now Bill, it belongs with you and where you go, I go. For better or worse it's an adventure I want to share with you. I'm not like John you see, and perhaps you could teach me how to fly after the war? John was telling mother how much he liked Harrogate. Perhaps it might be a good idea to take up Mr Graham's offer at first, then we could see about flying later?' Bill agreed, overjoyed at Mattie's response.

They picked up John at five o'clock and although Jean asked them in for a while, Mattie hastened to say they were late and expected home. As John kissed Jean goodbye Mattie whispered in Bill's ear.

'Frightful snobs, not your cup of tea at all!'

They played cards after dinner then, as the night was clear, Bill and Mattie went for a walk in the grounds.

'I shall write every other day Bill, and pray for you every night. All I ask is that you take care and come back to me. I love you so much my darling.'

When they returned to the cloakroom Bill gave Mattie her brooch. 'Oh it's lovely and so appropriate! I shall be so proud to wear it Bill.' She showed it to her parents as John handed them both a brandy.

No-one discussed the war or the events of the following day. Mattie discussed horses and Pamela questioned Bill more about the Dales. John had lapsed into silence once more. Stewart Kenting then recharged their glasses and made a toast.

'To 12 squadron, an early end to the war and to their safe return!"

Tomorrow was going to be a trying time for all of them, and as though by mutual consent they all retired early.

Having said goodbye to John's parents Bill packed his kit into the Ford and sat beside Mattie. It was settled that John would drive them to Norwich, and as he made his farewells Thomson started the car. Sat in the back and surrounded by baggage, Bill and Mattie were content to huddle together. They said little, aware of nothing except each other. Only too soon they were at the railway station and with Thomson carrying John's luggage they strode onto the platform.

'Mattie, I shall kiss you now and then you must return home. I cannot bear to see you wait in this cold wind and it's better you go now my love!' Finding a quiet place they kissed and said goodbye. Then she was gone, only to give her brother a hug and a kiss before hastening out of the station with Thomson running behind her.

Their train arrived 20 minutes later. 'Well John, here we go, back to reality once more. We part here I suppose, you to first class and me to steerage. See you back at the squadron if not before!' With a sharp salute he gave John a wink, then throwing the kitbag over his shoulder went to find a seat. John watched him go, envious of his friend's confidence.

Chapter Eighteen

Wednesday 21st November, 1917

Bill arrived at the squadron in the early afternoon and immediately dumped his kit in the mess. After cleaning himself up a bit he went down to 'A' Flight lines to what was going on. There seemed to be no flying, which wasn't surprising considering the cloud and rain, but since the ack-emmas appeared busy he thought he'd chat to some of his friends. Finding 'Smokey' Black working in the cockpit of C.989 he asked what was happening.

'I see you decided to come back then Bill! More bloody modifications as you can see!' Bill looked inside the cockpit. 'As you can see, we're twisting some of the instrument dials around, the idea is that ASI, RPM, oil pressure, and such will have their needles vertical when at the correct condition, easier to check so they say!' Bill agreed it was a good idea. 'We are also replacing the old ring-and-bead with an Aldis sight, supposed to give you a better aim with the Vickers.'

Bill laughed, remembering his last success with the Vickers was pure luck. 'Some hopes Smokey, some hopes.'

Talking to his fitter Bill caught up with the war. Evidently there had been a big tank attack at Cambrai only yesterday. 'The rumour is the tanks found hard ground and advanced about five miles, lots of prisoners and guns captured so they say. Hey! Did you hear we captured Passchendaele?'

Bill remembered reading about it in the *Herald*. 'Yes, I saw it in the papers about two days after I got home. But coming back I heard that the Jerries captured it back again on the 10th, is that true?'

Smokey said he thought so. 'Where is Passchendaele Bill? That battle's been going on since July but I still don't know where the hell it is!'

Bill had flown over the area a few times. 'It's about seven miles north of Ypres, in French Flanders, which is why they call it the 3rd battle of Ypres. It's flat arable country, full of mud now of course. Those poor buggers in the 2nd Army must be having a terrible time Smokey, fighting and trying to stay alive in all that mud and death. I know, I've flown over it!'

Bill reported to Captain Webster who welcomed him with genuine pleasure. 'Hello there Proctor!

I didn't think you would be here until the morning, take a seat I have some news for you. Is Mr Kenting here do you know?' Bill said he was unsure as he hadn't seen him yet.

'I see congratulations are in order sir!' Bill smiled as he referred to the ribbon of the MC now adorning his Flight Commander's chest.

'Thank you. I suppose I've been here long enough to qualify for a gong, that's what decorations are about these days I'm afraid – survival!' He handed Bill a sheet of paper.

'Congratulations to you too Flight Sergeant!' It was true, the official signal from Wing HQ said so; he'd been promoted! 'Not before time 'Flight', and I'm sure you are in line for a decoration too.' Brian Webster came over to shake his hand.

'Something else – as you can see, we are not doing much in this sector at present, mainly the weather of course, but 12 Squadron have been 'volunteered' to send six machines on a detachment to 15 Wing at Droaland, shouldn't be more than a couple of weeks. Anyway, its been decided 'A' Flight shall send three, and three will go from 'B' Flight.' He took Bill to the map. 'Droaland is here, about ten miles west of Ypres. We need experienced crews up there Flight, so consider yourself volunteered as they say! All the Harry Tates are being modified, once again, but have to be ready for departure on the 23rd. That's what – Friday!'

Bill asked what they would be doing there. 'Well I can't say really, but I imagine it will be CPs and visual reconnaissance. Not to worry, 29 Sqdn are there with SE5as, and there's 45 Sqdn with its Sopwith 1½ Strutters. If there are any CAPs to be done then that would be 45's job. As soon as the weather clears we shall be busy supporting the tanks at Cambrai – you heard of course?' They talked on about the war in general and the air war in particular. 'We hear the Huns have a mixed bag of excellent machines these days. 'Richthoven is now in charge of a whole Jagdstaffeln, which is the same as one of our 'wings' by the way. Intelligence say this 'flying circus', as the Huns call it, is comprised of Jastas 4, 6, 10 and 11. Richthoven moves them about along the front, mainly by rail it's thought. Known as the Jagdgeschwader 1, or JG1, they now fly Albatros IIIs and Vs, Pfaltz IIIs and Fokker DR1s – triplanes. You know some of these machines already, and none of them are any real threat to our SE5as or Camels, but they are to us! So

346

take care Flight; you are just as likely to meet the Red Baron and his boys up north as you will in our 3rd Army sector.'

Bill went to the stores, then back to the mess. He had some sewing to do! It took him all of three hours to sew his new emblems of rank on tunics and greatcoat. There was a Royal Crown badge to be placed above the three chevrons, and the old four-bladed propeller replaced with a new one that came with a star. It was worth it, another shilling a day in fact. He would see John in the morning, then air test C.989 for their new detachment. But now he would write to Mattie, he had so much to tell her.

John was delighted with Bill's promotion and tapped Mattie's letter with his index finger. 'No doubt you will have told the brat, eh? Well done Bill I'm so pleased for you. I'll get this off to her without delay. Better waste no time in letting your folks know either.'

Before Bill could mention their detachment to Droaland, Brian Webster called them into his office. Lt. Don Larkin and his observer Lt. Mike Austin were already waiting, and as they entered Lt. Browning and Sgt Nettles joined the group. Captain Webster wasted no time in coming to the point.

'You three crews and your machines have been selected for a short-term detachment to Droaland. You will be accompanied by three crews from 'B' Flight. As some of you know, you are to go tomorrow. So check your machines and air test them before the day is out. Your riggers and fitters will go too. Mr Larkin got his second pip a couple of weeks ago, and as senior pilot he will be in charge of the detachment. From what I know, your duties will be visual recce and contact patrols. They need you there to support 2nd Army against the Boche counter offensive at Passchendaele. Evidently they are short of experienced reconnaissance crews, so don't let us down!'

Bill completed their air test by 1130 hours, then went to make arrangements for Smokey and Percy to follow them to Droaland. As he walked to the orderly room the sergeant clerk called his name.

'We were just going to look for you Flight, there's a telegram for you!'

Bill opened the military telegram without delay:

Bill,
It's Maggie. Badly injured yesterday. Playing on log pile at mill, badly crushed. Very serious. Could be fatal. Please come as soon as possible.
    Dad.

Bill leant against a desk half stumbling against a chair.

'Bad news Flight?' Bill simply showed the telegram to the clerk. 'I must go home, is the C/O in his office?' The clerk didn't know but doubted he could get leave, particularly since he had just returned from home. Bill never heard him, and ignoring their warnings, knocked on Major Kemp's door and walked in.

'Sir!' Roger Kemp looked up from his chair, startled and angry at the intrusion.

'What's this Proctor?' The adjutant, a one-armed ex pilot, broke off his conversation as Bill saluted.

'Sorry to intrude sir, but I've just received this.' He handed the C/O his telegram.

Major Kemp was sympathetic but was already shaking his head as he handed the paper to Captain Taylor. 'I'm sure the adj will say the same thing I have to say Flight Sergeant. Unfortunately you have no grounds for compassionate leave. If it was either one of your parents, or your wife, yes! But brothers and sisters no! I'm very sorry!' Raymond Taylor seemed to understand Bill's distress and put a hand on his shoulder.

'If you had some leave to come we could manage it lad. But since you've just returned from home leave our hands are tied. I know how you must feel, but there's nothing we can do I'm afraid.'

Bill exploded. 'You know I've never asked for anything sir. My leave was well overdue when I finally did get it! Now I need to see our Maggie. Christ she's only 12 years old and God knows what pain she's in. It's not for me sir, but for a poor little girl crushed by logs, she might well die. I've got to go or what the hell am I fighting for?'

The C/O signalled Captain Taylor to take Bill out.

'Come on lad, let's talk about this, it's been a shock I know.' Bill allowed himself to be moved into the adjutant's office, angry and distressed. Sitting on a canvas chair he broke down, sobbing quietly. The adjutant handed him a large whisky and ordered coffee from the Sergeant Clerk. Ray Taylor knew the symptoms, he also knew that Roger Kemp didn't. The young pilot had been flying too long and home leave was all too short. The stress was still there, coiled like an over-tightened spring. waiting to be released. He'd even known those who would never go on home leave a second time, the fear of desertion being too real to contemplate. He also knew about the young pilot's fearless reputation. Everyone on the squadron did. This too he'd seen before, it was rare but very fragile. And unlike true bravery it could break for any number of different reasons – like the one facing him now. The young warrior was close to breaking point, and the same lack of caution could easily induce recklessness.

'Listen to me Flight! I know how it is, I've been there myself. There is nothing you can really do to help. I know you feel you should be home to help your family. And I won't give you any hope that we can get you home, there is no chance of that! But supposing you were home, would you come back to us? I know I wouldn't myself. Then I would be a deserter and would regret it the rest of my life. She may get better son, but whichever way it goes you cannot change what will happen.'

Bill had listened to Captain Taylor's words. They were hard but they were honest. His sobs were less frequent as he took deep breaths, not noticing his glass had been filled twice.

'Sorry sir!' The reaction was automatic and strengthened by discipline. 'What can I do, what the hell can I do, the poor lass!' Ray Taylor comforted him for a full hour, now joining him with the rest of the bottle.

'I know you are due to go on detachment tomorrow. I could always arrange for that to be cancelled, Captain Webster would understand. But I don't recommend it. I think it's better you go. The flying will take your mind off things. Maybe you shouldn't answer this message right now! But perhaps I should?' Bill gave him a questioning look.

'I doubt you could say the right thing. I don't think there is any real comfort you could send at this time. But I could send a telegram right now, saying you were away for a week or so, and that you could only get compassionate leave for next of kin. I would of course send our deepest regrets on your behalf. Then, when you feel more up to it, you can send your own telegram.' Bill got up to leave. 'I shall make sure all your mail gets to you. Flight Sergeant Scully can fly it up with spares and such like!'

Thanking him, Bill agreed then went for a walk. He recalled how many times he'd warned Maggie about playing on the log piles. Most of all he wanted to know why and how it had happened, but he already knew. The adj was right, there was nothing he could do and he was too upset to write at this time. He found John and told him the sad news.

'Oh my God Bill no! The poor child; and they won't let you go home I suppose!' Bill related his experience in the C/O's office, and Captain Taylor's advice. 'I think he's right Bill, leave it at least a day or two. Maggie is bound to be in good care and no one can tell you much at this stage I imagine.' He saw Bill looking at C.989. 'That's not going to do you or Maggie any good! Even if you got home what could you

349

do? I've heard of married men deserting because they had heard their wife was carrying on with another chap and ended up in jail. But from France its desertion in the face of the enemy, no matter what the reason. You could end up before a firing squad Bill!' It started to rain heavily, and as John ran for cover Bill just stood there.

Early the next morning they left for Droaland in two flights of three. Bill had not slept and looking hollow-eyed and unshaven his flying was mechanical as he followed Lt. Larkin to their new field. On their arrival the six crews were told to report to a Lt. Colonel Ransome who could be found at the 45 Sqdn site.

'I'm from 15th Wing and am the chap responsible for you being here. Which of you is Lt. Larkin by the way?' The meeting went on for some time, Bill wasn't even listening as he sat at the back of the group. 'Now I shall be here in my capacity as Wing Intelligence Officer and as you can see, we have all the photography we need at present.' He pointed to the hundreds of prints, enlargements and loose mosaics lying around the room. But what we now need is detailed intelligence concerning the forward locations of our infantry. Since the Boche pushed us back on the 10th we've had to leave a number of positions, and many of our chaps are isolated in small pockets in either company or platoon strengths. It's your job to fly CPs and tell us where they are. Our hosts here are 45 Sqdn, and they can help you out with any problems you may have. They will be conducting counter-attack patrols as may be required based upon the information you can give us, and we have Wing approval to detail 29 Sqdn's machines for top cover on both CPs and CAPs. Mr Larkin, please stay behind, the rest of you will be escorted to your accommodation. Have lunch, then return here by 12.45 pip-emma.'

'I don't like this Bill, I mean why us? I know for certain there are at least two Harry Tate units in the 2nd Army, so why send for us? CPs under a Hun offensive! It's bloody murder!' Bill said little, just shrugging his shoulders. As they departed to their respective quarters John looked at his pilot's back. He would need to shake him up a bit or they would both be killed!

'Don't NCO pilots shave on 12 Sqdn, Flight Sergeant?' Bill looked up as the PMC of the Sgts' Mess took stock of him. Bill found himself gazing into a large red face complete with 'Kaiser Bill' moustache and bald head.

'Sometimes!' was all he said. He noticed the Warrant Officer had no flying badge but wore a colonial campaign medal and the Long Service and Good Conduct medal.

'Say Sir! When you speak to me Flight Sergeant!' Bill looked him over.

'Piss off you fat bastard before I deck you!' Peter Nettles stood amazed as he was told to stand still while the PMC called out for two Flight Sergeants to put Bill under close arrest. Left in a single room with a Sergeant MP standing on duty outside Bill smiled to himself 'Fuck 'em, he wasn't going to be pissed about by a shit like that.' He'd been told that the PMC, a certain W/O Blackman, was also the station Warrant Officer in charge of discipline! Peter Nettles was told he would be brought forward as a witness to Bill's gross indiscipline.

John Kenting was disturbed from his early lunch by a message – would he please see Sergeant Nettles in the anteroom.

'It's Flight Sgt Proctor sir!' Peter Nettles told the story. John was not too surprised but he knew he would have to intervene. As he walked with Nettles to the Sgts' Mess he could also see that the matter would have to be dealt with officially. It would be a serious charge, and Bill was entitled to be represented by an officer from his own unit – himself. As he walked into the Mess he had already formulated a plan.

'I'm sorry sir, we cannot ignore such matters. Discipline has to be maintained, no matter what the accused has come here to do.' John was right, his pilot was going to be kept under close arrest. The matter had already gone to the station HQ and Bill would be brought up against the Station Commander in the morning. Yes, he would be allowed to act as his officer representative, and Sgt Nettles had to be there as witness. John was allowed to see Bill in the meanwhile.

'What on earth made you do it Bill? Good God man that was just plain stupid!'

Bill shook his head. 'Just had enough John, and that fat bastard just made me blow up!' John knew he could take advantage of the situation. If he were to act for Bill he couldn't be flying.

'I shall tell them of your telegram, let me have it.' Bill objected.

'That's personal John, nothing to do with this.' They argued a while before he eventually handed it over.

'Don't worry Bill I'll soon get you off!'

Lt. Col. Ransome was not happy. 'You are here to do a job Kenting, this whole matter has gone too far. Why couldn't your pilot just say he'd not had the time to shave or something? Being abusive was stupid.'

John explained the young aviator's state of mind. 'I know it's no excuse sir, but considering his problems and his past excellent record I'm sure I can get him back on operations.' John knew it wasn't all that serious if Bill apologised. But by the time it had been sorted out it could mean two or three days off flying – two more days of security. New flying crews had an expected life of three weeks over the lines these days, and his own pilot was breaking up!

Bill appeared before Colonel Henry Topper DSO, MC, RA at 1000 hours. The charges were read out in front of W/O Blackman, who had drawn up the charges, and Lt. Kenting RFC the accused's defending officer.

Looking reasonably smart, considering he was not wearing his best uniform, Bill stood smartly to attention as his father's telegram was passed to the Colonel.

'I understand the pressure flying crews have today Lieutenant Kenting, and although I'm not one of you, I fully understand the terrible strain you chaps must be under.' As the elderly Colonel said this he looked pointedly at W/O Blackman, who stared ahead without blinking. 'Nevertheless, despite the awful tragedy to your young sister Proctor, we cannot have such indiscipline. And from a Senior NCO it is without pardon, if true! Now what do you say to these serious charges eh?'

Bill looked at John and thought he had better moderate his answer if only to avoid embarrassment to his friend.

'I cannot remember exactly what I said to the Warrant Officer Sir. I was very tired and upset, as Mr Kenting points out.' Tapping a pencil on his desk the Colonel continued,

'But do you admit to threatening Mr Blackman. Flight Sergeant?'

Bill said 'No!'

'Bring in your witness Mr Blackman!'

Peter Nettles made a smart entrance. 'You know the charges brought against Flight Sgt Proctor do you not Sergeant?' Peter confirmed he knew. 'Tell me what happened as you remember it.'

'Flight Sgt Proctor and I entered the Mess and had just signed the book when the PMC arrived Sir!'

Warrant Officer Blackman then asked if 12 Sdqn pilots ever shaved and Flight Sgt Proctor said they did!'

As Blackman was about to protest the Colonel waved him aside.

'Continue Sergeant. Did you hear Flight Sergeant Proctor threaten Mr Blackman?'

'No sir, not at all.'

'May I speak sir?' Colonel Topper nodded his assent. Turning to Peter Nettles the burly Warrant Officer asked him if he heard Bill say 'Piss off you bastard or I'll deck you!'

Peter cleared his throat before answering. 'Yes sir, I did; but he said it to me not you!' Colonel Topper asked Nettles to explain,

'Well sir, we'd been having an argument before we entered the Mess and when W/O Blackman requested that Flight Sergeant Proctor should address him as 'Sir' I simply gave Flight Proctor a push to wake him up! He was rather tired Sir!'

As W/O Blackman continued to argue he lost his temper. 'This man is lying Sir!' Already tired of the entire proceedings Colonel Topper banged the table.

'Sergeant Nettles is *your* witness Mr Blackman! And if he says he was addressing Flight Sergeant Proctor then you have nothing left to substantiate your charges.' Then turning to Bill he asked him if this was so and if true why didn't he tell W/O Blackman he was addressing Sergeant Nettles?

'I'm afraid I didn't get the chance sir. Too much shouting going on at the time! Then, before I knew what was happening I was being marched to my room.'

'Thank you Mr Kenting there will be no further action. But Flight Sergeant! Take care in future. I have some serious doubt about the circumstances of this charge. Nevertheless, it remains unproved so I have no alternative but to give you a caution here. Which means nothing goes on your record sheet. This charge is dismissed. March out!'

'You were a bloody fool Bill and damned lucky. I'm not very happy about Nettles lying like that either!' Bill waited for Peter Nettles to catch up with them as they left for the 45 Sqdn lines.

'You're only unhappy because it didn't lasted another day! Don't worry John, I'll try to get myself a court martial next time.' When they arrived at the lines it was close to midday. They found 'B' Flight had already flown, and Don Larkin was waiting for them, but not dressed for flying.

'How did it all go then?' John said nothing, leaving the explanations to Bill.

'Well thank goodness that's over; a fine start I must say! Anyway 'B' have just taken off for an initial look at the area. We shall then need to mark these mosaics as soon as they come back with their reports. Lieutenant Coombs will have dropped messages on any front line units they see today, telling them to lay out panels and use signalling lamps for our CPs tomorrow. Naturally we shall then fly to those positions and drop appropriate messages. These will be determined by Colonel Ransome later this evening. So we must concentrate on the maps and carefully inspect these mosaics as soon as we return from lunch.'

'Thanks Peter, it was good of you to lie for me; you took a risk though. Why?' Bill was walking up to the Sgts' Mess for lunch as he thanked the young observer for his help.

'I can't stand those types Bill, all bullshit and no idea what we do. If I'd left it to you I think it would have gone badly. I doubt Mr Kenting could have got you off with anything less than a severe reprimand, maybe worse!' Better watch our step in the Mess from here on Bill, I don't trust these bastards.'

It was close to 3.30 pip-emma when 'B' Flight returned and Colonel Ransome was waiting for their news.

'We found about three units in company strength sir, and many more scattered units perhaps in platoon strength or even less. But they were certainly holding out, possibly because the Boche didn't know they were there. They seemed well concealed too. But they made their presence known to us as we flew over. I think they will require ammunition, food and water sir. Some of these units are cut off too, behind advanced Jerry positions from what I can see. Fortunately there was complete cloud cover at about 1,500 feet and no Huns in sight.' The rest of the afternoon was spent with all crews searching maps and interpreting photographs. At last, by about seven pip-emma the Colonel came up with a plan of action.

'Right! You 'B' Flight chaps get to bed; you'll be flying again later tomorrow morning. Report here by 10 ack-emma. Mr Larkin's crews will remain here while we mark up some of these loose mosaics.'

It was nearly ten when they finished working on the photographs, even then it required the assistance of two 45 Sqdn photographers to assist with marking.

Ransome called them all together. 'I want your chaps to fly to these marked positions at 0800 Mr Larkin. Drop food and water at these locations marked in blue and also drop these packets of marked loose mosaics. I want them to know where their nearest support can be found.'

Trevor Browning was concerned. 'Surely this is dangerous sir? If we miss these positions and the photos land in German hands they will know where everyone is!'

Ransome agreed. 'Good point Mr Browning. Which is why you have to get them as close as possible. If you see any Boche close by then don't do it. But those lads need supplies, it's a risk we must take I fear, and the very reason we need experienced CP crews like yourselves. Even more important, we need to get our forward scattered units into a cohesive force. I suggest one of you fly about 800 feet or whatever height you need, to watch out for any Aldis lamp signals from the ground, while the other two crews make the CPs.

John spoke up. 'Will we have top cover, sir?' Colonel Ransome said he would arrange it. 'I think it better if we do this CP without top cover sir.' Everyone looked at Don Larkin.

'Lt. Coombs said they met no opposition, and even if the skies cleared I doubt the Huns will come down to our level. As I see it, our main danger comes from the Jerry infantry, and bringing in the SE5s just might attract the very fellows we don't want to meet! And from what Coombs has told us we might still have the advantage of surprise – tomorrow at least!'

Bill could see that Captain Taylor was right. Going back into action was possibly the best thing he could do! For most of the day his attention had been caught by immediate problems, and although Maggie was still on his mind, he had to postpone any serious thinking about her while he concentrated on flying matters.

'How much food and ammunition can we carry, that's another problem!' Don Larkin looked at him with interest. 'If we're flying very low then the only problem is with ground troops isn't it sir? So my question is, why bother with the guns and ammo we normally carry? If we remove the Vickers, the Lewis, and all the ammo we normally carry, we could have more room to carry supplies for our lads in the front line. We would also have extra speed if we needed to leave in a hurry, once we've deposited our presents.'

Don Larkin smiled. 'Damned good idea Flight! Naturally this is a matter for each crew to consider. But it makes good sense. Colonel Ransome liked the idea but was worried about their lack of protection. Don't forget, it's ultimately important you get back here.'

John repeated his request for top cover from a different angle. 'Perhaps if we have 29 Sqdn ready to help if required?'

Don Larkin thought a full minute before suggesting a final plan. 'I suggest we do the following. I shall fly with Lt Austin at something like 600 feet, depending on conditions, and will be responsible for looking at the overall picture. Mr Browning and Sgt Nettles will join Flight Sgt Proctor and Mr Kenting doing low level CPs. If you are agreeable to Flight Sgt Proctor's idea, say so now. Obviously we are looking at an increased supply load of about 100 pounds, if we remove your guns. But we must decide now, as our ack-emmas will have to prepare the extra load of supplies and remove the guns tonight. I also think we should adopt Mr Kenting's plan and ask 29 Sqdn for a flight of SE5s in readiness.'

As they broke up John came over to talk to Bill in private. 'I wish you would let me know about your ideas before spreading them to everyone else. To be honest I am not happy about flying unarmed. As the Colonel said it's mainly a question of us getting back here with the information, not handing out food to the infantry.'

Bill was genuinely sorry. 'Sorry John, you are right I should have asked you first, it won't happen again. But why didn't you say no?'

John shrugged his shoulders. 'How do you think I would look when the other crew had already agreed?'

The morning looked ideal for their mission. The stratus cloud base was about 800 feet, with some lower flecks of grey stuff floating below. As planned, Don Larkin took off first and flew directly to their recce area. Bill took off next followed by Trevor Browning. The distance to be flown was only a matter of fifteen miles to a CP line of about three extending between Langemarck and Gravenstafel. The entire terrain was one of utter destruction; Ypres itself a mass of rubble. But beyond, as they travelled a further four miles to their target line, Bill had to identify his position from craters, lines of wire, broken trenches and destroyed guns, all shown on enlarged photographs.

As expected the extended outposts had seen them coming and had put out their markers. By arrangement Bill had taken the northern end of their CP line, leaving the southern part, between St. Julien and Gravenstafel, to Lt. Browning. He made two runs over their line then, dipping the nose cruised over the blue marked outposts at 60 mph. Turning again he could see the infantry scrambling out of their pits and collecting the packets of photographs which John had thrown out. On his second run he knew John would be dropping the ammunition and food as best he could. Light archie was now reaching up to them, with the addition of some m/g tracer, but it was badly aimed and ignored as they turned once more for a final run.

Looking up, Bill could see Don Larkin's Harry Tate and Morse flashes from their signalling lamp. As he was only 150 feet above the flat landscape he estimated that Larkin would be no higher than 400 feet. Their task completed Bill turned west, keeping the RE8 at less than 200 feet.

They were the first to land at Droaland, and as John dashed to report to Colonel Ransome, Bill inspected his machine with Smokey and Percy Parsons. Smokey walked around C. 989 blowing on his hands.

'Christ Bill it's cold – must have been freezing up there!' Inspecting a triangular tear behind his own cockpit, Bill climbed up to inspect the interior of John's office. It didn't take long to find where the shrapnel had come out. 'Phew. Mr Kenting was lucky this time Bill. Must have missed his arse by a couple of inches!' Bill saw the exit hole on the starboard side just behind his seat. Mercifully it had not only missed him, he hadn't seen it either. Bill called Percy over.

'Do us a favour Percy, patch this up so Mr Kenting will never know; it could easily spoil his lunch!'

Hearing the approaching sound of a machine they all looked up to see who was arriving.

'Mr Larkin I think.'

Bill agreed. 'Funny, I thought Mr Browning would have followed me, I've been expecting him these last ten minutes.' Don Larkin taxied alongside and cut his engine. Leaping out of his cockpit he threw his gauntlets on the lower wing and was violently sick. Bill approached Mike Austin, now collecting his Aldis lamp and maps from the rear cockpit. 'Anything wrong sir?' Ashen-faced, Larkin's observer withdrew his helmet and looked at his pilot.

'You never saw it of course. Just after you turned for home Trevor Browning was hit as he reached Langemarck. Forced landing – burst into flames as they struck the ground. Don came down low to see if anyone survived. Just a mass of flames – no one got out!' John Kenting arrived with Lieutenant Coombs, and as the latter talked to Don and Mike, John went over to C. 989.

'What are you doing Parsons?' Busy with needle and thread Percy never even looked up.

'Bit o' patchwork in't back 'ere sir. Bloody shell near got 'im in't backside this time sir!' Too late he realised it was Lt Kenting. All officers' voices sounded the same to Percy. John looked at the holes and left immediately.

'It appears that we've been rumbled chaps!' Colonel Ransome was addressing all the crews in the map room. 'What Mr Larkin's chaps did this morning was truly excellent but they have paid a heavy price with the loss of Mr Browning and his observer.'

Bill spoke up. 'Sergeant Nettles sir.'

Looking uncomfortable Ransome continued in his pinched, metallic tones. 'Ah, yes of course. Sgt Nettles, two very brave men! I shall see if we can get them some posthumous recognition, very gallant chaps.' John now joined them, looking very pale and sick.

'As I say, we've been rumbled. The Boche will be ready for us if we try that again. So what I propose is that 45 Sqdn use their machines to bomb and strafe the Boche while you chaps do your CPs. If the cloud base rises we shall use 29 Sqdn for top cover. In this fashion we should be able to keep the Jerry infantry busy while you fly your CPs. Thanks to your good work our scattered troops now have the necessary information to group together and have supplies to make themselves effective. Mr Larkin tells me there were signs they were joining forces before he left. Mr Coombs will take his chaps out now, and will have the comfort of knowing that 45 Sqdn will cover him with their CAPs. Meanwhile, well done 'A' Flight! Get some rest and we'll see you here for a briefing at 12.15 pip-emma. I want you up at 1400 hours.'

The three officers dropped Bill off at the Sgts' Mess, then took the Crossley to their own quarters. Tired and out of sorts, Bill sought out the PMC. He found him in the bar, surrounded by his cronies.

'Sir. I have the duty to tell you that Sgt Peter Nettles of 12 Sqdn RFC, was killed in action this morning! I'm here to ask you to make sure his room is opened for me now, so that I can pack his kit for return to his unit. This is a standard procedure on 12 Sqdn, just as it is for all aviators killed in action. If you require further authority, contact Lt Col Ransome detached to 45 Sqdn.' Not even trying to avoid the contempt in his eyes, Bill kept his voice calm. The effect was electric. And as the bar fell into a deathly quiet, Bill turned on his heel. Embarrassed, W/O Blackman put down his drink.

'I shall see to it right away Flight Sergeant.'

Having packed Peter's kit, Bill had a sandwich and coffee for lunch and decided he would post a telegram to his father right away.

Dear Dad,
Only just learnt about Maggie. Beyond grief for you, Mum and Eileen. Deeply sorry. Cannot get any compassionate leave. Will write later tonight. Please tell me what happened, write to me at Avesnes.
    Give Maggie all my love and may she get better soon. I love you all. Your devoted and heartbroken son.
Bill

It wasn't adequate, and he couldn't find the words he wanted to say, even if he knew what he wanted to say. Poor Maggie, if only they can keep her free from pain. Crying without restraint he fell on his bunk, the pain for Maggie being mixed with the sadness of Peter Nettles' death. Later he would need to write to Mattie as she would have to know. Bill apologised for his lateness when he arrived at the map room.

'Sorry sir, I had to look after Sgt Nettles' kit.' Col Ransome was very understanding.

'Yes, of course. But it looks as though your observer is unwell Flight Sergeant. So I'm afraid you will have to fly with Cpl Sandbag this afternoon. There was general amusement as Ransome referred to the 160 pound ballast Bill would need for his solo flight.

'What's wrong with Mr Kenting? I hope it's nothing serious?'

Mike Austin dismissed John's illness with contemptuous ease. 'Only the usual Flight, only the usual.'

Colonel Ransome enquired further. 'Exactly *what* is Mr Kenting's illness Lieutenant?' Don Larkin broke into the conversation, giving his observer a warning glance as he did so.

'Mr Kenting has bouts of gastric problems sir, it seems to be getting worse.'

Col Ransome contemplated the problem. 'We have a battalion of Seaforths this side of Langemark, and they need to contact some of their platoons still occupying what is left of Langemark's railway station. I want you to find those positions and drop these messages to them.' He then handed them a bundle of weighted message bags. 'Each one of these carries a message ordering them to retire westward and to find their own battalion if possible. Both of you will be escorted by two of 45's machines. They will divert any ground fire as required.'

The mission went well. There was little ground fire at first, but by the time they'd made contact and dropped all their messages it became intense. As he turned for home Bill noticed a small group waving to him from some wrecked railway trucks. Having dropped all his messages, Bill flew over them at about thirty feet, pointing his arm westward and rocking his wings. Then, just to make sure, he levelled-off at 100 feet and fired a green signal flare in the same direction. Looking back he couldn't see them any more but hoped they'd got his message correctly.

On landing Bill noticed one of the 1½ Strutters was badly shot up and the ambulance in attendance.

'The observer's badly wounded Bill, riddled with bullets they say.' Smokey Black looked concerned as he inspected 989 with Percy. 'You'll need a new prop Bill, its edges are like hacksaw blades! Where the hell you been?'

Bill laughed as he explained. 'Brick dust! I remember flying through it, trying to contact some lads on what remains of Langemarck station.'

Percy shook his head. 'At this rate we'll 'ave bugger all left.' Bill noted that Don Larkin's machine had been badly hit in the tail. It looked like both aircraft would need a day off. The spares had to be transported from Avesnes before repairs could be made, so it wasn't until the 28th that 'A' Flight's detachment was flying again. John had changed considerably during this period. Hardly speaking to anyone he'd reported sick and complained of head pains every day.

Pat Scully had flown up the day after 989 was grounded. There were some letters for the detachment and orders for Lt Larkin, a few spare instruments and most important of all, a telegram for Bill.

It was from his mother:

Dear Bill,
Thanks for your telegram. Hope you are well. Maggie cannot be moved and is as comfortable as doctors can make her. She sleeps a lot which is a mercy. Don't worry we know you cannot come home. Captain Taylor explained in a telegram. Please thank him. Letter on its way.
Bless you son, love from all.
Mum

Bill felt comforted knowing his parents understood why he couldn't get home. He would certainly have to thank Captain Taylor, the kindly adjutant had given him good advice.

When the new propeller and tail unit arrived there was a letter from Mattie. He read it over and over again. She had written it as soon as he left her, and its contents brought him back to another world. So much could happen in a few days, she didn't refer to John. Perhaps she hadn't received anything from him yet?

Lieutenant Larkin's orders made it clear that since the detachment had lost a machine and its crew, and since the squadron couldn't replace either at this time, he was to rotate all five machines for flying while keeping two in reserve.

'This morning's CP is a line running five miles east of Ypres down as far as Kemmel, that's about 12 miles all told. Our troops are retiring so we are to look for ground panels and lamp signals. Our height will be 800 feet down to 200 feet. I want you at the top Bill, then Harry at 400 and myself at the bottom.'

Lt Harry Moore was a cheerful Lancastrian. 'I object to a bloody Yorkshireman being at the top, but fully agree you should be at the bottom old lad.' Bill grinned, surprised at Don Larkin's familiarity. Sharing the general mirth he saw that John could only muster a weak smile, possibly not understanding the old Yorkshire *v* Lancashire joke.

Lt. Larkin continued, 'And John! Please look out for lamp signals.' As they walked out to 989 Bill enquired after his friend's health.

'Bloody awful these days Bill.' He took hold of his arm. If we get bounced by any Huns get out fast, I'm not fit for any air fighting these days,' Bill looked at him. He was sweating heavily under his flying clothes and didn't look at all well.

'What did the MO say John? Really you shouldn't be flying in my opinion. Maybe its the flu?'

John lifted his eyebrows. 'The MO never said anything about influenza, maybe that's what it is?'

Bill referred to rumours now prevailing. 'Heard talk in the mess last night. It's said that with this latest revolution in Russia thousands of refugees are coming west, and spreading what they call Asian flu as they come. Certainly a number of the chaps seem to have the symptoms.'

The three aircraft took off together and flew to their CP line at 500 feet before staggering their heights and distances from each other. The cloud base was about 2000 feet with scattered wisps of grey stuff down to about 1200 feet.

After ten minutes the archie started but never came close. Bill noticed bright signalling flashes, and turned to see if John was responding. He froze in his seat as he saw the approaching flight of five machines climbing to reach them. He hardly noticed the archie had stopped, and as he tried to make out the shapes of the closing aircraft John opened up with the Lewis. Bill knew it was panic, they were too far away, but the Lewis kept firing. Turning again he saw the four rearmost shapes descend to attack the two RE8s and the three 1½ Strutters supporting them.

He could recognise them now. Four Albatros were attacking his friends below, while their leader, a Fokker Dr1 triplane kept on coming. Obviously Bill's RE8 was his intended target! John's Lewis gun had stopped, and as he turned once again Bill saw him struggling in an attempt to replace the empty drum. The 'tripe' was closing in as John desperately hit the magazine with a gloved fist.

It was time to do something and Bill decided to seek the company of friends. He could see them about 200 feet below, circling as they tried to fight off the attacking scouts. Better the sanctuary of confusion than trying to fight the agile triplane.

Turning gently he allowed the heavy RE8 to drop, then straightening up, put the nose down and chopped the throttle. Fooled into the belief he was dealing with a tyro, the Fokker pilot lost an easy kill, and as he flicked into a following descent lost his quarry among the milling

361

aircraft below. Joining his friends Bill knew he'd only delayed the inevitable.

Already one of 45 Sqdn's machines was smoking earthwards, and the chimneys of an injured RE8 were belching oily black smoke. Bill fired his Vickers as a DIII crossed his sights, he wasn't even near! He noticed a bright orange explosion out of the corner of his eye as someone hit the ground, then his upper wing shredded as a concentrated burst took them from the flank. Pushing the throttle forward Bill tried to regain lost height. The flapping wing fabric being enough to remind that he had lost too much lift to keep flying much longer. As he turned for home he saw the all-red triplane climbing, its flock of gaily coloured Albatros following as they disengaged from the fight. Looking up he could see why. A flight of six SE5s had joined the fray! Flying into the prevailing wind Bill managed to retain a decent height but he was down to tree top level by the time he landed. He smiled at the thought, just as well there were no trees left standing in Flanders!'

'Holy shit Bill! If you bring 989 back like this again I'll charge you for overtime!'

Bill laughed as he jumped down. 'Go on Smokey, you know it keeps you in practice.'

He waited for John to step down as he inspected their damage.

'What the devil are you playing at? You could see my gun had jammed yet you insist in trying to use a Harry Tate like a blasted scout!' John hadn't even waited until they were distant from their fitters, and his face was red with anger as he berated Bill for his tactics. Bill walked off to 45's crew tent.

'It got us away from that tripe John, do you know who that was?'

'I don't care who the hell it was! It was a stupid thing to do and if it wasn't for those SE5s we would never have come out of it.'

Bill stopped him there. 'Maybe so but do you realise what would have happened if we hadn't dropped into the throng? That was Richthoven in that flying venetian blind and you with no gun because you wasted a whole drum before he was in range!' They argued on, only finishing as they reached the crew tent.

Bill stripped out of his heavy flying clothes and waited for the rest to land. There could be no doubt now. John was certainly in a poor way. Never had he ever attacked him like that before. Even now he was sulking with a cup of cocoa in his hand, not even anxious about the rest of the flight. As they returned Bill counted only three machines. One RE8 and two 1½ Strutters. He dashed up to the line. It was Don Larkin and Mike Austin.

'Was that Mr Moore in trouble sir?'

Lt Austin nodded. 'That's right Flight, did you see him land?' Bill said he hadn't.

'Thanks for joining us Bill.' Don Larkin stepped down and came over with his hand outstretched. 'That was quite something, coming down to help us out like that!' Shaking his hand Bill had to disabuse him of any thoughts of bravery.

'When Mr Richthoven's on your tail you'll fly to the devil himself sir!' He explained his engagement with the Red Baron and the jammed gun.

'I never saw a triplane – did you Mike?'

'I saw it well enough! And it was him all right!' The newcomer had just landed. 'Grant Thomson, 45 Sqdn. Saw the bastard follow you down son.' Lieutenant Thomson smiled at Bill then gave him a playful punch in the chest. 'But next time you play with the red bastard please do the honourable thing and let him shoot you down rather than bring him to play with us.' They laughed a lot before they were joined by the remaining 1½ Strutter crew. Addressing himself to Don Larkin he reported on the fate of the shot-down Harry Tate. 'They're alive, I saw them land and saw them both wave, sorry to say they are now guests of the Kaiser. Our lads were not so lucky, exploded on impact.' Bill recalled the bright orange flash – now he knew!

When they all arrived at the map room, John was talking to Colonel Ransome. 'So we lost another crew and another machine Larkin. This is getting too expensive!' Don Larkin gave him the good news.

'Moore and Case were taken prisoner sir, it's all in one of the 45 crew's reports. But yes, we lost an RE8 and Flight Sgt Proctor's machine is badly off. Their rigger tells me it will take two days to repair, and the engine needs looking at so I'm told.'

Ransome took his time before speaking. 'It appears you chaps have done more than enough, I'm sending you back tomorrow. Our 2nd Army are still falling back and we have a war of movement for the first time in three years. We cannot use CPs at present as 15 Wing are mainly engaged in assisting our troops with offensive CAPs. So you go home, with our thanks for a job well done and some commendations to come. Thank you gentlemen.'

Due to weather and problems with 989's engine, Bill did not fly for a week. It was now the 6th of December and since his return to 12 Sqdn he'd hardly seen John. He'd received a long letter from Eileen. She mentioned she'd had a letter from John, posted from Norwich just before they left, and another one saying how sorry he was to hear of

Maggie's accident. Evidently the doctors gave little hope that Maggie would ever walk again, for apart from her mangled legs she had also been crushed across the pelvis. There were broken ribs and internal bleeding too. Heavily sedated against the pain, she rarely spoke, and now they say her very life was in danger. Her final words told him the worst. 'I pray our poor little Maggie might die rather than suffer so. I know that sounds terrible Bill but I cannot bear to see her pain!

There was a note from his mother too. She was bravely facing up to things, as she always did. But he could see her grief across the tear-stained page. It would appear she had been playing with a group of five other kids after school. Their playing must have loosened the chains binding the logs, and as Maggie was leaving the pile they broke loose - pinning her under two rolling logs.

Mattie had received his news concerning Maggie, and knowing his love for her, gave him much comfort in her letter. She had written to his mother and asked if there was anything she could do to help and had said she would gladly go to Dacre if there was need.

'Bill, I fear your family may be too proud to accept my help, you must tell them I want to help – anything, money or a nurse, anything.' Dearest Mattie, just like her!

They were detailed for an artillery shoot on the morning of the 7th and as John joined him he seemed in better spirits.

'Not seen you for a while John how are you?' They discussed their news, mainly letters from home.

'How is Maggie, Bill?' He told him of Eileen's letter and her fear for Maggie's life. 'She tells me she received a letter or two from you John and has written to you here, did you receive it yet? John said he hadn't yet, but would be writing to her again soon anyway.

Escorted by DH2s they completed the shoot against moderate archie, but saw no enemy machines until they were returning from their target. As Bill dived for home their escort followed. It was an ominous sign. The DH2s would protect them, but were not keen to oppose a superior enemy. When this sector became active again he knew they would need SE5s or Camels if they were to survive.

The weather clamped down again, and all flying was suspended as rain and sleet fell over the entire front. While the ack-emmas slaved over their machines Bill took the opportunity to visit Simone. Soaked through, despite his protective ground sheet, he parked the motorcycle in a barn and entered the house, removing his wet outer clothes as he did so. Calling for Simone he looked into the kitchen and there she was – a finger to her lips as she nursed her baby.

Chuckling at Bill's surprise she smiled as he came to kiss her.

'Oh, Bill it has been so long and I was so worried for you!' He told her he had been away, and this was his first opportunity to come. 'See Bill, your godchild is a boy! Is like Tom no?' Bill couldn't see any likeness at all, just a round pink-faced bundle who took no notice of him at all.

'Just like Tom Simone, just like him. I suppose I shouldn't be surprised but I didn't know he'd arrived! Where is Jean Louis?' Simone told him her father was at the local market.

'He comes back later. I told him dinner at six o'clock.'

Simone brought him some of Tom's civilian clothes so she could dry his uniform. 'Now you nurse young Tommy while I make coffee.' Bill told her about his leave and Mattie, then told her about Maggie. Simone could see his distress, he'd spoken of his little sister so often.

'It is so tragic Bill, I only hope she gets better.' She changed the subject by reading him Gertie's last letter.

When Jean Louis arrived he was overjoyed to see him and immediately opened a bottle of wine. Simone had dinner already prepared and it was almost like old times. She was much happier now, the baby had made all the difference. They discussed the christening and told Bill it would be arranged for a Sunday in January, naturally he would have to be there.

Before he left he promised to return as soon as he could, and thanked Jean Louis for the brandy and wine he gave him.

'Return soon Bill. Simone enjoys your visits as much as I do. You are our only company these days, but it's a blessing she has the boy!'

On the tenth Bill was tabled for two shoots. One at 1000 and one at 1300 hours. A watery sun shone through a layer of high cirrus and Bill knew they could expect enemy scouts soon after they arrived above the target. They were ranging guns onto a Boche gun emplacement between Loos and Lens, but in the five minutes since their arrival there had been no archie! John had no sooner tapped out the code for their battery's first shoot when Bill spotted them in the south east. About 2000 feet higher they were too far off to identify, but there were six of them and their own escorting DH2s were at the same level. Bill banged on John's cockpit and pointed his arm at the approaching scouts.

Immediately sending a hasty CI to indicate they were returning to base, John rapidly wound in their trailing aerial. Wasting no time Bill made a gentle turn to the west and as soon as he was on course made a rapid descent through 2000 feet. It was two to one, and the DH2s had no chance. John could see one of their escorts falling in flames from the first pass of the Pfaltz, the remaining two making a gallant attempt to fight a descending battle. By the time Bill was down to almost ground level, John saw one DH2 falling out of control and the other fleeing westward with two Huns on his tail. Within minutes three Pfaltz DIII were down to their level, trying hard to make slashing attacks from beam and astern as Bill passed over the British trenches. Climbing from an abortive attack one of the Pfaltz took a prolonged burst from John's gun while the remaining two received ground fire. Then, content with their two victories the Huns left them alone.

Brian Webster received their report and immediately threw on his flying clothes. 'It's ten-to-one those Huns will be returning home, and the target will probably be unprotected for the next 45 minutes or so.' He shouted for Lt Tyson, his observer, as he made contact with the C/O of 5 Sqdn. 'Yes, I know! But I have an order from Wing here, Sir. This target must be ranged and destroyed by the 98th battery today. My crew told me, yes sir, I'm very sorry. But if we hit it now we can be pretty sure it will be free of those scouts and unprotected apart from the usual archie … thank you sir … I'll be over the target in about 15 minutes.' As he left for the lines Captain Webster told them to prepare for their next shoot at 1300 hours.

John Kenting gave Bill his maps and codes. 'Tell Corporal Miller to fly with you Bill, I'll have to report sick.' Without further explanation he left for the latrines.

Bill had never flown with Arthur Miller before. Originally a 'C' Flight instrument technician, Cpl Miller had qualified with 'B' Flight some months ago and was reputed to be an intelligent observer. Bill took him over the maps and explained his own methods of flying shoots.

'I'm sure there won't be any problems Flight Sergeant, as it happens I was flying that area only a week ago.

'It's Bill from here on Arthur. I'm sure we'll make a good team. How's your gunnery by the way?'

'Fucking hopeless Bill, but I can send at 15 words a minute and I'm good with maps!'

Bill was pleased. Their target, a fortified crossroads at Wytschaete, was well camouflaged and very difficult to find, but the 87th RFA demolished the guns and supply sites within minutes. There was no doubt in his mind that Arthur Miller was good at his job! There had been no archie until the shells came over, obviously the Jerries didn't want to advertise the concealed installations. Now he was on his way home, the escorting DH2s keeping watch above.

'It looks as though Cpl Miller will have to substitute for Mr Kenting

Bill! The MO has put him on gruel and water from what I hear.' Brian Webster had safely returned and was very pleased with the two shoots they had completed.

'Is he in a bad way sir? He took off to the latrines just after you left and said he would have to report sick.' A snigger from Mr Austin was swiftly quelled with a single look from the Flight Commander.

'According to the doc it could be a gastric ulcer. So he's being kept under observation for a week or more. But tell me Flight! What do you think to Cpl Miller?' Bill said he was an excellent observer.

'As you know sir, I've spent some time as an observer, and map reading and identification of targets wasn't my strongest point. But Arthur Miller – he's very good; he spotted the concealed positions at Wytschaete almost at once and directed the battery right on target. I'm very happy to have him sir.'

During the next 12 days Bill managed to see John twice during his regular visits to the medical centre. He needed to pass his letters to John and always asked if he could see him, but mostly he was only allowed to leave them with an orderly. On his last visit he managed to spend a good half hour with his friend.

John had received more letters from Eileen, and some from home, including notes from Mattie. 'It doesn't sound too good about Maggie Bill, and Mattie tells me she had a letter from your mother.'

Bill told him about Mattie's offer of help. 'Hopefully Maggie might pull through John, but it's doubtful. I'm beginning to think like our Eileen now – if she doesn't get better soon maybe its better she goes. I can't bear to think of her suffering.'

John agreed. 'All the same, it makes me feel a bit of a fraud stuck here with gastric problems.'

Bill handed him some letters for home and for Mattie. 'Would you look after these for me John, at least I know my letters get off quicker than anyone elses while you're stuck here. When do you expect to get back to flying?'

'According to the Doc I'm just a liability at present; it's these stomach cramps I keep getting. He's even suggesting I should be grounded – permanently!'

Christmas came and went with little activity on either side. There was the usual serving of dinner in the Airmen's Mess, and Bill made a special presentation to Smokey and Percy, handing them a bottle of Jean Louis' wine and a bottle of brandy. After the dinner he went to the farm to celebrate Christmas with the three of them. He'd tried to see John, but the corporal in charge of the ward said Lt Kenting was now an 'out-patient' and celebrating Christmas with Lieutenant Smith-Cooper. When Bill asked who the latter was, the corporal looked surprised.

'You must remember him, he's the doctor who saw you when you first came here.' He gave Bill a sly smirk. 'I can see you don't remember me either! Everything all right now is it?'

He flew only twice between Christmas Day and the 4th of January. But they were only air tests of two new machines, and even these were restricted to 500 feet within the circuit. The weather was foul with low ceilings and strong winds, but it suited Bill fine. Knowing the weather could lift at any time he persuaded Simone to bring the christening of her son to an earlier date, and on Sunday the 4th he attended their church at Freyent. There were only two others besides themselves, old friends of Simone's mother, and with the weather so bad they declined to return with them for an evening meal. Bill had brought his godson a pure silver spoon and a soft toy rabbit. Simone was surprised and kissed him for his kindness. Thomas William Bolton, aged six weeks, simply made a rude noise.

On the morning of the 5th of January, Bill took Cpl Miller on another shoot, but the weather made them turn back before they even reached the front line. On his return he found a telegram waiting for him. Fearing the worst he broke it open.

Dear Bill,
Sadly our poor Maggie passed away last night. The funeral is on the 7th. Dad has bought a wreath for you. She'll be at peace now the poor mite. Letter following.
Love from us all,
Mum

As there was no flying for the rest of the day he left the lines and spent two hours in the Mess. He tried to write, but after tearing up everything he'd written he went for a walk in the rain. He needed to talk to someone, someone close. Eventually he ended up at the Officers' Mess and asked for John, but he wasn't there.

It was three pip-emma when he returned to the Mess and to his quarters. Alone and despondent he drank the brandy Jean Louis had given him. By five pip-emma he'd finished the bottle. Tired and sad beyond measure he cried himself to sleep.

Missing breakfast except for three cups of black coffee, Bill shaved and walked down to the lines. The sky was only a few hundred feet above the field and he was thankful, for he was at least one and a half hours late!

As he walked into the crew tent he could see a party in progress. An arm was flung about his shoulder and a beer mug thrust in his hand. 'No flying today Bill so you can relax!'

Bill looked up to see Lt Don Larkin at his side. 'What's all this sir?' As he looked about he could see the C/O, Brian Webster and just about all of 'A' Flight's crews, including John. 'It's a good day for 'A' Flight Bill – you included!'

'Ah there you are Flight Sergeant! Congratulations!' Roger Kemp transferred his beer as he shook Bill's hand. 'Congratulations on your MID, well done.' Surprised, and yet not too surprised, Bill thanked the C/O who quite obviously had put him forward for the 'Mentioned In Dispatches'. Motioning for the Adjutant, Major Kemp stepped aside as Captain Taylor handed him the small metal Oak Leaf. 'It can be worn now of course, but eventually it should be pinned to your campaign medal, when we get them!' Aware that the celebrations were not just for himself Bill smiled as he looked about.

'Seems I'm not the only one to celebrate sir.'

Ray Taylor took him to the edge of the tent. 'You're the only one that's not been honoured properly I can tell you that!' There are three new recipients of the MC here this morning and you've done as much and more and only get an MID – I'm quite disgusted!'

Bill looked closely at the Adjutant. He was drinking with his right hand while he used the stump of his left to nudge him in the side. He was also very drunk! 'Lieutenants Larkin and Austin did good work of course, and so did you with Mr. Kenting. The four of you took on similar missions with similar risks and received similar commendations! I know because I sent all your records to 3rd Wing myself. But you get an MID and they get MCs! You were recommended for a Military Medal Proctor and this is not right!' Bill looked closely at the Adjutant's MC ribbon.

'None of them here lost an arm either sir. But I've often heard it said that only the wearer of the medal knows its true worth. You know what the Army's like Sir, it possibly got lost in the post!'

Captain Taylor smiled at him. 'You're a good chap Proctor. Wait here, I'll get us something stronger.' Though not cynical by nature, Bill couldn't help feeling that awards and recognition only went to the favoured. He'd seen more MCs than MMs about, and remembered Tom's words on the subject. 'Officers need 'em Bill, a pretty ribbon or two makes them look right for one thing. It also imparts a necessary distinction between us and them. Officers are expected to be bloody heroes, so on a percentage basis we must get less recognition. But since they can't ignore the bravery of 'other ranks' we only get medals for being exceptional. Or in my case when somebody else was exceptional for him. It all belongs to the same kind of thinking that gets them a Cross while we get a Medal – if we're lucky!'

Raymond Taylor returned with two large whiskies on a small tray. 'Did you know Mr. Webster has been posted home?' Bill was surprised. 'This little affair is really for him, he goes back tomorrow, and Mr Larkin takes over as Flight Commander. No doubt his Captaincy will be … promulgated in due time. But to more important matters lad. How is your little sister?' Bill told him.

'God it's always the innocent, even in civilian life. Perhaps it was for the best; I know she was very badly injured poor child. Did you know I received a very generous letter from your mother?' Bill said he knew. 'There was nothing we could do son, I know Major Kemp sounded a bit off when you burst in, but he saw me later and was quite concerned about you.' Bill really didn't want the drink, but downed it just the same.

'Shall I get you another sir?' Captain Taylor said no. 'I can usually get away with it, my walk being decidedly lop-sided when I'm sober, but I still need to work today so I'd better be off. Come and see me soon lad, I think we can get you some leave in March – if Jerry lets us alone that is.'

Bill couldn't understand why John was not joining him. Perhaps he didn't want to disturb his conversation with the Adjutant? But he was still chatting with fellow officers when the C/O left with Captain Taylor. More curious than concerned he walked over to the group.

'Congratulations gentlemen, the Adj just told me of your awards!' There were similar congratulations to himself, but he could see the embarrassment on their faces.

John put it into words. 'It's all wrong Bill. You should have received the same, the MM that is.' A refill for his whisky came immediately.

'Oh I think I'd rather settle for two weeks leave to be honest – anyway your good health gentlemen!'

The following day was much brighter and while a number of photo-reconnaissance sorties were flown by 'A' and 'B' Flights, Bill and Arthur Miller were detailed for a CP along a quiet sector of the front. They saw little activity either on the ground or in the air and as no ground markers were visible they returned to make their usual report to the Flight Recording Officer. Usually a junior officer detached from 3rd

Army, Bill was surprised when he saw John Kenting sitting at the RO's desk.

'Now that surprised you didn't it!' John grinned as they walked into the tent. 'The MO says I'm fit for light duties, so I'm here for the next month, learning the trade so to speak.' They made their report and as soon as Arthur left, the two could speak more openly.

'I was so sorry to learn of Maggie's death Bill – is there anything I can do?' Bill thanked him, but said he thought it was better that she had died. John could see he didn't want to talk about her and gently changed the subject. 'I doubt if I shall ever be flying again Bill. Paul thinks I'm a total liability in the air these days, and I think he's probably right!'

Bill shook his head. 'Paul?'

John apologised. 'Oh yes, sorry old lad, that's Lieutenant Paul Smith-Cooper, the doctor! He's a very decent chap. Keen chess player too, we always have a game on the go.'

Bill felt a pang of cold fear. Was it really true that medical records were strictly confidential? He recalled Smith-Cooper now, pleasant and professional. He had met him during his early days on 12 Sqdn, before John had joined them.

'Have you heard much from Mattie?'

Bill told him she was now writing almost every day. 'She means everything to me John. You know I'm even getting a bit scared! Not about flying you understand, but since Maggie's death? Well, it just doesn't make sense John. Here am I alive, but innocent little Maggie has to die! It's not just that either. I have Mattie and she's with me all the time John! Her letters give me such strength and a belief in our future.' Bill gave a wry smile. 'I only hope my old girl friend never leaves me!' Seeing his friend's expression Bill explained. 'Lady Luck John, Lady Luck! She mustn't desert me now!'

Chapter Nineteen

Monday 7th January, 1918

With Don Larkin now Flight Commander, Bill noticed a more relaxed atmosphere on 'A' Flight, but he was deeply concerned at the
comments directed against John and his 'illness'. Although only a few
'A' Flight officers were involved, he noticed Mike Austin was chief among
them, and Don Larkin did nothing to stop rumours of cowardice. Not
that it was openly referred to in such brutal terms, on the contrary, it
was only discussed in humour, but he noticed that John never entered
the crew room these days unless it was necessary. Nevertheless, it was
convenient that as 'A' Flight's Recording Officer, John had his own tent,
and Bill could visit him at will.

There was little flying at this time, mainly due to the very low ceiling
of stratus that prevailed over their sector, but priority sorties were building up and Bill had been selected for a high altitude photo reconnaissance job as soon as the skies cleared. Evidently it was important,
because a Major from 3rd Army Intelligence came down to discuss
details.

'It's been five weeks since we've had any reliable information concerning German concentrations along our front, and under cover of
this damned cloud they'll certainly have been making preparations. We
can expect some new thrust from Jerry as soon as the ground hardens,
using new weapons such as tanks and flame throwers for example. But
we must have photographs if we are to anticipate a spring offensive
correctly.'

Major Kemp was looking at the most recent weather predictions
while Don Larkin studied the sector map-sheets with Bill and Cpl Miller.

'From what I can see it might be possible in a day or two. There's a
clear patch of weather coming in over the west coast and if we time it
right I think we might make it on either the 9th or the 10th! What is
your calculated altitude Mr Larkin?'

Don Larkin took a second look at the figures. 'Since we don't
really know what the weather may be like, there could be all kinds of
cloud at different levels. We've allowed for a number of options. Ide-

ally 12,000 feet would give us all the cover we need in the shortest possible flight time, but if we have to go lower then it's going to take longer and the threat of interception is higher.'

Roger Kemp thought a moment. 'It makes sense to calculate for every 1000 feet down to 5000. If we have cloud at that ceiling then we shall have to consider a different approach. But from what I have here, the weather chaps tell us we can expect perfectly clear skies, the only question is when and for how long. So I shall leave it to you; in the meantime Flight Sgt Proctor's crew are to stay on top of this until the mission is completed – no other duties Mr Larkin, this is top priority!'

With all their options pre-calculated and a stack of plates packed for every contingency Bill and Arthur Miller waited for the promised weather. Consistent with clear skies comes the cold.

'It's going to be chilly up there Arthur! I think we should see about better clothing don't you?' Bill was aware that almost all of his flying had been done below 8,000 feet, and that he could expect it to be much colder at 12,000, but that wasn't his only problem. The Harry Tate's performance at 12,000 feet was something outside his own experience, and the fact made him cautious. According to specifications it would take about half an hour to climb to that height, and as this was close to its ceiling he knew performance would be impaired.

Taking every precaution against cold and frostbite, Don Larkin issued them with Sidcot flying suits. Designed for high altitude work, the tightly woven Sidcots would keep them sufficiently warm against temperatures close to minus ten Centigrade. At high altitudes open cockpits were never comfortable and in winter, crews would return literally frozen stiff. To remove, or worse, lose a glove would usually result in frostbite, often leading to the loss of fingers. Consequently, Bill and Arthur were issued with Muskrat lined gauntlets with silk inners. Although a necessary protection against frostbite, they also made camera operation easier.

As it turned out the clear weather missed their patrol sector completely, and it wasn't until the 15th that a second opportunity arose. Arthur Miller checked his camera and plates with care and studied the maps for a final time before preparing for flight. Like Bill, he dressed in silk pyjamas, then woollen long johns before putting on two pullovers inside his uniform. Finally, and only ten minutes before takeoff, they applied whale oil to faces and necks before putting on the Sidcots and heavy wool-lined fug boots.

Lieutenant Larkin saw them off. 'You'll have six SE5as as cover Bill, join up with them here, above Albert, before you cross the lines at

12,000 feet. The weather will stay like this for a couple of hours I imagine, so get your pictures and get back soonest. Approach from the south-west and fly straight onto the Bapaume–Cambrai road, I think Cpl Miller knows he only needs four photographs but he's been told if there is any doubt about the exposures he's to do it again! These photos are important Flight, which is why 29 Sqdn's SEs will be backed up with six Camels from 3 Sqdn. You won't see them, I hope, because they will be at 16,000. Good luck!'

The climb to 12,000 took them all of 32 minutes, by which time they could feel the cold biting into every part of the body. As they passed 10,000 Bill could feel how sloppy the controls were becoming, and although the RE8 still responded to his touch, he couldn't feel the rudder bar beneath his boots.

As he circled slowly around the ruins of Albert, Bill saw their escort 1000 feet above them, still climbing as they fell in behind. Passing over the front he approached their photo-line in good time, and responding to Arthur's blows on an appropriate shoulder, put the Harry Tate on a straight and level path along the Bapaume to Cambrai road. Looking up and ahead he caught a brief glimpse of numerous streamlined forms diving onto him, then they were gone, hidden from view by the RE8's upper wing. Turning his body left and right he could see the SEs flying in different directions and knew the fight had begun.

Two swift blows on his right shoulder told him to turn 180 degrees. As he made a slow coordinated turn Bill could see the air battle now fully engaged. It looked like Albatros Vs and Fokker triplanes against the clearly outnumbered SE5s. Then he lost them as he straightened out and flew back towards Bapaume, keeping his eye on the road below.

Within less than a minute they were being attacked, and responding to his observer's directions to descend, Bill put the RE8 into a steep dive for their own lines. He could hear Arthur's Lewis and hoped his gunnery was better than he'd previously claimed. An Albatros passed below, and was immediately followed by an SE5a – it was good to have friends he thought!

Arthur's gun started up again, three two-second bursts then a long one before it stopped abruptly. They were now at 5000 feet and turning in his seat Bill watched as Cpl Miller put two hands together, then pointed to his four o'clock. A yellow and blue triplane was climbing slowly, aflame and streaming smoke, Bill saw it flick over before it fell from view. He grinned at Arthur's frozen blue cheeks, now mixed with grey powder streaks across an oiled face. His gunnery can't be that bad he thought.

374

'Bugger me! Thar's dun it agin, tha just don't care do thee? Look at them thar holes!' Percy's greeting brought him a playful cuff from Bill's gauntlet as he carefully put his frozen feet on the ground.

'Always complaining, you dizzy Yorkshire git! We brought it back didn't we? And you'll be pleased to know that our Arthur shot down a bloody Hun!' The ack-emmas were ecstatic, and while they hoisted 989's crew on their shoulders, Percy counted the bullet holes in their machine.

They were busy making out their report to John when Don Larkin burst into the RO's tent. 'Well done you two! The plates look splendid and are now being printed. As soon as you've finished here, please come with Mr Kenting to the C/O's office.'

Twenty minutes later they knocked on Major Kemp's door. 'I first of all want to congratulate you both on downing that Hun, a splendid bit of shooting Corporal. The victory was confirmed by both of your escorting squadrons. The photography is excellent and within the hour the prints will be on their way to 3rd Army Intelligence. I have already been in contact with Wing HQ and have recommended that Cpl Miller should receive immediate promotion to Sergeant.' Looking up at the astonished Corporal, Roger Kemp smiled. 'I have no doubt it will be confirmed within a day or two!'

Bill turned to his observer and shook his hand. 'And you said you couldn't shoot? Must have been pure luck!'

The next eight days were spent on shoots until the 23rd of January, when 3rd Army's forward troops found they were increasingly infiltrated with enemy patrols and raiding parties. Under these obvious signs of an approaching offensive, 12 Squadron was put on full alert and all crews were doing at least two recce sorties a day.

'Have you done oblique photography before Arthur?'

Sgt Miller tapped the air camera with a gloved hand. 'Not from 1000 feet I haven't and I hope this will be the only time. I like to think I might actually see the photographs I take, but the Boche archie is pretty bad around Vimy these days.'

Bill didn't like it either. 'It's not so much the 1000 feet that worries me but the reason for it – flying just below cloud base makes it simple for archie to find our range. So I'm going to fly in cloud at 1500 feet, then pop out when we should be just past the target. Hopefully you'll be able to locate our position, then we fly west to the target, take your photos, and beat it back home.'

Bill hated flying in cloud, and although he could rely on his compass, without visual references it was difficult to know which side was up after a few minutes! Tying a coloured streamer onto each wing strut helped, but he still hated the disorientation.

The plan went well, and Arthur soon had their position when Bill turned under the cloud base. Flying towards Vimy it took four minutes before they were spotted, and another two before they were ranged by archie east of the town. Rocked and blown by gunfire, the turbulence made photography difficult but as soon as it was completed Arthur gave the thumbs up – to seek cover in the clouds once more.

Feeling relatively safe, Bill climbed into the cloud. But the archie still followed him, now illuminating the cloud's interior with orange light and shell fragments. Climbing higher he changed course then dropped to cross their lines at 800 feet. Setting course for Avesnes Bill checked the RE8 as far as he could, all seemed well and Arthur seemed to be busy in his cockpit.

With a deep sigh of relief Bill switched off and climbed out of the aircraft to see Smokey dragging steps up to Arthur's cockpit. Turning to look down he shook his head.

'Sorry Bill, Sgt Miller is dead!' Gently they handed him down while Percy went for the ambulance.

Don Larkin joined Bill in the RO's tent as he made out his report to John, 'I never even knew he was dead, poor old Arthur! A bloody fine observer, not only did he get our position when we came out of the murk, but I'm sure you'll find those obliques are bang on target! It must have been one of those damned shells in the cloud that got him.'

Don Larkin left them to check on the photographs Bill had brought back. 'You're on rest for three days Flight, it will take at least that to get you a fresh observer!'

John came over to put a hand on his shoulder. 'I'm sorry Bill, it must have been a tricky job from what I have in your report.'

Bill nodded. 'It doesn't get any better John.' Then changing the subject he asked if he'd heard from Eileen recently. Looking embarrassed John said he had, but was behind in his letters to everyone.

Collecting his mail Bill was overjoyed to see there were two letters from Dacre and one from Mattie. At least he would now have a couple of days in which to answer them. Opening Mattie's first, he read that she'd heard from John, who had told the family he was now grounded. 'Perhaps it's just as well, since it was obvious from his letters that he could no longer face flying. But I worry about you Bill! Please my love, take the greatest of care and come back to me soon.'

He then opened Eileen's letter and left Jane's until last. Eileen gave him the full story of Maggie's funeral and the following wake. 'So many people came to the service Bill, just about the entire school too. As you know, everyone loved her.' It seemed that Mum and Dad were coping well enough, but her mother worried her a lot. 'Please get home as soon as you can Bill, she worries about you more than ever nowadays.' She also mentioned John, or rather his lack of writing after the letter concerning Maggie's death. 'Perhaps he's too busy, because he hasn't answered my last four letters! Yet we've heard from you two or three times. Please tell me if he's alright?' Bill was concerned, should he tell Eileen that he was sick, or perhaps leave matters for a little longer? He decided to tell her that John was just sick and would no doubt be writing later.

Jane's letter was very sympathetic. More than most, she knew exactly how close Bill and Maggie were and how much her death would hurt him. She said plainly that she still loved him and would always be there for him, even knowing that he was deeply in love with Mattie. It was a wonderful letter but it made him very sad.

Lieutenant Paul Smith-Cooper wasn't looking forward to their chess game that evening. John had appeared at the usual time, the chess table was as they left it the previous night, and the whisky bottle to hand. He liked John, unlike most of the officers he could speak to him whereas most of the others tended to look down on non-combatants, even medics like himself. But it had to be faced, John would have to go back to flying. He knew John's condition was nothing more than nerves. True, there were gastric problems and headaches, and he also knew many flyers who suffered from the same condition – but didn't care to admit they were just scared! The order was clear and came from 'A' Flight's Commander, now a Captain, and endorsed with Major Kemp's signature.

'Owing to squadron commitments and operational requirements, it is essential that all aircrew must be made available for flying duties unless there are severe medical problems that must keep them grounded.'

They'd drunk over half the bottle when Paul showed him the order. John looked at his friend.

'Surely I'm not fit Paul? You've said so many times in the past, and my health hasn't changed as you know.'

The MO shook his head. 'It makes no difference John, they are quite adamant. I even checked with the Chief Medical Officer at Wing, and I particularly mentioned your case. He could only say that this was war and everyone had to grin and bear it! I'm sorry John, my hands are tied.'

'When will I have to go back to flying Paul, did they say?'

Paul told him it was with immediate effect. 'From my conversation with the C/O he tells me you are needed urgently. But at least you will be with your old pilot, Flight Sergeant Proctor. And I know you and he are good friends.' John agreed; there wasn't a better pilot on the squadron, but he still looked very concerned. 'Well he must be one of the most experienced John, as I remember he came from 4 Sqdn and was here some time before you arrived!' Paul gave them both another tumbler of whisky.

'He's quite a lad your pilot John! Did you know he came to us with a dose of clap?' John Kenting was too full of self-pity to hear correctly.

'Sorry Paul, what was that?'

'Proctor! Your young pilot, I was just saying he likes the girls!'

John didn't understand. 'How do you know that? I can't say I've noticed it and I think I know him pretty well.'

Smith-Cooper was half-drunk and arrogant. 'If there's one thing we medics know it's our own men. When Proctor came to us, his first visit was here – I treated him for a dose of clap!'

John wouldn't believe him, which prompted the MO to take out Bill's medical records from the filing cabinet.

'There you are see? Gonorrhoea!'

Horrified, John looked at the document more closely. 'But he doesn't have it now is that right?'

Paul took the document back and locked it away. 'Now for God's sake don't mention I told you this John, I'm not supposed to divulge private records, even though I'm often asked to! But yes, it cleared up some time ago as you could see – don't worry it's not infectious! As I say, your lad likes the ladies, and in my experience I find that once a chap's had a dose of clap he usually goes back for more; now with syphilis…'

John made a hasty departure from the medical centre. 'Good God. Poor Mattie!' He would confront Bill Proctor right now. But then he remembered, he wasn't supposed to know! Wracked with misery he returned to his quarters. He knew he would have to tell her before it was to late and he'd been responsible for bringing the dirty blighter into his own home! Never again would he ever be deceived by these common bastards, they were all the same!

Captain Larkin welcomed John back to flying with a sly wink to Mike Austin. 'I hope you're up to it John? You'll be flying with Flight Sgt Proctor of course. As you know, we lost Sgt Miller a couple of days ago.' John waited until he was alone with Don Larkin before mentioning his request.

'If it's all the same to you sir, I would like to fly with someone else – just a change you know!'

Don looked at him with interest. 'But Bill Proctor is *your* driver John. He's not only one of our best pilots, but I thought he was a bit of a pal of yours?'

John realised he was on difficult ground. 'It was just a passing thought really, in case you thought I wasn't flexible.' At that moment Bill came into the crew room.

'Here you are Flight – you've got your old observer back!'

Bill came over with a bundle of maps in his hand. 'Good morning sir, glad to see you are flying again.' John mumbled something and walked away. Puzzled, Bill went to the duty board to see what the morning had in store for them. Then, quietly came up to his old friend. 'An easy one this morning John, a shoot just over our lines north of Albert. Take-off in about 40 minutes, I've got the maps, codes and frequencies already for you.'

Knowing that John would be displeased with the order to resume flying, Bill took little notice of his friend's surly attitude. But although he never responded to conversation he did discuss the mission in neutral tones. After the sortie they reported to the new RO sent down that morning then returned to the crew room.

'Anything wrong John? I mean you've hardly said a word all morning; is it anything I've done, or not done?'

John looked at him, at the point of speaking his mind. 'No, its just me. I'll be fine in good time.'

Bill produced the letters he'd been busy writing. 'Would you pass these on for me John – two for Dacre and one for Mattie?' John said he would, as soon as he had the time.

On returning to the crew room Bill was summoned to Captain Larkin's office.

'As you know, 'B' lost Flight Sgt Scully and his observer two days ago, so they pinched an experienced pilot from 'C' Flight. Your machine, C.989, is due to go to St. Omer for a major overhaul in two day's time, and since we have no reserve machines at present, I'm sending you to 'C' as an observer driver until we get C. 989 back.'

Bill was quite pleased. 'That's fine by me sir. What happens to Mr Kenting?'

Don Larkin chewed on a pencil. 'W/O Benton was taking a rest from operations Bill, which is why he was sent to 'C'. But he actually belongs to 'B' Flight. Similarly, the C/O thinks I should take this opportunity to send you on a semi-rest period. Naturally W/O Benton

379

will need an observer, so Mr Kenting goes to 'B' Flight, and you are to report to Captain Wickens tomorrow.'

John was pleased with his transfer to 'B' Flight and the relief from having to fly with Bill. With luck he might receive a slight wound, anything that would get him out of flying would do. Meanwhile he had to write to Mattie. Taking Bill's three letters from his pocket he decided he would read them. The letter to Eileen was of little interest, apart from Bill's comments concerning himself. He decided that he would ignore Eileen from now on and sealed the letter ready for posting. The letter to Jane Graham was more than interesting. Here was further proof of Bill's duplicity and womanising. Oh yes! Bill had told him all about Jane and their childhood friendship, but he could no longer believe it was limited to that, not now!

Finally he read the letter to Mattie. Lies, just lies! He tore the letter to Mattie into shreds, then placed his censor stamp on the two letters for Dacre. Picking up his pen he wrote to his sister.

Dear Mattie,

I trust you are well my dear? Unfortunately I have some very distasteful news concerning Bill. By distasteful I must admit to finding this letter very difficult. But no point in beating about the bush, so here goes.

Bill Proctor is an utter scoundrel! I have recently seen his medical records and have been told by the medical officer who treated him, that Bill Proctor came to 12 Squadron with a nasty venereal disease, to be blunt, gonorrhoea! To think I brought him into my family, and even supported his 'affection' for you! It makes my flesh creep to think of him kissing you, the filthy swine. I'm sorry my dear I feel so very responsible. Obviously he had been with some French whore or other. But you must end it right now Mattie! I suggest you tell him it's all off! Tell him why as well. Unfortunately I am unable to see him about this matter as it would compromise the MO, who is my friend. I also know he has a girl-friend in Dacre, he writes to her. He told me she was just a friend but I have reason to think he's lying.

Thank God we found out in time. I am so very sorry my dear. Please write to him as soon as possible and have done with the man.

Affectionately yours,
John

Bill reported to Captain Bert Wickens on the 28th January. His new Flight Commander seemed to be very friendly, but as he was relatively knew to the squadron he didn't know him.

'I'm told you've worked with this Flight before Flight Sergeant?' Bill told him of his experiences with Tom Bolton and the wireless training he'd done. 'That's excellent, I see you've also been an observer as well, so you are just the man we need! What I want you to do is teach a group of five ack-emmas in the gentle art of map reading. They've already done their gunnery and are now struggling with Morse and wireless. We have an Avro 504 for you and an old RE8 for some familiarisation flights. Come along, I'll introduce you to your students.'

By the 4th of February Bill was making good headway with his trainee observers. He used the Somme for initial map reading exercises, then planned to take them on a three-legged course to Boulogne via St.Omer. Following the Somme was easy of course, but he expected his students to put a time to each of the points he'd plotted on their maps. He could then check if they were identifying map points correctly.

Bill sought out John in the 'B' Flight crew tent and gave him more letters for Mattie. Still unaware his erstwhile friend was destroying them, he found John rather preoccupied, not exactly unfriendly but he knew something was wrong. Training flights kept him busy throughout the day, but he enjoyed flying the Avro. He found his 'C' Flight machine was equipped with a Gosport speaking tube. Introduced by the Smith-Barry flying school at Gosport, it provided reasonable communication between instructor and student, but was hardly useful for operational sorties due to its inconvenient nature.

The ack-emmas were doing well, and by the 6th he'd already taken two of them to Boulogne and back, but then the bad weather set in once again and he had to be content with classroom exercises. Although he wasn't worried, Bill realised he'd not received a letter from Mattie for four days; it was the longest period yet!

On the 7th he found her letter waiting for him in the Mess letter rack. The weather still precluded any flying so he knew he would be able to read it in the classroom while his trainees did navigation exercises on their maps. Opening her letter Bill smiled in anticipation, and hoped she was still well.

There was only one page, and as he looked at the opening line his heart near stopped.

Bill,

Although I find it too cruel to believe, John tells me you have, or have recently had gonorrhoea. I know little to nothing about such things, but the nature of the disease is too horrible for me to discuss. I can understand why you didn't tell me. What I cannot understand is the false nature of a person I dearly loved - or thought I loved.

John has told me I should have nothing further to do with you. Of course he is right. You have broken my heart, and broken the trust John and my dear parents have put in you. Please do not write, there is nothing you can say.

Goodbye,
Mattie

Bill felt cold; so many feelings numbed his mind while his stomach heaved. He wanted yesterday again.

'You all right Flight?' One of the ack-emmas must have asked him a question.

'Yes, of course, go ahead.' He forced himself to listen, trying hard to get back to reality. Feeling the bile rush to his mouth Bill dashed from the room retching violently against the outer wall. Breathless he stayed there, gulping in large mouthfuls of air. After five minutes he returned to the classroom and told them to continue on their own. 'Too much of the local red last night, carry on lads, I'll be back later!'

Bill went to the mess and cleaned himself up. It had stopped raining now, and looking up at the cloud base he knew there was room to fly.

'I have the lads doing map exercises sir, but if possible I should like to take the Avro up for a small weather check. It's just possible I might be able to give one of the trainees a revision exercise this afternoon.'

Captain Wickens was pleased. 'I can see why you came recommended Flight! By all means go ahead, I like to see initiative in a senior NCO.'

Finding a break in the clouds Bill took the Avro up to 2000 feet and into clear skies. The wind on his cheeks the clear blue skies, they helped – but only when he freed his mind from all thoughts. After 20 minutes he came down to find the airfield under cloud once more. As he taxied back to the lines he felt better. He had his answers now.

Bill reported to Captain Wickens to tell him that although the cloud was thin, the weather was not suitable for navigation training. He then returned to the classroom, there was work to be done!

By evening his 'answers' fell apart. He thought he could keep the pain away by hard work, but try as he might he couldn't push Mattie out of his mind. He was tempted to read her old letters again, to see if there was a chance, surely she couldn't deny her love for him! He took her last letter and read it once more. 'Please do not write, there is nothing you can say.' He wrote three letters to her that night but tore them all up! She was right – there *was* nothing he could say, and for perhaps the first time he felt real shame about his VD record. Exhausted he fell into fitful sleep.

It wasn't until the 16th that Bill wrote home. Already he knew his folks would be worrying, but he made suitable excuses and told them his safe job also meant more work. Eileen had written to him and evidently she'd found a new boy friend. He smiled to himself, Eileen – she always managed to stay away from deep emotions – she was lucky! He hadn't mentioned Mattie in his letter; what could he say? There were other problems too. John still acted as his censoring officer so he would have to face him sometime.

Finding a suitable time Bill walked over to 'B' Flight to seek him out. He found John Kenting in the crew tent.

'I have a letter for your inspection, Sir!' John found it more difficult to face Bill since he was totally unprepared. 'And I would like a private word with you, Sir.' Bill walked out of the tent still holding his letter, John following.

'This letter is to my family in Dacre. I shall not be writing to your sister any more, as you *must* know Sir!' Bill knew his tone bordered on the aggressive, but there was still the feeling that John had dealt him a foul blow.

At last John looked him in the eye. 'What the hell can you expect? Do you think I would allow my own sister to have anything to do with a man like you?'

Bill hadn't even rehearsed his thoughts. 'The least you could have done was to talk to me before telling Mattie. God man! I'd been flying over the front for more than a year before you came to France. You have no idea of the circumstances. Did you ever think there could be a reason why I got a dose, which was cleared up a long time before I even met Mattie I might add! I know you got the information from the doc and I'm seriously thinking he should be reported for releasing confidential medical reports! Had a good laugh at my expense did you!'

John Kenting listened. Looking at Bill he could see genuine anger; perhaps he should have spoken to him before writing to Mattie.

'There is nothing to laugh at concerning such a foul disease, and

383

you deceived me as well as Mattie! In any case, you have no proof it was the MO who told me, and no one is going to be concerned about a VD case I assure you!'

Bill lost his temper completely. 'Naturally, all you bloody officers stand together, anyway, you know where you belong now don't you! There's no need to be slumming it with the likes of me, or Eileen, anymore.' John started to interrupt but got no further as Bill got it off his chest. 'Well I'll leave you to them, they all think you're a bloody coward anyway – even if you did win an MC in the usual officers' raffle!' With that he walked away.

John Kenting hesitated, almost at the point of ordering Bill to return, but it was a private argument and could never be taken further without disclosing their relationship. At least it was all over now, but it was Bill's final and cruel remark that hurt and surprised him most. He never knew that Bill was aware of his fellow officers poor regard. A coward? Perhaps Mike Austin, could there be others? He looked down at the MC ribbon on his chest. Surely no one could believe him to be a coward – except himself. Finally, he resolved to get another 'A' Flight officer to censor Bill's letters. It wouldn't be difficult, not since he was now on 'B' Flight.

By the 27th of February Bill had completed his work with the ack-emmas. They would now receive further lectures on artillery work then be handed to the operational Flights for duties and final mission qualification. Captain Wickens thanked him and hoped he might be able to steal him from 'A' Flight on a regular basis.

'The trouble is I know I won't get my way on this Flight! The Boche are definitely up to something, and everyone knows they will attack somewhere – soon. Anyway, many thanks for all your hard work.'

On his return to 'A' Flight Bill reported to Captain Larkin.

'Do you have anyone in mind for my observer sir?'

Don Larkin looked surprised. 'Mr Kenting of course! You two are an experienced crew Flight, and I've only three experienced crews - counting Mr Austin and myself. But 989 will be ready for collection tomorrow, so the C/O said he will fly you to St. Omer to bring it back. By the way Flight, I'm not sure what you've been doing, but the C/O wants to see you immediately!' Bill saluted and left his Flight Commander's office with deep concern. Perhaps John had reported him for insubordination? As he left Don Larkin's smile turned into a grin. 'About time!'

'Good morning Flight Sergeant! Did Mr Larkin tell you we are flying together tomorrow?' Bill said he'd been informed. 'It's the only chance I get to fly these days, doing silly little jobs like this. It's not easy seeing you brave chaps risking your lives every day. Not when I'm not allowed to go over the front lines. I know every squadron commander is in the same boat but that is no satisfaction.' Embarrassed, Bill said nothing. 'Nevertheless there are times when I get some pleasure out of this job, such as now.' Roger Kemp came round the desk with a small box in his hand.

'Flight Sergeant William Proctor! On behalf of the General Officer 3rd Army, I have the honour and pleasure to award you the Military Medal.' Wide-eyed Bill accepted the box, now opened to reveal the medal. 'Let's have a look at it shall we Flight?' Bill remembered Tom's award of the same medal and the words 'For Bravery in the Field' engraved on the front. Major Kemp handed Bill his citation. 'I'm told that MM citations are very rare but as you can see yours is a very special award. Delayed far too long in my opinion, as you can read, it has been awarded for continuous bravery in the execution of a number of dangerous missions.' The C/O shook Bill's hand then looked at the medal more closely. 'I don't know if you know this Flight, but only MM recipients have their name engraved on its edge, the MCs don't have that!

Before he left, Roger Kemp handed him a large glass of whisky, and joining him, toasted his award. 'What would you say to a Commission Flight Sgt? I've had numerous good reports from all my Flight Commanders, and I certainly agree you should be put forward.'

Bill coughed, spilling some of his drink. 'Thank you very much sir. But I think I would prefer to remain a member of the Sgts' Mess.'

As Bill walked out of the C/O's office a group of orderly room clerks applauded his award, one of them coming forward with two MM ribbons to sew on his uniform tunics. Bill thanked them and backed out of the room, completely overcome with embarrassment and emotion.

It was nice to see 989 again, and as Major Kemp returned to Avesnes, Bill inspected his old RE8 before signing for its release from the aircraft park. He was quite well-known at St.Omer these days, and a number of the ack-emmas congratulated him on his medal while he prepared the machine for flight. Strangely enough he felt affection for his old bird, and as he flew south he realised that despite the sadness of recent weeks he was lucky to still have his flying.

On reading the mission allocations Bill saw he was scheduled for a shoot the following morning, the 1st of March. His observer was to be Lt. Kenting! Turning round he saw that John was waiting for him.

'Congratulations on your MM Flight Sgt, well earned! Shall we check over our mission?' They found it an easy task, the battery was well-known to them, as was their target.

'I've already flight tested 989; she's all ready to go, and your Lewis has been checked out too – Sir!' John looked at him without saying anything. 'Seeing as you haven't flown in 989 for a month or more, perhaps you would like to test the Lewis gun – Sir!'

John Kenting decided to ignore Bill's taunting attitude. 'You now have a new censoring officer in Lt Barlow. Please hand all your letters to him in future.' Bill just nodded. He knew Nigel Barlow, a recently arrived observer who had spoken to him a few times.

They completed their shoot without even speaking to each other. On their return Bill let his observer do all the talking to the RO, then went back to 989 to talk to Smokey and Percy.

Bad weather set in again the following day and was to continue until the 8th March. With too much time on his hands Bill spent a couple of days tuning up 989's engine. Although familiar with the RAF 4a, he needed more practical experience, and Smokey Black was only too pleased to help.

It was a good time to write letters too. He wrote to his mother and sent her his citation for the MM. He couldn't tell the whole story of course, but as she had never met Mattie it was sufficient to say they had decided not to marry. He joked about being a free man again, as though it was of no concern to him. But he knew he could expect more searching questions from Eileen!

There was a letter to Sam as well, he'd been neglected for months, but he never mentioned the break with Mattie. Finally he wrote to Jane. Dear faithful Jane. He knew she would be glad to learn of his medal! Perhaps, when he finally came home he and Jane…?

Chapter Twenty

Friday 8th March, 1918

Levelling off at 3000 feet, Bill looked down on the shattered town of Flesquieres. Still in enemy hands he'd expected considerable archie, but this was intense! He was waiting for John to give him the sign to fly directly towards their battery, but in the meantime he flew an oval pattern, waiting for the first shells to land about their target. Within a minute they arrived, the first salvo exploding beyond and to the right of the gun installations being bombarded. The second part of the bracket fell short but was more or less on line. John's signal came almost instantly and as Bill turned, he checked the sky for unwelcome visitors.

Automatically he dropped height, most of the archie seemed near to 4,000 feet now, and with the amount of metal coming up, it would soon find them unless he changed course and height more often. Bill could even hear the British shells coming over, they were obviously in their flight path! Turning and climbing Bill could see shells now exploding about the target, but there was too much smoke to see if they were an OK – a direct hit. Turning to the tap on his helmet he saw John indicating their return to base.

Still climbing Bill waited for the shell smoke to clear. Surely John wouldn't signal a CI – return to base – until he could clearly see the effect of the British guns? Again, another tap on the shoulder, and John's agitated face signalling a CI. There was another rush of noise as British shells rained down on the smoke. It was true; John must have signalled the battery it was an OK, even though he couldn't possibly see the effects of the first explosions. Again fierce taps on his helmet. Bill shook his head and levelled off at 4,000 feet. Glancing upwards he found their escort of three SE5s spaced above them. As the smoke cleared he could see large craters about their target, but the gun pits were still intact!

Turning in his cockpit Bill pointed to the Boche guns and shook his head. John was still pointing to the west when they were shaken by a close one, then the archie stopped. Spotting a group of dots to the east Bill took the hint and made a shallow dive for their own lines.

Upon landing Bill was quite prepared to forget the whole incident, even though he knew John had been in panic, and the mission a complete waste of time and artillery shells! But John wanted to pursue it.

'When I signal a Cl that is exactly what I mean, do you understand! There was far too much archie for me to get any more accuracy than we achieved, and from what I saw we made hits on the target. In future you will obey my commands! In fact there won't be any future – I shall see the C/O and get a new driver!'

Bill could see the fear on John's face and felt sorry for him. Covered in sweat and trembling like a babe he was almost out of control.

'I'm sorry John, I thought you were confused. We never even hit the target – you know that!'

'I know no such thing, and don't you John me! We're finished!' Bill let it go. John could tell his own story to the RO, he no longer cared.

At three pip-emma Bill was called into the C/O's office, where he found Captain Larkin and John Kenting already sitting down.

'Please sit down Flight Sergeant, I have called this meeting to discuss some rather disturbing news just received from 108 RFA.' Bill looked over to John; 108 was the battery they had ranged only that morning.

'I have the RO's report here Lieutenant Kenting. In it you say the 108's third salvo actually hit the target, then you signalled an OK to the battery. Is that correct?' John said it was. 'The problem is that your escort say the gun pits were left untouched, and the 108 say you signalled a Cl immediately after your OK. If this is true it appears you left the target before you should have done, isn't that so?'

John played with his cap. 'There was a lot of smoke sir, I thought the shells had made a direct hit, then I signalled OK. To the best of my knowledge the gun pits were straddled and hit. Smoke prevented perfect confirmation Sir.'

'What do you have to say Flight Sergeant? I notice you made no comments to the RO!' Bill made to get up, but the C/O waved him down. As he did so Bill noticed John's white face staring at him.

'We had a lot of heavy archie sir. My main concern was keeping a decent track around the general area and changing height and course. I only saw smoke around the target sir, but was convinced we had struck the installations.'

Major Kemp gave Bill a brief smile and dismissed him. 'Thank you Flight; you can go now. We won't make a mountain out of this confusion.'

As soon as Bill left the office Major Kemp had another question for John. 'This squadron has an excellent reputation for artillery cooperation Mr Kenting and I don't want any more complaints from the batteries we serve. Now you and Flight Proctor have a well-earned reputation on 12 Sqdn, but today's effort was below par – why?' John gave much the same explanation as before.

'Captain Larkin tells me you requested a different pilot? Do you have some problems with Proctor?' John was becoming confused, his brow shining with perspiration.

'Well, not problems exactly sir. I just thought I would like experience with another pilot.'

Roger Kemp looked at Don Larkin for a moment. 'Proctor is one of our best Mr Kenting! Captain Larkin tells me he refused your request and I support that. We can expect a Jerry offensive within weeks or days, and I cannot countenance crew changes at this time. I have to say your record hasn't been too good recently, quite a lot of time off sick and now this! Let's improve shall we!'

The following morning brought them a CP under a low cloud base. John looked more at ease as he approached Bill in the crew room.

'Are we ready to go? I believe we are to follow the Flesquieres salient is that right?'

John said it was, and pointed to the markings on his map. 'This cloud dictates 500 feet maximum, but I intend to approach the line from the Jerry side – in cloud. That way we should surprise them when we dive into the clear at about 300 feet. We can't miss the obvious line of our trenches and as soon as we reach this point – here, we look for any panels our lads might have put out.' Knowing how John feared CPs at this height he expected some discussion, but none was forthcoming. As they walked to their machine John stopped him short.

'Thanks for yesterday!' Surprised, Bill said nothing. 'You could have said a lot; I know I should have waited for the smoke to clear, but that archie really had me worried.'

Bill understood and shrugged it off. 'Well who cares eh! Must have done some poor Jerry a favour though, so we can always put it down to a Christian act of mercy.' John actually smiled.

Bill slipped out of the protective cloud to find they were on the western outskirts of Cambrai. Shocked into action he instantly climbed back, seeking refuge within the wispy grey cloud base. He could easily see Flesquieres in front of them and noting his heading, estimated the magnetic bearing that would bring them to the southern edge of the salient. Noting his altitude, Bill crept higher into the cover of dense cloud and changed course. As the cloud base seemed to be around 480 feet, he planned to descend to that in about six minutes or so, when they should be able to see the most advanced positions of the British line. Gently lowering the Harry Tate, Bill descended until he caught a glimpse of the cratered terrain below. He could see their own forward trenches ahead and to the right – it was time to go down. Turning in his seat he pointed to the British forward line, John responded by showing the Aldis lamp!

A white signal flare brought their attention to a trench some 400 yards ahead where a lamp was flashing Morse code. Bill throttled back and levelled off at 200 while keeping his feet busy on the rudder bar. They were taking hits as they weaved among the trench line, mostly small arms fire but there were a number of flashes suggesting mortar fire too. Rocked by a close explosion Bill climbed into the cloud again. He knew they were most vulnerable in the climb, but it was suicidal to stay as they were. At close to 600 feet he turned to see if John was injured. He was greeted by a bleak smile and a wave of his message pad, John then ducked into the cockpit to use his Morse key.

Circling over their recent position until John had sent his W/T message, Bill then went south for another minute before lowering them to 450 feet. There were some panels laid out indicating the location of concealed Jerry gun pits, and as they received more concentrations of gun fire Bill returned to the clouds once more. So it went on until they reached the Somme, then they returned home.

Inspecting 989 they found no less than twelve bullet holes! Bill wanted to discuss future strategies.

'The obvious trick is to stay just under the cloud base if we can – it's safer that way. But if you don't find it possible to observe detail then we shall have to go lower, what do you think sir?' John Kenting had been in a cold sweat from the moment they popped out of the cloud at Cambrai. Although not a fatalist he was now confident that survival was impossible. All he had to do was accept that fact and live with the fear. He looked at Bill closely. Confident as ever and without any sign of fear, Bill Proctor could even rationalise their chances of survival!

'I managed to read the Aldis signal in time because it was all coded and simple. They needed more ammunition and signal flares. But it was difficult to see the panels; what was it 500 feet?'

Bill told him it was closer to 450, and made a suggestion. 'Perhaps if we stay at 500 feet, or even higher, but always just below the cloud, then you can use the binoculars as I fly a circle. But with all this concentrated infantry fire it's too dangerous to go low.'

John agreed. 'I also think it's easier for me to see our infantry's lamp signals when under cloudy conditions, they could certainly read mine without trouble. So yes, let's keep just below the cloud in future.'

By keeping to this profile, the crew of 989 could manage to stay out of trouble while the cloud remained low, but they knew these tactics would need to be changed when the skies cleared. Bill found it easier to talk to John by adopting a familiar but disciplined mode of conversation. Now and again their Christian names would slip out, but for the most part they talked without reference to their former friendship.

It was generally accepted by British Intelligence that General Ludendorff would attack any day now. It was also known that Ludendorff's 2nd and 17th Armies would seek out Albert, Bapaume and Arras as their main objectives. They also reasoned that either the British 3rd Army, or the 5th Army to their south, would take the initial assault.

Just before five o'clock on the 21st March, a massive German barrage of almost 6000 guns struck along a 40 mile front. From the Sensee river in the north to the Oise in the south, the morning air vibrated with flame and shock. As predicted, Ludendorff's spring offensive was aimed at the British 3rd and 5th Army fronts in the Somme sector. It was a morning filled with mist and fog, and worst of all poison gas! The noise was deafening, and even at Avesnes bugle calls were not heard as officers rushed to their posts and telephones.

For two hours the barrage fell upon camps, billets, HQs, ammo dumps, artillery positions, airfields, communication trenches and horse lines. German intelligence had been accurate, all the important rear areas had been ranged within minutes and gas-drenched in the soggy air. The British front line was first bombarded with trench mortars, then blasted with the heavy guns before the barrage returned to the rear areas once more. Systematically, the barrage continued to devastate rear and front line positions then, at 0940 the German infantry rose to their feet and charged forward.

Fog was the German's main ally! By 1000 hrs all of 12 Squadron's aircraft were in the air, but little could be seen until nearly 1100. Bill was given a CP over Doignies and Flesquieres and as they flew over the smoke-filled terrain he could plainly see pockets of mustard gas lying heavily among the craters. Communication with most of their batteries was impossible and failing further instructions most of the squadron returned to base early.

As the afternoon wore on, the advancing infantry were preceded by Hun scouts, Albatros, Pfaltz, Fokker and Rowlands, all sweeping forward at less than 50 feet as artillery duels took place between opposing batteries. While covered by other Jastas flying at 2000 and 8000 feet, the ground attack machines had a devastating effect, bombing and firing their Spandaus into forward and rear defences.

In the following days it was obvious that CPs were the only reliable source of information for field commanders, and each of 12 Sqdn's crews were given their own area of responsibility. By the 23rd of March things were getting desperate and all Scout Sqdns were ordered into ground attacks against attacking infantry. By the 25th, even 12 Sq

Don Larkin put it plainly. 'Think of it as a normal CAP but at 50 feet above Jerry helmets!' There was even a general order from 3rd Army GHQ. 'Very low flying is essential – all risks are to be taken.'

Armed with eight Cooper bombs and extra drums for the Lewis gun, Bill took off with the rest of his squadron. Even elements of 'C' Flight flew with them, their old BE2s making a brave sight as bombing aircraft! Surrounded by other squadrons they swept into the Germans at 50 feet, dropping their small bombs and raking the enemy with their guns. As usual Bill found the low flying exciting. The slaughter was terrible but highly effective in slowing up the advance and most of all, giving valuable respite to the British troops. Three times they flew against attacking infantry before nightfall gave them rest.

On the 26th Bill and John were called to Captain Larkin's office. He had a special mission for them.

'The pressure is still on ground attack, and we have to put all our aircraft to that task. But 3rd Wing need some photography west of Flesquieres. Evidently it's very important otherwise we wouldn't be allowed to divert two aircraft for the sortie, and you two gentlemen know the area better than anyone, so you get the job.'

Bill interrupted. 'You said two aircraft sir?'

'Yes, we are going to need two machines, both flying at 5,000 feet. Unfortunately I cannot get you any cover. All the scouts are dedicated to ground attack. I can't even get you a couple of DH2s. I'm afraid Wing think you must take some risks here, just as the infantry are doing. I then suggested that since time was of the essence there's a much better chance of them getting their photographs if we covered the area with two machines. It takes half the time and gives you a better chance to get home before the Huns see you. They wouldn't wear that either, until I told them I could put up an old Avro that would be useless for ground attack!'

Bill laughed. 'No problem sir, I used to do a lot of photography in the old Avro!'

'Exactly Flight! It's still a good aeroplane, a bit slow, but it compares well against an RE8 when flown by an experienced pilot. Which is why *you*, my lad, are going to fly it!'

John Kenting enquired about the other crew. 'I have a new pilot for you John – Sergeant Bond. He's been with 'C' Flight for a couple of months and is a decent pilot so I'm told.'

Bill cut in to give his support. 'I worked with Harry Bond while in 'C' Flight. He's a good pilot sir, and has some photo experience in quirks, I checked him out on the RE8 myself.'

Don Larkin continued. 'As I said earlier, you two have the most experience over Flesquieres so I need one of you in each machine. Bill in the Avro and Sgt Bond will drive you in 989 John.'

'Who will be my observer sir?'

Captain Larkin gave him a huge grin. 'Corporal sandbag!'

Bill laughed. 'He was a Sergeant last time he crewed with me. What happened – lost some of his sand?'

'Dead right Flight! As you know the Avro only needs a little ballast when it's correctly trimmed. But you will have a fixed Lewis on the upper plane, so that adds a bit of weight. Naturally the gun has to fire outside the propeller disc. Have you ever fired one like that before?'

Bill said he hadn't. 'If I meet a Pfaltz it won't make much difference sir – not in an Avro 504!'

The Flight Commander smiled grimly, 'Let's hope you won't need it! You see we don't even have a spare observer on the entire squadron! Did you know the five ack-emmas you recently trained are now flying as gunners on ground attack? You take off at 1030 hours. Sgt Bond will be here for briefing in ten minutes. He's now picking up the plates from our photo section and will bring all the exposure details with him. Let's work out the photo calculations now John, so when Bond comes we shall have both maps ready.' Don Larkin called out to Bill. 'What speed do your recommend for both machines Flight?'

Bill suggested 90 mph. After a few minutes John had the answers. 'Scale is 1:10,000 and at 90 mph we need to make an exposure every ten seconds.' Captain Larkin measured out the flight lines on the map. If you do these two lines John, that will mean a total of 18 plates and a magazine change. Flight Proctor can use the entire magazine on his single line, a total of 12 shots. Each of you take a spare magazine, just in case.'

While John examined his camera Bill checked over 989 with Sergeant Bond. 'Take care of her Harry, she's a good old bird! Smokey and I tuned the engine recently and she's nicely trimmed. I'll take off first in the Avro and we'll climb to 5,000 feet before approaching our photo area. Keep your ASI at 90 mph for both your flight lines and Mr Kenting will do the rest. Now remember! Waste no time on this sortie! If the Huns see us they'll come after us like a shot. So when you've finished descend and scoot back soon as possible, finished or not! That means you'll be following me, since I'll be finished before you and already on my way home.'

As Bill pre-flighted his Avro he noticed the Lewis gun stuck on the upper wing. Complete with its 97-round drum, the assembly looked quite aggressive, but without practice he doubted he could hit anything, despite the ring-and-bead sight mounted ahead of the windscreen. He checked the gun cable leading to the joystick, then looked at the camera mounted against the starboard side of the fuselage. Situated over a cut-out in the lower wing, the camera was simple to operate, particularly with its semi-automatic plate changing device. A large stop watch was firmly attached to the instrument panel, but Bill usually counted the seconds for the next exposure, ten seconds was easy!

Looking up he could see a high overcast to the west, but he knew they would have clear skies for the next hour. It was time to go! Waving to 989's crew he scrambled into the front cockpit and prepared for take-off.

At 5,000 feet Bill looked behind to check that Harry Bond was with him. Then reducing speed he let them come abreast. Making use of hand signals he confirmed their readiness and, once satisfied, gave the signal for them to part, Bill to the north of the salient and Harry due east.

Although good landmarks were now very few, Bill had little difficulty in completing his photo line. From start to finish he finished the task in no more than two minutes, and waiting no longer turned the Avro for home. Crossing the western part of the salient he took a brief look to the east, hoping to see 989 completing its second run. What he did see drew a sharp intake of breath. The unmistakeable profile of a Fokker triplane was descending on Harry Bond's RE8!

John Kenting could hardly be blamed for not seeing the enemy scout. Intent on his work, and with only three more frames to go he never saw the danger until too late. The Fokker pilot had marked them well, making a classic approach from out of the sun!

Part of a top-cover from Jasta V, 21 year old Gefreiter Hans Bock was on his second operational flight and new to the Fokker DrI. Most of the Jasta were now equipped with Albatros DIIIs, but were expecting the excellent Fokker DVII within weeks. As a new, but very com-

394

petent pilot, Hans Bock was content to be given the slow but highly agile Triplane. Like most young scout pilots his hero was Richthoven, a legend who had made the Fokker Triplane almost as famous as his name.

With two companions from Jasta V, Bock was providing top cover at 6,000 feet when his section leader signalled him to return to base. Oberleutnant Lindenberger respected the youngster's skill with the Dr1, but the fight below was too chaotic and dangerous for the inexperienced. With a wave, the two Albatros fell away leaving an angry Hans Bock to return home.

As he turned the Fokker eastwards, Bock saw a flash of sun glinting from Harry Bond's RE8, only 1000 feet below! Recognising the lumbering RE8 as an easy victim, he positioned himself with care then dived!

Harry saw the Triplane first and rolled immediately to the right. Startled by the evasive action John peered over the top of his cockpit at the same time as Bock's twin-Spandau brought a hail of bullets across the port wings. Still keeping on right rudder, Harry lost height before straightening out of the turn. Then he turned west once more as he searched desperately for the enemy.

Hans Bock brought the Tripe around within seconds and attacked from the rear. Now fully aware of their danger John brought the Lewis onto the approaching enemy – there wasn't even time to be afraid! Seeing the threat, Bock side-slipped to his left then fired a short burst as he climbed into the slow moving Harry Tate. A total of seven Spandau bullets smacked into Harry Bond's cockpit, four smashed into the instrument panel, one clipping the reserve fuel tank, and three mangled Harry Bond's left arm from shoulder to wrist. In shock, Harry only remained conscious through the airstream now falling on his face, and recognising he'd nearly lost control brought the machine level and into a shallow dive.

A small stream of petrol leaked from the reserve tank, leaving a white trail in the cold air as Harry tried to anticipate the next attack. He'd no idea of their height, the altimeter being in ruins, but if he could get low enough to force-land he knew they might have a chance, providing he didn't faint through loss of blood. Through dulled eyes he saw the Fokker coming in for a frontal attack and kicking the rudder made a flat turn to the left in order to give his observer a clear shot.

Hans Bock recognised the strategy, and as his quarry turned away opened up at 60 metres, the twin streams of fire cutting through canvas, flesh and bone as they broke both of John Kenting's legs.

In great pain, Harry turned to see the damage. Feeling the hits and knowing the Lewis hadn't returned fire, his worst fears were realised as he saw John writhing in pain and clinging to the Scarff mounting. Without any defence they were completely at the Hun's mercy and he knew they could expect none! All he could do was hope and fly to the earth below.

Realising that 989's crew stood little chance against the Tripe, Bill turned the Avro around to help. His direct orders were to return as soon as photography was completed, but if 989 was shot down it never would be! As he approached, Bill saw two of the Fokker's attacks, but Harry Bond seemed to be doing well with his descending turns. Looking at his altimeter Bill estimated the RE8 to be about 3000 feet, and coming directly towards him.

Seeing the approaching British machine Hans Bock turned from his fourth attack and climbed away. He knew the RE8 was crippled, its observer either dead or wounded, but he needed to make sure if the new arrival was a threat or perhaps another possible victory!

It was obvious the RE8 had been hit, and as Bill made a sweeping turn over 989 he could see very little movement in either cockpit. Glancing up he noted the Triplane was still there, circling like a hawk. Bill knew he would be down again. Coming as close as he dare, Bill saw Harry's death-white face as it turned slowly in his direction. Then it turned away as the injured pilot slumped forward. John's pain-filled face hung over the Scarff ring, a weak wave of recognition indicating he was still alive. Bill noted that 989 was in a steady descent, and might even survive a forced landing if Harry could stay conscious!

One RE8 almost dead – and an old Avro! Gefreiter Bock knew he had every advantage and decided to attack the Avro first. A final check of the surrounding sky made sure there were no other threats then, without further delay he pointed his Fokker towards the Avro which was slowly turning towards him.

Bill saw the Triplane coming down, and waiting until it was at extreme range fired two short bursts from the Lewis. He never expected to hit the closing scout, but his enemy's reaction would tell him a lot! Hans Bock slipped aside, his lack of experience now obvious to Bill as he continued to fly eastwards. Looking over his shoulder he twisted round to see the Fokker make a climbing turn towards him. Bill could expect another pass from the rear, and he knew he could never turn in time to face it!

John Kenting watched as the Fokker diverted its attention to Bill. The two machines were flying away from them now, but he could see that Bill was making a fight of it! Bill! What chance would he have in that old crate and why did he come back? It was suicide!

Looking down, John could see they were approaching a British rear trench system at about 1000 feet. With great pain he swung his body round to face the front. Harry Bond was still alive; he could see his slight head movements as the pilot made an approach to some open land ahead.

Fighting to keep awake Harry decided to drop 989 onto the first open patch he could find. Now at 400 feet he could see there was sufficient room between a line of communication trenches. With blurred vision he side slipped to the left then straightened up. Figures were moving, running this way and that, then he lost the horizon! Pulling back on the stick Harry flared and stalled the RE8 from ten feet above the ground. It was more an arrival than a landing, but as the undercarriage collapsed 989 slewed into a pile of empty ammo boxes, throwing Harry forward onto the cockpit combing. Already unconscious John was pitched over the side and thrown clear.

Conscious of intense pain, John awoke to find himself in the back of a Commer ambulance bouncing its way to the BNM at St. Omer. Both legs were bound with a tourniquet, and the RAMC Corporal at his side was kept busy attending them. His patient had lost a lot of blood and he'd also broken an arm in his fall. Dimly, John could see Harry Bond opposite, then he fainted again.

As the Corporal supervised their arrival at St. Omer's BMH the attending surgeon shook his head. 'This one's dead I'm afraid! Lost too much blood Corporal. And this one? It's going to be touch and go!'

Epilogue

Gefreiter Hans Bock was pleased. His first kill had been witnessed in the field and confirmed by 2nd Army observers. Though proud of his achievement the young pilot was vaguely dissatisfied. He couldn't erase the sight of 'his' Tommy as he shot him down, his bullets striking the pilot as he closed to less than 50 yards. The Avro never stood a chance, and its brave pilot must have known that when he came to the aid of his comrades.

John Kenting became fully conscious late in the evening of the 28th March. In great pain he learned there would be further operations on his legs, and could expect to be in traction for some time to come. For Lieutenant John Kenting MC, the war was over. As it was for Sergeant Bond, who died of his wounds!

Months later, the squadron told him that Flight Sergeant William C. Proctor MM, was officially reported as missing in action. A telegram to the same effect had already been sent to his family.

Over the years John realised he'd cheated not only death but the truth itself. In hiding from his own limitations he'd denied Bill's valour to common knowledge. He had never spoken of Bill's self-sacrifice to anyone, not to his own or to Bill's family. Despite his cruel rejection of their friendship and the wrecking of his love for Mattie, Bill Proctor came back to save his life! Too late did he recognise the true meaning of comradeship, that selfless bravery was a rare and precious thing!

It had been 78 years and more, and very few days passed without him thinking of Bill. Mattie had married three years after he came home, but Bill Proctor's name was never mentioned at *Saddleworth* again. He'd found no comfort in his marriage to Jean Matlock, and even less for the job that came with it!

And now, old and infirm he headed this great parade, the sole representative of WWI veterans. A stir of small flags caught his attention. Schoolchildren for the most part, their chilled faces showing little interest for the huddled figure pushed in the wheelchair. The bands had started again, and as they struck up 'Colonel Bogey' he held the memories back.

Childless and sad, he sat weeping. If only he'd died on that fateful day! But perhaps he did? For John Kenting knew his youth had flown with his friend, and precious memories were held hostage to regret and sorrow.